I0822413

SHOCK AND AWE

A SPECIAL EXPLOITS THRILLER

MICHAEL RYDER

THOMAS PUBLISHING

Shock and Awe

This book is a work of fiction. The names, characters, places, and incidents are products of the writer's imagination or have been used fictitiously and are not to be construed as real. Any resemblance to persons, living or dead, actual events, locales, or organizations is entirely coincidental.

ISBN-13: 978-1945320248

DEDICATION

For Dad

ACKNOWLEDGMENTS

The author gratefully acknowledges the assistance of the many subject-matter experts — in microbiology, infectious disease treatment, pandemic response, environmental pollution mitigation, software development, supercars, motorbikes, and close-combat fighting — who reviewed early drafts of this manuscript and generously offered guidance to ensure that this story, fanciful though it may seem, remains rooted in the realms of the real and the possible.

Any inaccuracies that exist are solely the fault of the author.

AUTHOR'S NOTE

MY FIRST ENCOUNTER with Special Exploits occurred on a downtown San Francisco subway platform at rush hour, when a disheveled man bumped into me and knocked my commuter bag off my shoulder.

"Sorry, dude," the man said. Without even looking up from his hoodie, he stumbled away, leaving a cloud of booze and sweat in his wake.

A momentary annoyance, hardly worth remembering. Which explains why, when I got home and found a sealed envelope in my bag, I didn't make a connection to the man in the hoodie. Not at first.

The envelope wasn't mine — I hadn't put it there — but it had my name on it and the words: "For your eyes only."

Who'd slipped it to me? Someone at work? A friend?

I opened the envelope. Inside it were eight photocopied pages of what looked like a government report, typed on an old typewriter, single-spaced. On the first page, at the top, were the words: "Special Exploits: Case 11348-X."

As I scanned the pages, it quickly became apparent that I was reading a mission report written by a skilled obfuscator. Instead of specific people, places, and objects, the report employed euphemisms like "biological materiel," "asset enabled," "target surveilled," and "zone of contamination." The report overflowed with intentionally opaque sentences like "requisitioned necessary inventory of subterfuge-assisting devices for in-field activation" and "improvised alternative method to initiate deployment of disruptive countermeasures."

No amount of bureaucratic obscurantism, however, could disguise the drama of sentences like: "To prevent a global pandemic, the team determined that standard operating protocol would not apply."

What the hell?

My phone rang. Still distracted, I picked up. "Hello?"

"I trust you are enjoying the report," a man said. He sounded old, his voice soft and wispy.

"What?" I asked. A stupid response, I admit — I'd heard just fine — but the voice, and the words, had jolted me.

The old man stayed silent.

"Who is this?"

More silence. He was playing with me.

Fine, I'd play along. "Yes, I'm enjoying the report."

"I am glad to hear that," he said, each word carefully enunciated. "Would you like the remaining twenty-one pages?"

I looked at the bottom of the eighth page. The last line cut off mid-sentence.

"Yes."

"Good. You will agree to two conditions." He said it as a statement, not a question, like he was used to giving orders.

"What conditions?"

"First, you will write about this and publish it — a fictional version."

"Why would I do that?"

"It is time people know."

"Know what?"

"How the world really works," he said softly.

"You're saying the report is real?"

"Every word."

This was easily the weirdest call I'd ever had. Who the hell was on my phone?

"Why me?"

"You are hungry and ready. You have a flair for turning reality into fiction and the sensibility to entertain while you educate. You will tell the story the right way."

I appreciated the confidence — truly, I did — but my primary reaction was wariness. I felt as though I were being led into a trap.

"Who are you?"

"You need not know."

"This is a joke. Someone put you up to this." I threw out the names of friends who might be capable of such a prank.

He answered with silence.

"That's it?" I said. "That's all I get?"

"Yes."

It was my turn to stay quiet.

The old man waited. He was better at this game than me. Infinitely better.

I gave in. "How do I know anything in this report is true? It has no names, no places."

"You will receive three specific pieces of information. Then you will know. Before you receive this information, however, you will agree to the second condition."

"Which is?"

"You will not reveal these three pieces of information,

ever. When you write your account, you will fictionalize all names, dates, biographical details, and locations."

"To protect the innocent?"

"To protect the guilty and to protect yourself," he said, his voice momentarily strengthening. "There are no true innocents, Mr. Ryder, not in this world."

That's when I got my first chill. I hadn't, until that moment, absorbed the implications of the envelope and the voice on the phone. This stranger had selected me. He knew things about me.

And I understood something else.

"Today, on the subway platform, when your guy slipped the envelope into my bag, you had him bump into me on purpose. You wanted me to remember."

"Yes," he said. "Good."

"If this report is real, isn't it classified? Is it even legal for me to have something classified in my possession?"

The old man chuckled. "Yes and no. But you need not worry."

"Why?"

"Because for all intents and purposes, Special Exploits does not exist."

"So if I bring this report to the police or the FBI...?"

"They will conclude that you have written a piece of fiction."

"Except you're saying it's not."

He must have sensed my anxiety, because he added, "As long as you abide by the terms of our agreement, Special Exploits will keep you safe."

Sweat trickled down my neck. With a start, I realized my hand was trembling. Either I'd attracted a delusional lunatic or — probably worse — the old man was the real deal.

"I will call in twenty-four hours," he said. "If you ask for the three pieces of information, we will have an agreement."

"And if I don't?"

"Then you will never hear from us again. Good night, Mr. Ryder."

The line went dead.

Since you're now reading these words, you know what happened next. Regarding the three specific pieces of information, I'll only say that they proved enlightening.

And terrifying.

I doubt I'll ever know why Special Exploits — that's what I've decided to call them — want this story told. My best guess: For reasons unknown, it's in their interest to show us, as the old man put it, "how the world really works." I also believe, on a more human level, that they want us to appreciate how difficult their jobs are, the sacrifices they make, and the lengths to which they will go to protect us.

I'm choosing to believe they're the good guys. I hope, after you read about Case 11348-X, that you'll agree.

Michael Ryder
San Francisco, California

CHAPTER **ONE**

Executive Boardroom
Kasson & Kasson Chemicals
Zurich, Switzerland

IN THE HOURS following the blast that blew apart Building 2B in the Kasson & Kasson experimental research campus outside Zurich, the company's top executives gathered in their glass-and-steel corporate boardroom on the top floor of Kasson Tower, in the heart of Zurich's financial district, and quickly learned that they'd been the target of a flawlessly executed precision attack.

The elements, once pieced together, painted a frightening picture: Malware to disable the perimeter alerts. A false alarm to distract the security staff. Jammers to disrupt communications. Traces of black-market plastic explosives on the laboratory's door locks. An open gas valve in the building's basement, next to the melted remains of a timed igniter. A lone camera capturing a fleeting glimpse of a three-person team, clad head to toe in black, darting away seconds before the building was destroyed.

When the executives received confirmation that, as feared, key biological samples in Lab 2B4 were missing, a debate ensued about the company's responsibilities and liabilities.

In typical Swiss fashion, the discussion began as a calm, precise analysis of their options, but the implications of the theft were such that decorum and protocol soon yielded to baser forms of expression.

Kasson & Kasson had survived worldwide depression, war, and financial crises in the decades since its founding, but today was quite possibly the company's darkest hour. Fear, anger, blame, and despair engulfed the boardroom.

Kasson's chairman was ninety-two years old — a Swiss legend going strong into his tenth decade. Through shrewdness and force of will, he'd built the company into a multinational conglomerate.

While the others raged, he listened, weighing options, then made up his mind.

"Gentlemen," he said over the arguments. "Gentlemen!" he repeated, more loudly.

The arguing stopped. The room went quiet. The exhausted executives turned toward their chairman.

"I have made our decision. We will ask for help. The right kind of help. Bring me a telephone and leave the room."

A phone was placed before him.

He waited for the others to exit, then picked up the receiver and, from memory, punched in a series of numbers, his fingers bony and mottled with age but showing no hesitation.

"I would like to speak with the Director. I'm afraid we have a problem."

CHAPTER **TWO**

Nine days later
Downtown Los Angeles

JACK FORD STEPPED out of the elevator and into an all-white, windowless room that was brightly lit and empty except for a woman — white blouse, white slacks, white heels — seated in a white chair behind an elegant white desk.

The woman was lovely, with mocha skin, flowing black hair, and dazzling green eyes.

His pulse quickened. A new agent. He liked new agents. They had a freshness, an enthusiasm, that couldn't be faked.

He'd been a new agent once. He'd even had her job: greeting visitors with a bullet or a smile.

The new agent gave him a smile. "They warned me about you, Agent Ford," she said, her voice as appealing as the rest of her — smooth and husky, with a hint of a Brazilian accent. Sao Paulo, perhaps.

He ran his fingers along the edge of the desk. "They?"

She tapped the surface of the desk, projecting the *National Snooper* on the white wall behind her. Deftly, she zoomed in on a photo of him dancing on a table in a crowded nightclub, drink in hand, tuxedo shirt unbuttoned, arms flung wide, blond hair wet with sweat. Above the photo was a headline: "Party-Boy Jack Wrecks Vegas Hotspot!"

Rather breathlessly, the article read, "Celebrity wild man Jack Ford has been banned for life from the Heavy Metal Hotel in Las Vegas after he and his entourage trashed the hotel's red-hot Libido Lounge and turned the Presidential Suite into a den of sex and sin! No charges have been filed, but a hotel spokesperson confirmed that Ford, playboy heir to the Abernathy Industries fortune, 'will never again be allowed to use the Heavy Metal Hotel as his personal pissing ground.' When asked for comment, a spokesperson for Ford laughed and said, 'Jack loves the Heavy Metal. Maybe he'll buy the place so he can go back.'"

The *Snooper* certainly hadn't minced words.

He turned to Miss Brasil. "In my defense —"

She stopped him with a smirk. "They want you in Conference Room A."

Such inviting green eyes. He leaned in closer.

"A pleasure meeting you, Agent...?"

She held his gaze, a hint of mischief in the arch of her eyebrow, and pressed a button under the desk. The door behind her clicked.

"Last room on the right," she said, very crisply.

A flirt, this one. She'd fit right in.

Conference Room A was dolled up as an interrogation room — standard issue, movie-ready, and quite convincing. His bosses did enjoy their stagecraft: Featureless gray walls. Fluorescent lights humming faintly and casting an appropriately harsh glow. The requisite metal table and two metal chairs. Cameras in each corner, red lights blinking and aimed straight at him. A faint whiff of disinfectant wafting from the tiled floor.

A nice touch, the disinfectant. *We cleaned up the blood and piss from our last guest*, it said. *Make yourself comfortable.*

Idly, he wondered who the room was for — who they planned to scare, persuade, turn, or break.

The door opened and a sensationally attractive brunette with warm brown eyes and ruby-red lips walked in, carrying a folder stuffed with papers. Jennifer Calhoun, Deputy Commander of Special Exploits. A decade or so older than his thirty-two, she was dressed, as usual, in a white silk blouse and black skirt, with her hair pulled back in a bun. Sexy as hell, of course. When she wore glasses, as she often did, she became the kick-ass librarian of every teenage boy's wet dreams.

"Have a seat, Agent Ford." Her voice was warm, as always, just as it was always "Agent Ford" and never "Jack." Professionalism, as well as boundaries, mattered to the Deputy Commander.

Steel scraped against tile as they pulled out chairs and sat down. The cold of the metal chair seeped through his white slacks. He watched her eyes glide over his dark-blue blazer and white dress shirt, which was open at the collar.

"Looking nautical today," she said.

"Benefit at the Marina tonight."

"Not anymore. But we'll get to that."

He waited. This was her meeting, after all.

She placed the folder on the table. She always had a folder with her and always, at some point, read something from it or pretended to. But she never wrote anything down.

She opened the folder and gave him a sympathetic look. "We're doing a tune-up today."

For a nanosecond, his lips tightened. The Deputy

Commander's psych debriefs were increasing in frequency, the last barely two months earlier.

"Great," he said, keeping his tone light. "More pointless mind-fucking."

"Before we get to that, tell me about last night."

"Where should I start?"

"The beginning. Pretend it's a briefing."

"Do I sense a critique?"

"The Secretary called you 'cheeky.'"

"Aww, so she liked me."

He saw the barest hint of impatience in the Deputy Commander's eyes. He sat up straighter and said, "Dieter Strauss. German national. Thirty-six years old. Financial adviser to drug kingpin Carlos Zamora. Touched down in L.A. three months ago to buy his way into the movies and engage in some old-fashioned money laundering, Hollywood-style. My assignment, courtesy of you: deploy the tools to track his every contact, every breath, every piss, and every fart."

"Not exactly the language we use for briefings, Agent."

"Noted. Strauss is a tough target. His security is top-notch. You don't become Zamora's go-to money guy if you're not smart and careful and paranoid. But no man is an island, not when your girlfriend is one Andrianna Barzon, age twenty-four, a fashion model with dreams of becoming an actress.

"We set up the usual physical and electronic surveillance, but needed more. The obvious entry point was Andrianna. She started taking a yoga class on Melrose, so we had Agent Dawes strike up an acquaintance and invite her to a party at a producer's pad in the Hills. Andrianna and Dieter showed, and I made sure they were introduced to a certain fun-loving celebrity wild man."

"Referring to yourself in the third person? Interesting."

"The tune-up's already begun? Interesting."

"Go on, Agent."

"By the end of the night, after a lot of booze and some harmless fun with a blowup doll —"

"Agent."

"Long story short: Dieter believed he'd made a well-connected new Hollywood buddy. Three days later, when I passed Dieter my invite to a Producers Guild event, he bit. His swag bag included a year's supply of his favorite after-shave, laced with a cool new tracking tool: an invisible, odorless liquid with a chemical signature visible from space."

He paused and cocked his head. "How does that work, by the way? How is something like that even possible?"

"Stay focused, Agent Ford."

"A week later, at a fundraiser in Malibu, Andrianna and I had a chat about jewelry — expensive jewelry — and how it symbolizes affection and commitment from the giver. I gave her a card for DeLuchs Jewels on Rodeo and told her to ask for Eduardo. She dragged Dieter there the next day. Four days later, a custom diamond necklace was delivered to Dieter's pad and inspected and cleared by Dieter's security team."

He paused and took a breath. Calhoun waited attentively. Listening was a skill she excelled at.

"Which brings us to last night and to my little shindig at the Heavy Metal Hotel that apparently got me banned for life, which is a bummer because that place is super-fun."

Calhoun gave him a sympathetic smile. "The world is full of hotels that haven't banned you yet, Agent Ford."

"The point of the party was to make sure Dieter and Andrianna — and Andrianna's necklace — made an appearance. All three did. In the crush at the bar, I switched Andrianna's necklace for a duplicate equipped with a super-tiny, nearly invisible audio recorder made of a newfangled plastic polymer and programmed to transmit in short, intermittent bursts to avoid most radiowave communications warning systems."

"The switch was seamless?"

"Seam-free. We get anything yet?"

Calhoun nodded. "She placed the necklace on the dresser when she got home. While she was in the shower, Dieter called Zamora to confirm the timing of the payments for his next shipment. We got every word. With luck, we'll get weeks of solid intel before the battery dies."

She closed the folder and gave him her warmest, most inviting smile.

Uh-oh.

"You didn't bring anyone home with you last night."

He fought the urge to frown. He should be glad his boss encouraged him to have an active sex life. Supportive work environments were all the rage these days.

"I didn't fuck someone, and now you're worried."

"After a successful op, your usual pattern is to celebrate with a roll in the hay."

"I can't believe this."

"You had any number of potential bedmates, yet you went home alone."

"Didn't I tell you? I had an epiphany. I'm joining the priesthood."

She shook her head and leaned forward. "You left your own party before midnight and drove from Las Vegas to L.A. in less than three hours, hitting one-forty on the open stretches near Barstow. When you got home, you went straight to your building's gym and worked yourself into a sweaty mess, jumping rope and pounding the punching bag like you wanted to kill it."

"Your point?"

"You know why we do these debriefs. If you're not at the top of your game, we need to know."

"I'm fine," he said, no longer bothering to hide his impatience.

Her brown eyes didn't give an inch. "Are you? We've never had an agent with a cover like yours. Your colleagues can immerse themselves in a role — businessman, thug, doctor, waiter, guard, escort, architect — and discard it. They can move on. You can't. You're playing a version of yourself. You can't escape who you are."

He'd heard it all before, too many times. But beneath the familiar words, he detected something different. Was the Deputy Commander actually concerned?

She continued her staredown. "People look at you and see a rich, superficial asshole, an irresponsible party-boy, a light-weight trading on family connections and charm. Men resent your looks and wealth and think you've done nothing to earn what you have. Women see the same and don't trust you because they know you'll sleep with anything that moves."

He was reminded again of why he disliked Calhoun's psych debriefs: her insistence on rehashing the same litany of insults.

She leaned in. "You understand why I push on this."

"You want to know if it bugs me that people think I'm an undeserving douche."

"Does the cover still fit?"

"My clothes are fine."

"Let's talk about your family."

He quelled the flash of irritation. "Let's not."

She frowned at that, or maybe at her earpiece. She fingered the flap of the folder while she listened to what was being said into her ear.

"All right," she said, then stood.

Usually the Deputy Commander was more determined,

the tune-ups going on for hours. He took a stab at why she'd cut it short. "Tell me about the new op."

She walked to the door, opened it, and turned toward him. "Patience, Agent Ford. For now, stay in here. We'll buzz when we're ready."

CHAPTER **THREE**

At that moment
Outside the same building

DR. LUCY KIMBALL stared at the building in front of her, then again at the directions she'd hastily written down. The call had come from nowhere: a polite but firm request — instruction, really — to drop what she was doing, get in her car, and drive downtown. Her help was required — again.

On most days like today, she kept her shoulder-length brown hair pulled back in a no-nonsense ponytail. Her glasses, a tad too big for her face, had an annoying tendency to slip down her nose. Her blouse and pants fit loosely, on purpose, to ensure comfort during her long days and nights in the lab. On her feet were the same cross-trainers she ran in like clockwork three times a week. When she wore her white lab coat, her body — slim and naturally feminine — disappeared into a shapeless muddle.

Today of all days, she should be in the lab. After months

of methodical prep, she was close to a breakthrough. She'd had that tingling sense before and was feeling it again.

Instead, she was here, staring at a scribbled note. She didn't have to do this. She didn't have to become part of their world again. She could walk away.

But she couldn't walk away.

They need you, her inner voice said. *And that excites you.*

With a mixture of reluctance and anticipation, she crossed the street and stepped into the bustling entrance of L.A. Body Works, the city's hottest fitness club, which occupied four floors of a huge, converted warehouse in the city's downtown district. The lunchtime crowd had the place hopping. Beyond the front desk were rows of running machines and weight-lifting equipment.

"Can I help you?" a fresh-faced attendant asked.

"Yes. A friend signed me up for a day pass," she said, as instructed.

"Your name?"

"Kimball. Lucy Kimball."

The attendant looked through a file.

"I see you have a Platinum pass. Lucky you. The changing rooms are to die for! Do you know how to get there?"

She looked at the note she'd scribbled. "Fourth floor?"

"That's right." The attendant handed her a card. "Just take this card and insert it into the door lock."

A minute later, the elevator opened to the fourth floor. Unlike the rest of the gym, this floor was quiet, devoted to rooms for sports therapy, massages, and the Platinum changing areas.

She inserted the Platinum card in a slot next to the door marked, "Women's Lounge." A light flashed green. She turned the handle and entered.

Following the instructions, she walked past the rows of lockers, showers, and sinks to a door labeled "Storage." She looked around to confirm she was alone. Another card slot, another insertion, and she opened the door. The room looked like a storage room should, with shelves on the walls filled with cleaning supplies, toilet paper, and towels.

She stepped in, flipped on the light, and closed the door behind her. On the back wall, a fire extinguisher and an ax hung in a glass box marked, "Break in case of emergency." To the side of the glass box, hidden in the shadows, a final card slot was buried in the wall.

She hesitated. She could still turn back.

No, you can't, her inner voice said.

She inserted the card into the slot. For a few seconds, there was silence. The storage room went dark. A hum kicked in and soft green light bathed her.

She was being scanned, she realized.

The storage room shook and started moving upward. The room was not a room, but an elevator.

A few seconds later, the room came to a stop. The shelves along one wall vanished into the ceiling, revealing a door.

She opened the door and stepped into a bright white, windowless room occupied by a woman seated at a white desk.

The woman smiled at her. "Please continue through the door behind me. Oh, and Dr. Kimball?"

"Yes?"

"Welcome to Special Exploits."

CHAPTER **FOUR**

LUCY STEPPED OUT of the white room and into a construction zone — or more accurately, into an unfinished office space. Along one wall a row of offices looked nearly complete, but the rest of the floor (and she could see almost all of it) was wide-open. In one corner, she counted eight people around a cluster of folding tables, working intently in front of computer screens. Surrounding them like spectators were rows upon rows of flat-screen monitors suspended by wires from the exposed ceiling.

Several people glanced her way, but none made a move to greet her.

She heard a quiet cough and turned to find a woman behind her. The woman was older than Lucy's thirty-two — early forties, perhaps — and an inch or two taller. She had brown hair pulled back into a sleek bun and excellent skin, with warm brown eyes and a reassuring smile. She looked very athletic beneath a form-fitting white blouse and dark skirt.

"Dr. Kimball," the woman said, extending her hand and

giving her a firm, brief handshake. "I'm Jennifer Calhoun, Deputy Commander of Special Exploits. We appreciate you coming in on such short notice. Any trouble with the directions?"

Lucy found her voice. "No, the directions were clear."

"I'd suggest a tour," Calhoun said, nodding toward the open space, "but there isn't much to see."

"Did you just move in?" Lucy asked, curiosity winning out over nerves.

"Recently, yes, but we're nomads. We don't stay put for long."

"The storage room, the elevator — I had no idea."

"Thank you. Some details are important to get right."

Lucy glanced at the group clustered around the computer screens. "Is that your team?"

"Part of it, yes. They're the day shift: analysts, researchers, a satellite expert, a cryptographer, and a hacker — essential support for our agents in the field."

The Deputy Commander's willingness to share information was unexpected. Also comforting and reassuring.

Quite unlike the man striding toward them. She'd met Commander Nathan Grant once before, soon after her return from England, when he'd appeared unannounced in her lab to thank her in person for the help she'd provided, or so he'd said.

Then and now, she found him unsettling, intense, and intimidating, with tremendous energy contained — barely — beneath his stoic exterior. Mid-forties, thick black hair going grey at the temples, hard grey eyes, and full, sensual lips pressed tight with tension. His broad shoulders strained the fabric of his tight black pullover.

She'd often wondered whether Commander Grant had had ulterior motives for visiting her lab. His call this morning had proved he had.

"Dr. Kimball. Thank you for coming."

His hand engulfed hers, and once again she felt his magnetism. Since his call, she'd been trying, without success, to identify exactly what generated that pull. Yes, the man was confident. Yes, he was good-looking — astonishingly so. Yes, he was tall and muscular and physically imposing. But none of that came close to explaining his special, persuasive skill.

Somehow, with just a few words, he'd pulled her out of her normal routine. The routine she worked so hard to keep focused and productive. The routine she cherished and protected fiercely.

He'd done it simply by asking. She hadn't even tried to say no.

"Let's get started." The Commander guided her to an all-glass room along the wall that was probably meant to be a conference room. Aside from a round table and four office chairs, the room was empty.

She saw him press a device in his ear.

"Ready," he said.

He walked up to the windows and gestured toward the spectacular view of the Los Angeles coastline. "I assume you're familiar with the city?"

"Of course," she said, stepping toward him and the view.

"More than nine million people live within ninety minutes of this window. We need your help protecting them."

From anyone else, the statement would have seemed dramatic and even pompous, but the man pulled it off effortlessly. How? What was his secret?

Behind her, she heard the door open and a man's voice say, "Yo, Commander."

She knew that voice, but that voice couldn't be here. It wasn't possible.

She whirled around.

And felt a jolt of shock — even horror — at the sight of Jack Ford, asshole extraordinaire, staring at her in surprise.

"You?" he said. For a split second, anger flashed across his face.

Heat rushed to her cheeks. The humiliation — the betrayal — of their prior encounter came roaring back. Nausea surged through her.

What in the hell was going on?

She saw Jack gazing angrily at Calhoun, but Calhoun had eyes only for her. "Dr. Kimball, my apologies. We meant to tell you sooner that Agent Ford would be here."

Somehow, Lucy was able to say, "*Agent* Ford?"

"Yes, an agent with an unusual cover. He's here because he needs to understand what he's up against."

Lucy kept her focus on Calhoun and away from *Agent* Ford. She didn't need a reminder of how ridiculously attractive *Agent* Ford looked, with his unruly blond hair and dazzling blue eyes. How breezy and confident and carefree he looked in that crisp blue blazer and white slacks, with his white collared shirt open at the neck, like he was ready for a spin on the family yacht.

No, she'd seen more than enough of that lying, manipulative jerk.

"I don't understand what this is about."

She heard the quaver in her voice and hated it. Who were these people? What did she know about them? Nothing, except this: They'd lied to her, deceived her, duped her, and made a fool of her. Had anything they'd ever said to her been true?

"Dr. Kimball," Commander Grant said, interrupting her train of thought. "Right now you're beginning to realize that what happened between you and Agent Ford on the flight from London wasn't what you thought. You're wondering what else we've kept from you and how much of what we've told you is true. Let me be clear: We have kept a lot from you and will continue to do so, for your own safety and ours. Compartmentalizing information is an operational necessity."

He gestured toward Jack. "Would you have come today if you'd known Agent Ford would be here?"

She hesitated.

"You aren't sure," Grant said. "Neither were we. But we know you have important information to provide that could mean the difference between failure and success in the field. If we had even one more day to prepare, I would have sent someone to your lab to interview you in person — I wouldn't have called you in — but with this mission, time is of the essence."

The Commander stepped closer and looked directly into her eyes. "You're here because you've demonstrated the ability to be discreet. What you did for us in England was very much appreciated, but it was your discretion afterward that impressed us most."

Her head whirled with anger and uncertainty. She wanted to turn on her unheeled sneakers and get the hell out. These people were liars and users, but they were also serious. They didn't mess around. They'd brought her in for a reason.

She took a deep breath. She'd dealt with this crew before and managed to survive. She could do it again. She'd give them what they wanted, then get the hell away as quickly and efficiently as possible.

"You haven't told me why I'm here," she said as calmly as she could. "What's the big emergency?"

"Phosphorin has been stolen," the Commander said.

Her mouth opened.

Phosphorin — stolen?

Four words. A wallop to her solar plexus.

Involuntarily, she took a step back.

What he'd said wasn't possible. Aside from samples

stored in a secure CDC facility, her lab was the only place on earth with phosphorin. She'd been at her lab this morning. Nothing was amiss.

"From the CDC?"

"From Kasson & Kasson Chemicals in Zurich."

She gasped. "Kasson was denied permission! They wanted to research it, and we told them no. How did they get it?"

"They bought it from someone in your lab or at the CDC. The source is under investigation, but that's not our focus."

Horror rushed in. The implications were terrifying.

"Our orders are simple and clear," Grant said. "Find the phosphorin, and retrieve or destroy it by any means necessary."

CHAPTER **FIVE**

LUCY RESISTED the temptation to collapse into a chair.

Phosphorin stolen? It seemed impossible.

No more weakness. Not in front of these people.

"Who stole it from Kasson?" she asked.

"We'll get to that," Grant said. "But first, we need your expertise. You know more about phosphorin than anyone."

"What do you need to know?"

"Start wherever you like. We'll ask questions."

The three agents took seats at the table and looked up at her expectantly.

They were used to this, she realized. They dealt with emergencies and catastrophes all the time. They brought in experts from various fields and disciplines, learned and absorbed the information they needed, and then went out and — saved the world?

Still shaky, she pulled out a chair and joined them. Commander Grant was to her left, Deputy Commander Calhoun to her right, and *Agent* Ford dead ahead.

If she swiveled her gaze back and forth between Grant and Calhoun, she could avoid looking at *Agent* Ford. Yes, that would work.

She took a deep breath and exhaled. Her heart rate slowed.

With her eyes on Calhoun, she began a narrative she'd repeated so often and to so many scientific colleagues and government health officials that she could recite it by heart. "Three years ago, in a remote, abandoned mine in the Andes, Chilean scientists discovered a new species of bacteria in a subterranean steam vent. The bacterium feeds on sulfur and white phosphorous and has the unusual ability to survive and thrive at high temperatures. The scientists named the bacterium phosphorin."

She felt herself calming as she moved through the account. "A few months after the initial discovery, a team of researchers, including two colleagues from my lab, returned to collect more samples. An earthquake struck and a landslide buried the road to the mine. The team radioed in and said they were fine. They said the mine had collapsed and a falling boulder had crushed their power generator, but no one was injured, their shelter was undamaged, and they had sufficient food and water to wait for workers to clear the road. They'd collected phosphorin samples before the quake. Their battery power was running low, so they told us we shouldn't worry if we didn't hear from them. They communicated twice in the next day. After that, we heard nothing."

A familiar tightness gripped her throat. Even after three years, talking about it hadn't gotten any easier.

"Seven days later, a work crew cleared the road and made it to the mine, where silence greeted them. The camp appeared deserted. They found signs of a struggle — equipment knocked over, backpacks emptied, sleeping tents uprooted. As they got closer, they found vomit and blood.

When they tried to open the door to the main shelter, they found it locked from the inside. A piece of wood had been hammered to the door with a warning written on it in English and Spanish: 'Do not enter! No entrada! Peligro! Enfermo! Highly infectious airborne agent attacks lungs and gut. Five dead, three dying. Save yourself. Call CDC. Stay away! Tell Nancy I love her.'"

She swallowed. "The warning was written by my colleague Gabe. He and Nancy had just gotten married."

"Take your time, Dr. Kimball," Calhoun said. "No need to rush."

Lucy gave Calhoun an appreciative glance. "Fortunately for all of us, Gabe's note scared away the road crew. They ran back to their trucks and called in.

"Three days later, when the CDC and Chilean health authorities broke down the door, they discovered the researchers dead. All showed evidence of extreme respiratory and gastrointestinal distress. All had bled out. Somehow, the last one to survive — Gabe — had taken the bodies and wrapped them as best as he could in plastic and had done the same to himself."

"To reduce the risk of infecting whoever found them," Calhoun said.

"He was like that — brave." She shook herself and continued. "When the phosphorin came to our lab, I was offered the opportunity to study it. Phosphorin was strongly suspected as the cause of their deaths, but we didn't know how the bacterium had killed them. We ran a series of experiments. We started by feeding the phosphorin its usual sulfur and white phosphorous diet, but found no evidence of lethality. Next, we decided to see what else it could eat. Phosphorin, as it turns out, can consume pretty much anything without issue."

She paused.

"Except sugar. When fed sugar, the phosphorin respond differently."

"When you say sugar," Grant asked, "do you mean any kind of sugar?"

"Any substance with a high concentration of sucrose or fructose, including syrups and soft drinks."

"Is that what happened?" Jack asked. "A soft drink accidentally spilled onto the phosphorin?"

"We think so," she said, glancing at him for the first time since sitting down. "Possibly during the earthquake."

"And the different response?" Calhoun asked.

"The act of feeding on sugar triggers a fundamental change in the phosphorin at the enzymatic and cellular levels, and also at the genetic level. The idea that food can change an organism's DNA isn't new, of course, but the ease with which phosphorin can alter itself to new environmental conditions is rare. This genetic change is important. When phosphorin transforms as a result of its exposure to sugar, it creates a byproduct called sucronal phosphoral excrete."

"The dreaded sugar shits," Jack said.

She shot him another look. Given the seriousness of the subject matter, was this really the time for tacky jokes?

"You'll have to excuse Agent Ford," Calhoun said. "Sometimes, if he doesn't lighten the mood, he doesn't know what to do with himself. Too many late nights partying for the paparazzi, too many brain cells destroyed …."

Lucy continued. "The excretion has a distinctive smell that many people would think of as citrusy or lemony. That aroma is the reason companies like Kasson want to research it, to see whether they can develop it as an air freshener."

"So," Jack said, "what happens if the little buggers don't keep getting their sugar?"

She glanced at him again, surprised that he had asked the right question.

"The transformed phosphorin will die within twenty-four hours."

"From your tone, I'm guessing that matters."

"Living phosphorin isn't dangerous. Dead phosphorin, mixed with its excretion, is lethal."

"That's highly unusual," Grant said. "Do we know why?"

"Not yet, but I have an idea. I'm designing an experiment to test my hypothesis. I'd be working on it right now if I wasn't here."

"Was your colleague right?" Calhoun asked. "Can this mixture of dead phosphorin and excretion be spread by air?"

"Yes, and by other means. If frozen or dried out, it's fairly stable and can be added as an ingredient to pretty much anything, liquid or solid. For example, to a water supply, or an air conditioning system, or a bomb."

"A bomb?" Grant asked. "The blast doesn't destroy the phosphorin?"

She shook her head. "The bacterium is naturally resistant to high temperatures and can withstand brief periods of extremely high heat and pressure, like you have with an explosion."

Tension rose in the room.

"Dr. Kimball, here's the question we've been leading up to," Calhoun said. "How does it kill?"

"Phosphorin acts as a trigger, turning our own bodies against us."

"Explain."

She took a deep breath. "Most of us carry three to five pounds of 'good' or 'healthy' bacteria in our bodies at any given time. Most of the bacteria are in our gut, but the bacteria are everywhere on us and in us, including in our lungs and on our skin. These 'good' bacteria prevent infection and aid in digestion.

"When our good bacteria are exposed to dead, transformed phosphorin mixed with sucronal phosphoral excrete, they begin acting differently. The first change occurs in our lungs, where phosphorin interacts with the colonies of benign bacteria that flourish there. The second change is in our gastrointestinal tract — the small and large intestines and colon, but also the esophagus and, to a certain extent, the stomach."

Jack shifted in his chair. "I don't like where this is going."

"There's nothing to like. In our lungs, the phosphorin triggers our good bacteria to begin reproducing and dying at an accelerated rate. This activates our body's immune response. A very vigorous response — too vigorous. In layman's terms, the immune system goes ballistic. It attacks with everything it has. And when the bacteria die, they leave a toxic mess that, in turn, kills our lung tissue.

"The response in our intestines is, if anything, worse. In our gut, the phosphorin triggers a reproductive response with Group A streptococcus bacteria that, in most people, live comfortably in balance in our bodies."

"Is Strep A what I think it is?" Jack asked.

"It's commonly referred to as 'flesh-eating bacteria.' The bacteria don't actually eat flesh — they kill flesh — but that's really not the point. The Strep A bacteria, after its exposure to phosphorin, go haywire and attack our gut the same way they can attack our skin or connective tissues. Quite literally, we die from the inside."

"Geesh."

She nodded. "Individuals exposed to a mix of dead transformed phosphorin and its excretion feel fine at first. A day or two later, they start coughing and feel short of breath, like they have a chest cold or a touch of the flu. Four to five days after exposure, with mucus and blood choking their lungs, they begin vomiting and passing blood and dead tissue. Within a week, they're dead.

"From nearly the moment of initial exposure, they're highly infectious. When they breathe, and especially when they cough, phosphorin is expectorated and, in aerosolized form, it can find its way into someone else's lungs. That person gets infected, and the spread continues."

Grant's grim expression became even grimmer.

"We've given it a name: Phosphorin Fever. It has the potential, if it enters the general population, to kill millions."

For a moment, no one spoke. Aside from the faint hum of the overhead lights, the room was quiet.

"Let me guess," Jack said. "Dr. Kimball is here because she's developing a treatment."

She noticed his flippant tone had vanished.

"Is there a vaccine?" Calhoun asked. "Can we be inoculated?"

"There's no vaccine, but we have an experimental treatment. If administered quickly and accompanied by proper medical care, it can work."

"Explain," Grant said.

"First, an immunosuppressant is administered, targeting the lung infection. Second, we've developed an immune modulator to treat the Strep A infection in the gut."

"How does the modulator work?" Calhoun asked.

"We've constructed a protein that mimics the protein in the phosphorin excretion that interacts with Strep A. The idea is that if we can flood the gut with our protein, then the Strep A bacteria won't interact as much with the phosphorin excretion. If it doesn't interact as much, then the body's bacterial balance is less likely to be thrown out of whack."

"Survival depends on a lot of factors lining up," Jack said.

"Timing is key. The sooner the treatment begins, the better the odds. The amount of exposure is also important. A person with significant phosphorin exposure is less likely to pull through."

"What are the effects of the treatment?" Grant asked.

"For up to a week, you are terribly sick — diarrhea, vomiting, dehydration, breathing difficulties, blood loss, hallucinations. And with your immune system compromised, you're vulnerable to other types of infection. But with proper medical care, you can get through it."

"You know this through human trials?"

"One human: me. I've been through it."

Sudden interest flashed in their eyes.

"Accidental exposure," she said. "Fortunately, I had already developed the immune modulator and had formulated the treatment, and it worked."

Something imperceptible rippled through the room, or maybe she imagined it.

Calhoun smiled. "Well, I'm glad you survived. We couldn't rely on you otherwise."

"How much of the immune modulator do we have?" Grant asked.

"Enough for a few hundred people."

Grant's frown deepened.

"How is phosphorin transported?" Calhoun asked.

"Before it gets fed sugar, it's quite hardy and can be transported easily. But once it's fed sugar, the bacterium becomes unstable. Without careful handling, it dies."

Jack sighed. "What does dead phosphorin smell like?"

"It smells a lot like the harmless lemony aroma the bacteria give off when they're alive and feeding on sugar."

"A lot like? Not the same?"

"There's a subtle difference."

Jack glanced at Commander Grant, and the Commander held Jack's gaze.

"No," Jack said. "No way."

"Deputy Commander Calhoun," Grant said, "why don't you show Dr. Kimball your office?"

"You're sure?" Calhoun said to Grant, and he nodded. "Even though...?"

"Yes."

Lucy frowned. Something important had just happened, but what?

Calhoun stood. "Dr. Kimball, or can I call you Lucy? I'd like to tell you more about Special Exploits and the work we do."

CHAPTER **SIX**

JACK WAITED FOR the two women to close the door behind them. No way the Commander meant what he'd said. No fucking way.

The good doctor looked good — damn good. Furious, of course, her lips tight with anger, her lovely brown eyes radiating vividly the depths of her dismay. He had watched her racing over her options, trying to figure out how to get the hell away from him.

She was still making the same bad wardrobe choices, he'd noticed — the same shapeless blouse, the same loose pants. And she was still giving off that "Don't hit on me, I have important work to do" vibe.

He shifted his attention back to the Commander.

"No," he repeated.

"The mission calls for it," Grant said.

"No."

"I don't like it either, but we have no other choice."

"She's a civilian."

"Who did surprisingly well in England."

"She's untrained."

"She demonstrated grace under pressure, initiative, flexibility...."

"Her role was limited. She lied to a guy."

"With a gun in her face."

"She doesn't know what we do, how we operate, or how we accomplish our missions."

"Calhoun is telling her now."

"She'll be a liability in the field. I can't be effective if I have to be her goddamn babysitter."

"You don't even know what the mission is."

"I don't need to. Including her is a mistake."

Grant shrugged. "More to the point, you don't know what dead phosphorin smells like. She does. You won't be effective without her."

"Goddamn it!" Jack exploded. "The woman doesn't like me. She fucking despises me, and we both know why."

"She's a good person who actually cares about people, Agent Ford, just like you do, at least most of the time. She knows the stakes."

It was like talking to granite. Time to switch gears.

"Commander, you've been out of the field and chained to a desk for, what, a decade? You may have forgotten about this little thing called chemistry. Funny thing, chemistry — either it's there or it's not. You can't fake it."

Jack leaned forward in his chair. "Dr. Kimball and I have what's called 'anti-chemistry.' She oozes dislike for me. It's like she bathed herself in 'Eau du I Hate Jack.'"

Commander Grant smiled, something he rarely did. There was something frightening in that smile, an implacability.

"Agent Ford," he said, his voice a low rumble, "you were selected for Special Exploits because of your Special Forces training, your combat experience, your privileged background and all the useful connections it provides, and, most importantly, your rare and valuable capacity to charm anyone in varied and inventive ways, as you've demonstrated countless times."

Grant stood up, walked around the table, and came to a halt behind Jack.

Jack tensed and willed himself to not look back, to not respond. The Commander's powerful hands took hold of his shoulders. A rush of displaced air brushed his cheek as the older man leaned down.

"So I want you to stop your goddamn whining," his boss said, breath hot in his ear. "No one cares."

Jack wanted to push the Commander away and tell him — to his fucking face — to kindly back the fuck off, but he resisted the urge as Grant added, "You'll have thirteen hours on your private jet tonight to charm the living shit out of Dr. Lucy Kimball. If she isn't putty in your hands by the time you touch down — if stopping a catastrophic epidemic isn't enough incentive to change one woman's mind — then give me a call when you land and tell me this uptight scientist has you beat."

Jack snorted — couldn't help it.

The mouth left his ear. The hands left his shoulders. The Commander walked to the conference room door and gave him a look that hovered between exasperation and resignation. "Life is about priorities, Agent Ford. It's about doing what's important and giving your all to accomplish it. For some reason — God, fate, random chance — you have talents that can make a difference. Don't squander them."

The Commander opened the door. "There's a lot to go through in the next few hours. We'll use the briefing room. Are you on board?"

The fucker knew he was on board. Why was he asking?

He gave the Commander a theatrical sigh and stood.

"Only if you agree to stop lecturing me about the meaning of life."

Grant let the comment pass. "I mentioned your family's private jet. You'll be using it, which means — "

No way. He couldn't mean —

Grant smiled, a genuine one this time. "You'll be dining with your mother this evening. She insisted, as a condition for lending us the jet."

"You really are a fucker, Commander."

The smile widened. "With pleasure."

CHAPTER **SEVEN**

TWO ROOMS AWAY, in Deputy Commander Calhoun's office, Lucy and Calhoun sat across from each other on facing chenille-clad sofas. Unlike the bare-bones encampment on the other side of the door, Calhoun's office was fully decorated, with solid walls and recessed lighting. Its neutral color palette— Berber carpeting, walnut wall paneling, cream curtains — conveyed a softly whispered message: *Relax. You're safe. Nothing bad will happen here.*

The scientist in Lucy took in these details and gleaned the decor's psychological intent, but that was hardly her focus. No, her focus was on the utter ridiculousness of what Calhoun was proposing.

"No way," she said. "No. I can't do that. I won't."

"I know it's a lot to take in," Calhoun said. "Before you say more, let's have some tea."

Calhoun picked up an antique copper teapot from the coffee table and poured steaming tea into two cups.

Lucy regarded Calhoun in silence.

"You pour a lot of tea, don't you?" she said abruptly.

The Deputy Commander smiled. "Every now and then, yes."

"It's deliberate, isn't it? Part of your act."

Calhoun set the teapot down. "I've found the act, the ritual, of sitting quietly and watching a cup fill with steaming water, offers reassurance and familiarity to civilians who have just been asked to go well beyond their comfort zones."

"I assume you have training?"

"Once upon a time, I trained as a psychologist."

Lucy picked up the teacup and inhaled. "Jasmine?"

"Fresh from my favorite shop in Chinatown."

She took a sip. "It's delicious."

"Thank you." Calhoun picked up her cup and sipped, and waited.

The silence lingered.

As Lucy brought her lips to the cup a second time, she asked herself why she felt so angry. She'd already said no, so why was she upset?

Because they need you. She brushed the thought away.

Because you're scared.

"I'm not the right person to send out on a mission," she finally said. "I don't know the first thing about being a secret agent."

Calhoun put her cup down, waited six long seconds, and said, "Lucy, you're the only person we can send. How many people on this planet know what dead sucronal phosphorin smells like?"

Lucy didn't answer.

"I can guess your other concern," Calhoun said.

"Good. Then I don't have to explain why I could never work with Jack Ford."

"Would it help you to know that Agent Ford was on a mission when the two of you met on that London flight? That he had no choice but to do what he did?"

"No, it doesn't."

"Even if it happens to be the truth?"

"I don't know if I believe you. You've shown me I can't trust you."

Calhoun nodded. "I respect your honesty, and I understand — truly, I do. There's too much you don't know. Who are we? What, exactly, is Special Exploits?"

Lucy put the teacup down, leaned back, and folded her arms against her chest. "Do tell."

Calhoun poured more tea, slowly, taking her time.

As the silence stretched, Lucy realized her mistake. Curiosity was a weapon, a hook, and she'd bit.

"What I can tell you is this," Calhoun said. "We're a small team — an elite team. Our field agents are handpicked from military Special Ops and intelligence agencies. They're highly trained and combat-tested. They're tough, smart, dedicated, and deadly."

"I thought Jack Ford barely graduated high school, enlisted in the Army to piss off his mother, and got kicked out of the military because of a sex scandal. What's so elite about that?"

"I assume you read that after the two of you met?"

Lucy flushed. "Yes, in a profile of the Ford family dynasty in *The New Yorker*. The article mentioned his dismissal from the military as one of the many ways Jack Ford has embarrassed his family."

"There was a lot more to his dismissal than what ran in that piece," Calhoun said. "Agent Ford was Special Forces at the time. We asked the reporter and his editor to keep that detail and several others out of the final article, for reasons of national security. They agreed."

Calhoun picked up her cup and took a sip. "Agent Ford would probably tell you what happened if you asked him. Now, where were we? Ah, yes, Special Exploits."

Calhoun was playing her, tempting her with knowledge as bait. And it was working.

"You're good, you know that, right?" Lucy said quietly. "Go on."

Calhoun chuckled. "You see that I'm manipulating you, but you decide that you don't care. I like you, Dr. Kimball."

Unable to stop herself, Lucy smiled back. "You were saying?"

"Yes, I was saying. Agents are recruited for Special Exploits because of two defining qualities. The first is empathy."

"Empathy?" she said, surprised. "I'm sorry, I don't see that."

"I use the word with care. Let me ask you: How would you define it?"

Lucy considered the question. "I would say that empathy is the capacity to think and feel oneself into the inner life of another person."

"I couldn't have said it better," Calhoun said. "Would you agree that a person's abilities to observe, learn, remember, and reason are essential to a person's capacity for empathy?"

She nodded. "I would."

"Our agents are excellent at reading people and situations. They are exceptionally good observers and listeners. They have to be. The more they see and remember and learn, the more they can figure out about our targets. What do our adversaries care about? What motivates them? What are their weaknesses? How can we gain the advantage? How can we defeat them?"

"Okay. I get that."

"The second quality we recruit for is charisma. Or, as I choose to define it, the ability to charm and persuade."

"Charm? In what ways?"

"In every way. For example, our agents are excellent negotiators. They've used their powers of persuasion to help resolve many serious crises. Those same skills also help when they go undercover. They have to be convincing to succeed in their missions."

"So they're like actors."

"Except our agents have to stay in character, nonstop, for days or weeks or even months at a time."

"It sounds exhausting."

"It is, but they're chosen because they're up to the task." Calhoun paused, then continued. "There's one other arena where their charisma comes into play: the physical."

"Do you mean what I think you mean?"

"Yes, Dr. Kimball — seduction. It's definitely a weapon in our agents' arsenals. Our agents will, when needed, use sex to accomplish their missions."

Lucy nodded. "I see."

Calhoun looked dubious. "I doubt you do. Most people don't, not at first."

"Like James Bond," Lucy said. "He sleeps his way through every movie he's in."

"Special Exploits goes far beyond what you see in mainstream movies."

"Well, I do get it. You're forgetting I've had … exposure."

"Not really, Dr. Kimball," Calhoun said. "Forgive me for being blunt, but what you experienced on the flight from London barely qualifies. You really haven't seen anything at all."

Calhoun stood. "There's someone I'd like you to meet."

Lucy rose with her. "My answer hasn't changed."

"I know. You're welcome to leave at any time. If you do, I promise you'll never hear from Special Exploits again."

Calhoun walked to the door and opened it. "You can learn more about us, or not. The choice is yours."

CHAPTER **EIGHT**

THREE DOORS DOWN, in the dark, windowless briefing room, banks of monitors covered every wall, casting a dim light over the table and four chairs in the center of the room. Jack dropped into one and threw his legs up on the table. He watched Grant expertly manipulate a remote and bring up a selection of images and videos on the main wall.

"Let's talk about the break-in at Kasson," Grant said. "Dr. Kimball doesn't need to know more, but you do."

With precision, the Commander took him through the sequence of events the thieves used to execute the theft.

"You know what this feels like?" Jack said when Grant finished. "Like one of ours. This is how we would have done it, if we'd wanted the world to know we'd done it."

Grant nodded. "Agreed."

"Not many people could pull this off. It narrows the list of suspects."

"The Director has concerns — "

" — that it could be...?" He left the name unspoken: La

Société pour le Barbare Acquisition de Richesse Extravagante, or SABRE — an organization of elite criminals for hire and a major focus of Special Exploits' efforts.

"It could be," Grant said, "except there's an auction. Whoever did this is selling the phosphorin to the highest bidder."

Jack considered that for a moment. "An auction doesn't feel like SABRE. If they'd stolen the phosphorin, they would have delivered it to their client quietly and without fuss."

Grant nodded. "Then we're on the same page."

"We're looking for a rogue player with resources and skills."

"Yes."

He sighed. "Rogues suck. So many possible reasons for their rogue-iness."

"On a related note," Grant said, "let's discuss how Kasson got the phosphorin in the first place."

"Kasson told us everything they know?"

"Yes, but they were careful, and so was the seller. Double anonymity, using a middleman we have yet to track down. Kasson doesn't know who sold it or even whether it came from the CDC or Dr. Kimball's lab."

"Don't tell me you think Dr. Kimball is involved."

"We doubt she is," Grant said. "But it remains a possibility."

Jack felt his gut rebel at the thought. Why? Because the mission became exponentially more dangerous if it turned out Lucy Kimball was a snake?

Grant continued. "The lie she told about being accidentally exposed — "

"Proves only that she's a terrible liar."

"Most likely, yes. But it could be part of a deeper game."

Jack sighed. "So either I'm being saddled with an

untrained civilian who hates me, or a criminal who's playing us like a fiddle."

Grant ignored the complaint. "If it's the latter, then you know what to do."

Lucy looked toward the door that led to the elevator and then toward Calhoun, who stood waiting for her in front of an office three doors away. She could leave right now, and probably should. Or....

Damn it. The hook was holding, at least for now. She could almost feel its tug.

She pivoted toward the Deputy Commander and followed her into a large, open room that appeared to be a combination of a hair salon, makeup room, and special effects studio. Brightly lit mirrors covered every wall. Along one wall were two adjustable salon chairs with rinsing stations. On the opposite wall were comfortable chairs and makeup desks. In the back was a motley assortment of wigs and what looked like rubberized masks on mannequin heads.

Her eyes came to rest on a man carefully applying bushy eyebrows to a mask. He was in his mid-thirties, tall with short black hair, and had muscles in all the right places, as his tight white t-shirt and blue jeans revealed. He glanced back toward the door and smiled, giving her a flash of brown eyes, dazzling white teeth, and a hint of stubble on his olive skin.

"Paul," Calhoun said, "you have a customer. A potential customer. Be nice."

"New jeans," Paul said. "You like?" He did a full turn for their inspection, giving them the opportunity to admire his muscular butt from every angle.

"My new secret weapon," he said, aiming a playful wink

at Calhoun. "I'm hoping the Commander will take one look and realize he's been in love with me all these years."

Calhoun smiled. "Lucy, this is Paul Tyler, head of character design for Special Exploits."

"Character design?" Lucy asked.

"I help you create the person you'll become for the mission," Paul said. "Or rather, the person you'll become if you agree to help us. Like a makeover show on TV, but with higher stakes."

"What do you mean, 'the person I'll become?'"

"The best way to explain is to show you. Here, take a seat." He guided her to a salon chair and stood behind her so that they could look at each other in the mirror.

He pointed to her ponytail. "Would it be okay if I loosen this, and maybe give your hair a trim?"

She glanced at Calhoun, half-expecting the Deputy Commander to encourage her, reassure her, or tell her that Paul was fabulous. But Calhoun simply stood there, waiting, letting her know, through her silence, that the decision was hers alone.

It was only a trim, after all. "Okay."

"Perfect." He undid the band and let her hair spread across her shoulders. "You have great hair. Why do you keep it back?"

"It's easier. Long hair doesn't work in the lab."

"So for you, the lab is everything."

"Right now, yes."

He ran his hands through her hair. "I think the new Lucy — your cover name will be Lucy Keen, if you agree to help us — will wear her hair long, full, and natural. We'll shape it a bit, but keep it shoulder-length and the same color."

"Why Lucy Keen?"

"'Lucy' because that's your real name, and it's nearly impossible to not respond to your own name when you hear it. And 'Keen' because it's similar to your real name, but different enough."

He picked up a pair of scissors and started taking a few experimental snips.

"Also," he said, "the name 'Keen' subconsciously reinforces a key element in your character's approach to life. Any woman who dates Jack Ford is, by her very nature, eager for excitement."

Looking steadily at him, Lucy said, "You know I think Jack Ford is an asshole."

His snips didn't miss a beat. "He can be many things, as you'll see."

In the mirror, she saw Calhoun press her ear. A few seconds later, the Deputy Commander said, "Lucy, I'll be leaving you in Paul's capable hands."

Lucy watched the sway of her hips as she walked away. "Deputy Commander Calhoun is an impressive woman."

"That she is."

"Are she and Commander Grant together?"

"Why do you ask?" Paul replied in a distracted voice, his focus on her hair.

"She likes him."

"You sound sure."

"I am. So what's going on?"

He stopped snipping and looked at Lucy's face in the mirror.

"Deputy Commander Calhoun doesn't share her feelings. Neither does Commander Grant."

"Sometimes, a woman knows."

He continued looking at her as if weighing what to say next. "In my experience, many scientists are brilliant at research and terrible at understanding their fellow human beings, but you seem comfortable with your intuition. Do you often rely on it?"

She nodded. "It helps my research. I get a sense, a feeling, about a direction or an experiment, usually before I can verbalize or rationalize a reason for it."

He turned his attention to layering. "The answer to your question is no. Calhoun and Grant are not together."

"But they want to be, right?"

He didn't answer. She looked at his face and could tell he was holding back.

"Come on. Let's say I actually do this. I'd need to know how this agency works, right? I'd be trusting you with my safety and letting you throw me into God knows what, right?"

"Listen," he said, then sighed. "There's stuff you need to know, and stuff that's dangerous for you to know."

"The more I understand, the better I'll do out there."

"I like you," he said, putting the scissors down. "Let's get you to the rinsing station."

He guided her to another chair and leaned her back over the sink.

"We have three ironclad rules in Special Exploits," he said as he ran warm water through her hair. "The first rule is: Do whatever — and whomever — it takes to complete the mission."

"Whomever?" she repeated, looking up at him.

Calhoun had said much the same thing, but it hadn't really sunk in, and she realized how shocking she found the idea.

He turned the water off and picked up the shampoo.

"You heard right. We go there. We were picked because we can go there. Most people don't have that capacity."

The implications rattled through her head as he squeezed a dollop of shampoo into his palm and lathered her hair. With his fingers, he lightly massaged her scalp.

"I can feel the tension you're carrying. Can you?"

His fingers seemed to dissolve into her skin. "That feels wonderful. Keep doing that."

"As you wish."

"You were saying, about the second rule?"

"Post-mission debriefs. In person. No exceptions."

"Which is another way of saying be safe out there? Get back home alive and in one piece?"

He nodded. "The Commander would never put it that way. He likes to play the hard-nosed boss, but deep down, he cares."

"And the third rule?"

"The third rule," he said as he finished lathering up her hair, "is the tough one, or at least it was for me."

He turned on the water and began rinsing the shampoo from her hair. Until this moment, he'd been animated in his manner, but thinking about this third rule, whatever it was, had brought him closer to ground, like a stabilizing weight.

He finished the rinse and sat her up, then took a towel and softly dried her hair. "Come on, it's time to give Lucy Keen her fabulous new 'do."

He sat her up and guided her back to the salon chair. She wanted him to hurry up and tell her about the third rule. She wanted to prompt him, but held back. He was working up to something.

"Before I took on character design, I was a field agent," he said after unwinding the towel from her head. He picked up a comb and ran it gently through her damp hair. "I loved it — the excitement, the danger, but most of all, the sense of purpose. I stopped some truly evil shit and saved a lot of people."

"The details of which you can't share."

"That's right."

He picked up the scissors and began snipping in earnest.

"On my last mission, something unanticipated occurred, something I wouldn't have predicted in a million years."

"What happened?"

"I fell in love."

Her eyes widened. She hadn't expected that.

"With?" she prompted.

"His name is Carlo. That's him," he said, pointing to a snapshot on the makeup station next to a row of lipsticks. Lucy had noticed the photo earlier but looked at it more carefully. A handsome man in his early thirties, with dark hair and a shy smile, stared intently at the camera.

"He's a landscape designer. We live in Santa Monica, near the beach."

"He's not part of Special Exploits?"

"A civilian, like you. We met because of my mission. He got caught up in it and ended up helping me complete it."

He ran a hand through her still-damp hair. "No perm. No highlights. We'll use the blow-dryer a bit to frame your face. Lucy Keen is in med school at UCLA, so she doesn't have a whole lot of time to spend on her hair."

"UCLA? That's where I went to medical school."

"We need Lucy Keen to be as much like Lucy Kimball as possible," he said, resuming his snips. "We want you comfortable in your new skin, if you agree to help us, of course. The real you graduated from UCLA med school six years ago, but Lucy Keen is in her third year of med school there. The two Lucys have attended the same classes in the same buildings with the same professors, lived in the same neighborhoods, and eaten in the same restaurants."

"How similar, exactly?"

"Let's see. Ask me about a detail from your past you'd be surprised would be in Lucy Keen's file."

She thought for a moment. "Who taught my anatomy class?"

He turned toward the makeup table and opened a folder. "Dr. McGuilders. Last semester. Lucy Keen got a C."

"Why a C?"

"Because she threw up in her cadaver."

She laughed, amazed. "How did you find out I did that? And how did you create the transcript?"

Paul pointed toward the door. "For the past few hours, the team out there has been creating Lucy Keen's electronic history, which started with researching Lucy Kimball. You'll see what we've come up with soon enough. But first, your face."

She stood and moved across the room to a makeup station.

"Unlike Lucy Kimball, Lucy Keen has a bit of a wild streak," Paul said as she sat down. "Most of the time, she's a serious med school student, but every once in a while, she lets loose. She likes to party. It's how she met Jack and why they hit it off."

He scrutinized her face in the mirror. "She wears more makeup than you do. You really are very attractive — high cheekbones, great skin, nicely formed nose and chin, lovely eyes, long eyelashes, and nice lips."

Unaccustomed to either the scrutiny or praise, she felt a blush rise in her cheeks.

He turned to his makeup kit and rummaged through it. "And easily embarrassed. Good to know."

What Paul had said about her becoming another person sounded so casual and easy, but it wasn't. They expected her to be someone else, someone like her, but not.

They wanted her to be a party girl.

Even more outlandishly, a party girl who'd hit it off with Jack.

"You were telling me a story," she said, the edge in her voice betraying her doubts.

He glanced back at her. "I was. And hey, I know this isn't easy. We're asking a lot. We wouldn't if the stakes weren't so high, and if we weren't confident you could pull it off. Ah, here we go."

He turned back to her with eyeliner, blush, and lipstick in hand.

"Close your eyes." He started applying the eyeliner. "So, where were we…? The third rule. The third rule is: Don't fall in love."

She felt her heart thump. Another unexpected answer.

"What happens if you fall in love?"

"You're fired. You're out. You can no longer be a field agent."

"So when you fell in love...."

"I got yanked from the field."

"Why would Special Exploits do that?"

"Keep your eyes closed while I apply just a hint of blush." She heard him rummaging for a brush. "It's Grant's rule. He has a whole speech about it. He loves to recite it like a spoken-word poem. The damn thing is imprinted in my brain."

"Recite it. I want to hear it."

Paul applied the final soft brushes of blush to her cheeks.

"Keep your eyes closed for now. Let me put on the lipstick and then we'll do the big reveal."

The tip of the lip gloss stick touched, pressed, then glided over her lips, and he ran the brush through her now-dry hair.

"Okay," he said, "open your eyes."

She looked at the woman in the mirror and gasped. She was her, but at the same time, not her. The new haircut, soft blush, and glistening red lipstick somehow made her cheekbones look higher and her neck longer. And her eyes — my God, her dark brown eyes looked twice as large. They seemed mysterious, deep, and inviting.

"You're a genius," she breathed. "I never knew I could look like this."

He grinned. "Are you ready to check out the wardrobe we've selected?"

"Sure," she said, suddenly quite curious. "But wait, how do you know my sizes?"

"How do you think?"

She thought for a moment and got it. "The elevator captured my measurements when it scanned me."

He smiled.

"One more thing. I want to hear Grant's love poem."

"Love poem — that's rich. No, I don't think so."

She leaned back in the chair and folded her arms. "I'm not moving until I hear it."

He sighed, then glanced at the open door, cleared his throat, and said, in a very credible imitation of Grant's growl:

Love is the enemy.
Love distracts you.
Love dulls your edge.
Love makes you hesitate.
Love kills.
If you fall in love, you're out.
And don't invite me to the goddamn
wedding.

She couldn't help but laugh. Paul's mimicry was spot-on.

"When I got back from my last mission, Grant knew. Somehow, the bastard knew. He knew before I did. It's like he sniffed it out."

"Scientifically," Lucy said, "that might be possible. We're learning more about how body chemistry changes when a person is in love. Some individuals may have the ability to pick up on that."

"If anyone can, it's Grant. The man is deep. Okay, time to get you to wardrobe."

Lucy gave herself a final look in the mirror, then stood up. "I have to ask. Was the Commander right? Was he right to pull you from the field?"

Paul didn't answer for a moment. He turned away from Lucy as he returned the blush, lipstick, and eyeliner to the makeup case.

"I can't tell you that," he finally said. "All I know is, when I'm not with Carlo, I'm thinking about him, wondering how his day is going, wondering what we'll do when I get home, what we'll have for dinner, what we'll do this weekend.

"I still miss the missions like crazy, but I had to make a choice, and I chose Carlo. It's as simple as that."

As they walked out of the makeup room, she said, "You never told me if Grant and Calhoun are interested in each other."

"You're right," he said with a smile. "I didn't. Let's go try on some clothes."

CHAPTER NINE

IN THE DARKENED briefing room, Jack sat with Grant and Calhoun, who were focused on the monitors on the wall.

"Your point of entry is a party," Grant said. "And here's your host."

The main screen popped up a picture of a man in his late twenties, attractive but not model-handsome, with dark hair, a mischievous grin, and an impish gleam in his brown eyes.

"Sergei Eristov," Grant said. "Self-made billionaire and programming wizard. While still a student at Moscow University, Sergei created what is now the most popular online game on the planet, Gang Bang. More than fifty million people worldwide play Gang Bang every day."

Calhoun said, "I'm familiar with Gang Bang, but only on a superficial level."

Jack jumped in. "It's awesome. You and your friends play criminals, and you gang up to rob banks, smuggle goods, run protection rackets — you name it — all inside this incredibly detailed, immersive online world. The goals are to make money, buy fancy houses, throw big parties, travel, acquire special skills or powers — you know, the usual. But you also put a lot of your money into weapons, safe houses, bodyguards, and other kinds of protection."

"Bodyguards? Safe houses?"

"When you and your gang aren't committing crimes or having fun, you're fighting other gangs, either attacking them or defending yourselves. For territory, for money, for revenge...."

Grant added, "Jack heads up the Hollywood Hillz crew."

Calhoun looked amused. "I'll confess I don't understand the appeal. Why do you and your rich pals play Gang Bang when you could be out nightclubbing?"

"You wouldn't understand this, Deputy Commander, since you never accept my party invites, but sometimes my friends and I don't feel like getting high or laid. Sometimes, we just want to kick back and chill. I mean, how many times do you really want to hop in the sack with the same people?"

"Let's talk about hopping in the sack with the same people," Calhoun said. "Specifically, you and Vienna Hastings."

Jack sighed. So the tune-up wasn't over. "This again?"

"Clearly, the two of you have hit it off, and not just for the benefit of the paparazzi."

"So what if we have?"

"Fourteen confirmed fucks and counting," Grant said, clicking to multiple computer screens that showed him getting physical with the sexy shipping heiress. "That's out of pattern for you."

He shook his head. "You guys worry too much. You really need to get a life."

"You know why we track this," Grant said.

"Vienna and I are friends with benefits. That's all. We

understand each other. We've got the 'poor-little-rich-kid' thing in common."

Grant stared at him intently. What he saw appeared to satisfy him. He turned back to the monitors.

"When a person plays Gang Bang," Grant said, addressing Calhoun, "he creates an avatar, an online representation of himself."

Grant clicked a screen and up popped a fearsome, hulking mountain of muscle and menace. "Meet Jack's character, Wulf Avenger: mob boss and owner of the hottest casino in Bangland."

"A fun guy," Jack said. "Grunts a lot. Total hard-ass."

Calhoun leveled her brown eyes on him. "Interesting. Your alter ego is monosyllabic and physically off-putting. Tired of relying on your charisma all the time, Agent Ford?"

He held her stare. "Okay. What's going on?"

"You tell me," she said, not backing off.

What was her problem? She knew he loved laying on the charm. She knew he was great at it.

After several seconds of silence, Grant pushed on. "Sergei Eristov has several characters. His public character looks just like him and is exactly what you'd expect from the CEO of a successful, high-profile company."

"I hear a 'but' coming," Jack said, turning toward him. "Nice suspense-building technique, by the way. Adds an edge to your briefings."

Grant ignored him. "Computer geniuses are exceptionally good at covering their tracks. Sergei's taken great care to keep parts of his online life hidden."

"But...." Jack prompted.

"As a result, we do not yet have a full picture of him, or his activities, or his interests."

"But...."

"Which means we're operating with less intel than usual."

"Do I even need to say it again?"

"Fortunately," the Commander said, "we've been able to identify the secret character Sergei uses most when he's in Gang Bang. He's spending a whole lot of quality time pretending to be...."

Grant clicked the room's main screen and a character appeared — a computerized version of a man they all knew extremely well: Thick locks of blond hair. Shockingly blue eyes. A nose broken one time too many. A strong jaw. A wide, easy grin that revealed a cocky, devil-may-care attitude.

"Look familiar?"

"Holy shit."

"It gets better. His character spends half his time dressed like this."

Grant clicked again and the screen showed Sergei's character walking, nearly nude, through a luxuriously furnished mansion. It was odd seeing the character's broad shoulders, powerful arms, impressive pecs lightly dusted with blond hair, eight-pack abs, tight ass, and long, muscular legs. Truly, the resemblance was uncanny.

"And, the piece de resistance ..." Grant said, zooming in on the screen.

Jack's eyebrows went up at the closeup of the character's impressive package, barely encased in tight, black rugby swim trunks.

"He's done his research," Grant said. "He finds you quite fascinating."

Jack whistled.

"He's watched your sex tape several dozen times. He took your proportions exactly and used them for his character," Grant said.

"So ... he prefers men?"

"Based on what we know, he sleeps with women — high-priced escorts."

"So this super-awesome, super-fantastic character that's based on me — I mean, how can I not be flattered? — is about ... what?"

"Best guess?" Calhoun said. "Keeping in mind the lonely, nerdy, computer-obsessed, socially awkward teenager he was just a decade ago, our theory is that Sergei admires you and wants to emulate you. He's attracted to the idea of being the ultimate party-loving, rich-boy hedonist. He doesn't want to have sex with you. He wants to *be* you."

"Our best guess," Grant repeated. "No guarantees with this one."

"A serious case of hero worship?"

"Most likely."

"Okay," Jack said, already formulating his approach. "I can work with that."

They heard the door open. Grant clicked off Sergei's character.

Lucy stepped in, nervous apprehension on her face.

For a second, no one breathed. She looked, in a word, sensational. With a few bold changes, Paul had turned the serious scientist into an elegant swan. A simple black cocktail dress hung by straps from her bare shoulders and accentuated her slim curves. She'd slipped into heels, which changed her posture and pushed out her chest. With her shoulder-length hair brushed to frame her face and neck, and soft blush accentuating her cheekbones, she looked like a different person. Most astonishing were her eyes, which seemed impossibly large and dramatic.

"Lucy," Calhoun said, "you look incredible."

Lucy smiled self-consciously, grateful for the confirmation. "Paul suggested I try this out."

"Have a seat," Grant said. "We're just getting started."

Jack noticed Calhoun glance his way again. What was up

with the Deputy Commander? Surely she wasn't worried about him and Dr. Kimball?

"Have you heard of Sergei Eristov?" Grant asked Lucy as she sat.

"The Russian whiz kid who started Gang Bang?"

Grant nodded. "How familiar are you with Gang Bang?"

"A couple of my colleagues play it," Lucy said. "I'm aware of the basic idea."

"Good. You and Agent Ford will be attending a party this weekend at Sergei Eristov's compound on the Greek island of Synkonos. Sergei bought the island two years ago. He's spent millions turning it into his private playground."

Lucy's breathing stopped and her eyes widened.

"Lucy, are you okay?" Calhoun asked, placing a hand on Lucy's shoulder.

"Just taking it all in. Go on."

Grant continued. "Sergei's party is an annual event. It's an elite gathering, invitation-only, for people at the top of their fields in technology, entertainment, business, government, and science. It is, without question, the most coveted invitation of its kind in the world."

"Why are we going?"

"We'll get to that. But first, more background. The invitation list is a closely held secret. Invitations are sent days before the party. At this point, we know about half of the invitees. We're chasing down the rest."

"For three years running, he's invited you," Calhoun said, looking at Jack.

"I was otherwise engaged?"

"Yes."

"Special Exploits has never infiltrated the events?"

"No," Grant said. "You'll be the first."

"Staff?"

"What you'd expect for maintenance, support, kitchen,

and security. Sergei pays well. Most have been with him for years. In addition, for each event, he hires talent."

"Talent?" Lucy asked.

"A euphemism," Calhoun said.

She waited for Lucy to frame her followup question. It took Lucy a few seconds to get it.

"Escorts? Prostitutes?" she finally asked.

"That's not how I would characterize them. Most are models from the world's leading modeling agencies. They are paid a lucrative appearance fee — this year, close to $50,000 — to participate in, and help facilitate, various activities."

Calhoun paused and waited for Lucy to prompt her.

"So they're expensive prostitutes."

"That's not what I'm saying," Calhoun said. "Look at it from the models' perspectives. They're in a competitive, ruthless business built on sex appeal. They're hardworking, focused, aware of their attractiveness, and comfortable using their looks to advance their careers. They're being paid a huge sum to spend a weekend mingling with, connecting with, and possibly forming ongoing relationships with the world's most influential people."

"So you're saying they're...?"

"I'm saying they are career professionals making the most of an incredible networking opportunity. Also, I'm saying that, when it comes to the world's top models, you won't find a lot of judgment or inhibition."

Lucy's cheeks flushed. "You mean, like the kind of judgment I'm showing."

"Yes, that's exactly right." Calhoun leaned forward. "Dr. Kimball, will this be a problem for you?"

"What do you mean?" Lucy asked, though she clearly knew what Calhoun meant.

"I want to be explicit. If you choose to help us, we do not expect you to change your values or participate in activities you are not comfortable with. However, we hope you can temporarily suspend whatever judgments you might have about sex so that you and Agent Ford can focus on retrieving or destroying the stolen phosphorin.

"Can you do that, Dr. Kimball?"

Lucy blinked, obviously uncomfortable with three pairs of eyes on her reddening face, and obviously hating being put on the spot like this. But beneath the discomfort, Jack sensed her weighing Calhoun's question. Could she suspend judgment for a greater cause?

"Yes," Lucy said. "I can."

"Good," Calhoun said.

Ever so slightly, Jack relaxed. At least when the inevitable judgment-fest took place, he could remind her that she'd promised.

"Let's go into what we know about this year's event," Grant said. With a click, he popped up the invitation on the screen, handwritten in bold, beautiful calligraphy:

Dear Mr. Ford,

You and a guest are invited to join Mr. Sergei Eristov for a full-immersion journey back in time ... to a city of swagger and style ... danger and desire ... where the stars played ... and the mob ruled.

Las Vegas, baby!

Jack sat up. "Vintage Las Vegas? Sinatra and the Rat Pack? Sun and sin? Gambling and gangsters?"

"Right up your alley, isn't it?" Calhoun said.

"What does 'full immersion' mean?" Lucy asked.

"Sergei's events are famous for their themes," Calhoun said, "and for their lavish attention to detail. He wants you to believe you've traveled through time to another era. For his first big party, 'Ancient Rome,' he built a coliseum, complete with chariot races and gladiator fights."

Lucy's eyebrows rose. "He built a coliseum? For a party?"

Calhoun nodded. "For his 'Roaring Twenties' party, he recreated a Prohibition-era speakeasy and had it raided by cops, with guests carted off to a jail he'd also built, which they then broke out of. Last year, his theme was 'Space: Beyond Earthly Restraint.'"

"Let me guess," Jack said. "Brave astronauts boldly exploring sexy new worlds?"

"Exactly," Calhoun said.

"Alien abductions? Unexpected probings?"

"That too."

"Damn. Wish I'd gone."

The Deputy Commander turned back to the invitation. She scrolled past the event details and stopped at the end: "An important note for 21st-century visitors: Personal computers and mobile communications didn't exist in the 1960s, baby! Your groovy futuristic gadgets won't work. Plan accordingly."

"Sergei has jamming in place?" Jack asked.

"Very effective jamming, covering every inch of the island. We've been trying to break through, so far without success. Something else: We don't have the schematics for the main compound yet, so we don't know what's inside it."

Jack grinned. "So if our satellite coms, surveillance bugs, spy cams, and geo-taggers won't be of any use, then…."

"You seem excited," Lucy said. "Why?"

Calhoun answered for him. "He gets to loot the Vault."

Jack shot Lucy a huge grin. "The Vault, baby, the Vault! Finally, after years of relentless and, I must say, impressive pleading, we get to play with some of the coolest, baddest spy tools ever devised. Totally old school. Totally cool."

He saw her almost smile before she managed to stop herself.

"Tools like what?" she asked.

"Oh, you'll see," he said and turned to Calhoun. "I'll handle that part of the prep."

"Back to the event," Grant said. "Dress code is what you'd expect: Black tie, cocktail, casual, sports, swim." Turning to Lucy, he added, "Paul is putting together a wardrobe for you now."

"For the party itself," Calhoun said, "we expect the usual Vegas elements — gambling and stage performances. It's likely that Sergei's interest in mixed martial arts will also come into play."

"A night at the fights," Jack said. "Classic Vegas."

"As with his previous parties," Calhoun continued, "you can expect a full-on, no-holds-barred bacchanal, with an emphasis on role play."

"Role play?" Lucy asked.

"You and Jack will very likely be invited to play characters appropriate to the party's theme and era," Calhoun said. "For example, Jack might step into the role of a high-roller, and you might be a showgirl."

Grant brought up a satellite photo of Synkonos and zoomed in on a twisty trail that snaked across the island. "It appears he's also set up an off-road motorbiking course."

With that final detail, Jack got it. He let out a short laugh. "That means...."

He left the rest unsaid. Grant and Calhoun nodded.

It meant Sergei had designed the party with one person in mind: Jack Ford. It meant Sergei had read Jack's interview in GQ, in which Jack had expressed his appreciation for the boisterous, man-centric style of the early 1960s, as epitomized by the Rat Pack and Vegas. It meant he was catering to Jack's well-publicized enthusiasms for motorbiking, mixed martial arts, partying, gambling, and sex.

It meant Sergei planned to observe and learn from the world's greatest playboy in his preferred environment.

It meant he really did have a fan — a superfan of the epic sort. He didn't know whether he should feel flattered or like an animal in a zoo.

"What does what mean?" Lucy asked.

"It means Sergei has put together a weekend that Jack is likely to enjoy," Calhoun said smoothly. "Now, as we said, we're continuing to run down the confirmed guests. About half are from business — top executives, bankers, hedge funders, technologists. The other half are from politics, entertainment, sports, and science."

"Science?" Lucy asked.

"We know one attendee from your field," Grant said and pulled up a photo of Francois Le Coq, the eminent French biologist and notorious womanizer. The photo was quintessential Le Coq: resplendent in a tux, a beautiful blonde by his side, his full mane of silver hair sweeping over his head.

"Do you know him?"

"Only by reputation," Lucy said. "He spoke at a conference I attended last year, but we didn't meet."

"Have you met his wife, Marie?" Grant pulled up a second photo of the attractive, much younger blonde from the first photo. "His fourth wife. They were married two years ago. She's attending as well."

Lucy looked at the photo. "No, I don't believe so."

"We'll find out if she and Lucy ever crossed paths," Calhoun said.

Grant nodded.

"Commander," Jack said, "I assume the reason we're hitting Sergei's party is that someone there has something to do with the stolen phosphorin."

"That's right," Grant said.

"Do we know who?"

"That's where things become complicated."

CHAPTER **TEN**

LUCY WAITED FOR the Commander to explain. Surely the situation was already complicated?

"More specifically," Grant said, "I mean this is where things become virtual. The person who stole the phosphorin is auctioning it to the highest bidder, and every aspect of the sale, at least so far, has been conducted inside Gang Bang."

Grant turned to a screen and pressed a remote. "Ten days ago, a Gang Bang character named YokoNoNo posted in the Gang Bang Weapons Bazaar."

He pressed the remote and zoomed into a message that read: "Presenting high-octane, superior-performance helicopters. Onboard rockets installed. Now seeking all legitimate entreaties."

"A simple puzzle," Grant said, "if you look at the first letter of each word."

Lucy spelled it out. "Phosphorin Sale."

"The message was posted shortly after the theft from Kasson."

"Where did the trail lead?" Jack asked.

"Players who responded to the notice were screened for seriousness of intent and financial means. Three players passed the screening and were invited to a meeting yesterday, eight days after the theft from Kasson."

"Do we know what they were told at the meeting?"

"We do. We captured it."

The monitor zoomed into the online world of Gang Bang. From their viewpoint, they were flying through the clouds, above a city far below. They swooped down, careening between skyscrapers, low enough to touch cars and buses, and flying past utility poles before landing on a busy street. The cacophony of the city washed over them.

Lucy gasped. "It feels so intense."

Calhoun nodded. "It's an impressive and dramatic entry into the game."

"The entry route is different each time," Jack added. "Some gamers — they're called 'entry loopers' — focus almost exclusively on starting and restarting the game, and then map out and share their game-entry trajectories."

On the street, other gamers' characters pushed past them. Most were human, but Lucy saw aliens, animals, and mythological creatures mixed in. Some walked alone, but most moved together, in groups.

Ahead of them, they heard gunfire.

"Hold on," Grant said. They peered around a corner and saw two gangs in battle: ninja warriors, dressed in black, swords slashing, facing off against 1930s-era gangsters armed with machine guns. The ninjas surrounded the gangsters, who stood in a defensive circle, guns blazing. The ninjas batted away the bullets with ease as they advanced, step by step.

One of the gangsters yelled out an instruction to his cohorts. He waved his arm in a wide circle. A force field appeared around the gangsters.

The ninjas roared in frustration and pressed their attack, attempting to hack their way through the barrier, but it was too late. With a pop, the force field shimmered, and the gangsters vanished into thin air.

"What was that?" Lucy asked. "How did they disappear?"

"Gangs with a sufficient quantity of combined skills can create force fields and teleport," Grant said.

"Gangs that fight together, survive together," Jack said. "A core rule in Gang Bang."

Grant clicked the remote, and the view took them along a sidewalk, past busy cafes and stores, and into a dark alley. Rats scurried under their feet. Lucy could almost smell the dampness.

They stopped along a blank brick wall.

"The only way to access the meeting is to follow the path the participants took into it," Grant explained.

He turned to the wall and said, "Zero Alpha Seven Five Three Three."

The brick wall shimmered away, and in its place stood a community message board crammed with posters and fliers.

Lucy read the messages: "Samurai sword, hand-forged by Level 37 master," one said. "Anti-tank missiles, captured in raid on Nosa Nostra weapons depot." And "Assassination Training by Level 43 killer."

"The weapons bazaar?" she asked.

"One of the many portals," Calhoun said.

Grant intoned, "Alas, regardless of their doom, the little victims play! No sense have they of ills to come, nor care beyond today."

Lucy looked at him, a question in her eyes.

"The entry code. Our seller is a fan of the 18th century English poet, Thomas Gray."

As he spoke, one of the fliers on the message board shimmered.

"Welcome," it said. "Click to continue."

Grant pressed the remote. For several seconds, there was nothing. She became aware of a low rumble that grew into a roar. The view in the monitor blurred.

"We're entering the instance," Calhoun said.

"The instance?"

Onscreen, they lifted off the ground, bare inches from the building's vertical brick wall. Gaining speed, they shot into the blue sky, the city in all its sprawling glory below. Seconds later, they were in the clouds, gusts of wind buffeting them as they hurtled into the upper reaches of the atmosphere. She saw the curved horizon line of the planet, and with a final push, they were in the silence of space, floating above the planet — a luminous globe, blue and green and brown similar to Earth, but with continents in unfamiliar shapes.

It was dazzling. She shook her head in admiration.

"Think of an 'instance' as a unique point in space-time," Calhoun said. "It's the real-world equivalent of being invited to a meeting down the hall, except when you walk into the room, you're on Mars, years in the future."

"So it's very private."

"That's the intention. But because it's electronic, it can be hacked."

Their onscreen view shifted from the planet, toward a bright light in space. She sensed they were picking up speed. They hurtled toward the white light, closer and closer. She heard a keening sound, almost a whistle: metal under pressure. Their velocity increased, and she fought the urge to cover her eyes with her hands.

And then, with a quiet pop, the white light vanished. They were in a large, tastefully furnished room, with rich red carpeting and wood-paneled walls, decorated with paintings by Rembrandt, Cezanne, and Van Gogh. In the center of the room were three comfortable leather chairs, arranged in a semi-circle, facing a podium on a small stage with red velvet curtains. Against one wall was a table with appetizers and drinks. In the background were the soft, soothing sounds of Schubert.

Pop. A scorching-hot dominatrix in a black latex catsuit appeared. She wore a mask over the upper half of her face. In her hand, a whip, seemingly with a mind of its own, curled sensuously over and around her body. The whip's tip flickered over her nipples, causing them to harden. The woman smiled with satisfaction at the sensation, a hint of tongue moistening her ruby-red lips.

She took in the room with a swift, haughty glance.

With a second *pop*, an alien creature appeared. It was vaguely humanoid, with an enormous head atop a squat body and dark green skin oozing sweat or perhaps oil. The creature's wide mouth opened, revealing decaying yellow incisors and a rough, thick tongue. It had multiple arms — Lucy counted fourteen — like a Hindu god run amok.

Behind the creature was a cage hovering in midair, filled with fluffy white and softly mewling baby seals.

The creature said, with a nod of respect to the latex-clad woman, "I am Ming."

The dominatrix inclined her head. "You may call me Messalina."

"May I enquire about your weapon? Is it possible I am in the presence of the legendary Whip of Woe?"

"You may, and you are." The tip of her whip flickered quizzically, as if assessing Ming.

"Truly, this is an honor."

There was a third *pop*, and before them stood an elven warrior who bore a startling resemblance to the actor Orlando Bloom wearing elf ears. He was carrying a bow, with a quiver of arrows slung over his shoulder.

"Hello," he said. "I'm … um … Borlando."

The others looked at him with disappointment.

"Really?" Ming said. "That's the best you can do?"

"What are you, Level 2?" Messalina sneered.

"Can we try to be civil?" Borlando asked.

"Or what?" Ming sneered. "You gonna shoot us with your scary arrows?"

"Level 2 arrows have 3 damage per second," Messalina said. "Practically useless." She took a step toward Borlando. "I suggest you go home, little boy. Leave this business to the grown-ups."

Borlando stood his ground. "How do I express disdain?"

"Control Z, press twice on the space bar."

A look of disdain appeared on Borlando's face. "Unlike you losers, I don't waste my valuable time in a bullshit online fantasy world."

Messalina's eyes blazed. "You dare insult me? Show some respect to your superiors!"

"Fuck you."

Her whip snapped. The bow flew out of Borlando's hand.

"You bitch!" Borlando said.

As if on cue, Messalina and Ming swiveled and advanced on Borlando, who blinked, took a step back, and assumed a defensive crouch.

"The newbie bores me," Ming said.

"On the count of three?" Messalina said.

They heard a new *pop* and turned toward the sound. The red curtain on the stage parted.

A young Japanese schoolgirl stood before them. She bowed politely and gave them a cheerful smile.

"Welcome. I am YokoNoNo. You may call me Yoko." She giggled. "Please, I place a high value on courtesy. I would be terribly distressed if two of my honored guests slaughtered my third honored guest."

As she spoke, Yoko's black hair transformed into writhing snakes and her bright wide eyes turned fiery red.

Ming and Messalina stepped back.

"The legendary Medusa Death Helmet," Ming said. "Truly, an honor."

Messalina added cautiously, "My apologies to our hostess. No disrespect intended."

"None taken," Yoko said with a giggle. The snakes and red eyes vanished. "I expect you have so many questions. Please, do take a seat. I do so hope my answers will be satisfactory."

The guests sat in the leather chairs.

Ming spoke first. "I would like assurances. What can you tell us about how you acquired the item up for bid?"

"But of course," Yoko said. With a snap of her fingers, a large video screen materialized behind her on the stage. She and the podium glided to the side to give her audience an unobstructed view.

"I'm sure you have all investigated the theft. What you are about to see is footage from a camera mounted on a helmet worn by a member of the extraction team inside Kasson Building 2B."

The screen cut to a video recording of a room — a real room, in the real world. The person wearing the helmet camera made a full turn. The room appeared to be a laboratory, dark and quiet. The camera moved toward a locked container against one of the walls. The video showed hands applying plastic explosive to the handle of the cabinet and inserting a fuse. The person wearing the camera ran behind a lab table and ducked. They heard the sound of a small explosion.

A few seconds later, the holder of the camera ran back to the cabinet and opened it. Inside were sixteen petri dishes. A hand picked one up and held it to the camera. The label read: "Phosphorin Sample 13C." The cameraman opened a custom carrying case and placed the sixteen petri dishes inside.

The video screen went black.

"How else may I be of assistance?" Yoko asked.

Ming shifted in his seat. "I would like assurance that the item you stole from Kasson is — to use the scientific term — the real deal."

Yoko nodded. "Of course. Each of you has been sent a sample for testing, deliberately degraded to ensure it cannot be used for any purpose other than to verify that it is, as you said, the real deal."

Messalina arched her back in her seat, causing her breasts to stick out even more. Ming eyed them with interest.

"I appreciate your thoroughness in providing us this information," she said. "I have an additional question."

"If I may guess," Yoko said, "you would like proof that the item actually works."

"Yes, that would be lovely."

"Kindly direct your attention to the screen."

CHAPTER **ELEVEN**

ON THE VIDEO screen, the words "Day 1" appeared as a computerized female voice said, "The demonstration began filming eight days ago."

The screen cut to a video feed of a real-world room. The room was windowless and all white, with a bed, toilet, sink, and shelf with basic foodstuffs.

A door to the room opened, and a young woman — a prostitute, judging by her provocative skirt, tight tank top, bad perm, and flashy jewelry — was escorted in by two men in hazmat suits. She appeared frightened but defiant, demanding, in German, for the men to tell her what was going on. The two men pushed her onto the bed and left the room, closing the door behind them.

The computerized female narrator said, "The room is pressure-sealed with a closed air system. The phosphorin will be introduced — now."

There was a loud hiss. The woman jumped.

"Oh my God," Lucy whispered.

The computerized narrator continued. "In five minutes, the air in the room will be completely replaced with new air. The only phosphorin remaining in the room will be in the woman's lungs."

The screen went black, the words "Day 2" appeared on the screen, and the view returned to the white room. The woman was sitting on the bed, crying. She coughed. She appeared to be coming down with a cold.

The door opened. The woman looked up, fear and hope on her face. The men in hazmat suits brought in a second woman, also a prostitute and also frightened.

The two women stared at each other, then simultaneously turned to their captors and begged the men to tell them what was happening. The men said nothing.

After two minutes, the men took the second woman by the arm and said, in German, "Enough."

The video cut to a different white room. The second woman was brought in by the men and locked in.

The computerized female narrator said, "The second room also has a closed air system. No phosphorin will be introduced. The second woman's exposure is from spending two minutes in the room with the first woman."

The video continued its day-by-day chronicle:

Day 3: The video cut between the two women, each in her own cell. The first woman appeared to be getting sicker, her coughs worsening. The second woman seemed tired and, by the end of the day, developed a cough.

Day 4: The first woman could barely get out of bed. She begged for help. Coughs wracked her body. The second woman appeared flu-like.

Day 5: The first woman began coughing up blood. The second woman wasn't far behind.

Day 6: The first woman passed out. Too weak to cough,

she choked to death on her own blood. The second woman died the same horrible death eighteen hours later.

Their rooms, once stark white, were drenched in blood.

In the auction room, the video screen went black. The three guests sat in silence.

Yoko giggled. "Impressive, yes?"

After a moment, Ming cleared his throat. "What is your plan for selling this?"

"All of you have the financial resources to meet my price point. You are all so very wealthy! I am motivated by profit, of course, but I am also careful to avoid excessive greed."

She giggled again. "So I have come up with a plan. We will play a game. You will compete against each other in challenge rounds. The first challenge will advance you to the second round. The second round will advance you to the final round. The final round will be between the two top players. The victor will win the right to purchase the phosphorin at the agreed-upon price. The losers will pay nothing."

"What if we don't want to play?" Borlando asked.

The others turned and glared at him.

"You are under no obligation," Yoko said. "I can remove you from this instance immediately if you would like. Do you wish to play?"

Borlando hesitated. After a moment, he said, "Yes."

"Does anyone wish to bow out?" Yoko asked.

"I'm in," Ming said.

"I love playing games," Messalina said.

Yoko beamed at them. "Such wonderful news. I am so excited. We are going to have such great fun. I will communicate the details of the first challenge within the next day."

"Will we see you again?" Ming asked.

Yoko giggled. "That will depend on your progress in the game. Thank you so very much for joining me today. Truly, it has been an honor. I wish all of you the best of luck!"

With a snap of her fingers, the instance ended.

CHAPTER **TWELVE**

LUCY LOOKED AT Commander Grant with alarm.

"The two women in the video…?"

Grant brought up police reports and mug shots on the screen. "Known prostitutes in Zurich. Neither has been seen in over a week."

"The video is real?"

Calhoun nodded. "Our techs have been over every second of it."

"What do we know about the buyers?" Jack asked.

"The characters are run by people using fake identities," Grant said. "The real individuals have been difficult to track down. They each took great care to eliminate any links to their real-world selves."

"But…," Jack said.

"But we've been able to identify two of them." He clicked and a face appeared on the screen of a man in his early forties, with short-cropped dark hair and an intense, unsettling stare. "Ming, the alien baby-seal eater, is a character created and operated by hedge fund manager Dick Hould."

"Ugh," Jack said.

"Why 'ugh'?" Lucy asked.

"Dick Hould is a gigantic asshole."

Calhoun stepped in. "As a trader, Hould is known for taking huge contrarian positions, usually shorts, that pay off when disaster strikes. Earlier this year, he bet against a major toy company before it was revealed that its toys were made with radioactive plastic. Two years ago, he bet against an aircraft manufacturer shortly before a wing on its high-profile prototype jet fell off during takeoff. Perhaps most famously, he made a killing investing in mortgage securities in 2006 and 2007, then sold and took out bets against the same securities a few months before the market crashed in 2008."

"What does he want phosphorin for?"

"Presumably, to create a disaster and profit from it. For example, he might invest in defense companies, then organize a terrorist attack. The possibilities are endless."

Lucy shuddered. With her attention fully focused on her research, she didn't spend much time pondering how the world really worked.

Grant clicked at the screen and a different face appeared, that of a handsome, dark-haired man in his early thirties with a wide smile and impeccably dressed in a coat and tie.

"No way," Jack said.

"Who is that?" Lucy asked.

"You're looking at the second potential buyer," Grant said. "The person using the Borlando character, Prince Ali Saad Bandar of the Royal Kingdom of Gudan on the Arabian peninsula. Well-known for his high-profile, strategic investments in some of the world's top companies."

"The reason we find this surprising," Calhoun said, "is that Prince Ali is a capitalist, through and through. He's also a progressive voice in his country — a supporter of education, equal rights for women, and democratic reform."

"Dude's a major player," Jack said. "I met him once at Wimbledon, when he was dating Helena Gornichova, the tennis star."

"We tied his Gang Bang character to a computer in the Prince's quarters in the Gudan Royal Palace," Grant said. "If it isn't him, it's someone close to him."

"Setting him up?" Calhoun asked.

"Possibly," Grant said. "Or he's after the phosphorin for reasons unknown. It's possible we were wrong about him. Someone in the Gudan ruling family is funding terrorist training camps in the Sudan. It could be him."

"And Messalina?" Jack asked.

Calhoun shook her head. "Nothing yet."

"Let me guess," Jack said. "Prince Ali and Dick Hould are invited to Sergei Eristov's private bash."

"Yes."

"So the thinking is that Messalina has been invited as well."

"Yes."

"Which means the sale could go down there."

"Yes."

"Which means Sergei Eristov could be involved."

"Him or someone close to him."

"Which means the phosphorin could be there."

"Yes."

"Do we know what the first round of the competition will be?"

"We don't," Grant said. "We hacked the instance we just watched, but we have yet to isolate the subsequent communications."

Calhoun added, "Given Sergei's obsession with historical accuracy and the communications jamming he has in place, it's very likely the competition, if it does take place at the party, will rely on older methods of communication."

"Notes passed in study hall?" Jack asked.

Calhoun nodded. "Drop points. Code words. Visual clues."

"Interception could work," Jack said. "It's unlikely the competitors know who YokoNoNo is, or who they're competing against."

"Agreed," Grant said. "In case one of the rounds takes place in Gang Bang, we've created duplicates of Ming, Messalina, and Borlando for you to inhabit."

Lucy watched with growing anxiety as the three Special Exploits agents hammered out the mission's logistics — proposing, modifying, rejecting, and accepting plans and details with dizzying speed. Clearly, the three of them were comfortable working together. They relied on each other and trusted each other.

Just as clearly, they were missing the forest by spending too much time focusing on the veins in the leaves on the trees.

"Can I say something?" she asked. The three agents stopped talking and looked at her. "For my benefit, can I summarize what we know?"

"Please," Calhoun said.

Lucy cleared her throat. "The summary is: Two suspected bidders are attending Sergei Eristov's party, and that's it. That's all we know."

She looked at each Special Exploits agent in turn.

"We don't know who stole the phosphorin. We don't know where the phosphorin is. We don't know why the seller is selling it. We don't know why the seller chose to turn an auction into a competitive, multi-round game. We don't know the terms, timing, or playing field for this game. We don't know who one of the bidders is. We don't know why the bidders want the phosphorin. We don't know if our host is involved. And we don't know to what extent, or why, this Prince Ali fellow, who you thought you knew, is involved."

Lucy turned to Grant.

"Your plan is to send him," she said, pointing to Jack, "to the party with an untrained human bloodhound — me — as his sidekick. You can't promise backup inside the party, given the exclusive nature of the invite list, and you can't promise tech support, given the use of communications jamming technology. You don't have building schematics, so you don't know what's inside the compound. Basically, you're sending us in blind and alone."

Her face flushed as she finished. She hadn't meant for her recitation to sound like an accusation, but that was how it had come out.

Commander Grant regarded her with his usual seriousness. Quietly, he said, "Every statement you made is correct. What you're not acknowledging are five facts."

He sat up even straighter and aimed his eyes at her.

"One: We have the world's foremost phosphoric expert on our side. Our enemy, whoever he or she is, does not.

"Two: Agent Ford is exactly the right man for this mission. He has all of the necessary skills and attributes to succeed.

"Three: Our enemy doesn't know what we know, which could be to our advantage.

"Four: Special Exploits will find a way to provide backup, even if it means storming the compound in broad daylight."

Grant leaned in, his dark eyes glowing with intensity.

"Five: Never forget the stakes are enormous, and we're on the side of right. Never underestimate how much that matters. Knowing that, believing that, feeling that, makes all the difference in the world."

He looked at Agent Ford, then at Calhoun, and then back at her.

"It's time for your decision, Dr. Kimball. Are you in, or are you out?"

Her chest tightened, squeezing the air from her lungs. This was insane. This couldn't be happening. It was too much. There were too many gaps. Too many unknowns. How could they succeed? They couldn't. But they had to. Because if they didn't —

"In," she said before she knew she'd said it. She breathed in sharply. "I'm in."

CHAPTER **THIRTEEN**

Pacific coast, south of Los Angeles
Later that day

THE ORANGE SUN hit the ocean as Jack zoomed along the winding hillside road, his McLaren 650S hugging the curves with ease.

Man, he loved his elegant beast — ferocious yet refined, powerful yet controlled. He'd been behind the wheel of some incredible dream machines — the Ferrari 458, the Porsche 918 Spyder, the Bugatti Veyron — but something about the McLaren reached deep into him and reverberated through him on a ferociously primal level. From every angle, at every speed, on wide-open highways, and in the tightest of turns, his baby's bold muscular beauty felt utterly, completely right.

All day — ever since he'd walked into that conference room and been confronted with Lucy Kimball's shocked, furious eyes — he'd been looking forward to this moment of crisp, controlled performance and to this respite from the inherent messiness of mission prep.

Grant and Calhoun insisted Lucy was essential to the mission — that she alone possessed the knowledge needed to help him in the field. Yes, they tended to be right about these things. And yes, as they had ever so reasonably pointed out, the only thing Lucy Kimball had to do on this mission was inhale.

To her credit, she seemed game — a quick learner, observant, cautious, aware of the stakes, and capable, or so it appeared, of pushing through emotional responses to focus on the mission's objective.

But still, even if all she had to do was lounge by the pool and look good in a bikini, the op was a hell of a lot to ask of a civilian. Especially this civilian, given their past encounter. Lucy Kimball didn't like him and never would. She'd never trust him, which made her a menace. A single slip would expose them both to a world of hurt.

With a caress of his fingers on the beautifully finished hand-stitched leather steering wheel, he turned onto a winding residential road. The homes he passed became progressively grander, the lots larger, until eventually they disappeared entirely. For several long minutes, he and his McLaren had the road to themselves.

The road ended at a massive stucco gate, Mediterranean in appearance, with wrought ironwork painted cobalt blue. As Jack pulled up, the sensor at the gate scanned the car and license plate. With a smooth flourish, the gates opened, and he was home.

His great-grandfather Harland Abernathy, a Texas oil speculator, had ventured to California in 1912 and, on a whim, purchased 10,000 oceanside acres south of the growing city of Los Angeles. Most of the land had been sold off over the past century, but eighty acres at the top of the bluff remained in family hands.

He drove past the feathery pepper trees that lined the

half-mile drive up to the main house, catching glimpses of his childhood at every bend and curve: The dry creek bed where he and his older brother, Danny, had played war games. The water towers he'd climbed, and fallen from, and climbed again. The stables where he'd learned to ride like the wind on the back of Ruby, his spirited mare. The playing field he and Danny had torn up with their games of soccer and rugby. The big red barn his parents used for fundraisers and galas, next to the entrance to the magnificent formal garden, modeled after Versailles and masterminded by his grandmother in the last decade of her life.

As he rounded the final turn, he knew that if he looked to his right, he'd see the family's private chapel. He kept his eyes firmly fixed straight ahead.

The main house came into view: a two-story, Spanish-style stucco mansion with a red-tiled roof, perched dramatically on a bluff overlooking the Pacific.

He pulled into the eight-car garage and turned off the engine. He took a deep breath, hopped out, and, as he always did, completed a full walk-around inspection of his baby to check for scratches and dings. Satisfied, he turned toward the garage entry door and stepped into the main house.

For a few seconds, while standing silently in the main hallway, he let the house seep in, absorbing the lacquered carved ceiling panels, the red-and-gold Chinese teapaper wall covering, and the formal portraits hanging on the walls. His grandmother had decorated the hallway decades ago, blithely ignoring concerns about the clash of periods and colors. Though not his style, he appreciated its odd beauty.

He heard the faint sound of music and conversation coming from the kitchen and caught the welcome aroma of grilled steak. As he passed the formal dining room, he saw, as he always did, his father, Walter Ford, at the head of the table, holding dinner guests spellbound with tales of hunting with presidents, horse-racing with queens and sheiks, and buying and running companies.

His father had loved his two sons, but he'd pushed them, too, and not just in school and sports. Meals at the family dinner table had been a mix of graduate-level history seminars and high-pressure public debates, often with prominent witnesses. Walter Ford expected his sons to do more than listen and absorb. He expected them to participate and to explain, analyze, and defend.

The lessons had stuck for one simple reason: his father steered clear of abstractions. His focus, always, was people.

"Jack, why did President Bush lose to Governor Clinton?" his father had asked him one afternoon, a few months after the 1992 U.S. presidential election. "What was the President's key mistake?"

Jack quickly swallowed the bite of roasted squab he'd been wolfing down. His mother looked at him expectantly. Across the table, his brother Danny gave him an "I'm-gonna-enjoy-watching-you-blow-this" grin.

"The economy. It was barely out of recession," Jack said. He'd just turned fourteen. His voice was starting to crack. He'd grown three inches in four months. His interrogation was being witnessed by a lunch guest named George, a major figure in the Reagan administration, who was sitting across the table, looking on with quiet interest. He could see George wondering, Does the kid have it? Can he pull it off?

"The economy made the President vulnerable," his father said, "but what was the mistake that cost him the election?"

"The President broke his no-new-taxes promise."

"That certainly disappointed his base, but no, it wasn't the crucial factor."

"Bill Clinton is a great campaigner. The President underestimated him."

His father shook his head. "The President had a very good

handle on Governor Clinton's strengths and weaknesses as a candidate."

George nodded in agreement. "Without question."

"Ross Perot," Jack said, pulling out his last card. "The President knew Ross Perot and thought he'd drop out of the race, but he was wrong. Perot hung in."

"Did Perot cost the President the election?"

Jack remembered snippets of a different dinner, weeks earlier, between his father and a different guest, a leading pollster. "No. The President needed two-thirds of Perot's votes to beat Governor Clinton, and there's no way he could have won over that many of those voters."

George shifted in his chair. "Not bad, young man. How old are you now? Fourteen?"

"Yes, sir."

"I agree, Mr. Secretary," his father said. "A good analysis of the political and economic environment facing the President, and certainly as good as what you read in the op-ed pages, but you're missing something, son."

"What's that?"

"You're missing the man."

"What do you mean?"

"Let me tell you a bit about the man who became our president," his father said. He sat up in his seat and rubbed his hands together, his eyes lighting up the way they always did when he told tales. "George Bush is a very impressive individual. Smart, tough, politically savvy, and very capable. Combat pilot. War hero. Elected to Congress. Head of his political party. At the height of the Watergate scandal, he told President Nixon, in the White House, to his face, that the Republican Party no longer supported him and he had to resign. Can you imagine being George Bush in that moment, telling the most powerful man in the world to pack it up and get out of Dodge? Then, of course, envoy to China, where I met him. Director of the CIA. Vice president. President.

"A good president. History will judge him well. He believed — and I agree — that he deserved reelection. He felt he'd earned a second term, so why did he lose?"

His father looked over at George. Something unspoken passed between them.

George turned to Jack. "Your father is about to tell you what he told the President last summer. The President wasn't happy to hear it."

"And you, Mr. Secretary?" his father asked.

"It's your thesis, not mine," George said, then sighed. "The hell of it is, you're probably right."

Walter Ford turned to his son. "Here's the thing about the presidency of the United States: If you work hard and prepare and sacrifice and the stars align and you have the great good luck to win that office, you get to be president for four years. If you want the job for four more, you have to apply all over again. The President loved being president — he knew he had important work to do — but he hated the job interview — resented it — so he delegated his reelection campaign. He let other people run it.

"And that," his father said with emphasis, "was his mistake. He didn't put his heart into the job interview. Voters saw that, clear as day. They saw a guy who took the interview for granted and acted like he was entitled. And nobody likes a guy who acts entitled."

George shrugged. "I like my 'Perot is a son of a bitch' theory better. Much more emotionally satisfying."

"The President didn't follow our family motto," Jack said.

His father chuckled.

"Family motto?" George asked.

His father chuckled again. "Tell him, son."

Jack turned to George. "*Ferociter*."

With a smile, George translated from the Latin: "'Fight fiercely.' Walter, I like this kid of yours."

"So do I," Walter said, looking at his son with pride. "So do I." He stood. "Enough talk. Let's saddle the horses, mix the martinis, and ride down to the beach."

Standing in the hallway, nearly twenty years later, the memory brought a pained smile to Jack's lips. His childhood had ended six months after that dinner, when, in the space of two weeks, he lost his grandmother in a car accident and his father in a plane crash in the Pacific.

His mother, devastated, had retreated to her bedroom, barely able to leave her bed. His brother, Danny, had been pushed off to college.

Not yet fifteen, grief-stricken, and bewildered, Jack had suddenly been very alone. The anger, the rebellion, the drugs, the fights, the sex had started then. By the time his mother pulled herself together, his transformation into teenage wild child was complete.

A middle-aged couple stood side by side in the kitchen, the woman turning steaks in the oven, the man on the phone. They turned at the sound of Jack's entry.

Jack gave them a big grin. "Hola, Rosita, Harold."

"Mr. Jack!" Rosita said. She bustled up to him and gave him a tight hug. "I miss you! You need to visit your mother more often. I want to see my favorite troublemaker in person, not just in the magazines."

He disengaged from Rosita and shook Harold's hand.

"Good to see you, Jack," Harold said.

"You, too, Harold."

The couple had been with the Ford family for three decades, Rosita running the house, Harold managing the estate. They'd remained even through his teenage reign of terror, when he'd done his best to drive them away. They'd hunkered down and waited him out, and when he was ready to listen, they'd told him what he'd needed to hear.

"Your mother's looking forward to seeing you," Harold said.

"But be careful," Rosita warned. "Her mood is snap snap snap."

Jack kissed her cheek. "Always got my back."

"Always," she said. "Now *vaya*. Let me finish in here."

CHAPTER **FOURTEEN**

STEELING HIMSELF, JACK pushed through the kitchen door and headed toward the sunroom overlooking the back garden.

Time to throw down with Mother.

Before her husband's death, Abigail Ford had been, happily and devotedly, a full-time wife and mother. Afterward, hesitantly at first but with gradually increasing confidence, she'd become an active player in the various businesses her husband had bought and built into Abernathy Industries. She'd joined the Abernathy board as the company's largest shareholder; eighteen years later, she was its chairman — an informed, discerning chairman. No major move was made at the company without her review and approval.

Ah, a mother's approval. The lengths to which he'd gone to avoid it.

His mother was at the sunroom's breakfast table when he walked in. She looked up from her newspaper.

"Mother," he said, stepping toward her.

"Give me a hug," she said, putting the paper down. She stood and gripped him briefly but firmly, then leaned back to scrutinize his face. "It's good to see you. You're looking well."

"Thank you."

"Considering."

"Mother."

"You're right, of course. Sit down."

He took a seat opposite her at the table.

Harold walked in with two glasses of water. "Dinner's almost ready."

"Thank you, Harold," Abigail said. "We'll have it in here."

Harold nodded and headed back to the kitchen.

"How are you?" Jack asked.

"Good. Busy with work. Traveling. We flew in from Singapore last night. It's good to be home. You?"

"Pretty much the same. A lot of traveling."

"Our friends in the media have been keeping me informed of your various doings."

"Oh?" he said as casually as he could. Here it was. The battle had commenced.

"Vienna Hastings," she said. "A charming girl, I'm sure, but apparently very much like her mother." She sighed. "Poor Peggy. Always chasing men, but only catching the wrong ones."

"You haven't met Vienna. Don't say that."

Rosita bustled in with two plates of steak and baked potatoes, followed by Harold carrying two salads, napkins, and silverware.

"Rosita, this looks great," Jack said. "Aren't you and Harold joining us?"

"No, we are not. You and your mother need your special time."

"But I need protection!"

"Jack, stop that," Abigail said.

"I'm sure your mother will go easier on you than she should," Harold said.

"Enjoy your meal together, both of you," Rosita said.

Abigail's eyes softened momentarily as she watched them vanish. "I don't know what I'd do without them."

"Agreed."

They allowed the ceasefire to linger as they ate in temporarily companionable silence.

He took a big bite of steak and, thus fortified, said, "For the record, Vienna and I are just good friends."

"More than that if *Fame Weekly* is to be believed," his mother replied. She put down her fork, reached down to the floor, and picked up the latest issue.

Dammit. She'd brought ammo.

She opened the magazine to a spread showing him and Vienna canoodling on the rooftop terrace of Hotel Lex in Hollywood, his hands cupping her face, her hands grabbing his butt. The headline read, "Vienna Stakes Her Claim!" and the subhead added, "The sexy shipping heiress tells friends, 'Jack better stop looking at other girls, because his ass is mine!'"

"Come on," he said. "You know better than anyone how they make stuff up."

"They don't need to make anything up. Your indiscretions take place in public. Now I know that —." She cut herself off, brought her napkin to her mouth, then said, "I'm concerned about you. And I'm concerned about your brother. Heaven knows what his constituents think."

"Danny and I are fine." His brother had won a seat in Congress three years earlier and was gearing up for a U.S. Senate run.

"Every time you do something, the media pounce — on him."

"Danny has his standard answer," Jack said evenly. "You've heard it a million times: he loves me, he doesn't understand or agree with everything I do, I'm my own person, and I make my own decisions."

His mother reached down again and picked up a recent issue of *Hey There* magazine.

"You've had a busy few weeks."

She opened the magazine to a two-page spread of him on a New Orleans balcony, with a Hurricane drink in hand as he tossed beaded necklaces to topless women in the street below. The headline: "My 24 Hours with Legendary Playboy Jack Ford."

"Believe it or not, I was in New Orleans for work."

She pulled out her spectacles and scanned the page. "According to the article, the only work you did was invite a group of young ladies to your suite for a night of drinking and sex. And how does *Hey There* know this? Because you had the reporter join in on the fun!"

"She was very persistent."

"And attractive," his mother said. Without warning, she threw the magazine at his chest.

"Ow!"

"Oh, please."

He rubbed his breastbone and set the magazine on the table. "It's important to cultivate good relations with the media."

"It's hard work, isn't it?" his mother said. "All this activity."

Without warning, she squared her shoulders and swiveled her entire body toward him.

He tensed, because he knew full well what was coming. She was hauling out her big gun — her "bunker-buster stare"

— to burrow through his layers and find his inner core. She'd been aiming it at him his entire life. Try as he might, he had never been able to fully withstand its impact.

Boom. Her eyes plowed in. "I know that your partying isn't just about enjoyment. It's about creating an image, an image that provides value. It's why that investment company hired you."

"I'm glad you see the method to the madness."

She intensified her focus. "You're thirty-two years old. Are you sure this is how you want to spend your time?"

"Mother —"

"Because let me tell you, young man, if you are not fully committed to what you're doing, if it stops being fun and starts being work, then your image will ring false. Your public and your clients will see it, instantly."

"Mother," he said, doing his best to hold his defenses, "when have I ever held back? When have I ever not gone all out?"

She maintained full-stare power for a few seconds more, and then switched it off.

"Never," she said with a sigh. "God help you, you've never held back, even when you should have."

"I love my job, Mother. And I love having fun."

She looked at him silently, then reached out and squeezed his hand. "All I ask is that you be careful."

He heard the sound of a helicopter approaching. He stood and walked to the window.

"I should get going. We'll be leaving from the air strip in about an hour."

"We?" his mother asked immediately.

"A ... new friend."

"Is she — I assume your friend's a she — in the helicopter?"

"It was more convenient that way."

"Bring her in."

"Mother —"

His mother stood. "I said bring her in. I would like to meet this new friend of yours."

CHAPTER **FIFTEEN**

THE HELICOPTER BANKED left from its track along the Pacific coastline and began its descent. The vibrations shook Lucy's seat. Even with the earplugs the pilot had given her, the roar of the engine and the whoosh of the blades were deafening.

They swooped over an expanse of rolling hills, toward a complex of Spanish stucco buildings at the top of a bluff. To one side of the main house, she picked out a tennis court, a pool, and an open playing field. In the back of the house was what looked like a formal garden, with a pathway leading up to an open-air, Roman-style plaza in a grove of trees.

She'd spent her afternoon with Calhoun and her team, completing the checklist they'd prepared for her cover. Paul had finalized her wardrobe and had taught her how to maintain her new hair and apply her new makeup. Calhoun had her memorize Lucy Keen's background, and a tech had snapped casual photos for Lucy Keen's Facebook profile. She, in turn, had provided detailed information about the regimen to treat phosphorin exposure.

Somewhat to her surprise, the lies had come easily. For her lab director, the story was that her aunt had taken ill and that she and her parents were driving to Monterey to be with her. For her parents, the story was that she couldn't make dinner on Sunday because she had to fly to Atlanta for a conference. She used the same lie with her friend, Joanie, when she canceled movie night on Saturday. Ditto with her neighbor, whom she enlisted to take care of Mr. Snuggles, her cat. If anyone called or emailed or texted while she was away, Special Exploits would respond for her.

She and Calhoun had also boned up on all things Jack. Calhoun had given her a stack of press clippings about Jack's very public antics: His nightclubbing and carousing. His fondness for getting naked in public — at beaches and pools, on hotel balconies and yachts, in mosh pits at rock concerts, at Burning Man, and even once at the Lincoln Memorial in Washington, D.C. ("He had his reasons," Calhoun told her. "I can't say more than that.") His pursuit of adrenaline thrills — motorbiking, fast cars, mixed martial arts. And, of course, his seemingly endless parade of women. Dear God, the man kept busy.

She had expected the tabloid stories to convey disapproval — to express shock and dismay while eagerly dishing out the salacious details — but the prevailing attitude, intermingled with expressions of concern, was affectionate. The reporters and editors of the tabloids appeared to *like* Jack Ford, and not just because he generated great copy. They called him "charming" and "fun-loving" and "good-natured," and they worried about his excesses and his stunts, much like a worried parent.

Calhoun had her watch his sex tape, the one he and his then-girlfriend, Brazilian pop star Estella, filmed and "accidentally" leaked to the Internet.

"It's essential you know all this," Calhoun had said with a

smile. "And it's not like it's unpleasant to look at. Say what you will about Agent Ford, but he's nice to look at, from every angle."

He was also, if the tape was to be believed, a skilled and generous lover. The segment that generated the most attention was the fourteen minutes and thirty-seven seconds he spent with his face buried between Estella's legs. The camera captured a side view, with Estella lying on her back on the bed, long legs sky-high, face contorted with pleasure as she moaned loudly, and her beautiful breasts heavy with arousal. Jack knelt at the foot of the bed, her legs over his shoulders, and his hands gently roaming up and down her body.

From the way Estella's body convulsed, from the way her stomach shook, and from the way she gasped and moaned and begged, it was clear that Jack's mouth and tongue were bringing her wave after wave of pleasure.

At one point, right after the nine-minute mark, he pulled back and said, "Tell me what you want."

"More. I want more."

"More what?" Slowly, teasingly, he licked his wet lips.

"Stop talking."

"Tell me," he said, his eyes dancing.

"Tongue-fuck me, you bastard!"

The tape was a worldwide sensation. Estella's record sales skyrocketed. Her orgasmic moans became the world's most downloaded ringtone. "TFMYB" achieved instant catchphrase status. A Brazilian TV network awarded Jack the title of "World's Most Talented Man." When the Vatican made the mistake of issuing a statement of condemnation, Estella skillfully fanned the flames — and ignited a social movement — by appearing on news programs to proclaim, "The Vatican is out of touch. God made females to enjoy life. Women should embrace their power!" Across Latin America, in election after election, female candidates rode a wave of "Placer es Poder" ("Pleasure Power") into office.

The helicopter touched gently on the lawn. With an arm covering his head, a middle-aged man ran out to the chopper. He shouted something to the pilot, who nodded.

The man opened Lucy's door. "Ms. Keen, please come with me. Mrs. Ford would like to meet you."

Lucy unstrapped herself and, ducking beneath the spinning blades, hurried across the lawn. She followed the man through the house and into a beautiful sunroom with glass walls and ceiling, filled with plants and flowers.

Jack and a woman who could only be his mother were seated at a round table in the center of the room. They stood as she entered. Jack stepped forward to greet her, giving her a quick peck on the cheek.

"Lucy Keen," he said, "I'd like to introduce you to my mother, Abigail Ford."

A thought flashed through Lucy's mind — an irrational, ludicrous, and unsettling thought — that Abigail Ford possessed the power to stop time. That in a single frozen second, Abigail had walked around her, inspecting her from every angle and cataloguing every detail of her makeup and outfit, from her helicopter-blown hair to the pink toe polish on her sandaled feet. And then, with a single fingernail, had sliced through her skull, popped open the top of her head, and reached in to cradle her glistening brain in both hands, absorbing her essence.

Even as she felt so exposed, the trained observer in Lucy captured impressions about the woman before her: Early sixties. Vital but controlled. Silver hair, expertly coiffed. Makeup lightly applied. A clear resemblance to her son in the cheekbones and intense blue eyes. A firm mouth, lips compressed. Tense. Displeased about something. About her son? About Lucy?

Time unfroze.

"Lucy, it's a pleasure to meet you," Abigail said with impeccable courtesy. "You've met Harold, I see. Please, sit down. Jack and I were about to have a post-dinner coffee. Are you hungry? Can we get you something?"

"Thank you, Mrs. Ford. Coffee would be lovely."

With a nod from Abigail, Harold slipped away.

Lucy slid into the chair next to Jack.

"I don't often have the opportunity to meet my son's friends," Abigail said. "He was just beginning to explain how the two of you met."

Jack looked at her expectantly. He was testing her — giving her the chance to try on her new persona. Or perhaps he was waiting for her to fail? Was the bastard hoping she'd flub it?

"Well," Lucy said, adjusting herself in her seat, "we met at a club. Jack's nightclub, Naked Lunch, on Sunset."

"Yes, he was saying. I understand it's quite the popular hotspot for the young crowd these days."

"It was my first time there, actually. A friend of mine knew someone who got us in."

"You're not a habitué of the nighttime scene, like my son?"

"I'm in medical school at UCLA. I like to ... let loose once in a while, but my coursework keeps me pretty busy."

"A future doctor?" she said. "Jack, you're setting your sights higher. A woman of substance."

He started to protest, but his mother pooh-poohed him.

"I adore my son," Abigail said, "but sometimes he drives me up the proverbial wall. Now, I'm quite familiar with UCLA and its medical school. We endowed a chair there last year. What is your specialty?"

"I'm considering pediatrics."

"Wonderful, that's just wonderful."

Harold entered the room with a pot of coffee, milk, sugar, and three cups on a tray.

"Thank you, Harold," Abigail said as he set the tray down. She picked up the pot and poured three cups.

"I understand you'll be accompanying Jack to Sergei Eristov's annual retreat?"

"That's right."

Lucy added a dollop of cream to her coffee and took a sip. "This is delicious. Thank you."

"You're welcome, dear. Do you have much experience moving in those circles?"

"No, not at all."

Abigail picked up her cup and breathed in the aroma. "Then a word of advice from someone who knows: If they try to push you around, don't hesitate to push back. They may be wealthy and influential beyond comprehension, but they're still human beings."

"I was going to ask you," Jack said. "Have you met Sergei Eristov?"

"Yes, briefly, last year at Warren's chalet in Davos. He's brilliant, but very young. Perhaps too young for the position he finds himself in."

"Too young?" he prompted.

"Experience informs judgment," Abigail said. "At least it should."

Lucy noticed Jack's eyes narrow by a fraction.

Abigail continued in a business-like tone. "If your firm is considering business with Sergei, I suggest paying close attention to his key advisers. I suspect they greatly influence his decisions."

"You've met them?"

"A man and a woman. Boris and Natasha."

Lucy's eyebrows rose.

"Yes," Abigail said. "Their real names. We checked. They were by his side constantly in Davos — hovering."

"Good to know," Jack said. He glanced at his watch. "Lucy and I have to get going."

"Of course." Abigail stood, clasped Lucy's hands in hers, and gave her another long, searching, unapologetically appraising stare. "A pleasure to meet you, Lucy. A final suggestion: Enjoy yourself, but don't let Jack distract you too much from your studies."

CHAPTER **SIXTEEN**

FORD FAMILY JET
12,000 FEET AND CLIMBING

THE JET'S WINDOWS were large and oval and positioned for optimal viewing. Of all the things to ponder, to process, to prepare for, this was what Lucy's overwhelmed mind had chosen to focus on: well-placed windows. With her head resting comfortably on the cushioned leather seat, she could watch the California coastline recede below her, no leaning forward required.

The jet banked right and continued its ascent. What a day. A day of firsts.

Her first ride in a storage closet.

Her first flight in a helicopter — jarring, unsettling, deafening, and a bit frightening. She'd watched the pilot maneuver four different controls simultaneously, using both hands and both feet to keep the chopper in the air.

Her first time in an aircraft hangar, where their transportation had awaited.

Her first personal customs officer, who'd greeted her with a smile, examined and stamped her Lucy Keen passport, and wished her a safe journey.

And now her first private jet. Upon boarding, Jack had guided her to the rear of the cabin, to facing sofas, and had left her to settle in while he went up front to talk with the pilots. She noted the cabin's luxurious design: fabric-covered walls, wool carpeting, and honey-brown wood veneers. Pressing a button on the armrest revealed a storage compartment in the arm of the sofa, with a tablet inside that acted as a remote control. She took out the tablet and flipped through the menu of options: Dimmable reading and table lights. Air and temperature controls. Satellite television. Internet connection. Film library.

At the sound of laughter, she glanced up and saw Jack talking, very animatedly, with the two pilots. He grabbed one of them in a bear hug, said something else, and the three men burst out laughing again.

Returning her attention to the remote, she stopped flipping and, intrigued by one of the options presented in the tablet's menu, moved her legs aside to examine the carpeted floor between the two sofas. She pressed the table and watched part of the floor slide away. In its place, a table rose and unfolded.

A vanishing conference table? These people lived in a different world.

A world she was now a part of, at least for the next few days. As a temporary spy, on a private jet hurtling north toward the Arctic and Europe at speeds approaching Mach 1. With this stranger — this confident, high-energy charmer who flirted as easily as he breathed — who'd settled into his seat before takeoff and now sat opposite her.

The charm was a facade, she knew now. A front. The man

behind the fun-loving exterior wouldn't hesitate to use her and discard her if necessary, just like before.

He looked good in his white linen slacks and blue sports jacket, his collared shirt open at the neck, his blond hair messed up just enough to make her want to reach over and brush it out.

She watched him take out a thick folder from his carry-on and place it beside him on the seat.

"Thirteen hours," he said, "depending on headwinds."

"I'm sorry?"

"Our flight."

"Ah."

"The sofas convert to beds," he said. "We can get some shut-eye."

"Good," she said cautiously.

He gestured to the tablet. "You find the controls for the window shades, air, lighting, and temperature?"

She flipped through the menu and pressed a button. The shades on the large, oval, well-positioned windows slid shut.

"Are we going directly to Sergei's island?" she asked.

He shook his head. "Synkonos is too small and hilly for a runway. We'll touch down on the island of Kasos in the Aegean. Sergei's private ferry will pick us up."

"How long is the ferry ride?"

"About thirty minutes." He unbuckled his seat belt and stood. "It's self-service on this flight — just us and our pilots — so how about I show you around?"

She followed him to the galley kitchen, where he pointed out the convection oven, microwave oven, fitted storage for china and crystal, and ice drawers.

"There's salmon and chicken in the fridge, plus veggies and fruits and salad and yogurt. Oatmeal is in the dry storage. Water and juice and sports drinks are in the drinks bin. Hungry?"

Her stomach growled. She was ravenous.

"I'll have some chicken and salad."

He pulled out the meat platter and salad bowl, then reached across her for plates.

"Silverware behind you, top drawer."

His arm brush across her back as he set the plates on the prep counter.

"If you want wine, we have a good selection." He gestured to a credenza in the main cabin.

Wine. A glass of wine sounded perfect.

She slipped past him, her shoulder brushing across his chest, and opened the credenza.

"Any preference?" she asked, scanning the selection.

"I'm good with water."

She glanced at him, surprised. "You were drinking water at your mother's house."

"It's important to keep my wits around Mother. Plus, jet travel dehydrates. So does alcohol."

"The food selection here is very healthy."

"Yep."

"Are you a fake drinker? A secret health nut?"

He grinned. "When I can be."

"You're famous for your excess."

He turned, a plate in each hand, and gestured toward their seats.

"I'm no saint, Dr. Kimball, but if I partied the way people say I do, I'd be dead."

He watched her tear into her dinner. She ate with gusto. Nothing picky about this eater. He'd been waiting for the right moment to broach the sensitive topic of their first encounter. With food in her, and two gulps of wine, now seemed as good a time as any.

"Should we talk about the first time we met?" he asked.

"No need," she said between bites, eyes firmly on her plate. "Deputy Commander Calhoun briefed me. You were on a mission. You can't talk about the details."

She said it briskly. Which meant she was still furious. He couldn't blame her.

"Good," he said, as if agreeing the matter was closed. "During our first encounter, you told me a bit — a tiny bit — about how you helped us in England by rescuing your colleagues from that gunman."

She looked up from her plate. "I had help — a lot of help — from your colleague. How is he, by the way?"

"Good. I spoke with him this afternoon. He sends his regards." (His colleague's words had been more specific: "This woman, this Dr. Kimball, is a rare one — courageous and intelligent and caring and capable of more than she knows. If you do not treat her with respect, I will track you down and beat you to a pulp.")

He glanced toward the file on the seat next to him, which was bulging with papers. "I read my colleague's account of the mission, and I heard your edited version the first time we met. Can I ask you to tell me about it again? This time with all the details?"

"Would that be helpful? For this mission?"

"We're partners now. The more we know about each other, the better."

"Okay," she said. "Where should I begin?"

"Wherever you want."

She took another sip of wine and looked at him for a moment. "Then I'll start a few minutes before the gun was aimed at my head."

CHAPTER **SEVENTEEN**

Eleven months earlier
University of Reading
40 miles southwest of London

THE CLICK OF Lucy's heels echoed down the corridor of the university's modern steel-and-glass laboratory building. She wasn't used to this particular pair of shoes and predicted a blister in her immediate future as she struggled to keep up with her host.

Until two minutes earlier, when he'd received a text on his phone, her guide, Professor Rupert Eddington, had been a genial host, acting for all the world like a department chairman who welcomed the opportunity to escort a visiting researcher around his campus. Now he was moving his rumpled bulk down the corridor with surprising speed.

"I apologize for rushing," Professor Eddington said, "but I was reminded that I have another appointment. After introductions, I'm afraid I'll have to take my leave."

He glanced over his shoulder as if he was looking for someone.

He stopped in front of a door at the end of the hallway, then leaned in and positioned his eye in front of the retinal scanner imbedded in the wall. The door clicked, and he stepped aside to usher her in.

"Everyone," he said loudly as he entered the room, "please gather round for introductions."

Six people in white lab coats looked up from their work. The room was large and, to her eye, well-equipped for the team's cutting-edge bacterial research. Along the back wall were a glass-walled conference room, a kitchenette, and a lavatory.

"Dr. Crimple-Smythe," he said, addressing a tall man with thick glasses and frizzy, thinning hair. "Let me introduce you to Dr. Lucy Kimball."

As they shook hands, Eddington's phone buzzed.

He looked at it and the color drained from his face. "Doctor, can you handle the introductions? Dr. Kimball, so sorry. Urgent appointment. Must run. So sorry."

He rushed out the door, leaving the researchers to exchange puzzled looks.

"Well, my," Dr. Crimple-Smythe said. "Most unusual. Dr. Kimball, I attended your talk this morning at the conference. Most impressed with your work with extremophiles."

"Thank you."

"Allow me to introduce my colleagues. I'm sure many of us have questions about your samples and tests."

She heard the lab door beep and open. A man walked in, sweating and out of breath as if he'd been running fast. He was in his late thirties, unshaven, and wearing a tweed coat over disheveled clothes.

"Where is Rupert? They said he was here."

"You missed him," Crimple-Smythe said. "He said he had an urgent appointment."

"Damn it!" The man looked as though he were about to cry.

"Arthur, why are you here?" a woman in a lab coat asked. "It's really not right, not after —"

"Shut up!" the man said. "Those are lies! Lies!"

He pulled a gun from his coat and aimed it at the group, moving wildly from person to person. Lucy gasped. Two of the researchers screamed.

"Are you part of it?" he yelled. "Were you in bed with him too?"

"Arthur," Crimple-Smythe said, shock in his voice, "please put the gun down. Rupert isn't here. He left."

"Shut up! He'll be back. He came here for a reason, didn't he?"

He noticed Lucy for the first time.

"Who are you?" he cried, swinging the gun toward her.

It was then that the horror hit home. This agitated mess of a man — this unhinged stranger — could kill her.

"Who in the hell are you? What are you doing here?" the man yelled again, louder, the gun trembling in his hand.

A jolt of adrenaline coursed through her. She had never faced mortal peril before. Never been challenged by a dangerous, unstable man. Never stared down the barrel of a gun.

"My name is Lucy Kimball," she heard herself say in a steady tone. "I'm a scientist visiting from Los Angeles. I'm here to discuss my research."

What came next surprised her as much as it did the gunman.

"Now it's your turn," she said angrily. "Who are you? Why do you have a gun in my face?"

The man gaped at her and took a step back.

"This isn't what I meant to happen. I'm sorry. I just ..." He stood there for an agonizingly long time, deep in thought, the gun still aimed at her.

"No," he said at last. "I will see it through. I'm sorry about this. Really, I am. Everyone, in the conference room. You can't leave yet. Hurry, please! I must think."

With the gun, he waved them toward the conference room.

Crimple-Smythe's face had gone ashen. "Arthur," he said. "You don't want to do this."

"I said shut up! Get in there! No talking!"

He hurried them into the conference room, then stood at the glass door and stared at them. Again, his resolve seemed to falter. "I'm sorry. I just need to see Rupert. Settle accounts. You can all go back to work soon. Sorry."

From inside the room, they could see Arthur pacing. For several long minutes, no one spoke. A woman cried softly on a colleague's shoulder.

"Who is he?" Lucy whispered to Crimple-Smythe. "Why is he here with a gun?"

"Arthur is a colleague of ours," Crimple-Smythe whispered back. "Or rather, he was, until —"

He was interrupted by one of his colleagues, who said to Crimple-Smythe, "I need the loo. I'm going to be sick."

Panic flared in Crimple-Smythe's eyes. He didn't want — couldn't handle — the leadership role expected of him.

Again to her surprise, Lucy found herself standing up and walking to the conference room door and knocking on the glass.

"What do you want?" Arthur said. "Sit down!"

"You need to let us use the bathroom," Lucy said. "One at a time. If you don't, this room will become rather messy."

Arthur hesitated.

"This man is about to be sick!"

Arthur relented and nodded. Lucy stepped aside, and the

researcher ran into the bathroom. Through the closed door, they heard him vomiting.

"Arthur," she said as calmly and evenly as she could. "What you want from Rupert has nothing to do with me, or with these people here. I'm a visitor. I'm here to present my research. These people are your colleagues. Rupert isn't here. You can let us go, if you wish. We shouldn't be involved in this, should we? You wouldn't want us to be in any danger, would you? I know you don't want to hurt us."

Arthur stared at her, his face impassive. She couldn't tell whether her words were having an impact.

"I'm not going to hurt you," he said finally. "But I can't let you out yet. I told you I need to think. Until I sort this out, no one is going anywhere. Please sit back down and wait your turn for the facilities."

She sat back down on the conference room floor. A few minutes later, the man in the bathroom returned to the conference room. One by one, the rest of the group took their turn.

Lucy was last. She closed the bathroom door behind her and expelled a huge sigh. She felt like crying. As she stood in front of the mirror, staring at her pale, anxious face, her mind leaped to her life in Los Angeles. To her research, which, since the phosphorin event, had taken on urgent, life-and-death importance. To her loving, supportive, but increasingly frail parents. To her cat companion Mr. Snuggles, her cozy Craftsman bungalow near the beach, her close-knit group of friends, and her colleagues at the lab, most of whom she genuinely liked. What in the hell was going to happen? Was there anything she could do about it?

Lost in her thoughts, she didn't register at first that something in the bathroom had changed. There had been a sound, very faint. Had something moved?

"Up here," a voice whispered.

She looked up and gasped. A masked man was staring at her from the air vent.

"I'm coming down."

She pressed against the door as the masked man slid smoothly out of the vent and dropped to the floor. He was dressed head-to-toe in skintight black clothing.

"Who are you?" she whispered. "Are you the police?"

"Something like that," the man whispered back. "I'm here to help."

Despite her circumstances, she found herself noticing how tall he was, and powerful and sleek, like a panther.

"No one needs to get hurt," the man said. "Arthur's made a foolish mistake, but he hasn't done permanent damage — yet."

"Why is he doing this?"

"He's had a difficult week. He's reached his breaking point."

"Why?"

The man shook his head. "No time to explain."

"Make time," she shot back, again to her surprise.

The man in black regarded her silently. His stance relaxed, slightly. "He believes he's been framed by Professor Eddington for ethics breaches. Yesterday he was suspended from his position at the lab. This morning he found evidence indicating his wife is having an affair, with Eddington."

"He's here for revenge?"

"He thinks he's here to kill Eddington. He thinks he can do it. Unless we can stop him, he just might."

She hadn't missed the man's choice of words. "We?"

"I need to keep away from the cameras in the hallways and labs. The lavatories are the only rooms in this building without video surveillance."

"Why do you care about cameras?" she asked. "You're the police."

"I didn't say that."

Now it was her turn to stare silently.

"You're wearing a mask. No one can tell who you are," she said.

"A common misperception. Suffice it to say, my presence would not be welcome."

"You're some kind of spy," she said.

"We don't have time for this."

"I don't know if I believe you. I don't know a thing about you."

The man stood still, just for a moment, then pulled off the mask to reveal a darkly handsome face, black hair, olive skin, green eyes, a prominent nose, and a strong jaw. He looked fierce — dangerous. She could see him astride a horse in the Sahara, sword raised in fury, battling invaders.

"If we are to be allies," the man said, "then you should know my face."

The weight of the moment descended upon her. This mystery man, who penetrated high-security laboratories and navigated air ducts with ease, was asking for help. Her help.

"You're obviously very capable," she said. "Can't you handle this yourself?"

"If I must. But as I said, if my presence here becomes known, then there would be … complications."

"Such as?"

"It's best you not know, Dr. Kimball."

She started. "You know my name?"

"You arrived from Los Angeles two days ago to present a research paper. In two days, you fly home. I watched you in the conference room. You kept a level head and you handled yourself with courage. I've decided I can trust you." He reached out and laid a hand on her shoulder. "Am I right? Can I trust you?"

From outside the door, she heard Arthur yell, "What's taking so long?"

To the door, she yelled, "Be right out!" To the man in black, she whispered, "I can't stay."

"I need your answer," the man said.

She felt short of breath. For several long seconds, she simply stared at this impossible stranger.

"The answer is yes," she said. "I'll help you."

"Thank you." He handed her a bottle of common pain reliever. "Arthur punched a wall this morning. His hand is in great pain."

"How do you know he's in pain?"

"Have you ever punched a wall?"

She shook her head.

"Trust me," the man said. "It is very painful."

"Okay, fine."

"Persuade him to take a pain reliever," the man said. "As soon as the pill's protective coating dissolves — fifteen minutes after swallowing — he'll be unable to stay awake. When he falls asleep, take the others and leave the building as quickly as possible. The authorities will handle the rest."

"The pill will make him ... sleep?"

"The active ingredient is flunitrazepam."

A powerful narcotic. "Strong stuff."

"In twelve hours, he will awaken with a bad headache, but otherwise be fine. More important, he will be alive and will have avoided a terrible, life-changing mistake."

"If a person pretends to take one and keeps it in her mouth, how long can it stay there before it dissolves?"

The man smiled. "About the same amount of time — ten, fifteen minutes. I see where you're going with this."

"My gut is telling me to trust you. I want to know if I'm right."

"If you're not afraid of a headache, then you have nothing to fear."

She stared into the man's eyes, searching for deception, but saw only appreciation and respect.

With a swallow, she nodded.

"A final suggestion," the man said, pulling the mask back over his face. "Tell the authorities what you wish, but it will be easier to not mention me. They will not believe you if you tell them I helped you. But they will believe you when you say you found the bottle of pills and saw an opportunity to use them."

"They won't believe me? Why? Because you're a secret agent?"

With a silent leap, he was back in the air duct. "Something like that. Good luck, Dr. Kimball."

And as if he'd never been there, he was gone.

She hid the medicine bottle in her hand and opened the door.

Arthur looked at her with suspicion. "You were in there quite awhile."

"I needed a breather. This experience has been ... overwhelming. Could I get a glass of water?"

"Water?"

"I have a splitting headache. Maybe the kitchenette has a first aid kit? I could really use an aspirin."

Before he could say no, she walked into the kitchenette, opened a cabinet door, and pretended to root around.

"What are you doing?" Arthur demanded.

She turned around and showed him the bottle.

"I found these. Would it be okay with you if I took one? My head is killing me. Anything to relieve the pain."

He snatched the bottle of pills from her and examined it.

"Go ahead," he said, handing the bottle back.

She found a glass, filled it with water from the tap, and opened the bottle of pills.

"Would it be okay if I took one now and kept one for later? They really take the edge off the pain."

Arthur nodded.

She popped a pill in her mouth. An act of faith.

She brought the glass of water to her mouth. Choosing to trust a complete stranger.

She swallowed and nearly panicked when she felt the pill go down with the water.

Shit. If her instincts weren't right, she was screwed.

"Thank you," she said, leaving the bottle on the kitchenette counter.

She returned to the conference room and chose a spot on the ground facing away from the door, next to Crimple-Smythe.

"I need you to watch Arthur," she whispered. "Tell me if he goes into the kitchenette or opens a bottle of pills."

The room was quiet, the researchers silent and tense.

The first wave of drowsiness hit about twelve minutes later.

"Has Arthur been in the kitchen or taken a pill yet?" she asked Crimple-Smythe.

"I don't think so. Why?"

"The pills will make him go to sleep, about fifteen minutes after he takes them. He thinks they're pain relievers."

"Why would he take one of those pills?"

"Because he saw me take one, and because his hand is hurting him." A second wave of drowsiness rolled through her. "I need you to pinch me hard if I nod off. I need to stay awake until he takes one."

Crimple-Smythe glanced nervously at the door.

"Pinch you? Where?"

"Anywhere it will hurt. As soon as he falls asleep, get everyone out. Leave us both here and call the police."

Soon after, she felt a pinch on her arm. "Wake up, Dr. Kimball. He's looking at you."

She forced herself to open her eyes and turned around to look at Arthur, who was staring at her from the doorway.

"Everything okay?" she asked.

"Fine," Arthur muttered. He stared at Lucy for a long moment. Abruptly, he closed the conference room door and walked away.

A few seconds later, right before she descended into unconsciousness, she heard Crimple-Smythe whisper excitedly, "He's doing it! He's helped himself to a pill! By jove, I think you've done it!"

CHAPTER **EIGHTEEN**

FORD FAMILY PRIVATE JET
49,000 FEET

JACK LISTENED CLOSELY as she wove her narrative. She told her story clearly and, it appeared, had handled her moment of pressure well. That was encouraging, though it failed to address his primary concern: How would she handle an op that was immersive, full-time, and open-ended? How long before, inevitably, she slipped up?

She finished the last of her wine, then continued. "A week later, Commander Grant visited me in my lab. He told me the man in the air vent was an agent who worked for him. He asked if he could call on me in the future if needed. I said yes."

She looked around the jet. "And here I am."

"Thank you," he said. "That was helpful. And the agent you met? One of the best. Kicks my ass in close combat and penetrates high security like nobody's business."

"He's very persuasive."

"The man has skills."

"Are all of you persuasive like that?"

"Yeah, we are. We have to be."

Her brow furrowed. "So you're tired of it?"

"Why do you say that?"

"You said you 'have to be' persuasive."

He tried to hide his annoyance. What in the hell was up with people lately? First Calhoun had probed him on his night of non-fucking and busted his chops about his Wulf character, and now this cool-as-ice scientist was parsing his every word. Even his mother, who knew nothing about his real work, had questioned his enthusiasm and commitment.

"Dr. Kimball," he said evenly, "I love my job, every part of it."

"You're not liking this part of it. You find me quite irritating."

She was right about that.

"You're mistaking irritation for concern," he lied. "I'd like to try something."

"Try what?"

"A demonstration. You game?"

She nodded, warily.

He gathered up the plates, glasses, silverware, and napkins from the table and took them into the galley kitchen. He returned a moment later and, using the tablet, had the conference table deconstruct itself and slide back into the floor.

He sat down opposite her, with no barrier between them.

"By the time this plane lands," he said, leaning forward, "you and I will want to be comfortable with each other. When we hold hands —"

He reached out and took her hands in his. Startled, she did her best to not jerk away.

"— we need to avoid reactions like the one you just had. Let's be clear: If you flinch, we're fucked."

He saw the effort it took for her to hold her tongue. Man, she wanted to lay into him.

Instead, she withdrew her hands and said, in a calm voice, "I can pretend to like you, and you can pretend to like me. Since you're the great pretender, why don't you teach me how?"

He smiled, impressed. He'd goaded her deliberately by intruding into her private space and using inflammatory language to elicit a defensive reaction. Instead of throwing up barriers, she'd swallowed her anger, acknowledged the criticism, and sought guidance from an expert.

"Happy to," he said. "Let's start with basic physical intimacy. When we touch, we want the world to think we're together. We want them to see that we enjoy each other."

"Physical intimacy? Because if you're suggesting —"

He shook his head. "I'm talking about holding hands. Give me your hands."

After a second's hesitation, she held them out. He leaned forward again and took them in his.

"Let's get to know each other's hands," he said. "What they look like, how they feel."

He watched her focus in. His hands were large and strong. They had weight to them and heat. They easily covered and encircled hers. As her fingertips glided over his calluses, her brow furrowed. He could guess what she was thinking: A Hollywood party boy should have smooth hands.

"You noticed the calluses on my hands," he said, "and you're wondering if they're consistent with my public image."

"Are they?"

"If you were a regular reader of *National Snooper*," he said, "you'd know that Jack Ford has recently discovered the thrills and dangers of off-road motorbiking."

"Oh?"

"A few weeks ago, according to the *Snooper*, I wrecked a custom-built, $100,000 bike. It's a miracle I escaped without injury."

"Is that so?" Lucy asked, a small smile making its way to her lips. "Did you really do that?"

"Wreck the bike? No way. I love that beauty. But I let media think so."

"Hence the calluses?"

"Ycp."

"Okay," she said. "I get it."

And she did. She began to see the logic of this handholding thing.

His hands moved over hers. They were curious; they wanted to know her. He slid his fingers through hers, then took hold of her hands and brought them to his cheeks.

"You have lovely hands," he said, staring directly into her eyes. "Smooth. Nicely proportioned. Surprisingly strong. You take care of them, but they're not ornaments. Most of the time, you apply a simple clear gloss to your nails and keep them fairly short. You rarely wear rings. You have a slight indentation at the top of your right index finger from using a pen, and a slight callus on your right finger and thumb from holding a pestle to grind up materials in the lab."

His eyes were a truly dazzling blue. She willed herself to hold his gaze.

"These points are suggestive," he continued. "I'm sure your lab has electric mixers and grinders and computers, so the indentation and callus indicate you were trained — I'm guessing as a teenager — to do your lab work and record it the old-fashioned way. You enjoy carrying on those traditions. You value them. Which suggests you had a mentor or mentors who were important to you, who trained you to be a scientist, who you remember with fondness and respect."

Despite herself, Lucy was impressed. Excellent observations and reasonable deductions, unless —

"You could have read about my background," she said.

He shook his head. "I haven't had time. Nearly everything I know is from what I've seen and heard, and from what I can sense right here, right now."

"What else do my hands tell you?"

"That you don't date often."

"Because I don't paint my fingernails?" He was going there? Really?

"No," he said. "The fact they're trimmed short isn't conclusive either — plenty of women avoid long nails, for work or other reasons — but throw in the lack of indentations or skin responses to rings or bracelets, and the case for a date-deprived existence becomes clearer."

"Is that all?"

"The clincher isn't your hands, but you."

"Me?"

"Your beauty," he said quietly, the blue in his eyes suddenly more intense.

Heat rose in her cheeks. She had to resist the impulse to pull her hands from his face.

"The only reason a woman as attractive as you isn't dating is because she isn't interested in dating. Or rather, because she's more interested in something else, something that consumes her time, energy, and passion."

"You're wrong about that," she said. "I've been seeing someone for a while now."

He shook his head. "No, I'm right. I bet you're asked out a lot. I bet several guys in your lab have unrequited crushes."

"The man I'm seeing —"

"Wait. Let me guess."

Abruptly, he let go of her hands and sat back in his seat. He was waiting for her answer.

"All right," she said, a hint of challenge in her voice.

He took a deep breath, a serious look on his face. "He works in your field or a related field. You met at a scientific conference. He lives in a different city. He's intelligent, attractive, probably divorced. Like you, he's a workaholic. You've been seeing him for six months, maybe nine months, but you've actually only seen him four or five times because you both have busy schedules."

She did her best to keep her face immobile. His guesses were direct hits. Every one.

"In many ways, this long-distance arrangement suits you. It lets you tell your family, friends, and colleagues you're seeing someone, which means they've stopped trying to introduce you to available men, or set you up on blind dates, or ask you out. That's a relief, because it means fewer awkward encounters and more time for your work."

"Anything else?" she asked with what she hoped was an even tone.

He leaned toward her. "You're trying to see a path forward with this guy, but you can't. More importantly, you're starting to ask yourself if you're making the right choices."

"So now you're a mind reader."

"Just someone trained to be observant. Can I guess about something else?"

"Oh, please."

"You wonder why your friends and family don't ask more

about him, and why they've stopped acting excited. The questions — are you moving to be near him, is he moving to be near you, is he the one, is marriage in your future — are becoming less frequent. You're wondering if they're starting to give up on you."

She folded her arms over her chest. "Anything else?" she asked, doing her best to maintain a neutral tone. God, this man was aggravating.

"Yes. You're worried you'll wake up one morning and find that ten years have passed and that you're still single, still a workaholic, and still in a long-distance, part-time relationship."

She'd actually had that thought this morning, in the shower, before the summons, before her life had been upended by this tornado of a day.

"I know how important your research is," he said. "I've seen the passion you bring to your work. The questions you're asking yourself are: Is the work enough? Or do you want — need — more?"

He shifted in his seat. "I think I know the answer, but I want to hear what you think."

She could only stare at him, at this smug, arrogant man who was so sure of himself.

And so right.

He watched the progression of thoughts flit across her face. He kept giving her opportunities to unload, lash out, or avoid, but she kept plowing forward. He bet she was one hell of a scientist.

"The polite thing for me to do," she finally said, "would be to compliment you on your insightful nature and thank you for giving me a lot to think about. If I wanted to shut down the discussion, I'd tell you that my relationship with

Steven — yes, he's a microbiologist, from Chicago, divorced with two kids — is something I enjoy and want to continue and see deepen. I'd tell you I'm asked out every now and then, but that my work takes priority."

"And if you decided to not be polite?"

"I'd tell you to mind your own damn business," she snapped. For the first time, she let her irritation show. "I'd tell you I don't appreciate being subjected to pedestrian pseudo-analysis by arrogant know-nothings."

He smiled, but said nothing.

"Here's the thing," she said. "I'm not here to be polite or impolite. I'm here to pretend, and you're here to show me how. You're the great pretender, not me. So I want you to tell me how I do, to critique me, after I do this."

He watched her anger vanish and her face transform as she took a deep breath and sat up.

She reached out and grabbed his hands.

"Agent Ford," she said, leaning in, her voice soft and tremulous. "I'm afraid I owe you an apology."

She took another breath, glanced at him shyly, then looked away. "I don't know how you know everything you just said, but you're right. You saw my inner truth."

Another pause, and with her voice filled with restrained passion, she said, "You were right about everything. My life is empty — empty without love."

Holy crap!

He burst out laughing. "Love it!" he said and laughed again. "Sorry, didn't see that coming. Hope I didn't cut short your big reveal."

She suppressed a smile. "How'd I do?"

"Really well." He glanced down at her hands in his. "See? A bit of hand-holding, a bit of banter, and already we're more comfortable with each other."

"Good."

He let go of her hands, stood up, and slid onto the sofa next to her, his shoulder just touching hers. "We need to get used to being side by side rather than opposite each other."

He reached for the files and placed half the stack in her lap. "A lot of reading to get through before we land, for both of us. Everything we need to know about who we are, how we met, our billionaire host, the people he's invited to the party, the location, the threat — you name it."

She looked at the papers. "I'm surprised this isn't in electronic form."

He shook his head. "For security, nothing beats paper. Old school, baby." He could feel the warmth of her shoulder against his. "It all gets shredded and flushed before we land. Any questions, just ask."

CHAPTER NINETEEN

THAT SAME MOMENT
YOKO'S AUCTION ROOM
GANG BANG

YOKO RAN HER fingers over the leather of the chair Borlando had occupied earlier. She sighed with contentment. Everything was proceeding according to plan. The game would be enjoyable and, she expected, conclusive.

She wondered who would win. Certainly not Borlando. The man behind that character lacked the experience and stomach for this game. His interest surprised her. What did he want the phosphorin for? Why had he decided to continue the game, even after she showed him what she was capable of? She would need to be careful with him and keep a close eye. It paid to know as much as possible about whom she was playing with.

Ming was a different matter. The man was pure, naked

ego. He lived to crush others. He would stop at nothing to claim the prize for himself.

Which left Messalina. A fascinating contradiction. In Gangland, she was a formidable, clever, ruthless force. But in real life? Professionally capable, of course, but a follower at heart. Hired help. Unless....

Yoko waved her hand. A large monitor materialized. She gave a series of commands and watched as information flowed across the screen.

Several minutes later, she giggled. Oh, how clever! She should have seen that sooner. How pleasant to be hoodwinked. She would need to play her best game to outwit the lovely Messalina.

"Zurich," she said.

A video feed appeared from the facility in which the two prostitutes had died. A man in a lab coat stepped in front of the camera.

"Is everything completed?" she asked.

"Yes," the man said. "Bodies of the two prostitutes incinerated. Rooms cleaned and decontaminated. Briefcases prepared and ready for shipping."

"Your team has assembled to receive payment?"

"Yes, as instructed."

"Oh, I am so very pleased!" she said, beaming. "As a reward for your excellent work, I am increasing payment for each member of the team by $20,000, with an additional $25,000 bonus on top of that for you personally, in honor of your leadership."

The man smiled. "That is very generous."

"It is what you deserve! Expect an armored truck with the payment in unmarked, non-sequential U.S. dollars within the hour. I look forward to working with you again in the near future."

"Thank you."

She nodded and signed off.

She waved her hand. A different video feed appeared. A man pulled on a black mask and turned to face the camera.

"Yes?" the man asked.

"You may proceed." She gave the man the address of the Zurich facility. "They are expecting an armored truck. All six are there. No survivors. And quietly."

"Understood," the masked man said.

She exited the video screen then placed seven calls to seven couriers in seven cities: New York, Tokyo, Hong Kong, Mumbai, Rio, Paris, and London. For each, the instructions were the same: Your job is to manage the transfer of a briefcase. The briefcase is enroute. No weapons are needed. There is nothing dangerous in the briefcase. At the transfer location, wear a pin of your national flag on your right lapel. A man will approach you with a secret phrase. The phrase is: "While the little victims play." Hand over the briefcase when he says the secret phrase and leave. One third of the payment — $10,000 — has been wired, with the remaining $20,000 to be sent when the transfer is completed.

One last task before she returned to the real world.

"Synkonos," she said. Multiple real-time video feeds appeared.

"Poolside." The monitor jumped to a feed of a large, beautiful pool.

"Zoom in on the waterfall."

The camera obeyed. Beneath the waterfall were statues of frolicking mermaids and mermen.

Yes, that would do.

"Staff list," she said. A list of names appeared. She read through them. No recent hires. Good.

"Model list." The staff list was replaced by portfolios of the models who had been hired for the party. She flipped through them and nodded, satisfied. All known quantities.

"Guest list." Names and photos appeared. Again, most were known quantities. She stopped at a name she didn't know.

"Lucy Keen." The screen showed her Facebook profile and public search results, with references to UCLA and results of local running races.

She'd never met or heard of Lucy Keen, yet something about her seemed familiar.

"Deeper," she said. The screen pulled up her college and high school yearbooks, her credit report, and her passport.

A serious young woman. How had she gotten mixed up with an alcoholic waste of space like Jack Ford?

"Keep searching," Yoko instructed. "Cross-reference for Jack Ford. If you find something, alert me immediately."

CHAPTER **TWENTY**

ELEVEN HOURS LATER
FORD FAMILY PRIVATE JET
25,000 FEET AND DESCENDING

LUCY AWOKE TO the aroma of coffee and the muffled throb of high-performance jet engines.

The past day hadn't been a crazy dream. Eyes firmly closed, she tried to dive back into sleep.

But that wasn't going to happen.

Light was flooding through the cabin's well-positioned windows. The plane banked left. She cracked open an eyelid and saw land. They were over Europe.

"Wake up, sleepyhead," she heard Jack say. He placed a cup of coffee with cream on the side table and sat on the sofa opposite her.

"Are we there yet?" she asked, her voice scratchy and dry.

"Landing in an hour, but we have stuff to go over. I need you alert and focused."

Alert? Now? With a grimace, she sat up. The blanket fell from her shoulders.

"You sleep okay?" he asked.

She had, she realized. "Like a rock."

"I'm not surprised. Not after yesterday."

She stretched her back and eyed her traveling companion. He looked fresh and energetic. How was that possible? How did he do that?

"Have some coffee," he said. "It'll help."

She brought the cup to her lips and sipped. The heat was bracing.

"Time for show and tell." He unzipped a small duffel bag and, one by one, took items out. She could tell he was fascinated by the items. He handled them with reverence, as if they were rare treasures.

"Is this the old-school spy gear?"

"Very old school."

"From the Vault?"

He nodded again as he arranged them in a line on the seat next to him.

"I assume the Vault's location is more permanent than the temporary command center I saw yesterday."

"Way more permanent. Way more secret."

"But you know where it is, right?"

He shook his head. "Grant knows. Calhoun. A few others."

"So how did you get there?"

"Blindfolded and driven in circles."

"But you have a good idea where, don't you?"

He shrugged. "It's a game with some of us, to see how much we can figure out."

"About the Vault?"

"About everything. What Grant told you about compartmentalized information? It applies to everyone."

"Does that bother you?"

"Not usually."

He picked up the first item from the duffel bag — a golden tube of lipstick. It gleamed in the morning light. "Okay, this one is for you."

He opened the lid, revealing a soft red that, she suspected, would work perfectly with her other makeup.

"Twist it right, lipstick appears," he said, twisting the tube right. "Twist it left, it's a gun."

He handed it to her across the table. She examined it with interest. This delicate little thing was a gun?

"How does it fire?"

"Apply pressure to the base after twisting it left."

"Is it accurate?"

"Close range only. One bullet."

"I've never fired a gun."

"Don't worry, you won't have to."

"So you brought it because...?"

He gave her a big grin. "Because I've always wanted a girlfriend with a lipstick gun!"

Lucy found herself smiling. She set the lipstick next to her on the sofa. "Okay, what else?"

He picked up the next item, which looked like a walkie-talkie.

"Satellite phone. It won't work on the island — Sergei's communications jamming will prevent that — but it does have one feature that could come in handy."

He handed it to her.

"Press the 7, 8, and 9 buttons simultaneously, and the phone becomes a stun gun."

Lucy covered the three buttons with her thumb and aimed it at Jack. "So all I do is ... press down?"

"Uh, don't point it at me," he said, not amused.

"Scared?"

"You've never been zapped."

"You have?"

"Too many times."

She put it down as Jack picked up the third item, a black pen. "We won't demonstrate this one either, because believe me, it's no fun."

"What does it do?"

"It really is a pen, but if you turn the handle right and press the tip down for eight seconds, it turns into a sonic nausea inducer."

"A what?"

"It's battery-operated. Good for thirty minutes. It emits a low-frequency sound, too low for human hearing, that disrupts the equilibrium in our inner ears."

"And because our inner ears are thrown out of whack —"

"— we get nauseous."

"What's the range?"

"Not far. Ten feet, tops. The closer you get, the bigger the impact."

"Why would you use this?"

"To weaken or disable someone, and make sure they're puking their guts out instead of concentrating on you."

"That's nice."

"Spycraft isn't pretty."

At the reference to what they would soon be doing, a wave of uncertainty rolled through her.

She stood up. "I have to get ready. Get changed. Put on Paul's makeup."

He stood with her.

"Hey, listen." He reached out and touched her shoulder. "It's your makeup now, not Paul's. You're gonna do great."

She looked into his eyes and, this time, kept her focus on him. "I have to do great, right? We don't have a choice."

She felt her stomach tighten.

As the kids were fond of saying these days, shit was about to get real.

CHAPTER
TWENTY-ONE

JACK HEARD THE bathroom door open and looked up.

The woman who stepped out may have felt shaky on the inside, but on the outside, she looked calm and put together. He noted with approval that her makeup was flawlessly applied and her hair brushed perfectly to transform the shape of her face. Her casual pants and blouse hugged her figure.

A spy for a day, and already her persona fit.

"Anything else before we land?" she asked as she took her seat.

"An additional wrinkle for our story."

"Namely?"

"Let's tell people you aren't feeling well. Something vague — stomach, travel-related. That way, we can excuse ourselves from whatever's going on if we need to and people won't wonder where we are."

"Okay."

"Also, we'll need a secret code to signal that we need to

chat privately, something innocuous we can say in front of other people. Just ask me if I'm tired."

"I should say, 'Jack, are you tired?'"

"Or some variation. If either of us says that, it means we need to go off and talk."

He heard the landing gears unlock and descend, and glanced out the window. The ground was fast approaching.

"Final thing," he said, "and this is important. Always assume we're being recorded — video and audio."

"Because they think you're a spy?"

He shook his head. "Because Sergei, our host, has a fondness for surveillance and a bit of a man-crush on yours truly."

"He admires you, does he?"

"He wants to see me in action — learn from the master."

Her eyebrows arched at that. "So he's going to spy on us?"

"Every moment he can."

"To watch you make your moves."

"Yep."

"On me."

"Yep."

"You don't expect me to...?"

"No, not at all."

"Won't he be disappointed?"

Jack smiled. "I'm fine with Sergei Eristov being disappointed, but are you okay with acting like we're dating?"

"Yes."

"Expressions of intimacy? Kisses on the cheek? Hugs? Holding hands? Sitting close?"

"Yes, I'll be fine."

"Occasional nudity?"

"Pardon?"

"I'm known for my lack of clothing. And since we'll most likely be watched non-stop...."

"You're treating me like I'm a prude. I'm not."

"Just making sure." He paused. "Remember, if you find yourself in a situation you're not comfortable with, just back out. I don't want you to feel like you have to do more than you want to."

From the way she pressed her lips together, he could tell she felt patronized, and maybe even insulted.

"You make it sound like we're going to a sex club," she said.

"We kind of are. This crowd gets pretty wild."

"You think I can't handle that?"

"I think you don't know," he said. "Listen, I can tell you're annoyed, and you know what? Too bad."

She blinked, startled.

"I've worked with civilians before. They're usually fine with the lies and deception and subterfuge, but there's an invisible line with sex that most won't, or can't, cross."

She wanted to protest. She wanted to tell him he didn't have to worry about her precious sensibilities.

"It's like you said," she said instead. "If I say I'm not feeling well, I have an out. Right?"

He looked at her, gaze steady.

"Right," he said. Doubt flared anew. "You're going to be fine."

With a bump, the jet touched down. Game on.

She would be fine. He just needed to keep telling himself that. At some point, he might actually start believing it.

CHAPTER
TWENTY-TWO

HARBOR
ISLAND OF KASOS, GREECE

LUCY STEPPED OUT of the limo, shielding her eyes from the dazzling midday sun, and onto a walkway ringing a small harbor. Dozens of small fishing boats dotted the water, their brightly colored hulls — oranges and blues and yellows and whites and greens — like dabs of wet paint on the harbor's blue-green water canvas. The sun here seemed brighter and more intense than the filtered rays of the Los Angeles sky. A soft breeze from the sea cut through the heat, carrying with it the scents of salt water and diesel oil.

Jack emerged from the limo behind her and pointed to their right. "There."

She followed his gaze. Docked at a large pier that ran along one side of the harbor was perhaps the weirdest-looking vessel she'd ever seen.

"Wow," she said.

"Wow is right."

So this was the ferry that would take them to Synkonos? The lower half of the vessel looked like a flat-bottomed transport ship, with a massive ramp at the bow that could be lowered to unload cargo. Grafted on top, as if sewn on by a mad scientist boat-builder, was what appeared to be an authentic Mississippi steamboat. The oddness of this maritime mish-mash had to be deliberate, serving the specific operational and entertainment needs of Sergei Eristov's island getaway.

They walked to the ferry and were met at the gangway by a grizzled man in a captain's hat. "On behalf of Mr. Eristov, let me welcome you. We have refreshments in the upstairs lounge."

They followed him onto the ferry and up a flight of stairs to a large, luxuriously appointed open room on the upper steamship deck, with sleek leather sofas and chairs arranged for comfort and conversation. At one end, two waiters were at work behind a long bar. Aside from the waiters, the room was empty.

"No other guests?" Jack asked, looking around.

"You and Ms. Keen are the only arrivals for this time window. Most guests arrive later today or this evening. The ferry will make round trips until everyone has arrived."

"How long is the trip?" Lucy asked.

"A bit under thirty minutes. Please have a seat or feel free to explore the roof deck. If you'll excuse me, it's time to get under way."

As if on cue, the engines rumbled.

One of the waiters, a tall blonde woman in tight black pants and a crisp white dress shirt, stepped out from behind the bar. She walked toward them with a tray, carrying two champagne flutes. The cut of her uniform emphasized her curves, hugging her rounded hips and accentuating her breasts.

"Welcome aboard," the woman said with a confident smile.

"Thank you," Jack said. He picked up both glasses of champagne, handed one to Lucy, and took a sip. "Armand de Brignac?"

"Of course." The woman flashed him a smile and took the empty tray back to the bar.

Lucy's eyes narrowed at the tightness of the girl's slacks. "I take it this is a high-end champagne?"

He took another sip. "The best."

Their waitress returned with a plate of caviar.

Jack's eyes widened. "Almas?"

"Yes," the girl said.

"Is that a special type?" Lucy asked.

"From an albino sturgeon," Jack said. "South Caspian Sea. You don't want to miss this. Here, watch."

He used his thumb and index finger to scoop up a generous dollop.

"Don't bite down and don't swallow. Let the eggs roll out in your mouth then burst. The flavor is out of this world."

She followed his lead.

"Oh, my," she said as her mouth exploded in pleasure.

Their waitress remained with them. She seemed unable to stop staring at Jack.

"Pretty good gig, huh?" he asked the girl, his tone friendly. "Not a bad way to spend a few days."

"You're Jack Ford, right?"

"I am. And you are?"

"Jenny. My name is Jenny Lynn Sparks." American, from the sound of her voice. Midwest.

"This is my date, Lucy Keen. Pleased to meet you."

"Pleased to meet you," the girl said, barely glancing at Lucy. "I recognized you, Mr. Ford. You're in all the photos. You're pretty famous."

Desire danced in her eyes.

But not for Jack, Lucy realized. For fame.

"I recognize you from somewhere," Jack said.

Jenny gave him a pleased smile. "I did a campaign for Herve Chin in the September Vogue, and runway shows in Paris, Milan, and New York."

"And now this," he said, waving his arms around. "Not bad, huh? Hanging out with billionaires? How many other models are here with us?"

"Eighty, I think? Mostly girls, but some guys, like David," she said, gesturing to the handsome young man behind the bar. Jenny paused, then blurted out, "I wish I was assigned to you!"

Assigned? Lucy was about to ask what she'd meant when she felt Jack's fingers on her lower back.

"That's too bad," he said, leaning in closer to Jenny, just slightly. "Who's your guest for the weekend?"

"Nigel something-or-other," she said. "I don't know much about him."

"So each guest is paired with a model?"

"Mr. Eristov calls us 'hospitality facilitators.'"

Lucy's shoulders stiffened.

Jack's grin grew even wider. "So you know what's planned for entertainment."

Jenny laughed. "I can't say anything. They made us promise! You'll have to wait and see."

"You're a tease."

She giggled.

"I'm going to take Lucy to the roof deck. It was very nice to meet you, Jenny Lynn Sparks."

Jack guided Lucy up the stairs to the top deck. The sun blazed overhead, but the steady sea breeze took the edge off the heat. Behind them, Kasos harbor was receding into the distance, the white buildings surrounding the harbor reflecting brightly in the sun.

Jack took her by the waist and pulled her in close, as if he was about to lead her on the dance floor. His hand felt solid and strong on her lower back.

He leaned into her ear.

"I can tell you have concerns about our hospitality facilitator," he murmured.

Did she ever. "Quite the euphemism. Were you just buttering her up when you said you recognized her?"

"Yep," he said.

"She's just a kid."

"Not really. She's twenty-two, twenty-three."

"Probably from some little town in Michigan."

"I would have guessed Ohio."

"No experience in the world."

"More than you think. She's probably been modeling for four or five years."

"She's in over her head."

"You're wrong about that. She knows the score."

"She'd do anything for fame."

"Pretty much."

He leaned in closer, his cheek touching hers.

"And that upsets you," he said, almost at a whisper. "You recognize that Jenny Lynn believes her looks are her main asset. You suspect she didn't get much education or family support growing up. You sense she's obsessed with fame. You worry her pursuit of it is foolish and ultimately pointless. You even feel an impulse to intervene, to help her, to guide her."

She liked how he felt against her, his body leaning into her, his cheek against hers. What she would have liked even more was some emotional support instead of yet another mental dissection.

"You think I'm the one who's being foolish and pointless," she whispered back.

"Yeah, I do," he said, an edge to his voice. "We're here for a reason."

God, this man was irritating. She pushed against him to step free. He didn't let go.

"The girl is not our concern," he continued. "You don't even have a reason to be concerned. Her skin and eyes and gums are healthy, which means she takes care of herself, which means she isn't an addict or bulimic. When her quest for fame fizzles, she'll settle for a wealthy husband. She might even end up happy. You need to stop thinking of her as an idiot and a victim."

"I'm not — "

"You are," he said, cutting her off.

With extreme effort, she held her tongue.

He reached up with one hand and brushed a stray hair from her forehead. "She's savvier than you think, but you can't see it because you're up on your moral high horse, racing into battle at full speed."

Her lower lip threatened to tremble. She willed it not to move. She would not let this man see her all worked up, not over a girl — a stranger — she knew nothing about, and not for any other reason either.

"Okay," she said. She took a deep breath. "We're here to save the world, one villain at a time, not one girl at a time."

"That's right. Now turn around and take a good look at Synkonos."

CHAPTER
TWENTY-THREE

LUCY SHIFTED AROUND, still in his arms. An island loomed ahead. It wasn't large — two to three miles long, perhaps — but its dark, rugged cliffs gave it an imposing aspect.

As the ferry chugged closer, she scanned the island's rocky shore for a pier or harbor. "I don't see where we dock."

"We're aiming for — there," he said, pointing to what appeared to be a narrow opening in the cliffs.

The engine revved down. The ferry slowed, carefully skirting jagged rocks that rose like sentries from the reef surrounding the island. As the ferry inched closer to the gap, the cliffs closed in around them.

Ever so gently, the ferry eased into a sliver of water that cut through the cliffs. The sun vanished, plunging them into shadows and turning the dark volcanic cliff rocks almost black. They eased through the gap in near silence; the only sound was the gentle throb of the ship's engine.

Ahead, bright sunlight bounced off water at the end of the passage, obscuring what lay beyond.

And then the ferry reached the light.

Lucy gasped as her eyes adjusted to the sudden brightness. They'd entered a small, almost perfectly round cove that was perhaps a half-mile in diameter. The cove's crystal-clear blue waters shimmered in the sun. A pristine white-sand beach lined the shore. Rising from the beach on all sides were the island's jagged black cliffs. It was as if someone had scooped out the center of the island and filled it with a garden of impossible tropical beauty.

"Incredible," she breathed.

"I see why Sergei snapped up this place," Jack said.

The ferry puttered across the bay to a small pier jutting from the beach, then reversed engines and docked.

"Shall we?" he said, gesturing for her to lead the way.

As they stepped from the gangplank onto the dock, a young man and woman — hospitality facilitators, judging by their form-fitting uniforms — stepped out from a building at the foot of the pier. The young man was tall and muscular, with olive skin and short dark hair, the young woman fair and willowy, with a creamy white complexion and an explosion of curly red hair.

"Mr. Ford and Ms. Keen," the young man said as he bounded toward them. "On behalf of Mr. Eristov, welcome to Synkonos." He flashed a brilliant white smile, his eyes lingering on Lucy. "I am Etienne, and this is Greta. We are your hospitality facilitators."

"I hope the ferry ride was pleasant," Greta said, a few unhurried, graceful steps behind him, her manner calm and composed. "Our job is to make sure you and Ms. Keen enjoy your time on Synkonos thoroughly." A slight emphasis on the last word hinted at possibilities.

The two of them were almost as beautiful as their surroundings. Lucy fought to keep her face neutral. Presumably, this pair of hospitality facilitators had been handpicked for them. Etienne and Greta, the hot and the cool, the bold and the not-so-subtle.

"Mr. Eristov offers his apologies for not greeting you himself," Etienne said. "He was called away on urgent business, but will return in time for evening cocktails."

"No need for formalities," Jack said. "Call us Jack and Lucy." He wrapped an arm around Lucy's shoulders. "How you feeling, honey?"

"Fine," she said, then remembered her role. "I mean, better. I felt out of sorts on the plane."

"We will take the very best care of you," Etienne said. "If you please, let us take you up to Villa Synkonos."

She heard a sound, a soft whir of machinery moving.

"Look," Jack said, pointing to the building at the foot of the pier. "See the cable line?"

Shielding her eyes from the sun, she followed a cable line running from the building on the shore. It stretched across the water to a cave at the top of the cliffs across the bay.

She gasped again. A gondola popped out of the cave and was zooming down toward them.

They watched as the gondola came to a stop and its doors opened. The ferryboat's crew members brought in their luggage. Etienne and Greta gestured for Lucy and Jack to enter, then followed them in.

Inside, the gondola appeared large enough to carry ten people comfortably. Benches lined the walls on both ends, with straps to hold on in the center.

Etienne closed the door. With a gentle whoosh, they were off.

The gondola rose rapidly over the bay. Lucy stared, transfixed, at the dazzling combination of blue water, white beach, and dark cliffs surrounding her. Just the day before, she'd been amazed by the incredible vistas in Gangland. What she was seeing now was even more spectacular.

"Impressive, yes?" Greta said. "We rise three hundred feet in two minutes."

"What's the top speed?" Jack asked.

"Thirty kilometers per hour."

Wind buffeted them. The gondola swayed.

"Please grab a strap," Etienne said. "Sometimes the —"

The gondola ground to a halt without warning. Before Lucy could lose her balance, Jack's arm reached around and steadied her.

"Thank you," she said, reaching up to grab a strap.

"The wind can be tricky in the bay," Etienne said. "The gondola is programmed to automatically stop if we sway too much."

They waited for the gondola to settle. A few seconds later, it resumed its trip.

"Look up ahead," Jack said.

The gondola was approaching the large cave near the top of the cliff. As they got closer, she could make out a loading dock inside.

"Is the cave natural?" Jack asked.

"Originally, yes," Etienne said, "but many of the caves and tunnels have been expanded, first by Greek resistance fighters during World War II, and now by Mr. Eristov."

"It's not just one cave? It's an entire system?" Lucy asked.

"Mr. Eristov is very proud of how he integrated the island's caves and tunnels into Villa Synkonos," Greta said. "I encourage you to ask him about it."

The gondola slowed and eased into the cave.

"We'll show you to your cabana," Etienne said, opening the gondola door.

Lucy stepped out and felt herself being drawn, almost pulled, to the mouth of the cave. She inched closer to the edge and stared down the near-vertical drop to the beach hundreds of feet below. The beauty seemed fake, like a photo in a travel magazine, perfectly staged and composed. Yet the island was real; it didn't get more real. A gust of wind whipped against her.

"Lucy," she heard Jack say.

She shook herself free of her reverie and joined him at the rear of the cave, where a stone staircase, carved into the rock, led upward. Greta and Etienne guided them up the stairs. They emerged into a beautiful, tropical garden. Palm trees rose toward the blue sky, surrounded by flowering plants that provided explosions of color — purples, yellows, reds, and whites.

At their feet, a cobblestone path branched in two directions. A red-and-blue neon sign pointed to "Casino" in one direction and "Pool" in the other.

"This way," Etienne said, leading them toward the pool. Through the trees and foliage, Lucy caught glimpses of what looked like private cabanas.

"Many of our guests will be staying in the cabanas," Etienne said, anticipating her question. "The property has more than two dozen of them. Your cabana is on the other side of the pool."

Rounding a bend in the cobblestone path, they found themselves at the edge of a large, wide-open courtyard.

Rising above the courtyard on one side stood Villa Synkonos, a glorious three-story modern compound, seamlessly integrated into the island's imposing cliffs. In a nod to Greek style, the facade was whitewashed to protect against the bright sun. Huge windows in the center of the building hinted at large, public rooms. Extending on both sides were wings of guest suites, each suite with a private balcony overlooking the courtyard and garden.

"Impressive," Jack said. "Sergei built this?"

"Construction took two years," Greta said. "The

compound is designed as a boutique resort. No expense was spared."

Overlaying the villa's architecture were the decorative elements of the weekend's theme: Vintage Vegas. Neon lights shaped like cocktail glasses, dice, playing cards, and showgirls ran up the walls of the villa. Poker and roulette tables stood at the ready in a corner of the courtyard.

Lucy's eyes slid to the opposite side of the courtyard, where a body of water appeared to vanish off the edge of the cliff. It took her a second to realize she was looking at an infinity pool, with the far edge completely covered by a seamless flow of water. The pool was large and wide, with a diving board on one end.

"This way, please," Greta said. She led them along the pool, past rows of lounge chairs, to a long bar. A waterfall rose behind the bar, and beneath the rushing water, Lucy made out intricately carved statues of mermaids and mermen. At the center of the waterfall, breaking free from the water, was a mermaid queen, arms raised to the sun as she surveyed her dominion with haughty pride.

Lucy turned around to take it all in again — the garden, the courtyard, the villa, the pool — and noticed something she'd missed next to the garden path.

A big, bright billboard rose over the garden, promoting "Synkonos Theater" and two big-name headliners:

Magical! One Time Only!
Robbie Armand & Carrie Esposito
Live in Synkonos Theater
Exciting 'N' Sensational! Tremendous! A Rare Treat!

Armand and Esposito? Two of the hottest pop stars on the planet?

"They're going to be here?" she asked Etienne, gesturing toward the billboard.

Etienne followed her gaze. "What Mr. Eristov wants, Mr. Eristov gets. They fly in tomorrow and perform Sunday night."

He led them past the bar, down a continuation of the cobblestone path, and through a lush jungle of trees and foliage.

They stopped briefly at a small, covered pavilion. Inside the pavilion, a heavy gate surrounded a cabling system, with a vertical rail track that descended into a large hole in the ground.

"Is that … an elevator?" Lucy asked.

Etienne grinned. "Unlike any elevator you've ever seen."

"It takes us to the beach?" Jack asked.

"Yes. There are also stairs to the beach," Etienne said, pointing to a set of steps to the side of the pavilion. "You can also take the gondola. But I recommend the elevator. After you've settled into your cabana, I suggest you try it yourself."

They continued until they reached a beautiful white cabana surrounded by a profusion of flowering plants at the end of the path.

Greta pushed open the cabana's heavy wooden front door and ushered them inside.

They stepped into an entry foyer, with the bathroom to the left and a closet to the right, and then moved forward into the main room. It was a single open space, airy and bright, with a king-size bed on one wall, a full kitchen on the other, and a seating area with facing sofas and a dining table and chairs in between.

All gorgeous, of course. A beautiful combination of leather and soft fabrics and polished woods and marble and gleaming stainless steel.

"Do you need help unpacking?" Greta asked as, behind her, support staff brought in their luggage.

"No, we're good," Jack said.

Greta picked up an information packet from the dining table and handed it to Jack. "Mr. Eristov is providing his guests with selected information about this weekend's activities."

"Selected?" Jack asked, flipping through the packet.

Greta flashed him a smile. "Mr. Eristov likes to surprise."

"Mr. Eristov does have one request," Etienne added. "He asks that you join him for cocktails this evening in the bar. Eight o'clock." He turned to Lucy. "I hope you're feeling better now that you're off the ferry?"

"A bit, yes," she said. "Thank you."

"You must be tired from your travels," Greta said. "We will let you rest."

Etienne added, his gaze still on Lucy, "If there is anything we can do to make your stay more pleasurable — anything at all — let us know."

They left. Jack closed the cabana door behind them and leaned against it, grinning at Lucy. "Somebody has a crush on Lucy Keen."

"Please."

Jack imitated Etienne's accent. "'Make your stay more pleasurable.'"

"Jealous?"

"Amused. Come on, enjoy it. People find you attractive. Deal with it."

She didn't answer. Instead, she picked up her luggage and placed it on the bed.

"We can unpack later," Jack said. "How about we explore?"

"Okay," she said. "Let me freshen up."

When Lucy disappeared into the bathroom, Jack stretched out on the bed, closed his eyes, and wound the tape back on everything he'd just seen. From the moment their plane had touched down, he and Lucy had been enveloped in a flawless procession of orchestrated comfort. The limo, the ferry, the gondola — all perfectly timed for their arrival. The landscaping, the architecture, the decor, the refreshments — uniformly elegant and selected with care. Their attractive hospitality facilitators (assigned, no doubt, after careful consideration) had guided them through a succession of visually stunning tableaus.

The goal was to impress, but there was more to it than that. He let his mind wander. Their host wanted to — what was it? — make them feel special ... distract them from whatever they'd left back home ... separate them, and this weekend, from their daily existence ... take them to a world where the fantastic was real.

The goal was to provide an immersive experience, and not just for him and Lucy. Every guest would receive the same welcome. Everything they'd seen, touched, smelled, and felt was exactly as the maestro of Synkonos had wanted it.

Which meant the real question was: Why did he want it?

He heard the bathroom door open. He sat up.

"I'm good to go. You ready?"

"Sure." He extended his hand. With the barest hesitation, she took it.

They left the cabana and made their way down the winding path and through the lush garden to the pavilion with the gated elevator shaft.

"Let's see where this hole in the ground takes us," he said.

He pressed a green button on the gate. Gears and cables sprang to life. Within seconds, a two-person carriage rose from the ground. The carriage looked as though it belonged on a ride in an amusement park.

The gate slid open. He followed Lucy into the carriage and sat down.

A computerized female voice said, "Thank you. Please fasten your seatbelts."

He found his belt and, with a click, strapped himself in.

"Thank you," the voice said. "Your next stop is the beach."

The gate closed, and the carriage dropped through the hole, into a small cave, and moved on a track through the darkness toward the cave's opening.

"Hold tight," the computerized voice said.

From his vantage, it looked as if the track ended abruptly at the mouth of the cave. He felt Lucy tense as the carriage reached the lip and hung there for just an instant.

Without warning, the carriage lurched over the edge, banked sharply to the left and — whoosh! — hurtled down the track along the side of the cliff.

The elevator was a rollercoaster! The wind whipped at their faces. Lucy gasped. Jack laughed.

The carriage turned and twisted as they careened up and down the edge of the winding black cliff. All too soon, the track brought them to the beach, and the carriage slowed to a gentle stop.

"Thank you for riding the Synkonos Express," the voice said.

"Wow," Lucy said as they stepped out.

He looked around to get his bearings. The carriage had taken them about a third of the way around the bay. The sandy beach extended on either side. Across the water, at the top of the cliffs, he could make out Villa Synkonos rising above the surrounding gardens.

He heard the faint sound of an engine and watched the ferry slip through the narrow passage, into the bay, and chug to a gentle stop at the pier. Four guests stepped off the gangway and were greeted by a pair of uniformed hospitality facilitators.

Like clockwork, the gondola emerged from its cliffside cave and zipped across the bay.

"A smooth operation," Lucy said.

"Very smooth," he said.

Polished and practiced, down to the smallest detail. If Special Exploits' suspicions were correct — if YokoNoNo was using this weekend as a cover for the phosphorin sale — then seeing through these details was critical, because somewhere within them, a devil lurked.

CHAPTER TWENTY-FOUR

LUCY GAVE HERSELF a final look in the bathroom mirror. She could do this. She'd be fine.

Her black cocktail dress, the one she'd worn in Los Angeles, still looked good on her. Her hair and makeup — scrupulously applied, following Paul's instructions — still disguised her true self. Lucy Keen, the medical student who'd somehow managed to snag one of the world's most eligible playboys, was ready for her debut.

But was she? Was Lucy Keen three-dimensional enough to survive a cocktail party with some of the world's most accomplished people? One of whom might be the dangerous criminal who had stolen a lethal biological agent and murdered two women to prove it worked? And three of whom were the amoral sociopaths scheming to buy it?

Jack joined her at the mirror. In his white cocktail jacket, blue open-collar shirt, and dark dress pants, he looked classic and sporty and — she couldn't put a finger on how he managed to convey this, though he did so in spades — up for anything. Maybe it was his eyes, so intensely blue and alive, or the way his smile invited her in. The man just plain radiated energy. No, more than that. The man radiated fun.

"Ready to mingle?" he asked.

No, she wanted to say, but didn't. She stepped past him and opened the cabana door. "After you."

The night air had cooled. Small lanterns in the garden cast a soft light over the path in front of them.

In the courtyard, the infinity pool glowed blue with underwater illumination. The neon lights of Vegas blazed on the walls of the villa. Hand in hand, they stepped into the main compound and walked down a long hallway, through the main lounge, and toward the sound of people talking and laughing in the villa's bar.

A hospitality facilitator greeted Jack and Lucy at the door. Her smile widened as she recognized Jack.

"Welcome to Synkonos, Mr. Ford."

"Thank you," he said, giving her a big grin.

They stepped inside. The bar looked like a gentleman's club, with rich wood paneling, booths, and comfortable chairs. Twenty or so guests had already arrived, the men in jackets, the women in cocktail dresses.

The room sparkled with diamond necklaces, champagne flutes, and dazzling white smiles. Bursts of laughter and excited conversation echoed through the room. In the corner, a man in a sequined blue tuxedo tickled soft jazz from a piano.

A hospitality facilitator appeared at their side, his shoulders threatening to burst through his tight white dress shirt. "May I get you something to drink?"

"A white wine?" she said.

"We are serving a Le Montrachet white burgundy."

"Which one?" Jack asked.

"The 2005 Marquis de Laguiche."

He nodded. "Excellent. And a vodka tonic for me. Hangar One, if you have it."

The facilitator stepped away. Jack leaned in.

"There," he said, nodding toward a group at the other end of the room.

A man, his back to them, was holding court with six guests: Sergei Eristov, their host. Jack took her hand and weaved through the crowd toward him.

Their host was an inch or two shorter than Jack. His curly brown hair was cut short. He was wearing a tailored black cocktail jacket with a white shirt and thin black tie. As she got closer, she saw a side view of a youthful, expressive, open face.

Sergei was gesturing excitedly as he made a point to his guests.

"No, no, let me say another way," he said. "I have sentimental attachment to Russian mother tongue, but I choose to use English. Is best language for future, because it has most words and is most effective way to capture and communicate ideas."

"English has the most words?" a guest asked.

"Eats other languages for breakfast, yes? Always hungry, like me." He laughed. "Now, to be clear, I advocate streamlined English, which is more efficient. I give it name: Ganglish. At first I think I brand it Gang Bang English, but Ganglish is easier to say, yes?"

"What do you mean by 'streamlined'?"

"Idea has appeal, yes?" he said, glowing with enthusiasm. "Rules are simple: Use present tense only. No unnecessary words. Drop articles if possible. Use acronyms if meaning is clear. You have trouble understanding, you tell me, yes?"

"It's a fascinating idea, Sergei," the guest said, "but aren't you missing something with your focus on efficiency? Aren't you losing the poetry, the beauty, the history, and the culture captured by language? Meaning is often referenced or evoked, rather than explicitly spelled out."

"Yes, excellent point, which is why Ganglish uses old language when it retains cultural or emotional relevance. For example, like language of old Las Vegas, which we use here this weekend. If you say, 'you pack of lousy, rotten rats,' or 'hop on, baby,' or 'get a load of this,' you feel connected to that time and place. Ganglish embraces words and phrases that keep their power."

The hospitality facilitator appeared at Lucy's side with their drinks.

"Thank you," Jack said.

Sergei glanced around at the sound of Jack's voice. His eyes lit up.

"We continue Ganglish discussion later, yes?" he said to the group.

He wheeled around, staring at Jack with something approaching awe.

Jack grinned and extended his hand. "Mr. Eristov."

"Jack Ford! I am so glad you are here!" Sergei looked as if he wanted to wrap Jack in a hug, but instead grabbed Jack's hand and shook it vigorously. "I look forward to meeting you for very long time."

"I'm thrilled to be here. Thank you for including us."

Sergei turned toward Lucy. "You are Ms. Lucy Keen, mystery medical student who appears from nowhere and sweeps Jack off feet."

"Oh, I don't know about that," Lucy said.

"I see why Jack has interest in you. You are beautiful. And brunette. Jack has attraction to brunettes, yes? Like Estella, yes?" He laughed. "You must be confident woman to date Jack, yes? He has so many opportunities."

His directness was startling, bordering on rude, and

momentarily threw her. But she sensed he spoke without malice.

"Lucy has tons of confidence," Jack said, wrapping an arm around her shoulders. "One of the reasons I like her."

"You have a beautiful island, Sergei," Lucy said, trying to change the topic. "I don't know if I've ever seen a view more stunning than the one this afternoon in the gondola."

"Is amazing, yes? Natural beauty is excellent starting point, but visual framing is key."

"You mean, like a stage?" Lucy asked.

"Yes, exactly like stage. Beautiful and intelligent — Jack, you pick well." He laughed again. "Why build gondola otherwise? Why place pier across bay from villa? Why build roller-coaster elevator to beach? Because of what one sees in those places. Nature provides backdrop, but composition and positioning are essential to maximize human visual experience."

A hospitality facilitator appeared at their side with a plate of appetizers. Lucy helped herself to what appeared to be a tiny flaky wonton. She took a bite, and a delicious mix of pulled pork and crunchy water chestnut jolted her taste buds.

She watched Sergei's eyes stray to the facilitator's curves as she walked away.

"Of course," Sergei said, "human visual experience is about more than rocks and sky."

Jack grinned.

"We hire best staff for weekend," Sergei added. "Very good-looking and sexy, yes? Recruited from top agencies."

Lucy tried to keep a frown off her face.

"You've done a bang-up job with the visuals," Jack said. "Stunning."

Sergei laughed.

"Speaking of," Jack said. "Our hospitality guides mentioned World War II caves. What are those about?"

"Yes, we use caves and tunnels to maintain environmental

conditions in villa. I offer guided tour tomorrow after breakfast. You have interest?"

"Totally."

A serious, dark-haired man appeared at Sergei's side.

"I apologize for the interruption," the man said, nodding briefly to Jack and Lucy. "Sergei, can I pull you away?"

"Not now," Sergei said. "Jack and Lucy, I introduce you to Boris Ignatiev, CTO of Gang Bang."

Lucy recognized him from his dossier: Sergei's right-hand man — thirty-four years old, shaggy brown hair, a good two inches taller than Jack. He'd be handsome, Lucy decided, if he'd relax and smile. According to his dossier, he'd been with Sergei since the start of Gang Bang.

Boris gave them a brief nod. "Welcome to Synkonos."

Jack said to Sergei, "Dude, if something needs fixing, no worries about us."

"It's a Grid issue," Boris said. "I will take care of it."

"Good," Sergei said, then closed his eyes. "No, I must know. What is issue?"

"Sector four is unstable."

"Is routing protocols."

"Agree. If you want full blocking...."

"Yes, must have," Sergei said. "Go with backup plan."

"Agree. If you'll excuse me," Boris said to Lucy and Jack before stepping away.

"The Grid?" Lucy asked. "What's that?"

The mission dossier hadn't included that term.

"Think of Synkonos as big testing ground," Sergei said. "Think of framing, but in different way than visual. What if framing is time? How can we reposition ourselves to experience earlier era?"

Sergei took a drink from a facilitator and continued. "In today's world, everyone connects instantly to information.

But in old Las Vegas, communication is only from copper phone lines."

"So to frame this weekend's vintage Las Vegas experience," Lucy said, "you've developed technology, which you call the Grid, to disrupt all wireless and radio communications on the island."

A smile came to Sergei's lips. "You keep Jack on toes, yes?"

"Only when he wants to keep up," Lucy said, smiling back. "So what is the Grid, exactly?"

"In simple terms, is ring of specialized weather balloons circling island, holding up web of thousands of super-thin, super-strong wires over Synkonos. Balloons use solar and wind energy to power self-sustaining electrical impulse in wires, which generates sufficient interference to disrupt radio signals, and even signals from satellites. In technical terms, is more complicated than that, but that covers basics."

"The Grid stops satellite phones? And cell service? And wi-fi?" Jack asked.

"Of course. How else do I recreate old Las Vegas?"

"I bet there's a lot of business and government interest in the tech," Jack said.

"That is what Boris says," Sergei said. "We work out kinks here at Synkonos, then launch new business for Gang Bang."

Behind them, they heard a man say, "Did I hear someone use 'new business' and 'kinks' in the same sentence?"

Lucy turned and stiffened. The voice belonged to Dick Hould, the hedge fund asshole behind the Ming character. He was short, early forties, with intense dark eyes, a wide mouth, and a full head of black hair graying at the temples. His tongue darted out and licked his lips like a predator sniffing prey. Even if she hadn't known he was trying to buy the phosphorin, she was certain she would have felt the same visceral dislike.

"Welcome to Synkonos, Mr. Hould," Sergei said, reaching out to shake his hand. "Do you know Jack Ford and his date, Lucy Keen?"

"Pleased to meet you," Hould said perfunctorily, his eyes dipping for a moment to Lucy's breasts before returning to Sergei. "I hope I interrupted an important conversation about a business opportunity involving Gang Bang."

"I delegate such talk to Boris and Natasha," Sergei said.

"Understand completely," Hould said. His eyes swung to Jack. "How about you, Jack? Any plans to enter the family business?"

"Not at this point."

"I heard your mother was in Singapore last week, working an Australian mining deal with the Chinese."

"Could be, but you're asking the wrong guy." Jack's tone was light, but Lucy heard, or at least thought she heard, tension beneath the affable facade.

Hould went still for a fraction of a second.

"Clearly you're an expert on beautiful women," he said, his attention shifting to Lucy. "Enjoying yourself, Ms. Keen?"

"I am. Are you here with a date?"

"Solo. How long have you and Jack been dating?"

"We met a few weeks ago."

Hould's eyebrows rose. "And now you're here. Well done."

A beautiful, redheaded hospitality facilitator appeared at Hould's side. She placed a hand on his arm and leaned in, her eyes catching his. "Mr. Hould, one of our guests would love to meet you."

"No one says no to Becca," Sergei said. "Very persuasive. We talk later, yes?"

Before Hould could protest, Becca slipped her arm through Hould's and led him away.

Jack chuckled. "Dude, that was smooth."

Sergei grinned. "You see what I do?"

"Totally."

"What am I missing?" Lucy asked.

"Sergei told the facilitators to step in and lead guests away after, what? Two minutes?"

"Yes, unless I laugh. When I laugh, two-minute timer restarts." Sergei laughed again. "Excellent technique to avoid boredom, yes?"

"I guess we should be flattered."

"I tell facilitators to never interrupt with you," Sergei said. "I wait too long to meet you. I hope we have great times this weekend."

Jack put a hand on Sergei's shoulder. "Dude, I feel the same way. This weekend's gonna be a blast."

To Lucy's astonishment, Sergei's face turned pink, and his eyes started glistening. Without warning, he grabbed Jack in a bear hug.

"Best time, I promise," Sergei said. "Best time!"

"The best!" Jack said with a laugh, hugging him back. "Love the enthusiasm!"

Carefully, Jack disengaged. As he did, a man and a woman approached.

Lucy recognized the man instantly: Francois Le Coq, the famed scientist, widely acknowledged for his leading role in the search for an AIDS cure. With his shoulders squared back and his mane of gray hair pulled over his head, he exuded authority, like a lion surveying his pride.

"Monsieur Le Coq!" Sergei said, shaking Le Coq's hand vigorously. "And Marie," he said to the striking blonde at his side. "So good to see you again."

"Thank you for having us," Marie said.

"I introduce you to Jack Ford and Lucy Keen."

Here it was — the first real test of Lucy Keen's cover. Francois and Marie had both attended a scientific conference with

Dr. Lucy Kimball the previous year. Would they recognize her?

"A pleasure, mademoiselle," Francois said politely.

"Lucy?" Marie said. "Very nice to meet you."

Not a flicker of recognition from either of them.

Good. So far, at least, Lucy Keen was working out just fine.

And so it went. The party swelled. Drinks flowed. Sergei stuck to Jack like glue. She and Jack were introduced, briefly, to guest after guest. The spotlight was on Sergei, with Jack running a close second. Lucy was in the conversation, but on the periphery, which had proven an excellent spot to be.

Nobody showed more than polite interest in Lucy Keen after learning she was in medical school and had met Jack only recently. Invariably, they offered a joke or two about doctors, asked about her planned specialty, and moved on. She had been deemed not special, not powerful, not accomplished, not famous, not connected, and not rich. Jack would tire of her soon. She would be treated with courtesy, of course, but not cultivated.

Boris returned and pulled Sergei aside. "You were right. It was the router. We fixed it with a physical rewire in the communications shed."

"We address with next release, yes?"

"Top of the list."

"Good. I stop thinking about it. You stop, too."

Sergei turned to Lucy to include her in the conversation. "Boris worries too much. I tell him to let go of cares, but he never listens. He is born worrier."

Boris frowned at that, but said only, "Ms. Keen, I hope you enjoy your stay. I'll let you get back to the party."

"No, stay here!" Sergei said. He reached for Boris and

stumbled. The drinks — he'd been downing them nonstop — were having an effect. "You work all the time, never have fun. But we have fun with Gang Bang, yes? We tell stories. We open people to new experiences. We change world, yes?"

"There is much more to be done."

"Yes! Many problems to fix, like climate change. I too see it like Boris, but I am confident we can adapt."

"It is not us I am concerned about," Boris said. "My worry is for the planet."

"See? Sourpuss! This weekend, I tell him to put worry on hold, enjoy life instead."

Boris gave her a tight smile. Clearly, he'd heard this before.

Across the room, another face from the Special Exploits files appeared: Natasha Dubronovitch, COO of Gang Bang. According to the file, Natasha and Sergei had been engineering classmates before she'd helped him start Gang Bang.

In her dossier, a single word had come up again and again: hard.

Hard-charging, hard-working, hard-edged, and interested in hardly anything other than Sergei and Gang Bang. In a rare interview with a French business magazine, she had described her role. "You can think of Gang Bang as a ship. Sergei has his hand on the wheel. He sets the course. My role is to ensure the ship is sound and goes where he guides it, at the speed he selects."

The interviewer had pressed her about Sergei's over-the-top parties, which Natasha organized, and whether they distracted from the business of running a multi-billion-dollar enterprise.

"I am aware of the criticism that our annual event is frivolous, indulgent, and unnecessary," Natasha had replied, "but I do not agree. The parties are laboratories for character play. It is best to think of them as research and development for future enhancements in Gang Bang."

The Special Exploits dossier noted her loyalty and protectiveness, including the rumors that she personally screened the women Sergei slept with to ensure they were disease-free and on birth control before allowing them anywhere near him.

In other words, Sergei's right-hand woman was a scary-smart, scary-loyal, detail-oriented control freak.

Which meant Lucy could relate, sort of, to the woman with the penetrating brown eyes and practiced smile cutting through the crowd and heading right toward her. Natasha wore a sleeved black cocktail dress and sensible low heels — selected, no doubt, for their easy transition from a work environment to an evening soiree. She was attractive in a sharp, angled way, but sexiness was not what she was about. No, this woman was all about being effective and capable.

Natasha reached Lucy and extended her hand. "Ms. Keen, I am Natasha Dubronovitch, one of your hosts. I am pleased to meet you."

"Likewise. Please, call me Lucy."

"I hope the accommodations are to your liking?" Her English was flawless, each word clipped and precise, with only a hint of a Russian accent.

"The cabana is lovely," Lucy said, "and the island is beautiful. Thank you for having us."

Natasha's eyes darted briefly to Jack, who had been pulled into a nearby conversation with Sergei. For a split second, distaste flashed in her eyes.

Interesting. Natasha was *not* a fan.

"It is one of our best suites," Natasha said, her attention returning to her. "I understand you are in medical school in Los Angeles."

"That's right."

"I considered medicine as a profession myself." For the next few minutes, Natasha peppered her with a series of well-informed and probing questions about medical school and modern medicine. Lucy found herself enjoying the grilling. With the focus on medicine and science, the pressure to pretend lessened.

"May I tell you something?" Natasha asked after a pause.

"Of course."

"I am not often surprised, but you are not what I expected."

Lucy realized she was being paid a compliment. "Thank you."

"If you'll excuse me," Natasha said.

As she slipped away, she felt Jack return to her side.

"How you holding up?" he asked.

"Fine."

"Need a refill?"

She was about to say yes when Jack said, "Shit."

She followed his eyes across the room.

A stunning blonde woman had entered the party. Heads swiveled. The woman rode the wave of attention with practiced ease. She seemed familiar, but from where?

"Do you remember your favorite drink at Naked Lunch?" Jack whispered in her ear.

After a second's pause, Lucy said, "The Cosmo Crump."

"The name of the tall bartender, looks like a sexy Mr. Clean?"

"Vince."

"Your friend who invited you?"

"Vince's sister Jane, my friend from high school."

"The color of the tile in the women's restroom?"

"Mirrored. Mirrored tiles everywhere." She stopped him with a look. "Why are you drilling me?"

"Because you're about to be interrogated like there's no tomorrow."

The crowd parted as the blonde vision headed directly toward Sergei.

"Sergei," the woman said, arms outstretched.

Sergei grinned. "You have arrived! Welcome to Synkonos!" The two of them exchanged cheek kisses. "I am delighted you are here. You are dazzling! A crown jewel for the weekend."

"Oh stop," the woman said, laughing.

"Lady Luck for our Las Vegas experience."

"So sweet," she said, reaching out to caress Sergei's cheek. "I hope Jack isn't getting you into trouble?"

Sergei laughed. "Not yet, but I have high hopes!"

The blonde laughed, then turned to Jack. "Hey, you."

"Hey, you," Jack said. He grabbed her for a hug.

The woman's eyes landed on Lucy.

"You haven't introduced your new friend," the woman said, turning to Lucy and extending her hand. "I'm Vienna. Vienna Hastings."

Lucy wanted to kick herself. Of course. Vienna-frigging-Hastings, pretty much the world's most famous woman. Heiress-turned-celebrity, fashionista, paparazzi fixture, and Jack's pal and occasional squeeze, she was even more stunning in person than on TV or in the magazines. Her blond hair hung straight and lustrous, her eyelashes lush, and her lips full and red. She was tall, too, towering over her by a good four inches.

Without doing a single thing, Vienna made her feel small, and inadequate, and like a fraud, which of course she was.

"I've always loved the name Lucy. I associate it with warmth and laughter."

"Thank you," Lucy said, unable to say more.

"And you," Vienna said, turning to Jack. "Until Sergei told me, I had no idea you'd be here."

"You are happy to see each other, yes?" Sergei asked, looking with interest from Jack to Vienna to Lucy and back again. Sergei had invited Vienna for a reason, she realized.

"I'm always happy to see Vienna," Jack said.

Vienna turned to Lucy and took her by her arm. "Now, if you gentlemen will excuse us, I'd like to steal Lucy for a few minutes. Girl talk."

"Of course," Sergei said.

Jack's eyes caught Lucy's, his meaning clear: Was she okay with this?

Her stomach fluttered, but she nodded at Vienna and said to Sergei, "Which way to the powder room?"

"Down hall, turn right," Sergei said.

And they were off, Vienna's arm through hers. Heads turned as they passed, acknowledging Vienna, but also reassessing Lucy. If the quiet medical student was close to Vienna Hastings, then perhaps she was worth knowing after all.

CHAPTER TWENTY-FIVE

"DUDE," JACK SAID, turning to Sergei, a grin on his face, "you trying to get me killed?"

Sergei laughed. "I confess I invite Vienna with special purpose. I want to see how Jack Ford handles juggle of two women."

"You'll find he does it effortlessly," said a voice from behind him with a smooth, cultured, Oxbridge accent.

Jack turned and grinned. "Your Highness. Good to see you, you old dog."

Prince Ali Saad Bandar, third in line to the throne of the Royal Kingdom of Gudan, stood smiling at them. A tabloid had once run a cheeky story comparing Jack and Ali that read, "Separated at birth? Consider the evidence: These fun-loving playboys were born the same year and are both impossibly handsome, impossibly charming, impossibly rich, impossibly fun-loving, and impossibly successful with the ladies. We're having an impossibly tough time figuring out which one we love/hate more!"

Ali grabbed Jack for a quick hug.

"No 'Prince' or 'Highness' nonsense this weekend. While I'm here, it's just plain 'Ali.'" He turned to Sergei. "I am honored by your invitation. Your annual events are legendary."

"I am very glad you are here. Honor is mine."

Ali glanced at Jack. "It's been … two years? London?"

"The after-party at Stella's," Jack confirmed. "Poor Stella."

Ali laughed. "I'm amazed that chandelier held up."

"Sergei, you didn't tell me Ali was gonna be here."

"A good surprise, yes?"

"How do you and Ali know each other?"

"Strictly speaking," Ali said, "Sergei and I are meeting now for the first time."

"Is okay to share with Jack," Sergei said.

Ali hesitated for a fraction of a second, then continued. "Gang Bang recently approached my kingdom with an interesting idea. Sergei's CTO, Boris, and I have been fleshing out concepts."

Sergei jumped in. "First we change virtual world with Gang Bang, now we transform real world."

"What's the idea?" Jack asked.

"Cheaper method to make fresh water out of salt water," Sergei said. "Boris keeps pushing me, so one weekend, I look at problem of desalinization. I am surprised. I see possibilities. I put together team. In four months, we have prototype from parts we buy retail. Cost is eighty thousand dollars. My machine can produce enough fresh water for one average household. Also, we work on second system for water purification."

"That's incredible," Jack said. "If the desalinization prototype costs eighty thousand...."

"Then cost of machine will be ten thousand when we standardize production," Sergei said. "Then five thousand, then three thousand, then less. In five years, like cost of new refrigerator."

"You're working to purify water as well?"

Ali nodded. "Set up a filtration layer around a farm, and Sergei's second system will purify the agricultural runoff."

"Less pollution in rivers and lakes — "

" — means healthier food and healthier people. We're testing in Gudan. If it works, it will transform my country. We will terraform the desert and grow our own food."

"You know," Jack said, "I've been using a certain word a lot here on Synkonos. The word is 'Wow.' Affordable desalinization, terraforming the desert, water purification, a floating grid that blocks all wireless communication...."

Sergei started to speak, but Jack put his hand up. "Hang on, I'm not done. The coolest elevator in the world...."

Sergei's grin grew wider.

"A kick-ass gondola, the weirdest-looking ferry I've ever been on...."

Sergei laughed.

"On a beautiful island, in a beautiful villa, with beautiful, um, hospitality facilitators, and you're only getting started, aren't you, Sergei? Am I crazy to think even bigger things are to come?"

"Not crazy, because you are right," Sergei said, clearly delighted by Jack's summary. "Big things to come!"

CHAPTER **TWENTY-SIX**

LUCY FOLLOWED VIENNA into the powder room. In addition to the usual stalls, sinks, and mirrors, the room included a beautifully decorated lounge with a chaise and chairs upholstered in sophisticated florals.

She watched Vienna step up to a mirror to check her face.

"Your hair is amazing," Vienna said, glancing at Lucy's reflection. "Who does it?"

Uh-oh. Her Special Exploits background story hadn't covered that.

"A friend of mine," she said. "Paul."

"Where does he work out of?"

Uh-oh again. "He's just starting out."

"I love it. Can I set up a consult?"

"Sure."

"You from L.A.?"

"Westwood."

"You go to UCLA?"

"I'm in med school."

"I applaud doctors. They give so much."

There was a pause as Vienna added a touch of lipstick to her lips. Lucy felt an urge to fill the silence, but Vienna beat her to it.

"Let me guess. You met Jack at the hospital when he crashed his motorcycle and needed stitches."

"No, I met him at Naked Lunch."

"Ah!" Vienna said, her eyes lighting up. "When?"

"A few weeks ago."

Vienna cocked her head. "Was I there?"

"I think so."

"But we didn't meet?"

"No," Lucy said. "I was with my friend. Her brother is one of the bartenders."

"Really? Who?"

"Vince."

"Mmm, Vince," Vienna said. "I love shaved heads."

She stepped away from the mirror and dropped gracefully into a chair.

"These shoes," she said, slipping them off. "My agent said I should tweet a photo wearing them, but they hurt! Plus, is it true we can't tweet?"

"Sergei blocked all wireless communications. He wants to bring back the Las Vegas from the sixties, before we had computers or cell phones."

"Why bring back *that*?"

Vienna took her phone from her clutch and turned it on.

"Nothing?" she said, staring at it. "Not even texts? How will we get anything done?"

"If you need to call someone, your room has a phone."

Vienna grimaced. "Attached to a *cord*. You have to, like, *stand* there."

"He wants the weekend to feel real."

Why was she defending their host? Sergei's party was his

business, not hers. Plus, for all she knew, he was a thief and a murderer.

"Is that why there's a showgirl costume in my closet?" Vienna asked.

Lucy blinked. She had one in her cabana as well, hanging in the closet. It had been there when they'd arrived. She'd meant to ask Sergei why.

"I have one too."

Vienna's attention shifted from her phone. "You try it on?"

"Not yet. You?"

"Of course." Vienna slipped her phone back into her purse and leaned forward. "Do you think we'll be performing?"

"Performing?"

The possibility hadn't crossed her mind, but Vienna was onto something. Sergei's parties were about playing a role and participating fully. At some point in the coming days, Lucy wouldn't just be dressing as a showgirl — she'd be a showgirl.

Vienna raised an eyebrow. "You didn't realize?"

Lucy felt that now-familiar tightness in her chest. Barely arrived and already in over her head. She took a deep breath to regain a semblance of calmness. "Sorry, this is all a bit much."

Something shifted in Vienna's expression. Sympathy, perhaps? Understanding?

"God, listen to me," Vienna said. "Going on and on about me." She stood and walked back to the mirror. "Thank you for letting me drag you in here."

"No problem."

"Can I share something?"

"Sure."

"I want to know more about Sergei. What do you think?"

"He's very … enthusiastic."

Vienna gave her a knowing smile. "You mean he's a pup."

"I don't know much about him or his company."

"Me either. I mean, I play Gang Bang sometimes, but I'm not serious about it."

"Serious the way Jack is?"

"Boys and their toys. Don't get me started."

"At least this weekend, there's no competition from a virtual world."

Vienna smiled. "Will you help?"

"With Sergei? He's available?"

"From what I hear."

"Not too puppy-like?"

"Everyone grows up eventually."

Somewhat to her surprise, Lucy felt the first thread of a connection with this celebrity icon. "Sure."

"Now, fun aside, I want to clear the air," Vienna said.

"About what?" Her stomach tightened. Here it was: what she'd been expecting.

"Jack."

"Yes."

"He and I are friends. I'm sure you know that. And every once in a while, when we're both unattached and available and in the mood, we have sex." Vienna said it matter-of-factly, looking her straight in the eye. "I want you to know that I'm not after him in any way, shape, or form. He's a buddy and a pal — nothing more."

"Thank you for saying that."

"I can see why he likes you," she said. "My advice? Enjoy yourself while you're here. Take this weekend for what it is."

Lucy turned to the mirror and adjusted her hair. Everybody was giving her that advice, and no doubt for good reason.

"Now," Vienna said, holding her arm out. "Shall we? We have a party to conquer."

CHAPTER **TWENTY-SEVEN**

THE COCKTAILS WERE still flowing an hour later when Jack leaned into Lucy and said, "Should we call it a night?"

Gratefully, she nodded.

He turned to Sergei. "Dude, Lucy and I are packing it in."

"What?" Sergei said, dismay on his face. "But night is young!"

"Lucy's not a hundred percent, so we're gonna head back to the cabana. Recharge for tomorrow."

Sergei cast an annoyed glance at Lucy, but his face softened when he saw the tiredness in her eyes.

"Yes, you must rest. Tomorrow is big day."

"See you at breakfast?"

"Yes, breakfast."

Hand in hand, they strolled through the villa, across the courtyard, and along the garden path to their cabana. The villa was quiet, the activity and energy concentrated in the bar.

"What did you and Vienna talk about?" Jack asked as they approached the cabana.

"Besides you, you mean?"

Jack shot her a glance.

Lucy said, "I hope this doesn't come across as offensive, but she's smarter in person than she seems in the media."

"It's her thing. Her persona is rich dumb blonde. The public eats it up. She and her team spend a lot of time crafting perfect stupid things for her to say and tweet."

"She wants me to help with Sergei."

"What do you mean?"

"She thinks he's cute."

"Good. Do that. Help her."

"She said she's okay with me dating you."

"Of course she is," he said, opening the cabana door and ushering her inside. "We're friends with occasional benefits. That's all."

She wondered about that. "You know why Sergei invited her."

"'To see how Jack Ford handles juggle of two women,'" Jack said in an impressively authentic Russian accent.

Lucy watched him walk straight to her suitcase, which was lying open on the bed.

He began moving her clothes to the drawers and into the closet.

"I was wondering when you'd get to that," she said.

"What do you mean?" he asked.

"You're a neat freak."

"Guilty as charged."

"Neat freaks are usually control freaks."

"The great thing about traveling together? We get to know each other so much faster."

He started hanging Lucy's evening dresses. "And yes, as you pointed out, I like things organized."

"Given that, there's something important I should tell you. Something that may upset you." She paused, then said, "Back home, right now, as we speak, clothes are tossed over my furniture, on my bed, and even on my floor, all unorganized."

A grin appeared on Jack's face.

"Will that knowledge gnaw at you, Mr. Ford? Clothes on a floor you can't get to? Are we over before we even get started? Have I uncovered a relationship deal-breaker?"

His grin widened. Her sense of humor — he was digging it.

"Your proud embrace of slobbery is only one of many dating hurdles we have to clear, Ms. Keen. We'll have to learn what we like about each other — "

"Before our differences send us running away, screaming in terror?"

"Exactly." He looked, with quiet satisfaction, at the clothes hanging on the rack. Then he picked up the suitcase and put it in the closet next to his. "Speaking of terror, would it be okay if I call the woman who runs way too much of my life?"

"Who's that?"

"My publicist."

"Publicist?"

"More like a stage mom, actually. A scary stage mom."

"No problem," Lucy said with an amused smile. "I'll give you some privacy."

She stepped into the bathroom and closed the door.

Jack stood there for a moment, thinking about her smile.

Focus, dude.

He picked up the rotary phone and dialed 0.

The operator picked up on the first ring. "Good evening, Mr. Ford. How can I be of assistance?"

"I'd like to place a long-distance call to Los Angeles." He gave her the number.

"Certainly, sir."

He heard the line ringing on the other end.

"I'll drop off the line now, sir."

"Thank you."

He heard an audible click as the operator dropped off. A reassuring sound, but meaningless. Protocol dictated he assume the line was tapped.

The phone rang two more times. Someone on the other end picked up.

"Gracie May Blowser, and this better be good," Deputy Commander Calhoun said in a brassy, vibrant voice completely different from her own.

"Gracie, it's Jack."

"Oooh, my handsomest client! Are you calling from the Mediterranean? Hang on, sweetie. Let me get my day planner! We got stuff to discuss!"

He heard the sound of her rummaging around a desk and smiled. Calhoun made the most of her opportunities to play different characters.

"First of all, how's the party? I'm so jealous! Is it fabulous? Tell me everything, sweetheart!"

"It's going great. Can't give you much now — have to get some sleep. We're getting up early tomorrow for a tour of some underground tunnels built into the cliffs during World War II."

"Fascinating, I'm sure," she said in a voice that indicated she couldn't care less. "But oh-my-god did I tell you I found out Vienna's going to be there?"

"I know. We just saw her."

"Talk about a surprise! How is your new girl Lucy taking it?"

"Actually, they're getting along fine."

"You know that won't last," she said with a guffaw. "Stay clear when those two go at it. Last thing I want are scratches on that adorable mug of yours. Don't forget, you have that movie premiere for *Avenging Transforming Aliens* next Wednesday night. I want you looking your best."

"Got it."

"But here's the thing. This is big, okay? We got a call from Nathan Ellen, the home furnishings retailer. They want to talk to you about a line of your own. Furniture for the stylish man, they said, and they want you. You! Can you believe it?"

"That's great. Set up a meeting."

"In New York, okay, honey? And I don't want you to put this off till later. You need to do this now, okay?"

"Is it okay if I get some sleep first?"

She laughed. "Aw, you tired, you poor thing? The new girl keeping you busy?"

"Now, now."

"Just for once, I want you to stop thinking about beautiful girls and start paying attention to lamps, leather sofas, and coffee tables, okay? And don't just fixate on one particular model. Think multiple options. I want you to go into that meeting with a big book of ideas."

He laughed. "Why do you always give me a hard time?"

"I want you to promise! Stop looking at girls, start looking at furniture! Right away, okay? This could be major. Do I need to ask for it in writing? We want to be on the right side of this opportunity, okay?"

"On it. Promise."

"And just in case you're wondering, no, I haven't found a replacement planner for the Cabo beach bash in August."

"I'm sure you'll find the right person."

"Don't I always? Oh! And you know how you asked me who was going to Sergei's party, and I told you nobody knew, but I'd try to find out?"

"Sure...."

"I got some names."

"I'm already here, Gracie May."

"Have you met everybody yet?"

"Not yet."

"Do you want me to help you or not?"

"Of course I do."

"Then listen, okay?"

He sighed. "Who do you have?"

"Federico Calvini, the race car driver? He's gonna be there. I knew you'd want to meet him."

"Very cool."

"The guy who runs Sky High Airlines, Derek Hanson, is gonna be there. You love those planes, right?"

"You know I do."

"And a bunch of names I'm not so sure about. You ever heard of Sarah Franz? Erica Sandoz? Hector Diamante?"

"No, no, and no."

"Well, sorry, I haven't Googled any of 'em yet, so you'll have to ask 'em what the hell they do."

"I don't know how I'd live without you, Gracie May. Now, the reason I called — "

"That's right," she said. "You called me! Whaddya want?"

"Is there room in my schedule for a trip to Gudan in the next couple of months?"

"A trip to what? A Gudan? What in the hell is a Gudan?"

"It's a country. Don't worry yourself about it. I'm only asking about my schedule."

"Honey, it's your schedule, you can do what you want.

But let's see." He heard the sound of calendar pages flipping. "You're booked — booked — for the next six weeks, and if you cancel on me, I'm gonna kill ya. But you're looking good seven-eight weeks out. You're gonna be in Milan for a few days. Is Gudan nearby?"

"Close enough. Pencil it in. I'll see if I can confirm it and call you back."

"You got me curious, sweetie. Is it a PR thing?"

"A business thing. But now that you mention it, sure, I see a PR angle. I can't tell you much, but it's something Gang Bang and Prince Ali are cooking up. If it works, it could do a lot of good. What do you know about desalinization?"

"Desali-what?" she said with a laugh. "Honey, don't bother explaining. I'll read up on it. But I love the 'Jack does good' angle. Your mother will appreciate that."

"Did you mention Mother for a reason?"

"She had her guy call up and ask about Lucy, like I know anything. Ha!"

"Thanks for the head's up."

"Don't jump on me for saying this, but I might be with your mother on this. There's something still a bit puzzling about that girl."

"Lucy's fine. Don't worry yourself."

"Okay, I'll back off."

"Listen, gotta go."

"Take care of yourself, sweetie. Call me tomorrow, okay? Don't get into too much trouble!"

With a click, she was gone.

He put the phone down. Calhoun had told him a lot.

Item 1: By saying that Lucy was still a bit puzzling, Calhoun was telling him that Lucy had not yet been eliminated as a potential source of the phosphorin purchased by Kasson.

Item 2: Mother had been making inquiries about Lucy,

which meant something about Lucy, or her cover, hadn't passed the smell test. If Mother had noticed something, then others might as well.

Item 3: The identity of the final mystery bidder (the name in the middle of the group of three names) had been established: Erica Sandoz.

Item 4: Calhoun hadn't brought up either Dick Hould or Prince Ali, which meant they remained on the list of suspected bidders.

Item 5: The identity of the seller (the Cabo planner) remained unknown.

Item 6: The movie premiere reference meant the game was definitely happening.

Item 7: By mentioning Wednesday night, Calhoun was telling him that the game would finish on Sunday night (three days earlier), which meant he had two days to figure out who the seller was and stop the game.

Item 8: By telling him to stop looking at girls and start looking at furniture right away, she was telling him the game had already begun.

Item 9: Leather sofas (the items in the middle of the group of furniture) would be used as drop points for instructions, most likely for the first round of the game. The reference to multiple options meant that each player would be directed to a different sofa.

Item 10: The instructions would be written down.

Item 11: The instructions would be placed on the right side of the sofas, most likely stuffed between the cushions.

At this moment, he knew that Calhoun was directing her team to learn everything they could about the desalinization project in the Gudan desert and the World War II tunnels built into the Synkonos cliffs. If either was relevant to the mission, she'd tell him when he called in the morning.

The outlines of the challenge were becoming clearer: Intercept the instructions for the game's first round. Keep an eye on Prince Ali, Dick Hould, and Erica Sandoz in case one of them could identify the seller. And for the rest, do what he always did: Improvise, play the moment, and be ready for whatever — and whoever — came his way.

CHAPTER
TWENTY-EIGHT

AS JACK RUMMAGED through his suitcase in the closet, he heard Lucy step out of the bathroom. He found what he was looking for, zipped up the suitcase, and closed the closet.

"I'm a little tired, but it's a nice night," he said. "Let's go for a walk."

"Sure." She was curious, he saw, about the need to talk privately, but she refrained from asking why. So far she was handling herself well.

Hand in hand, they made their way down the garden path and stopped at the elevator pavilion to admire the view of the bay. Below them, the white sand of the beach glowed in the moonlight. The warm Mediterranean breeze carried the faint sound of waves softly lapping the shore.

"I'm wondering about something," she said.

Before she could say more, he took her in his arms. "Let's dance."

With one hand on the small of her back, he began to waltz in time, softly humming a tune. After a second's hesitation, she eased into his rhythm, moving with a grace that surprised him. Together they glided around the pavilion. He dipped her down and brought her back up, swaying in the moonlight, cheeks touching.

"Even here?" she whispered in his ear.

"Even here," he whispered in hers. "Until we know better, assume every square inch of this compound is wired for sound."

"Then how do we talk?"

"Like lovers," he murmured. "Sweet nothings, whispered softly."

Her body felt good against his. He caught a hint of her scent. It was a shame she didn't like him. Such attractive packaging.

"Do you like furniture? Interior design?" he whispered.

"I guess."

"We need to check out some sofas."

"What are we looking for?"

"Written instructions stuffed between the cushions. Right side."

"You want me to take the lead?"

"Sure."

She broke free of his grasp.

"Here? I don't think so," she said in a normal voice. "I'm not that kind of girl."

"You have something else in mind? I'm at your service, m'lady."

"I want to check this place out, before everyone arrives and while it's still quiet."

He took her hand and pulled her back to him. "You sure you don't want to go back to the room?"

"Yes," she said firmly.

"Lead the way."

They walked through the courtyard and into the villa, this time stopping to take in the compound's public rooms. They strolled through the dining room and the library, and then past the bar, where the cocktail party was still going strong. While she oohed and ahhed over the decor, he noted the security cameras covering the hallways and entryways. The placements were standard — too standard. Almost as if their purpose was to distract attention from a more cunningly concealed surveillance system. Sergei wouldn't be satisfied with anything less than state-of-the-art. So where — and what — was it?

They found themselves in the villa's main atrium — a large, open lounge at the center of the compound.

"I love the furniture in here," Lucy said. "And look at these walls, the rug, the fireplaces."

She dropped onto a leather sofa facing one of the fireplaces. The flames cast a golden glow over her animated face. She was getting into her role, and enjoying it.

"Omigod," she said. "So nice and comfy."

He stood in front of her and held out his hand. "Come on, let's go to bed."

"The leather is so soft," she said, running her hand along the cushions. "I could sit here forever."

Her hand found something.

"Look," she said, holding up a scrap of paper.

Jack pulled Lucy from the sofa. "The cleaning staff missed something. Who cares?"

He took the scrap from Lucy and, without even looking at it, crumpled it up and tossed it into the fire.

"Be curious in the hallway," he whispered in her ear. "Open every door."

She pushed away from him.

"Aren't you curious?" she asked, leaving the lounge and heading down a long hallway.

"Lucy," Jack said, acting like a man who was patiently hoping his date would come around to his way of thinking.

"Come on," she said. "Where's your spirit of adventure?"

She tried a door, but it was locked, and then tried another.

On the third try, the door opened and she stumbled in. He heard her gasp and ran to join her.

She'd found the villa's security room. Against one wall, an array of monitors captured various views of the resort. Two men in suits, seated at the controls, had turned to face them. One of them, tall and imposing, stood and moved toward them with the ease of an athlete. He was an inch or two taller than Jack, a year or two older, his brow a bit too pronounced, and his dark eyes a bit too fierce.

"Ma'am, I'm afraid this room is not for guests."

"I'm so sorry," Lucy said.

"Hey, man, sorry about this," Jack said, giving the man a see-what-I'm-dealing-with look. "Didn't mean to intrude."

"No need to apologize, Mr. Ford," the man said. "I hope you enjoy your stay."

"Thanks, uh…," Jack said, extending his hand.

The man gave him an exceedingly firm shake. "Constantine Thanos. Security director."

"Come on, honey. Let's leave the man to his job."

Very smoothly, Constantine ushered them out. "Good night, Mr. Ford," he said, his gaze staying on Jack for a second before shutting the door.

Lucy leaned against Jack. "I upset him."

"Don't worry about it."

"He knew you."

"I'm sure he knows all of us. He's security. It's his job."

"No, I mean, he seemed to really notice you."

"What are you saying?"

"He doesn't like you," she said, but then smiled like she realized something. "Or maybe he likes you too much."

"Yeah, sure," he said with a snort, even though she was, of course, right. The signs had been clear: the flare of the nostrils and the way his mouth opened, just a fraction. Did that matter? Could that be useful? Probably not. Nevertheless, he filed it away.

Because he now had an additional goal: To get into that security room. To find out what was being captured by that video system, and what wasn't.

"I know you're not feeling well, but you've been a trouper today," Jack said as they got back to the cabana. "You ready for bed?"

She tensed slightly at that last word. "Yes," she said, "in a few." She stepped into the bathroom.

He sat on the bed and slipped off his shoes and socks, then stripped out of his clothes. If anyone was watching via hidden camera — he had little doubt someone was — he wanted to give them something to gawk at.

He opened the closet, carefully hung up his shirt and pants, and then reached down to rummage again through his suitcase. The hidden cameras in the room would see him bent over, looking for something, but viewers would be too distracted by the sight of his naked ass to care about what. While one hand moved items around inside the suitcase, the other opened the scrap of paper Lucy had found in the sofa — the scrap he'd switched for a substitute piece of paper to toss in the fire.

The scrap held a message: "Welcome, cherished competitor! The game begins tomorrow, after lunch. Instructions await you at the poolside bar. XOXO, Yoko."

He'd hoped for more, but it would have to do. He knew

where to look next, and one of the competitors — Messalina, Ming, or Borlando — did not.

He heard the bathroom door open and Lucy's faint intake of breath as she took in his naked form. She was shocked, of course. Even though she insisted she wasn't a prude, she kind of was. No doubt she was asking herself why he had to flaunt himself like this.

He zipped up his suitcase and shut the closet door.

"My turn," he said and stepped into the bathroom. He took a tissue, pretended to blow his nose, and threw it and the crumpled scrap of paper into the toilet.

A few moments later, when he came out, the room was dark. Lucy wouldn't be able to see him moving through the shadows, but she'd hear his bare feet on the hardwood floor and feel the mattress shift as he slid in next to her, just inches away.

"Good night, Lucy," he said softly.

She didn't answer.

He smiled in the darkness at the sound of her steady, regular breathing. The novice pretender was putting in some practice time.

As he fell into slumber, his mind drifted to the smile Lucy had given him earlier in the evening, right before he'd called Calhoun. The smile had been her first genuine reaction to him since arriving on the island. She'd been amused, and even, dare he say it, accepting.

In that second, she'd enjoyed him, and he her.

CHAPTER
TWENTY-NINE

Yoko's Auction Room
Gang Bang

WITH A WAVE of her hand, Yoko popped up the video screen. The masked man from Zurich appeared.

"Progress report," she said.

"Eliminations complete. Evidence destroyed. No complications."

"Thank you. The briefcases?"

"The courier picked them up an hour ago."

She already knew that, but it paid to be careful.

"As promised, your payment," she said. A console materialized in front of her. She clicked a few buttons.

On the screen, the man looked at his mobile device while payment transferred to his account.

"This is more than we agreed," the man said.

"A bonus," she said. "Well deserved."

The man paused, as if weighing what to say next.

"Your intentions, Fraulein…," he began.

He'd figured it out. She should have foreseen this possibility. He was, after all, at the top of his grisly profession.

He would be difficult to track down and eliminate. Did she have to take that step? He was asking for a reason. What was he after? Not more money — that wasn't his style — nor was he likely to alert the authorities.

No, his concern was for himself. He wanted to know how to be safe.

"It's a wonderful time for a vacation getaway," she said. "A small tropical island, perhaps. A cabin in the mountains. Someplace remote, away from other people."

"How long?"

"A few weeks. A month."

"Starting when?"

"No time like now."

The man nodded. "Until we do business again?"

"Auf wiedersehen."

The video screen went black.

Yes, she'd made the right call. Travel would keep the man busy for the next day or two — more than enough time for her next steps.

"Villa Synkonos," she said. The villa's security video feeds filled the screen.

"Bar." Video from the cocktail party was isolated and magnified.

"Start at 8:00 p.m. and fast-forward through footage." The screen went black for a second, then showed the bar quickly filling with guests.

She scanned the footage. Nothing unexpected. Good.

With a wave of her hand, she flipped to the video feeds showing each of the sofas in which she'd placed her welcome messages.

She watched Ming as he found his message. Good.

She switched to the next sofa and saw Messalina — the real Messalina — remove hers. She giggled, pleased that she'd figured it out. Oh Messalina, so delightfully clever.

That left the final sofa — Borlando's. She watched with annoyance as that wastrel, Jack Ford, and his squeeze-du-jour, Lucy Keen, flirted in the very spot. She saw Lucy's hand pull the scrap of paper from the sofa, and Jack, without even looking at it, toss it into the fireplace.

Idiots. Clueless fools. Yoko's eyes glowed red. Snakes burst from her scalp.

No, no, no, she told herself. Anger was not a constructive response. No plan ever worked perfectly. The unexpected must be expected.

"Cabana feeds," she said. "Jack Ford."

She flipped between the high-quality video cameras that captured the interior of the cabana from multiple angles. Nothing unusual. Jack and Lucy were getting ready for bed, Lucy in her nightgown in the bathroom brushing her teeth, and Jack rummaging through his suitcase, naked, of course, and parading around as usual. Such a narcissistic ass.

Yoko clicked off the cabana video. The snakes on her head dissipated like wisps of smoke.

Should she give Borlando a second chance? She clicked to the cocktail party and found him chatting up one of the hospitality facilitators. Rewinding, Yoko traced his movements back to his arrival on the island, hours earlier.

Borlando hadn't even tried to look for his welcome message. Was the clue not a priority for him? Had he decided not to compete? If so, why?

Something wasn't right. She'd need to keep a close eye on him. Perhaps even more.

She considered her options, then nodded. Yes, better safe than sorry. With so much at stake, nothing — and no one — could be allowed to get in the way.

CHAPTER **THIRTY**

JACK AWOKE TO find Lucy snuggled in the crook of his arm, snoring softly. She'd migrated to his side of the bed during the night and was wrapped around him, her face on his chest, her arm across his stomach. Her nightgown had ridden up her body and her warm belly pressed against his side, her bare leg covering his.

It was time to get up — today would be jam-packed — but he allowed himself to linger. This woman felt good. Damn good. It was nice to see that Dr. Lucy Kimball had a tactile side. A shame she had to be unconscious to express it.

He'd have to be careful when extricating himself. He was hard as a rock, his erection tenting the sheet.

Not a problem from his perspective, but how would his sexually repressed sidekick respond when she realized she was wrapped around an aroused, naked man?

She shifted against him, still asleep. Saliva dribbled from her open mouth. Without warning, she flung her leg over his hips, trapping his erection beneath her knee.

Her breasts were pancaked against his ribs. Ever so slightly, she started rubbing her crotch on his hipbone.

Damn. When this chick got going, she really got going.

He preferred the women in his life to be easy and uncomplicated, like Vienna and most of the women he bedded and sent on their merry way. For him, sex was a natural, carefree expression of human vitality. No angst, no worry, no jealousy, and — missions excepted — no agenda. The simpler the impulse, the freer the flow, the more pleasurable the experience.

Dr. Kimball was uncomplicated while unconscious, but wouldn't be when she woke up and realized she was grinding her clit against his hipbone. She'd be flustered, embarrassed, and irritated with herself for being turned on.

And she'd find a way to blame him.

Fuck, this woman was annoying. Why had he let Grant foist her on him? For her sake and his, he couldn't let her wake up like this. With a single smooth movement, he shifted his hips, lifted her arm, and slid out from under her.

Her eyes opened, unfocused.

"Time to get up?" she asked sleepily. She stretched beneath the sheet, her eyes closing again.

She had no idea. *Good.* It was better this way. Sexual tension was a distraction he couldn't afford.

"Wake up, sunshine," he said, getting out of the bed. "I'll be in the shower."

An hour later, in the villa's luxurious main dining room, Jack faced a different challenge — namely, how to maneuver surreptitiously under the relentless attention of his eager, anxious host.

From the moment he and Lucy entered the dining room, Sergei had attached himself like a barnacle. A hospitality facilitator had ushered them to Serge's table. Their host stood and pulled back Lucy's chair. Servers materialized to pour coffee. Sergei barely waited for them to sit down before telling them they must have the eggs.

"Classic American cuisine like you find in Las Vegas, but we make it special, yes? Eggs are Taiyouran. Do you know Taiyouran? Free-range. Chickens fed only natural herbs and leaves."

Within seconds, plates of piping-hot scrambled eggs, thick-cut bacon, and bagels were set in front of them.

Lucy picked up her fork to dig in, but Sergei motioned for her to stop.

"No, no, you must try with white truffle. Truffle is from Alba, yes?"

"Alba?" Jack said. "Nice." He leaned over his coffee cup and inhaled. "Is this … Kopi Luwak?"

"Yes," Sergei said, pleased. "You recognize."

"My favorite." Which, clearly, Sergei already knew.

While their server shaved white truffle over their eggs, Jack considered where Sergei might have picked up that coffee tidbit. From an interview? From a mutual acquaintance? Or, more likely, from investigators he'd hired to gather a dossier on him?

Which led to two more questions: What else did Sergei Eristov know about Jack Ford? And was there a moment, a second, in this weekend that Sergei hadn't designed, down to the tiniest, inconsequential detail, to appeal to him?

Lucy dug into the eggs and truffle.

"Oh my," she said after her first bite. "Sergei, this is amazing."

"You must try jam," Sergei said, passing her a jar.

She spread a dollop on her bagel. "What kind of jam is this?"

"Riesling. Infused with Goji berries."

"Omigod," she said as she took a bite. "Omigod!"

Sergei smiled, and in that second, he relaxed, his obsession with detail and effect melting away. He simply looked like a guy who enjoyed making people happy.

Jack picked up his fork and leaned over the plate, luxuriating in the truffle's earthy, musky aroma. He didn't know how these ugly little buggers made a meal taste so damn good, but they did, and Alba whites were the best, like little flakes of heaven. He scooped a bite into his mouth and closed his eyes as the fullness and depth of the experience rolled through him.

He opened his eyes. "Damn, Sergei. That's good."

Sergei grinned, delighted. "Only best for my friends!"

Between bites and banter, Jack surveyed the dining room. In scale, the room was large enough to comfortably seat the weekend's eighty guests, but its decor and design leaned toward intimacy. The walls were covered in grasscloth, with sound-dampening paneling in the ceiling. Floor-to-ceiling windows on one side offered a stunning view of the bay.

Across the room, Dick Hould had sat himself down with Francois Le Coq and his wife, Marie, and was no doubt being probing and unpleasant. Every few minutes, Natasha and Boris stopped at Sergei's table to discuss last-minute planning details. Prince Ali arrived with a gorgeous blonde hospitality facilitator on his arm. Of the remaining competitor — Erica Sandoz — Jack saw no sign.

Vienna, too, was a no-show, which was hardly surprising given that she usually slept till noon.

Sergei glanced at his watch. "It is time for cave-and-tunnel tour. You come, yes?"

"Absolutely."

They followed him from the dining room. In the hall, a group of twenty or so guests had already gathered.

A hospitality facilitator handed each guest a flashlight.

"Everyone, welcome," Sergei said. "Very happy to take you on personal tour of caves of Synkonos. As you may know, nation of Greece has six thousand caves, and many are extremely impressive and beautiful. Caves here in Synkonos are not biggest or deepest, but have important history and are useful to villa today."

Sergei led them into the courtyard, past the infinity pool, and down the garden path to the arched entrance of the stairs to the gondola cave.

"You remember cave you arrive at," he said, gesturing to the stairs. "Gondola cave is largest on Synkonos, but only one of many." Instead of walking down the stairs, he led them further along the cliff to a small, unobtrusive opening about twenty feet away.

"Please, follow me and walk carefully. Watch head."

The opening was the entrance to a tunnel, with a small alcove tucked to one side at the front, hidden from view from the outside.

Jack stepped into the alcove for a closer look. The little nook had possibilities. Casually, he bent down to tie a shoelace and placed his sunglasses on the ground. After tying his shoe, he stood and followed the others into the tunnel.

"As we move in deeper, cave narrows," Sergei said to the group. He turned on his flashlight and swung it over and around him. "Careful with head."

The guests pressed in, flashlights flicking on and running up and over the cave's floor, walls, and ceiling. Jack felt a gentle airflow — cooler than the outside — move past him toward the entrance.

Sergei's voice echoed from up ahead. "In second World

War, Greek resistance fighters use caves to fight Nazis. During construction of Villa Synkonos, we find cache of old weapons and other artifacts." He stopped and aimed his light at a flat sheet of rock along one wall. "Resistance fighters carve names here."

On the rock wall, Jack saw a date, 4 Απρ 1943, followed by nine Greek names. And then, at the bottom, a name in English that stopped him cold: A. Abernathy.

His mother's Abigail's initials before her marriage, and also those of his grandmother, Annelise. Mere coincidence, most likely. Abernathy wasn't a common name, but neither was it rare. Undoubtedly, there were others of the Abernathy persuasion who had a first name starting with an A.

Was that the explanation? Simple coincidence? Or had Sergei, who had designed an entire island to study the playboy habits of one Jack Ford, put the name there on purpose? Was it part of the role-playing game he expected to hear about soon? Were there layers to this experience he wasn't yet aware of?

Only one way to find out.

"Sergei," he said as he gestured for his host to step closer. "This name here, A. Abernathy. It's the same as my mother's maiden name."

Sergei peered closely at the names on the cave wall. Jack watched his face and body language.

"Do you have war heroes in your family?" Sergei asked.

"Not that war."

Sergei shrugged. He appeared to be looking at the name for the first time. "I do research. We find out who this is. Perhaps you have brave ancestors you do not know."

"Thanks."

"This is important to you?" Sergei asked, as if realizing he had an opportunity to broaden his connection with Jack.

"Curious, that's all."

"I find answers." He turned back to the group. "Tour continues, yes?"

They moved deeper into the tunnel. The cool air continued to flow past them.

Ahead, a shaft of daylight hit the cave floor. The tunnel widened into a large circle, perhaps forty feet across, the ceiling sloping above them like an overturned bowl. At the top of the bowl, a hole to the sky lit the room like a chandelier.

"Tunnel system has many openings to sky. This part of tunnel is more like a room, yes?" He gestured toward bags of concrete mix and a box of steel rebar on one side of the room. "We turn this space into subterranean cocktail lounge. Imagine with nice chairs and torch lighting, yes? Very mysterious and sexy, yes?"

"Is it possible to walk up there, at the top of the cliff?" a guest asked, gesturing to the natural skylight above them.

"Yes. Several paths from villa lead to plateau at top of island. View is very beautiful. At top is hill of white limestone. Sticks out like sore thumb from black igneous stone of cliffs. You can explore later, yes?"

He pointed to where the tunnel narrowed again. "Walk single file, keep head down, use flashlight."

One by one, the group stepped into the narrow gap. The darkness closed in, with only flashlights showing the way. Ahead, they could hear Sergei's voice.

"Tunnels have natural air flow due to difference in temperature inside and outside tunnels, so we use for Villa Synkonos. We drill ventilation ducts from tunnels into villa to provide fresh, natural air conditioning in main compound. Very green, yes?

"How extensive is the tunnel system, Sergei?" a guest asked.

"Very extensive. Not yet fully explored. We just scratch surface."

The group continued moving forward, single file, Sergei's voice echoing against the walls.

Just as Jack wondered how long they would have to remain bent over in the dark, he heard a door open ahead.

"Everyone, please step forward," Sergei said. One by one, the guests entered the gondola cave, Sergei counting heads to make sure everyone was there.

"Tour ends. Take stairs up to return to garden. Lunch in dining room at twelve thirty, yes? Very important to be at lunch for start of weekend Las Vegas experience."

Sergei led the way up the stairs, guests following.

Lucy held Jack back, waiting for the others to move ahead.

She whispered in his ear, "The temperature and humidity in the tunnels are ideal for storage of live phosphorin."

He nodded, and they walked up the stairs.

"Hey," he said when they reached the garden path, running his hands over his pockets, "I dropped my sunglasses. I think I know where."

"You want me to help?"

"No, go ahead. I'll catch up."

He walked to the opening in the cliff where the tour had begun, pretending to look for his missing eyewear. In the small alcove, he reached down, picked up his glasses, and then, as if intrigued by the geology of the walls, ran a hand over them.

"Fascinating," he said out loud.

If anyone was watching or listening, they'd learn that Jack Ford had an interest in old rocks. With his other hand, he reached into his pocket, took out his smartphone, and snapped photos. Simultaneously, the phone's hidden electronics sensor quickly and thoroughly scanned the alcove for hidden audio and video devices.

Even the tiniest working transmitter emitted a faint electromagnetic signal, but the sensor was showing —

Nothing.

Good. If he and Lucy needed a place to talk privately, away from microphones, this little alcove would do.

CHAPTER THIRTY-ONE

A LOW ROAR of conversation and laughter filled the dining room. Every seat at every table was taken. The last of the guests had arrived.

The meal Lucy had just polished off was as traditionally American and as delectably high-end as breakfast had been: a pizza with "very special dough, yes?" that required three days to rise and was topped with caviar, lobster, shrimp, organic mozzarella, and pink sea salt. Delicious, of course, especially when paired with a lovely Chardonnay — "a 2009 Kongsgaard with complex aromatics, hints of hazelnut, yes?" — selected by the house sommelier.

She stared in wonder at what a waiter now placed in front of her: an ice cream sundae with, as Sergei eagerly explained, Tahitian vanilla bean ice cream, Venezuelan Chuao chocolate syrup, and edible gold leaf, served in a sparkling crystal bowl.

It was barely past noon, but already she felt exhaustion — or was it sugar overload? — sinking in.

Sleep last night hadn't come easily, her mind refusing to

disengage from what she'd been thrown into. Over and over, in a seemingly endless loop, she replayed key moments from the past two days.

Moments like her eyes landing on Jack in that conference room in Los Angeles. Oh, the righteousness of her fury. But now she was feeling the first twinges of doubt. Was her anger justified now that she knew about Jack's secret spy job? Should she consider cutting him some slack about what he had done on the flight from London?

Her mind leapt to Jack's mother and to Abigail's laser-like dissection — a shock of a different sort. The older woman had been tense and wary. A mother's natural protective instinct, or was something else at play?

Another source of worry: last night's party. Had her ad-libbed lies about her haircut worked? Had Vienna been convinced? And what had Natasha meant when she said Lucy wasn't what she expected? Was that a compliment, as she'd initially interpreted, or had Natasha been telling her she knew who she really was?

She'd go crazy speculating if she let herself. So far, she was doing fine, and Jack seemed pleased. Even if she couldn't trust him for anything else, she supposed she should accept his judgment about the mission.

She glanced at her so-called partner with the big grin and easy laugh, who was leaning toward Sergei and quietly sharing a joke that, if she overheard correctly, involved a donkey, a farmer's wife, and a traveling vacuum-cleaner salesman.

She picked up her spoon and scooped a big gloppy chunk of sundae into her mouth. *Mmm.* The ice cream melted on her tongue in a vanilla-chocolate-gold mashup.

If she was going to be honest with herself, then she'd have to accept that much of her unease about Jack was due to her uncomfortable awareness of him. Last night, as he lay sleeping, naked and mere inches from her, she'd been confronted by a basic, inescapable, physiological fact: her body responded to him. He possessed physical qualities — musculature, height, bone structure, hair, eyes, smell — that her body was biologically predisposed to find arousing, along with an energy, a natural charisma, that magnified the impact of his physical traits. She wasn't alone in that assessment, she knew; Special Exploits had recruited him for the same reasons. She and Jack were at this party because their host, in the throes of a gigantic man-crush, had responded in a similar way.

Her physiological response could be due to something as simple and basic as her olfactory system sensing differences between her immune system and his. In any event, she couldn't stop her brain from increasing glutamate production in response to these external stimuli, and she couldn't prevent the excess glutamate from sparking increased synaptic transmissions in her anterior cingulate cortex.

And this was okay, she told herself. She was experiencing a natural chemical reaction — nothing less, nothing more. There was no need to beat herself up. Accepting reality would help her manage it.

The source of her chemical upheaval was now describing to Sergei, in rapturous detail, how beautifully his new car handled tight turns. A kid excited about his toy. Kind of cute, actually. Aside from a few moments of mission-centric bossiness (which, she allowed, might be justified), he'd been attentive and respectful toward her. She just needed to keep reminding herself that he was, at his core, an agent on a mission. His primary focus wasn't her. He'd use and discard her if he had to, without hesitation, as he had before.

She couldn't let herself be fooled again.

CHAPTER THIRTY-TWO

LUCY SENSED A chair moving next to her and snapped out of her reverie.

Sergei, standing up, gave a quick nod to Natasha. She spoke into her headset and the doors to the dining room swung shut. Shades dropped over the floor-to-ceiling windows. Lights dimmed.

A spotlight cut through the darkness and landed on Sergei. A hospitality facilitator handed him a microphone, and he said, "My dear guests, welcome to Synkonos! Welcome, welcome, welcome!"

The guests applauded.

"Or should I say," Sergei said, pausing dramatically, "welcome to Vegas, baby!"

Throughout the room, neon lights blazed to life on the walls and ceiling, transforming the dining room into a nightclub. The audience whooped and cheered.

"Yes, in this very moment, we are magically transported through time and space from Greek island in year 2015 to city of Las Vegas in year 1965. We gather at Hotel Synkonos, hottest new casino on Las Vegas strip. We are at center of epic battle. Two rival mob families fighting for control of hotel — and entire city!"

One of the guests oohed and everyone laughed.

"Yes, stakes are high," Sergei with a big grin, "and tensions even higher. Each of you has major role to play in battle for control of Hotel Synkonos, and soon you learn your role. But first, I must describe hotel, because setting is essential to understanding and enjoying game, yes?"

He briefly scanned the room, then continued. "But perhaps I ask you: When you think of classic Las Vegas, what do you think?"

"Gambling!" a guest yelled out.

"Girls! Fun! The Rat Pack!" said another.

"Strippers!" a man yelled, earning a round of whoops and cheers.

"Male strippers!" a woman added immediately to a general wave of laughter.

Sergei gestured to the closed doors of the dining room. "Yes to all. Hotel Synkonos is oasis of fun and games, of danger and desire, of vice and va-va-voom. Because what is Las Vegas without … beautiful showgirls?"

The dining room doors opened and the spotlight swung to a throng of statuesque women as they burst into the room. They wore stunning peacock-feathered headdresses and barely-there sequined costumes, with legs and cleavage and smiles that went on forever.

The room roared their approval.

The showgirls formed a line and, in time to music that started to play, started high-kicking to the heavens. A line of muscular men, painted head to toe in gold and wearing nothing but golden swim briefs, followed them in, marching in step. Each man carried a golden tray. On each tray was an exquisite jewel-encrusted golden chest, about twelve inches cubed, with rubies and diamonds forming an "S" on each side.

Sergei made his way to a small stage at the end of the dining room and jumped on it. The spotlight swung back to him. With a wave of his arm, the showgirls and golden men split off in pairs, each pair moving to a dining table. One pair made their way to the stage and stood next to Sergei.

"Round of applause for our entertainers, yes?" As the crowd responded, Sergei gestured to the showgirl at his side. "Like Jessica, yes? What a knockout! A real looker."

He turned to her and said, "You have something for me, Jessica?"

Jessica gave him a coy smile. "Have you been a good boy, Mr. Eristov?"

"I am always good boy," Sergei said solemnly.

"No he's not!" a guest yelled, to much laughter.

"Only because you asked so nicely," Jessica said. Reaching into her headdress, she plucked out a small gold key and handed it to him.

"Thank you. Now, I need assistance for next part. Ms. Vienna, can I ask you to join on stage?"

The audience applauded as Vienna stood and made her way through the crowd.

Sergei handed her the key. "Key opens lock on golden chest. If you please."

Giggling, Vienna stepped up to the golden man.

"Oh, my," she said, eyeing the man's muscular torso. "What a chest!"

She slid the key into the jewel-encrusted box and turned it. With a click, the lid slowly opened.

"Reach inside," Sergei said.

Vienna pulled out a golden envelope and handed it to him.

"Thank you, Vienna. This golden envelope is ticket, gateway, to your identity at Hotel Synkonos. Each guest has own envelope."

Guests at several tables turned toward their showgirls, but Sergei stopped them with a wave. "But do not ask for key yet! Soon, but not yet!"

He waved the envelope in the air. "So we have setting, yes? We know where we are. We are back in time, in days of old Las Vegas, at hottest new casino on the Strip, surrounded by glamour and gambling and girls.

"So now we turn to us, to who we are," he said, his voice lowering, becoming more serious. "In our own lives, we are all characters, yes? We play many roles. We are entrepreneurs, executives, technologists, innovators, scientists, entertainers, trendsetters. We are friends and rivals and partners. But here at Hotel Synkonos, for next two days, we become new characters. Every person has role to play, character to inhabit. Every person here.

"Look around," he continued. "The person next to you is gangster, showgirl, high-roller, federal agent, entertainer, journalist. Some of you are part of mob family, some of you are caught in-between. Every one of you has incentive to join winning side and share prize."

"What's the prize?" someone called out.

"Very nice, I promise," Sergei said. "But I keep secret for now."

He gestured to the showgirl next to him. "Our hospitality facilitators also have roles to play. They play entertainers, like lovely Jessica. They also play waiters, casino workers, escorts. We strive for realism, yes? And all of them can help you win points for your gang, if you offer right incentive...."

A low chuckle rumbled through the crowd.

Lucy felt a new tension in the room — an eagerness to learn what was to come. These people were born competitors. They wanted to play.

"Remember, is game. Role play. Every guest has goal. Every goal helps win prize."

Sergei paused and was met with an expectant silence. He had them. Barely three minutes into his pitch, they were his.

"So who are two mob gangs?" Sergei said. "First we have Avalon organization, very tough and successful. From Chicago, but moving out West. Head of Avalon organization is Anthony Avalon, very smart and powerful and ruthless. Anthony is played by … Francois Le Coq!"

Le Coq, surprised and delighted, laughed as the audience applauded.

Sergei waited for the crowd to quiet down. "Other group is Funicello gang. Runs West Coast. Also tough, also successful. See Vegas as their territory. Don't want Avalon organization in Vegas. Lots of bad blood.

"Head of Funicello gang is Francesca Funicello, also very smart and tough, maybe tougher than any man. Francesca is played by … Marie Le Coq!"

Marie gasped. Her husband laughed uproariously. They both stood as the audience applauded again.

"Watch out, mister!" she said, aiming her fingers at him. "I'll get you! Bang bang!"

"Yes," Sergei said. "Game is very exciting, so important to say now. Three big rules. Rule one: No violence. No fighting. We are pretend gangs, not real."

A pretend groan went through the crowd.

"Rule two: I tell you 'game word.' Like 'safe word,' but for game play. Person can say game word if they do not feel like playing. Game word is 'J. Edgar Hoover.' Hoover is big buzzkill in real life, yes? Someone says, 'J. Edgar Hoover,' they do not feel like playing and take break from fun and games, yes?"

While Sergei spoke, two of the gold-covered men carried a

large, golden drop box, about the size of a mailbox, to the stage.

"In game, we place drop boxes throughout compound, like this one, yes? If you learn information, you write down and drop in box. Rule three is no touching drop boxes, no stealing drop boxes, no breaking into drop boxes."

Faux-groans rippled through the crowd.

"Showgirls have key to your table's chest. Ask them nicely, and maybe they give it to you...."

The girl at Lucy's table winked at Jack. It was Jenny, their waiter from the ferry.

"Jenny!" Jack said, his eyes twinkling. "You look great in that costume."

"Thank you, Mr. Ford."

"Can we persuade you to give us the key?"

Jenny's fingers fluttered over a thin gold chain around her neck that disappeared into the valley between her breasts.

"I'll let you retrieve it, Mr. Ford."

Jack reached up, but she stopped him.

"But no hands."

"No hands?"

"Be creative."

Jack laughed, then turned to Lucy and shrugged. "Sorry, babe. Call of duty."

He stood and clasped his arms behind his back. With his eyes fixed on Jenny's, and with a wide, mischievous grin, he leaned over and buried his face in her bosom.

"Oh, Mr. Ford," Jenny said, giggling.

Lucy realized her lips were pressed tight. She forced her mouth and jaw to relax. Jack's face was not her concern. He could bury it in any heaving bosom he wanted to. But clearly, given her instinctive reaction of dismay, she needed to remind herself of that.

After a few seconds of rooting around, Jack slowly stepped away, the gold chain trapped between his lips.

"Well done!" Jenny said to cheers from around the table. She reached down, unfastened the chain, and handed Jack the key.

Jack took the key and turned, hand extended toward Lucy. "Will you do the honors?"

She nearly said no. This jerk wanted her to handle a key he'd retrieved with his mouth from another woman's bosom? Was he goading her? Challenging her?

So irritating!

"Of course," she said as smoothly as she could.

She took the key from his hand, stood up, and turned to the man carrying the box. Deftly, she inserted the key, turned it in the slot, opened the lid, and removed the envelopes inside. She sorted through them, found the one with her name on it, and passed the rest to the other guests at the table.

From the stage, Sergei said, "Everyone, please open your envelopes now."

She sat back down, slipped a fingernail under the envelope's golden flap, and carefully slid it open.

"Each envelope has two notecards," Sergei said. "First notecard is your character. Role you play in game."

She looked at hers, which read, "The future of Hotel Synkonos is in your hands. You are Lola Fontaine, a showgirl with ties to the Avalon gang. You are outgoing and headstrong, and perhaps too willing to speak your mind. You have been ordered by the head of the Avalon organization to befriend Daddio Donatelli, a top lieutenant in the Funicello crime family. Your goal is to convince Daddio to switch his allegiance to the Avalon gang, using every means of persuasion at your disposal."

She frowned. So she had to "befriend" someone, using "every means of persuasion." Who was this Daddio fellow?

"Now," Sergei said, "second card has today's task."

Hers read, "Introduce yourself to Daddio. Ask him about his favorite film. Write down the name of the film on this notecard and drop the notecard in a drop box. You have until dinner to complete your task."

Urgh. Chatting up strangers was not her cup of tea. Why did Sergei Eristov want her to do that?

Jack watched Lucy's face as she read her two notecards. She wasn't pleased. Around them, guests were sharing their notecards with each other, laughing and occasionally exclaiming with amusement.

Sergei's voice rose over the din. "This afternoon, game takes place in courtyard, by the pool. I see you all there! Remember: when you complete your task, you earn points. Gang with most points at end of weekend wins excellent prize."

Jack looked at his card, which read, "The future of Hotel Synkonos is in your hands. You are Bruiser DiMaggio, an enforcer in the Funicello organization. You're a tough guy, skilled with fists and guns, and a reliable foot soldier who has earned the respect and trust of Francesca Funicello. But you're finding your loyalties tested by your attraction to beautiful Daisy Avalon, daughter of rival mob boss, Anthony Avalon."

Jack flipped to the next notecard, which said, "Find out the card game a high-rolling whale named Harry Ashe likes to play most. Write the answer on this card and place the card in a drop box. You must complete this task before dinner this evening."

The contours of the game were emerging. Chances were

that everyone had a "find out X about Y" or "meet Z" goal for the afternoon.

Sergei was, very smartly, easing his guests into the game by making their first task relatively easy and painless. Jack knew from experience that people often felt self-conscious and distanced when trying a new role. They would joke about it, dismiss it, and even mock it. But gradually, inevitably, something shifted. They would start exploring the possibilities and opportunities. Without realizing it, they'd find themselves embracing the newness and becoming one with it. They'd make it real. Their new persona would free them to do things, and contemplate things, that they'd never otherwise do.

Given what he knew about Sergei and Gang Bang, chances were Sergei had more in mind than simply encouraging his guests to experiment with new personalities. Was his goal to continue learning how individuals interacted with, and possibly adapted to, the characters they played? Had he already mapped out the likely consequences of his social engineering? Did he want to see how accurately his map played out?

The game could also be something else, of course: an effective way to communicate with the prospective buyers of the phosphorin. If Sergei or someone on his team — like Boris, Natasha or the security guy, Constantine — was the seller, then the notecards and drop boxes were an innocuous way of exchanging information with Ming, Messalina, and Borlando.

He turned to Lucy and murmured in her ear, "Last night, at cocktails, you chatted with Natasha."

"Yes."

"Did you talk at all about this game, or the party, or the planning?"

"Nothing specific. Why?"

"Trying to figure out if she might be the organizer of this little Avalon and Funicello game we're playing."

"She probably is. She seems to run everything."

He leaned back and tried to catch her eye, but she turned her attention back to her sundae, which was apparently super-fascinating. Once again, Lucy Kimball was tensing up around him. The obvious reason for her tension was his boob-diving stunt with Jenny. But that would mean she was jealous, and she couldn't be jealous, because she didn't like him. She wouldn't care whose boobs he dove into. So it had to be something else. What was he missing?

He stood and held out his hand. She looked from her sundae and stared at his hand and then his face.

"Time to change," he said. "We're wanted poolside."

CHAPTER
THIRTY-THREE

LUCY STEPPED OUT of the cabana bathroom just as Jack was slipping into tight, black rugby trunks that left very little to the imagination. The black fabric made his golden skin glow. Her mouth tightened, even as her eyes widened. He turned around to give her a full 360-degree view. The suit hugged his muscular butt perfectly.

The man was such a show-off. Did he have any modesty at all?

"You're wearing that?" she asked.

"It's what Jack Ford, rich party boy, does," he said. "He likes to show off. And so does his hot new girlfriend."

He tossed her a bikini top and bottom, or rather, two pieces of black string with tiny bits of fabric in key places.

She looked at the strings in confusion. "Uh, what's this?"

"Your outfit. You need help putting it on?" He grinned at her.

"I can't wear this!"

"Sure you can."

She looked at the pieces of string, then at his trunks.

"Your swimsuit has, quite literally, a hundred times more coverage."

"I freely acknowledge the unfairness and sexism of our situation. It's sad — sad and outrageous — that men can't wear thong bikinis and be taken seriously. Women get all the breaks."

She glared at him. "That's not what I meant."

"I know," he said. "But you have nothing to fear. You're an attractive woman with a sexy bod. So hurry up. Chop, chop. Our presence is expected."

A few minutes later, they set off for the pool, Jack's rugby trunks leading the way, with sandals, sunglasses, and a towel around his shoulders completing his wardrobe.

Lucy wasn't ready to walk around nearly naked — not yet. She'd wrapped her towel snugly around her, covering herself from chest to thigh.

In the courtyard, Las Vegas in the 1960s was in full swing. The hospitality facilitators had changed from waiter uniforms to skimpy black swimsuits — string-like thongs for the women, swim briefs for the men — and were out in force, serving drinks, chatting with guests, splashing about in the pool, and in general, taking every possible opportunity to show off. Guests were reclining in lounge chairs by the pool, talking by the bar, and rolling dice and flipping cards at the gaming tables. The Mediterranean sun beat down from above.

The sight of so many sexy women and muscular men took Lucy's breath away. The facilitators all seemed so at ease with themselves. How did they manage that? The same way Jack did, she supposed. She saw eyes checking him out from all angles as they walked along the pool toward the bar.

And her? She'd have to take off her towel at some point and show everyone what she had on, or rather, what she barely had on. She didn't know how he had convinced her to wear this ridiculous thing. Had she ever been more exposed? Maybe once, in high school, when she and her classmates had snuck into a local pool for a late night skinny-dip. But that had been under the cover of darkness. The night had protected her.

Unlike here. It didn't take a Ph.D. in biology to comprehend how sexual the atmosphere was. She'd never seen so many barely concealed boobs and butts in one place in her life, with so many openly lustful, appreciative stares and so much flirtatious banter.

"What'll you have?" Jack asked when they got to the bar.

"Just some water," she said.

He turned to order, but she stopped him.

"Wait." She needed something stronger. She turned to the bartender. "What do you recommend?"

"The house special. A twist on the margarita."

"That sounds good."

"Make it two," Jack said.

At a table near the bar, she spied a burly man dressed in slacks and a dark golf shirt. The man had been with Constantine in the security room the previous night. He stood from the table with a theatrical sigh.

A curvaceous, thong-clad facilitator walked past him, carrying a tray of sweets. "Leaving so soon, Durgos?"

"Duty calls. Eight hours, all alone with the cameras," he said, "unless you join me, that is."

He playfully swatted her shapely ass.

"Durgos!" the facilitator said, pretending to be annoyed. "You naughty boy!"

Durgos grabbed two pieces of baklava from the tray of sweets. "I'll see you later?"

With a laugh, he turned and made his way into the villa.

"Honey?" she heard Jack say. She turned toward him. He

pointed to two unoccupied poolside loungers. "Why don't you snag us those?"

With a nod, she threaded her way through the tables and loungers and settled next to an attractive woman seated under the shade of a strategically placed umbrella. The woman was wearing a white-collared blouse, open at the neck, over a two-piece blue bathing suit. She was in her thirties, with short brown hair, a small mouth with full lips, lightly freckled skin, and a good figure. At her side was a tall, pink drink, and in her hand the latest issue of *The Economist*. Even in the heat, she exuded cool elegance.

"A bit shocking, isn't it," the woman murmured, with a hint of a Swiss accent.

"I'm sorry?"

"All this beauty parading about."

It was like the woman had read her mind, or her face. Was she that transparent?

"It takes some getting used to," Lucy said.

"I've found that one does eventually adapt. Temptations cannot be resisted indefinitely." The woman put down her magazine. "Allow me to introduce myself. Erica Sandoz."

"Lucy Keen."

"Are you enjoying yourself?"

"Very much," Lucy replied in what she hoped was a confident tone.

"How did you and Mr. Ford meet?"

Everyone, it seemed, was interested in the answer to that question. Everyone wanted to know how Lucy Keen fit into Jack's privileged world.

"At his club."

"And you hit it off."

Lucy glanced back to the bar and saw Jack engaged in an animated conversation with the bartender. In his black swimsuit, he was almost indistinguishable from the hard-bodied facilitators around him.

"I suppose so." She heard the doubt in her voice.

Erica gave her a keen look. "What do you do, if I may ask?"

"I'm in medical school."

"Have you selected a specialty?"

"Pediatrics."

"Ah," she said. "I see."

"What do you see?"

"You're that rarest of breeds: an idealist. Well, good for you. Had you said plastic surgery, I would have classified you as a mercenary, like me."

"A mercenary?"

"I suppose I should say image consultant. I present people to people, and to opportunities."

Lucy didn't know what that meant. It sounded rather vague. "Is that why you're here?"

Erica shook her head. "I'm here because I was invited. One does not decline an offer from Sergei Eristov to attend his legendary bacchanal. I'll dine out for years on the tales I'll tell about this weekend."

From behind her, she heard Jack say, "I'll do my best to make those stories good."

She turned and saw him standing there with a grin on his face and a drink in each hand. He gave Lucy her drink, wiped his hand dry on his swimsuit, and extended his hand to Erica.

"Jack Ford," he said.

"Erica Sandoz. I've heard about you, of course, Mr. Ford."

"Call me Jack." He settled onto the lounger next to Lucy. "What brings you here, Erica?"

"Simple good fortune," Erica said. "I met our host once before, but it was a brief conversation. I was flabbergasted to receive an invitation."

"A surprise for me, too," Jack said. He leaned in and lowered his voice. "So is what I'm hearing true?"

"What are you hearing?"

"About the plans for this evening's entertainment."

"Quite possibly. I met Mr. Eristov at a private party at Heinrich Koller's, in Berlin."

"I hear Heinrich's a bit of a...."

"Every rumor is true," Erica said.

"Which means you...."

"Make no assumptions, Mr. Ford, but I confess to enjoying myself."

"How do you spend your time when you're not enjoying yourself?"

"Image consulting. Branding. My main focus is repositioning."

"We should talk. I'm working with the Sinse Group. You familiar with them?"

"Of course. I'm surprised you're not involved in the family business."

Jack grinned. "Work with Moms? No way. Tell me what you've got going now."

Lucy listened as the two of them launched into a swift exchange of information. So this was how business got done: on one side, the scion of one of America's richest families; on the other, a public relations specialist for hire.

Clearly, Jack was doing what he could to draw Erica out. Did that mean — her breath caught at the thought — Erica was one of the Gang Bang players competing for the phosphorin?

She went over what she knew about this woman. Erica came across as sophisticated and cultured and cynical. But there was more to her than that. Erica was nervous about being here and worried she was out of her league.

So many layers.

Lucy picked up her margarita and took a gulp. The salt mixed with the sweetness, the lime adding a kick to the tequila. The heat on her bare legs felt wonderful.

She didn't belong in this hedonistic, transactional world, but here she was, stuck in the middle of it. She might as well enjoy herself.

She stood, removed the towel from around her shoulders, and spread it out on the lounger. She felt the sun's warmth on her skin.

She picked up her sunscreen and handed it to Jack.

"On my back, please. Don't let me distract you from your business talk."

"Mmm," Jack said, squeezing a dollop of sunscreen on his hand. He spread the lotion over her back and rubbed it in with slow, powerful motions.

Erica smiled and stood. "I'm afraid I must place a few calls. A pleasure meeting you both."

"We'll catch up," Jack said.

As Erica walked away, Lucy looked back at Jack. "Is she…?"

"Yes," Jack said.

"Anything you want me to do?"

"Just keep your eyes and ears open — and your nose."

CHAPTER
THIRTY-FOUR

THE SUN MOVED overhead. Guests mingled. Drinks and gossip flowed. Hospitality facilitators posed and played.

At the bar for a refill, with Erica Sandoz at his side, Jack glanced back at Lucy, who was staying put on her lounger and keeping a low profile. His eyes roamed over her slim figure, over the gentle curve of her breasts beneath the bikini top. Such nice packaging. Such a shame.

For the second time in two days, he reminded himself to focus on his job and, specifically on Erica, the player behind the impressively nasty Messalina persona, if Calhoun's intel was correct.

Erica's flesh-and-blood persona was cultured. Vivacious, too, once she had a couple of drinks in her. She laughed and flirted easily, yet underneath, Jack saw a professional. He had no doubt that, whatever Erica did, she did well.

"Who handles your P.R.?" Erica asked.

"Gracie May Blowser," Jack said.

"Who's she with?"

"She's solo."

Erica nodded. "I don't know her. My clients are mostly E.U. I don't handle Hollywood, though I'd love to."

"Is Sergei a client?"

"No, but wouldn't that be something! He attended a museum event I did last year in Prague." She looked over Jack's shoulder and waved at someone. "Now here's someone who is my client."

Jack turned to see Francois Le Coq and his wife, Marie, approaching.

Erica stepped up to Marie and gave her a hug. "So good to see you both." She turned to Jack. "Have you met?"

"Last night," Jack said. "You're looking lovely this afternoon, Marie."

"Thank you." Marie's hair was pulled back into a sleek bun. She wore a black one-piece bathing suit that hugged her body perfectly.

Francois wore board shorts and sandals. Despite his years, he exuded robust good health. Wiry grey hairs covered his barrel chest. His arms and shoulders remained muscular, his stomach firm.

"Why are our two crime bosses socializing with each other?" Jack asked.

"I'm winning him over to my side," Marie said.

"Madame Funicello, I will not be swayed by your undeniable beauty," Francois said sternly, a gleam in his eye.

"Then I must employ underhanded tactics."

"Give it your best shot, madame." He pulled her close and planted a kiss on her cheek.

Marie laughed and pushed away. "Stop! You brute!"

"Ms. Funicello," Jack said to Marie, "my name is Bruiser DiMaggio. I'm a loyal soldier in your organization, and I'm good with my fists. Just give me the word."

"Hear that, Monsieur Avalon?" Marie said to her

husband. "My loyal soldier — Bruiser? — is ready to defend my interests. So watch it!"

She and Francois tried to glare menacingly at each other, but Erica started giggling and soon everyone joined in.

A facilitator appeared at Marie's side and took their drink orders. Jack watched the interplay between Marie and Francois. They seemed well matched — both confident, both assured, and both enjoying themselves. Sergei had picked the game's rival gang leaders well.

He steered the conversation toward Francois and his research for an AIDS cure.

"The fight goes on," Francois said. "We will find a cure."

"I am very proud of my husband," Marie said, leaning her head against his shoulder. "I know he will win the Nobel Prize, very soon."

Francois harrumphed.

"No false modesty," Marie said. "I have already selected my dress for the awards ceremony. I am not joking!"

Jack smiled. "The work couldn't be more important."

Marie shrugged. "Of course, AIDS is yesterday's disease. I want Francois to expand his research — to tackle even greater challenges. He is a great man. He deserves the accolades. He can accomplish whatever he sets his mind to."

From her lounger, Lucy watched Jack work the crowd. He moved easily from conversation to conversation, his personality more than matching his abundance of physical charm. He had a technique, she realized as she watched him. He smiled and laughed, but most importantly he listened, focusing in on whoever was speaking as if he or she was the only person in the world.

At the bar, in a group with Francois and Marie, he was

aiming his charms at Erica, who was laughing with delight at something he'd said.

She felt a stab of insecurity, which of course was ridiculous. Jack Ford was an island unto himself, one she had no desire to swim toward. What he did, who he flirted with, was not her concern.

A shadow crossed her legs. She looked up and saw Vienna smiling down at her.

"May I?" Vienna asked, gesturing toward Jack's lounger.

"Please."

Vienna settled next to her. One of the facilitators, a dark-haired young man in wearing tight black swim briefs, approached.

"Would you ladies like a drink?" he asked.

Vienna regarded him with a smile, her eyes openly admiring his muscular frame.

"What's your name?" she asked.

"Diego," he said, smiling back.

"I don't know what I want." She pointed to Lucy's empty glass. "What's that?"

"The house specialty," Lucy said. "A twist on the margarita. Delicious."

"Two of those, Diego."

"Coming right up." He turned toward the bar, then swung back. "I want you to know, Ms. Hastings, that I'm a big fan." He shifted his hips, drawing attention to what was barely hidden beneath the thin black fabric of his swimsuit. "Really big. Anything you want, you let me know."

Vienna watched him walk away, a faint smile on her lips.

"So," she said, turning to Lucy, "what have we learned about our host?"

"Does that happen often?" Lucy asked, glancing at Diego.

"All the time."

"Must be difficult."

"Difficult?" she said, amused. "Hardly. So … about our host?"

"I saw Sergei this morning. He took us on a tour of the island's tunnels."

"And?"

"He's very proud of what he's built here — the whole compound. The whole island."

"What's up with that woman who works for him? What's her name?"

"Natasha. She's like his…." She struggled for the right description. "Right-hand woman?" That captured some, but not all, of what she was trying to describe. "Nanny?"

"Nanny?" Vienna said with a surprised laugh.

"I didn't mean it like that. She's like his … protector, maybe."

"So that means…."

"What?" Lucy asked.

"Nothing. Just thinking to myself. Where's Jack?"

Lucy pointed to the bar, where Jack was listening intently to Erica.

"He's always like that, you know," Vienna said.

"Like what?" Lucy asked, though she knew exactly what Vienna had meant.

"He can't help himself. It's a compulsion."

"What do you mean?"

"He walks up to complete strangers, and a minute later, it's like they're best friends. Last year at Cannes? He brought this guy, totally sketchy, to George and Brad's yacht party, and I was like, Jack, what's up with that guy, and he's like, 'I met him playing poker,' and I'm like, but he's gross, and Jack just laughed and said the guy was fun."

"Was he?"

"No! He got seasick and Jack spent half the party taking care of him."

Diego returned. Eyes on Vienna, he set their margaritas on the table next to their loungers.

"Diego," Vienna said. "What's the plan for tonight?"

He grinned. "I'm not allowed to tell."

"Mysterious. Will you be there?"

"Of course."

"Can I ask something?" Lucy said.

"Of course," he said, his eyes swinging her way, his gaze heated and direct.

Whoa. Lucy felt herself flush. Erica was right; the atmosphere here was difficult to resist.

"I'm supposed to meet a guest named Daddio Donatelli."

"Would you like me to find him and ask him to join you?"

She looked at Vienna, who nodded.

"If you ladies need anything else — anything at all — let me know."

Both women watched his tight backside as he walked away.

"What's all this about what's happening tonight?" Lucy asked.

"What do you think?" Vienna replied, casting a glance around the pool. She pulled out her mobile phone, pressed a button, and stared at it in disgust. "Argh. Stupid back-in-time nonsense!"

Lucy surveyed the crowd, getting friskier by the second.

Jack had warned her. He'd told her the party would get wild. With a sinking feeling, she realized she was indeed in over her head.

CHAPTER THIRTY-FIVE

FROM ACROSS THE pool, Jack watched Lucy and Vienna deep in conversation. Of all the guests here, Vienna posed the greatest immediate threat to Lucy's cover. He resisted the impulse to walk over and interrupt.

"A refill?" he asked Erica, pointing to her drink.

"Please," Erica said. "Vodka tonic."

Jack turned to the bartender. For the fourth time since he'd arrived, his hand casually slipped under the lip of the wood trim that lined the edge of the bar. Behind the trim was a small ledge — a ledge that YokoNoNo could have used to hide a message. He'd tried three spots already, so far without success.

This time, his fingers touched a scrap of folded-up paper. His pulse quickened. He'd found it. He left the scrap where it was. He was too exposed — too many angles for cameras to catch him in the act. He'd have to wait for a crowd to gather before he retrieved Yoko's next clue.

From across the courtyard, he heard Sergei's booming

laughter. Their host had arrived, with Natasha and Constantine in tow.

Sergei was wearing a black rugby swimsuit — identical to Jack's, of course — and it was obvious he'd been working out. The formerly skinny computer geek now sported actual muscles on what had once been a rail-thin frame. Natasha was in business mode, with a white blouse, slacks, and sun hat, as was Constantine in black slacks and a white golf shirt.

Sergei waved at Jack, and Jack gestured for Sergei to join him by the bar.

Natasha, he was amused to note, was unable to hide a momentary grimace when she saw him, and Constantine's eyes kept returning to Jack's rugby trunks. Lucy had been right about Constantine. He had an admirer.

"Jack!" Sergei exclaimed. He clapped Jack on the shoulder and looked him up and down. "We wear same suit! Like brothers, yes?"

"That's right, buddy." He nodded at Natasha. "Looking very elegant today, Ms. Dubronovitch."

"Thank you," she said. "Excuse me, I have to prepare for tonight."

"Do you know Constantine?" Sergei asked as she walked away. "Head of security for Synkonos."

"We met last night," Jack said, extending his hand. Constantine gripped it firmly, attempting to mask the self-consciousness Jack had been trained to understand the meaning of.

Sergei laughed. "Constantine works very hard when we travel, but here on Synkonos, he can relax. Is like vacation for you, yes? I tell Natasha we don't need security on Synkonos. We are island, middle of Mediterranean. Only people on island are people we invite. But Natasha says, what if kidnappers come in boat and take guests hostage? What if a guest becomes violent?"

He laughed again. "Very funny, yes?"

Jack didn't think either possibility was funny, but he laughed with him. He could tell Constantine wasn't amused either. Chances were the man had contingency plans in place for any number of possible disruptions.

"You've been with Sergei a while now?" Jack said to Constantine.

"Two years," he said.

"Constantine is very good at job," Sergei said. "He is fighting champion, mixed martial arts. I am learning now from him, yes? He is excellent instructor."

"A good man to have on your side," Jack said.

Something clicked. He felt an idea coming on, but he'd need more information before he committed.

"Hey, don't know if you know this about me," Jack said, "but I'm totally into mixed martial arts. Tell me more about the training you're doing."

"Ladies," Lucy heard a voice say.

She looked up at the unwelcome sight of Dick Hould, smug assurance plastered on his face. "Daddio Donatelli at your service."

Shit. She might as well get this over with.

"Thank you for coming over," Lucy said. "Have a seat."

Hould settled on the end of Lucy's lounger. He was dressed in board shorts and sunglasses. For a man his age — early forties, Lucy guessed — he kept himself in decent shape. No, it wasn't his appearance she found distasteful.

"Vienna," Dick said, shifting his attention to Lucy's companion. "I've followed your success with interest. I'm impressed with how you've branded yourself. There are lessons in your success for the companies I invest in."

"Thank you," Vienna said politely.

"Are you looking for venture partners?"

"I don't know. Maybe my people can talk with your people?"

Dick nodded, then turned to Lucy. "Ms. Keen, you wanted to see me. I was pleased to hear that."

"It's for the game," Lucy said.

"Of course it is," Dick said.

He licked his lips and her stomach tightened. Pretending she didn't know what this man wanted to buy was proving tougher than expected.

She picked up her margarita and took a big gulp.

"In the game," she said, trying to keep her voice light, "I'm a showgirl, and I'm supposed to introduce myself to Daddio Donatelli and ask him a question."

"A showgirl," Dick said. "Makes sense, pretty girl like you."

The way he looked at her made her skin crawl.

"The question is about film. What's your favorite film?"

"Scarface," he said without hesitation.

Of course. A film about a psychotic, egomaniacal gangster who destroys everyone around him in the most violent way possible.

"Why?" Vienna asked.

Dick glanced her way. "It's about a man who knows what he wants and doesn't let anything or anyone stop him. His only problem is, he doesn't do it smart enough."

"Smart enough?"

"Yeah. Guy dies in the end. Nothing smart about that."

Ugh. Lucy stood and wrapped her towel around her. "Sorry to be so abrupt. Nature calls. Dick, or should I call you Daddio? Thank you for coming over. Vienna, I'll be back later?"

Vienna looked at Dick with a frown, then nodded.

"I'll see you this evening," Dick said, looking at her towel as if he wanted to rip it away. "Count on it."

From his spot near the bar, Jack watched the interplay between Dick and Lucy. Clearly, she couldn't stand the guy, but the signs were subtle — a stiffness in her posture and the way she folded her arms together.

Sergei was describing a new hold Constantine had taught him when Lucy walked up and told him she was heading to the cabana for a breather.

"Just to freshen up," she said. "I'll be back soon."

As she walked away, Boris appeared at Sergei's side.

"Sector four," he said to Sergei.

"Again?"

"The balloon. It's losing altitude."

"Is chopper ready?"

"Waiting."

"Yes, I come. We do timing test, yes?"

Sergei turned apologetically to Jack and Erica. "I must add balloon. Is always case with new systems. Many tweaks. I return soon. Maybe thirty minutes."

"No worries, man," Jack said. "We'll be here."

"What's that about?" Erica asked as Sergei and Boris walked away.

"The Grid."

"The Grid?"

"You up for a dip? I'll show you."

She nodded and followed Jack to the infinity pool. They dove in, slicing through the water and surfacing at the edge near the cliff. From there, they had an unobstructed view of the bay below and the sky above.

"See the balloons?" Jack said, pointing out the ring of round, red objects surrounding them in the sky.

Erica shielded her eyes from the glare. After a moment, she said, "Yes. What are they for?"

"They're holding up a net of wires that cover the island and block radio waves."

"That's why my phone won't work?"

"Yep."

"Sergei mentioned a chopper. He has a helicopter here?"

"Don't know," Jack said, though he already knew that Sergei did.

For a moment, as they floated silently, he considered the puzzle that was Erica Sandoz. Something about her wasn't lining up. He tried to work out what he was sensing. She didn't seem to have Messalina's steely backbone. The whip-wielding online sociopath had an implacability that couldn't be faked.

Could it be hidden? Players in Gang Bang often adopted personas that were physically different from their flesh-and-blood selves. But assuming a different psychological persona was harder. One of the players in his Hollywood Hillz gang, a pixie-like starlet named Tina who weighed ninety-five pounds on a good day, played Gang Bang as a mountainous ogre named Berserker who loved breaking down doors and crushing opponents. The thing was, Tina loved doing the same in real life, though her destructive energy was aimed at the egos and ambitions of anyone who got in the way of her quest for stardom.

Jack raised his head. Faintly at first came the throb of an engine and the whip-whip-whip of blades slicing through air.

Without warning, a massive Huey helicopter roared over the roof of the villa, flying low over the compound before heading out over the bay. The cargo doors were wide open. Jack saw Sergei and Boris inside, holding tightly to straps.

"Is that one of those Vietnam War helicopters?" Erica asked.

"Yep," Jack said. "Amazing machines. Thousands still in use today."

"This big net over the island," Erica said. "How will the helicopter clear it?"

"Don't know. But if we watch, we might find out."

The helicopter approached the center of the bay, then slowed until it was hovering, nearly motionless. Carefully, it headed straight up.

"The net over the island must have a hole, a passage, over the center of the bay," Jack said. "The chopper is clearing the net by moving through it."

The chopper continued its upward ascent for several hundred feet. It then angled forward and headed toward one of the balloons.

Shielding his eyes from the sun, Jack made out Sergei and Boris moving inside the chopper. He watched them unspool a long cable and lower it to the balloon below. Somehow — with magnets, Jack guessed — the cable found the balloon's tether and attached itself to it.

The chopper swayed from a gust of wind, and Jack saw Sergei grab hold of a strap inside.

A few seconds later, the chopper righted itself and returned to its spot above the balloon.

Inside the helicopter, Sergei and Boris turned their attention to a crate of some sort, about three feet square.

Jack watched, fascinated, as Sergei pulled a cord. The crate popped open, and the contents began expanding.

It was another balloon, filling with gas.

When the balloon was half-inflated, Sergei turned and signaled to the pilot. The helicopter banked, and with a push from Sergei and Boris, the balloon slipped into the sky and fell toward the other balloon below.

But the balloon didn't drop far. Slowed by the gas filling it, it stopped falling, then began gaining altitude, rising enough to pull the cable tight. Gradually, both balloons rose higher, lifting the island's radio shield netting with it.

"That's incredible," Erica said.

Indeed. The lengths to which Sergei was willing to go to recreate a long-ago era were impressive — no effort, no expense, no imagination spared. What were the man's limits? If he was the one selling the phosphorin, could anything stop him?

CHAPTER THIRTY-SIX

RELUCTANTLY, LUCY PULLED the cabana door shut behind her and headed back toward the pool. She'd needed a break, an escape from Dick Hould and Vienna and, yes, from the frisky energy in the courtyard. Part of her — most of her — wanted to turn around and lock herself in the cabana, hop in the shower, wash off the sunscreen, curl up under a blanket in bed, and hide. Pretending to be someone else was hard work. Lucy Keen was tuckering her out.

But she couldn't run and hide. Jack wanted her at the pool. Her eyes and ears and nose were no use to the mission if they were buried under a comforter.

She paused along the path to admire a flowering bush that rose to eye level. The plant had been shaped into a giant lollipop on a stick by expert gardeners, its willowy branches covered with clusters of tiny lavender flowers. She leaned in and took in the faint fragrance. The tiny leaves reflected silver in the sunlight.

"Buddleia alternifolia," she heard a voice say.

She turned. Prince Ali was at her side, admiring the plant with her. He was alone, in sandals and swim trunks, with a towel around his bare shoulders.

"The fountain butterfly bush," he continued. "One of the Mediterranean's most beautiful flowering plants."

"You know your flowers."

"I pay attention to the beautiful ones."

He turned away from the plant and toward her. Like Jack, the prince radiated charisma that went beyond his good looks. His eyes, nearly black, were the kind a girl could tumble into if she wasn't careful.

"I also know a thing or two about useful flowers," the prince said.

"Useful flowers, Your Highness?" What did he mean by that? What was he saying?

"Please, call me Ali. Here I can be more than my title."

"Is horticulture a hobby?"

The prince's eyes flickered. She'd surprised him. Because she hadn't let him distract her? Because she knew the word horticulture?

"Jack did not mention what you do, back in real life," he said.

"I'm in medical school, at UCLA."

"Ah." He paused, then said, "I am not formally trained in horticulture. My interests are more agricultural."

"A gentleman farmer?"

Ali reached out and caressed a flower. "I like that phrase. Farming is more interesting than one might believe." He turned toward her. "Were you headed to the pool?"

"Yes."

"Join me for a walk on the beach. Let me tell you why I find farming so fascinating."

A million thoughts flashed through her head. Why did he want to walk with her on the beach? Did he know who she really was? Was Special Exploits right about Ali using the Borlando persona? If so, why was he after the phosphorin? What would Jack think about her going off alone with him?

Nervous tension fluttered through her, even as she straightened her shoulders and applied a smile to her face.

"I'd love to," she said. "Let's go."

Jack leaned against the bar, doing his best to come across as happy-go-lucky and slightly drunk. Through half-closed eyes, he surveyed the courtyard and considered, as dispassionately as possible, his frustrating lack of mission progress.

The poolside scene, at least so far, was a bust. Still no clue about who Yoko might be. The three phosphorin bidders — Dick Hould, Prince Ali, and Erica Sandoz — had all made appearances, but Jack hadn't been able to keep an eye on them full-time, so he didn't know whether they'd found their instructions from Yoko.

He had to assume at least two of them had. As for the third — his fingertips moved casually to the scrap of paper on the hidden ledge under the bar trim — at least this piece of intel was real and accessible. But he couldn't take it yet. He was still too exposed.

So far, the op was, to use the technical term, a suck-fest. Rarely had he gone into a situation knowing less about the players or parameters. Even worse, his gut told him that the briefing wasn't right. Special Exploits was missing something. He had the sense that *he* was missing something.

He'd call Calhoun again. With luck, she'd know more, but already he suspected it wouldn't be enough. He reached for his drink. It was time to shake things up, which meant it was time to find out what the video and audio surveillance covered, and what he could do to disable it and increase his options for covert action.

Doing that undetected and undisturbed meant doing something about Constantine, who even now was standing quietly in a corner of the courtyard, watching him and everyone else. The man never stopped observing. He was good at his job — too good.

How could he put the big guy out of commission?

Jack swirled the ice in his glass. The plan came with risks he would rather avoid, but nothing better had popped into his head, so there it was: the least bad option, preferable to not trying.

He heard a commotion and glanced across the courtyard. Sergei was back from his aerial escapade. Guests surrounded him, congratulating him and peppering him with questions.

Time to put "Operation: Disrupt Constantine" into motion.

When Sergei looked his way, Jack grinned and waved him over. As he did, he noticed Lucy's lounger remained unoccupied. A quick scan of the courtyard showed she hadn't returned.

He felt a flash of irritation, mixed with concern. She'd said she'd be right back. Where in the hell was she?

CHAPTER THIRTY-SEVEN

AT THE WATER'S edge, sand embraced Lucy's feet. The sun, dropping in the west, cast a golden glow. A soft breeze brushed past her as small waves gently tumbled ashore. With most of the guests still cavorting by the pool three hundred feet above them at the top of the cliffs, she and Ali had the beach to themselves.

She adjusted her sunglasses and glanced at the royal enigma beside her. Here she was, on a deserted beach, with a man who'd watched innocent women die; yet she didn't feel as if she was in danger. Was that because she was an inexperienced fool? Or maybe, just maybe, it was because she suspected Ali's motives for acquiring the phosphorin weren't evil? She felt an urge to confront him — to force him to explain his involvement in the scheme. Instead, she said, "I'm surprised an oil man would have an interest in agriculture."

Ali shrugged. "My family has ruled Gudan for three centuries. Oil is a recent phenomenon, an accident of geography. In the coming decades, sooner than we might think, it will be gone."

"Gone?"

"We do not possess the reserves of our neighbors. Our focus is now on turning our capital city into a center of information and commerce. We must create new revenue streams. There is no turning back. My people have tasted wealth and comfort. They will not accept a return to nomadic goat-herding."

"How does agriculture come in?"

"I do not know if Jack mentioned this, but I am working with Gang Bang on a new technology for inexpensive desalinization."

Lucy's eyes widened. "To terraform your desert?"

"Exactly," Ali said. "Today, we import most of our food and rely on deep wells for water. I want Gudan to become self-sufficient."

An idea struck Lucy. She almost said it out loud but managed to stop herself. A scientist at the cutting edge of bacterial research would have this thought; a medical student wouldn't.

"You're thinking about something," Ali said.

"Just random thoughts about the people I've met here," Lucy said. "So many of you are doing impressive things."

"Being a doctor is impressive and honorable."

"I suppose."

Ali turned to her and stopped. Behind him, the late-afternoon sun created a halo effect around his head. Lucy again felt the pull of the island — the temptations of so much beauty.

"Jack is growing up, isn't he?" Ali said, surprising her.

"What do you mean?"

"I cannot claim to know Jack well, but over the years, our paths have crossed. We share certain interests."

"Parties. Girls."

Ali laughed. "So direct. Yes, that is what I mean. But in the past year, my focus has changed. I find myself thinking less about my pleasure, and more about my people and their future, and about how to become, as you put it, a gentleman farmer."

He regarded her intently. "And Jack.... How do I say this? He attends the party of the year, and the person he brings is ... you."

She blinked, surprised again. "Should I be insulted?"

"On the contrary, Ms. Keen," he said, then reached out and took her hand. "On the contrary."

"Dude," Jack said to Sergei, "total bad-ass move with the chopper."

Sergei laughed. "I must confess, I am happy balloon fails so guests can see me in helicopter."

"Like something out of an action movie. Hey, can you get Constantine over here? I want to ask him something."

Sergei looked around, located Constantine, and waved him over.

When Constantine arrived, Jack took a step closer to the big man. Physical proximity was key for what was coming next.

He looked up into Constantine's face. "Sergei mentioned a move you taught him — the Kaan Krush — and it rang a bell. You wouldn't have learned it from Kaan Karaman, by chance?"

The brief flare of anger in Constantine's eyes was highly gratifying. Kaan Karaman, the reigning world champion, was renowned as much for his arrogance and disdain for his opponents as for his innovative moves, speed, and power.

"We fought once," Constantine said. "Unfortunately, he won."

"You and Kaan Karaman, in the ring?" Jack said. "No way. I love that guy. Incredible technique and power. Best fighter out there today."

Constantine's nostrils flared.

"I read that you know Karaman," Sergei said to Jack.

"I paid him to train me for two weeks last year. Guy's amazing. Taught me a ton."

Constantine's mouth tightened. Jack saw how he was coming across — as a rich dilettante, a lightweight, and an amateur.

Good.

"So Constantine," Jack said, inching even closer. "How'd Kaan beat you? Which of his moves put you out of commission?"

"Oh ho!" Sergei said. "Constantine does not like to talk about Kaan Karaman."

Constantine was, he could see, uncomfortably aware of Jack's physical presence. He was doing his best to stay focused on Jack's face, even though his eyes wanted to wander downward.

"I have great respect for Kaan as a fighter," Constantine said carefully.

Oh yeah, this was good. This guy hated to lose. Karaman was a flashpoint.

Jack laughed. "You have to. He kicked your ass."

Constantine tensed, and Jack grabbed him around the shoulders and pulled him in tight. One of the advantages of acting like an overenthusiastic party boy was that people half-expected him to breach their physical space.

"Hey, no offense. I'm sure you're plenty tough."

Frustration swirled behind the composed mask of

Constantine's face. Jack was close enough to catch a hint of the man's cologne, mixed with sweat from hours in the sun.

"You know, I've never had a chance to try out what I learned. Karaman taught me how to take down big guys like you." He stepped back in a fighter's pose, hands up, and started shadowboxing around Constantine.

"I'm sure he did, Mr. Ford," Constantine said, trying his best to remain polite.

"Hey now, come on. Don't go all fake on me," he said, pretending to land blows against Constantine's midsection. "Don't coddle me just because I'm your boss's buddy."

Constantine's eyes flashed. "With all due respect, Mr. Ford, I'm sure what you learned in those two weeks would not take you far in the ring against a top-level fighter."

Jack stopped dancing around Constantine and faced him directly.

"Dude, you are so wrong," he said, a challenge in his tone. "You don't know this about me, but I'm, like, a good fighter. And Kaan showed me exactly how to stop big guys like you. I bet my moves would work on you just fine."

Sergei, watching the exchange in rapt silence, jumped in. "Jack, you want chance?"

"What do you mean?" Jack said, pretending to not understand.

"We do exhibition match. Tonight, after dinner. My Greek champion versus Mr. Jack Ford."

He pretended to hesitate. "Sergei, a private word?"

He wrapped his arm around Sergei's shoulders and walked him a few paces away. Leaning in, he murmured, "You planned this all along, you sly dog, didn't you?"

Sergei grinned. "I do not lie. Cage is being constructed right now."

"What if I hadn't played along?"

"I have two fighters coming in ferry right now. But match with you and Constantine is better."

Jack leaned in closer. "What I'm really looking forward to is the after-dinner entertainment, if you get my drift."

Sergei chuckled. "You hear things?"

"Speculation is rampant. Folks can barely contain themselves."

"Consider match prelude to evening's main activities. You have concern my man beats you up too much?"

Jack's snorted. "Dude, no worries there. You've just given me all the incentive I need to stay out of harm's way."

"Unified rules, yes? Three five-minute rounds. Points. We accept wagers — we are in Vegas, yes? — and winner gets special sexy prize."

"Deal."

Jack steered them back to the group. "Okay, big guy. Sergei has proposed we put on a show. You and me, in the ring, going at it. I can try out those moves from Kaan, and you get the chance to show me that I'm full of it."

He stepped up to Constantine and stared him straight in the face.

"So what do you say, big guy? I'm game if you are."

"I do not hold back once I am in the ring, Mr. Ford." Though he spoke to Jack, the warning was aimed at Sergei.

"Like I said, dude, bring it on."

"No holding back," Constantine repeated, this time looking at Sergei for confirmation.

"Yes, Jack is okay with no holding back," Sergei said.

This time, Constantine couldn't conceal his smirk. "Then it would be a pleasure."

"Excellent!" Sergei said. "Tonight, after dinner, cage match!"

On the beach, three hundred feet below, Lucy found herself teetering on the edge. The hand holding hers was strong and confident. The man attached to it stood inches from her, shirtless and muscular and fit. If she leaned in, even just a bit, he'd read the signal and swoop in, his face closing on hers, his lips brushing —

What in the world was she doing? She blinked and took a step back. Ali's hand dropped away.

"I haven't known Jack for long," she said. "Barely a month. I don't know if he's growing up or not."

Ali regarded her silently, a small smile on his face.

"It's time to head back to the villa," he said. "Shall we?"

He turned toward the Synkonos Express rollercoaster, which awaited them further down the beach.

"No, wait," Lucy said.

He turned, looking at her expectantly.

She pointed to the steep, winding stairs cut into the cliff. "You up for a bit of a workout?"

"After you."

They climbed the steps in silence, pausing occasionally to catch their breath and take in the stunning views of the bay.

"I hope my question about Jack didn't upset you," Ali said.

"Your question wasn't about Jack."

"No?"

"You see Jack as an American version of yourself. Your question was about you."

Before Ali could respond, Lucy heard a faint sound from above, something shifting. A bit of dirt fell on her face.

"What the — ?"

"Look out!" Ali yelled. He pushed her against the side of the cliff, covering her body with his, barely a second before a large rock crashed onto the very spot they'd been standing.

She gasped in shock. For several long seconds, dirt and

rocks rained down on them. The cliff's jagged surface dug into her back.

When the rocks stopped falling, she opened her eyes and stared in disbelief at where they'd been standing.

"Are you all right?" Ali asked.

"I'm fine," she said, stepping out of his arms to brush the dirt off her hair and shoulders. "You?"

"Let's get up these stairs now."

Without hesitating, they dashed up.

When they reached the top, they stood for a moment, panting.

"There," Ali said, pointing to a spot on the edge of the cliff where the rocks had rested.

"A natural avalanche?" Lucy said.

"No doubt. Wrong place, wrong time."

Lucy continued to brush dirt out of her hair.

"I can't thank you enough. If you hadn't gotten me out of the way, I'd be — " She stopped. The enormity of what she had been about to say hit her. If Ali hadn't saved her, she'd be *dead*.

At that moment, Jack turned the corner of the garden path. His eyes narrowed as he took them in, disheveled and breathless.

"What happened?" he asked, running up to her, alarm in his voice.

"We're fine," she said. "We were walking up the steps from the beach. Rocks fell and almost hit us."

"You okay?" His eyes scanned every inch of her, searching for injuries.

"I'm fine. Ali pushed us out of the way just in time."

"You sure?"

"Yes." She took a deep breath. "But maybe we can go back to the cabana?"

Jack turned to Ali.

"I can't thank you enough." He grabbed him in a big bear hug. "You're the best. I owe you big-time. You okay too?"

"I'm fine. We were lucky." Ali tried to laugh, but the sound came out like a rasp. "Now let me go."

Jack stepped back. "You sure you're okay?"

"Yes, I'm fine. Now go."

CHAPTER THIRTY-EIGHT

BACK IN THE CABANA

JACK CLOSED THE cabana's front door behind him, plate of baklava in hand, and listened for Lucy. He heard the shower going.

Time to call Calhoun.

He placed the plate in the refrigerator, picked up the phone, and waited while the operator dialed. Seconds later, he heard the big brassy voice of Gracie May Blowser.

"How's the party, handsome?"

"Great. We're having a lot of fun."

"How's the new girl holding up?"

"So far, so good, except she and Prince Ali were walking up the cliff stairs and nearly got hit by falling rocks."

"Omigod!" Calhoun said, allowing her Gracie May voice to rise in tone and volume. "Tell me she's okay!"

"They're both fine. They were lucky."

"Is that island safe? What kind of place you at anyway? What's going on with those stairs?"

"The stairs are built into the cliff. Rockslides happen all the time. It was just wrong place, wrong time."

"It sounds very dangerous," she said, still agitated. "Last thing I want is for something to happen to you or your date. Can you imagine the headlines?"

"So it's the media you care about?"

"You know what I mean, mister!"

"Gracie, we'll be fine."

"I want you to call me every twelve hours, you got it? You have me worried now. I won't have you getting hurt out there on that god-forsaken island."

"Well," Jack said, pretending to hesitate, "then you won't wanna hear what I'm gonna say next."

"What's that?"

"I'm doing an exhibition MMA match."

"You're doing a *what*?"

"With a big guy named Constantine. Can you find out about him? I want to know more before I get in the cage."

"You're getting in a cage?"

"Gracie...."

"You're gonna give me a heart attack, pulling crazy stunts like this. How do you spell his name?"

He told her and, through the phone, heard the sound of her typing.

"Okay," she said after a moment. "Constantine Thanos was a professional mixed martial arts fighter for five years, and a Greek national wrestling champ. His record as a fighter is 26-1. He retired two years ago. I'm looking at an article that says he wants to get back in the ring and has been working hard all year to prepare."

Shit. So not only did the dude have skills, he was actively training.

"Any knockouts?"

Gracie was silent as she searched. "Fifteen knockouts. I'm

looking at a picture of him right now. Omigod, he looks huge — and mean!"

"I'll be fine."

"No you won't! You know how much I hate you doing crazy stunts like this." Jack heard her take a few deep breaths to calm herself. "What can I say to change your mind?"

"Nothing. I said I'd do it. You know how I am about that."

After a longer-than-normal silence, she said, "Is that why you called? So I can look up stuff about the man who's gonna beat the crap out of you?"

"The real reason? I just wanted to hear your voice. You remind me of home, Gracie."

Gracie snorted. "Save the charm for someone else."

He heard pages flipping in Gracie's day planner.

"Wish I had something exciting to share on my end, but it's been a slow weekend in La-La Land."

The bathroom door opened. Lucy walked out in a white terrycloth robe, with a towel around her head.

"Okay. Gotta go."

"You call me after you get out of that cage, you got it?"

"Got it."

He set the receiver down. Calhoun had nothing for him. By telling her he wanted to hear the sound of her voice, he was informing Calhoun he had nothing for her beyond what he'd told her about the rockslide and the exhibition match.

Time for the next item on his checklist.

Lucy was in the kitchen, bent over the refrigerator.

"How you feeling?" he asked.

"Clean." She pointed to the plate of sweets. "What's this?"

"Something for later," he said. "Promise you won't sneak any."

"For real?"

"Reals. Not even a bite. Have a seat. Let me get you something to drink."

Clearly. she understood something was up. She took a seat at the dining table. He opened cabinet doors and scanned the shelves until he found what he was looking for.

"You and Ali have a nice chat on the beach?" he asked, his back to her as he got her drink ready.

"He told me about his desalinization project with Gang Bang in Gudan."

"Interesting, isn't it?"

"And he asked about you."

"What did he ask?"

"If you were growing up."

He turned and gave her an inquiring look. "And you said...?"

"I told him his question wasn't about you. It was about him."

"Nice deflection."

She shrugged. "What else could I say? I barely know you."

"True that." He placed a mug in the microwave oven, hit the timer, and turned to face her directly. "Now about tonight. I think it'd be better if you rested up and had a quiet night in the cabana."

He watched her absorb what he'd said. In the past two days, he'd seen her expressions of fury, distrust, irritation, uncertainty, watchful interest, curiosity, and even a fleeting moment or two of — dare he say — appreciation. But this was his first encounter with stubborn resistance. Her eyebrows hunched closer to her eyes, her gaze sharpened, and her body went still as if preparing to defend her ground, all while sitting at the dining table, hair still wet from the shower, wrapped in a white bathrobe.

"There's no reason for me to stay in the cabana," she said.

"I'd feel better if you did." The microwave pinged. He

took out the mug and dropped in a tea bag. The aroma of jasmine filled the air.

He set the mug in front of her and took a seat at the table.

Her mouth tightened with irritation. "You made me *tea*?"

Keeping his eyes on her, he said, "Some of those rocks hit your head. We need to make sure you don't have a concussion."

Her eyes flashed her frustration. He knew she wanted to argue with him, engage in a frank and full discussion about exactly what was going on, and it annoyed her to no end that she couldn't. Had they been in a spot where their every word wasn't most likely being recorded, she would have said: *You're being silly. No one is trying to hurt me.*

To which he would have responded: *You can't know that.* Maybe the rockslide was no accident. Maybe someone tried to kill you. Maybe your cover — and mine — are blown.

That was the problem with this mission: There were too many maybes. After getting her back to the cabana, he'd returned to the cliff to check out the spot where the rocks had broken loose. He'd found no evidence of anything other than a random natural event, but his gut was telling him the rockslide had been deliberate. Someone had tried to kill her, or Ali, or both of them.

"You've had a long day, and I'd stay, except I did a dumb thing at the pool and agreed to a bet and, you know, I gotta make the peeps happy."

She looked at his get-up — satin fighting trunks, open-finger fighting gloves, and a robe with "Synkonos Fight Club" stenciled across the back — and shook her head.

"You're the one who's going to get hurt."

"Do I detect concern beneath the disapproval?"

She was about to protest, but he leaned over and kissed the top of her forehead. "I'll be fine. I'm pretty good at this fighting stuff."

Someone knocked at the door. He got up, went to the door, and ushered in Greta, the hospitality facilitator who'd greeted them the day before.

"What is this?" Lucy asked.

"I've asked Greta to stay with you."

"Why?"

He turned to Greta. "Lucy was hit by falling rocks on the cliff stairs a little while ago. She's okay, but she's going to take it easy and rest up tonight."

"Jack, I don't need this," Lucy said.

He continued talking to Greta. "I'd feel much better if someone stayed with her for the next couple of hours, until I get back, just in case."

"Of course," Greta said. She eyed Lucy without enthusiasm. Clearly, she'd been hoping the summons had been about something else.

"You guys can get room service and watch TV," he said. "There's probably a good selection."

"The food is excellent," Greta said, "but there are only three television channels, showing what was broadcast in Las Vegas in 1965. Tonight's shows include the *Donna Reed Show*, *Rawhide*, and Dr. *Kildare*."

His eyes widened. "Sergei got his hands on American television programming from 1965?"

"He believes that kind of detail is essential."

Lucy stood, walked to the kitchen sink, and poured her tea down the drain. She turned and faced Jack, annoyance radiating from her.

"Listen," he said. "I know this isn't your idea of fun, but do it for me, okay? I'll feel much better if you rest up here with Greta."

She stood there like a statue.

"Okay?" he repeated.

He saw her jaw loosen, just a bit. And then, finally, her shoulders dropped.

“Fine,” she said. “I’ll behave. Go. Get yourself beat up.”

CHAPTER **THIRTY-NINE**

JACK SHUT THE door behind him and headed down the garden path toward the main compound. With luck, his willful sidekick would stay put. Though his concern for her safety was real, it wasn't the only reason he wanted to ensure her absence. Despite her assertions to the contrary, Jack knew she'd be uncomfortable with what would go down after the exhibition match. The guests at this party knew how to play; Lucy did not. The last thing he needed was a civilian freakout.

Not when he had a fight to consider. And a post-match intrusion into the surveillance room. And the latest clue from Yoko, which he'd grabbed before leaving the pool.

The clue was in the form of a poem, or rather, assuming he was reading it right, a poetic mashup:

Oh, say can you see
...
... a swimming lad,
Picked him for her own,

Pressed her body to his body,
Laughed; and plunging down
Forgot in cruel happiness
That even lovers drown.

The first part was from the American national anthem, with the missing words: "by the dawn's early light." The second part, from a poem he didn't know, referred to something at the pool or down at the beach. The "her" referred to … who? There were tons of hot girls at the pool, but Yoko would have chosen something more permanent, more architectural, as her reference point.

In the courtyard, he stopped near the pool and looked around. Yoko would use something like....

Of course. Under the waterfall at the end of the pool, presiding ever so confidently, was the mermaid queen.

At dawn, Jack would rendezvous with a sea-maiden.

CHAPTER **FORTY**

Auction room
Gangland

YOKO REVIEWED THE security footage of the rockslide. Her timing was not at fault — the rocks should have crushed Ali — but he'd been very lucky. He and Lucy Keen had barely escaped with their lives.

No matter. There were other ways to handle the suspiciously disinterested Borlando.

The more intriguing question was: Why had Lucy Keen been with him? Yoko rewound the footage, watching Lucy and Ali as they walked backward along the beach, stepped backward into the Synkonos Express, flew up the track to the top of the cliff, and strolled backward along the garden path, where he had found her admiring one of the plants.

So he had approached her and not the other way around. *Good*. That behavior lined up. So far, there appeared to be nothing unusual about this young woman. Still, there was something about her....

"Video, Cabana 1." The screen switched to the interior of Lucy's cabana. Lucy and one of the hospitality facilitators were sitting on one of the sofas, watching television.

A quiet night in for Ms. Keen? Also not surprising. Her brush with death had probably shaken her. Perhaps she had no interest in watching her foolish beau get beaten to a pulp.

Speaking of....

She clicked off the video. She had things to do. Time waited for no Japanese schoolgirl persona. Ambitious plans like hers didn't materialize by themselves.

CHAPTER
FORTY-ONE

AS INSTRUCTED, JACK turned away from the main entrance to the villa and stepped up to a door marked "Staff Only." He knocked. A raven-haired hospitality facilitator with sparkling green eyes opened the door.

"Greetings, Mr. Ford." She was wearing the same black bikini she had been at the pool, but with one extra adornment: a waiter's collar and bowtie around her neck. "Mr. Eristov is waiting for you."

Jack stepped inside and found himself in the staging area of the event room. The space looked like the backstage area of a theater, with ropes and pullies and lighting and stage props on trolleys behind a huge red velvet curtain. Technicians scurried to and fro, making final adjustments. A gaggle of dancers, a mix of women and men in skimpy sequined costumes, awaited their cue on either side of the stage.

Sergei and Constantine stood together, stage center. Sergei was dressed in a slim black suit over a white shirt and black tie. Constantine was barefoot, wearing a dark blue robe and open-fingered gloves. He towered a good six inches over Sergei, his shoulders threatening to burst through the robe.

Jack frowned at the man's imposing presence, his doubts intensifying. He'd engineered the fight, but what if his oh-so-clever idea backfired?

Sergei waved him over. "Jack! Gear is okay, yes?"

"The gear's great."

"We open curtain in few minutes. You ready for match?"

In for a penny, in for a pounding.

"You bet." He turned to Constantine. "Remember, dude, don't go all pussy on me. If you hold back, I'll know."

Constantine's mouth tightened. "As I said, I will not hold back."

He looked again to Sergei for confirmation.

"Yes, I understand," Sergei said, his voice impatient. "Real match. All out. No holding back."

Natasha slipped her head through the curtain. "The dinner plates have been cleared and guests are settling in."

Sergei turned to Jack and Constantine. "Okay, we start. First is musical number, then I make introductions. When I say your name, you come to cage, yes?"

"Got it," Jack said.

"Sergei, you come from stage left, and Jack, you come from stage right."

Jack stepped across the stage and took his place in the wings. From across the stage, he could feel Constantine's gaze. The man oozed confidence, as if he knew something that gave him a secret advantage.

"Places, everyone!" Natasha said.

A spark of expectancy ran through the performers and crew — an alertness and a sense of shared purpose. The sound system roared to life with an up-tempo, big-band piece. At a nod from Sergei, the curtains swung open and the dancers burst onto the stage. Cheers and hollers rose up from the crowd. The dancers' costumes glittered in the lights, the sequins reflecting different colors — leopard spots on the men, the tawny hides of gazelle on the women. Their dazzling high kicks, acrobatic leaps, and catches mimicked the chase of predators versus prey.

Sergei's amplified voice carried over the music and dancing. "Synkonos is alive with energy, with grace, with beauty, with raw animal energy. And beneath that, Synkonos pulses with promise of a different sort."

The lights dimmed and the pace of the music dropped. Prey succumbed to predator. The twists and turns of the dancers slowed, becoming more pronounced. Limbs intertwined. Hands lingered. Hips thrust.

"We have much to experience this evening," Sergei said over the music. "Tonight, we witness exhibition of natural force like no other. Tonight we partake in rewards of a day and a game well played."

With a lush, shimmering crescendo of cymbals, the music pulled the dancers into a heaving mass of writhing bodies before snapping into sudden silence. The stage went dark. The audience, taken aback, tensed.

A single spotlight appeared. Sergei stepped into it, a grin on his face and a microphone in hand.

"We get to climax later, I promise! I tease you now, but for good reason."

Faux groans rippled through the crowd as the lights rose, enabling Jack to scope out how the event room was set up. The focus of the room wasn't the stage, but rather the eight-sided fighting cage sunk into the floor in the center of the room. Three levels of low, luxurious seating — couches and loveseats overflowing with cushions and pillows — surrounded the cage, and the guests were packed in tight, rubbing elbows and more. Every seat, from every angle, was positioned for an up-close view of the cage below. Facilitators in skimpy swimsuits and bowties circulated with hors d'oeuvres and drinks. The overall effect was decadent — the wealthy elite amusing themselves with violence and bared flesh.

"First," Sergei said, jumping off the stage and making his way into the cage, "update on first round of battle between Funicello and Avalon gangs for control of Hotel Synkonos. Nearly all of you place answers in drop boxes. We have ninety-five percent participation in first round — excellent first step. So now I tell you that in first round, Funicello gang scores forty-eight points!"

The Funicello gang members in the audience, including their leader, Marie, applauded loudly.

"And what of their rival, Avalon organization?" Sergei said. "Yes, they are also busy this afternoon. After first round, they score… fifty-three points!"

The Avalon gang erupted. Francois stood and led the Avalon gang in a cheer of "Avalon! Avalon! Avalon!" while the Funicello gang booed and hissed.

"Now, now," Sergei said as the laughter died down, "we only complete first round. Second round begins tomorrow morning, when we deliver envelopes to your rooms.

"Tonight, our dancers give us taste of animal energy. They show us hint of what is to come. Here, we know we can indulge our appetites for the physical. And what better way to demonstrate what Hotel Synkonos is about, what Las Vegas is about, than" — a drum roll started — "night at the fights?"

The crowd whooped, and Sergei continued. "I scour planet for fighters who bring incredible entertainment to Hotel Synkonos, who display physical qualities that make Hotel Synkonos special. And we are fortunate to have two such fighters with us tonight.

"First," he said, "maybe you already meet our Synkonos

director of security. But you may not know he is Greek national wrestling champion and mixed martial arts fighter, with professional record of twenty-six wins and just one loss. Give big applause to" — his voice rose and expanded — " Constantine Thanos!"

Constantine strode to the center of the stage and made his way, with his arms above his head, to the cage. He tossed off his robe and did a circle inside the cage, exhorting the crowd to cheer.

Jack watched with a sinking feeling. The dude was ripped. He moved with grace and displayed a level of confidence and ease with the crowd that Jack had not anticipated.

"So who do we get to go up against Constantine?" Sergei asked. "Who is brave enough — foolhardy enough — to step into cage with this monster competitor? Who else but one of our own — a guest with us here! Man famous for wild stunts. Famous for being crazy and getting away with it. Maybe this is craziest ever. I give you — Mr. Jack Ford!"

The crowd gasped and hollered and applauded as Jack stepped into the spotlight and made his way to the cage, grinning and with his fists pumping in the air. Three levels of eyes stared at him from every side, eager and calculating and amused. The closeness and tightness added an intensity to the overall atmosphere. As he stepped down into the cage, he could smell their perfumes, their drinks, their anticipation.

"Match is three five-minute rounds," Sergei said. "Fighters agree to rules. Winner is fighter who wins two of three rounds, or forces opponent to submit, or knocks out opponent."

Constantine gave Jack that same smug, knowing look.

Sergei continued. "Here at Hotel Synkonos, we take wagers. You can place bets with facilitators. Who here believes Constantine has edge?"

Most of the crowd roared its response.

"And who believes Jack can win?"

The response this time was more muted.

Sergei shrugged at Jack in commiseration. "Sorry, my friend — crowd thinks Constantine has advantage. But before everyone places bets, I should mention special prize. Because what is Hotel Synkonos without special Synkonos twist?"

Jack could sense the crowd leaning forward. Constantine gave him that same damn secret smile.

"Tonight's fight is prelude, warmup, for main event of evening, if you get drift."

Low laughter rippled through the crowd.

"Winner of match gets special prize: to choose who he can play with after fight. Do I have volunteers?"

The room stirred. Within seconds, a dozen hospitality facilitators rushed into the cage — ten women and two men. They arranged themselves in a line in front of Sergei, Jack, and Constantine.

Sergei turned to Jack. "You pick first, Jack."

Jack grinned and yelled to the crowd, "Now this is what I'm talkin' about!"

He walked up and down the line of models, smiling at each one, before stopping in front of a striking black woman.

He looked directly into her eyes. "What's your name?"

"Hazel." From the sound of her voice, she was Caribbean — Bahamas, perhaps. She appeared to be in her early twenties, eager and knowing.

He gently pulled her toward him, his gaze sliding from her eyes to her lips.

"How about it?" He leaned in for a kiss. "Sure you're game?"

"Mmm," Hazel said, her arms circling his waist. "I've had my eye on you all day. You better win."

Jack stepped back and said into Sergei's microphone, "I choose the beautiful Hazel."

The crowd whooped its approval.

"And now, Constantine, you pick playmate," Sergei said.

Constantine reached for the microphone. Sergei, taken aback, complied and handed it over. Constantine walked up and down the line of models, lingering in front of the two male volunteers.

He turned to the crowd. "I have a confession. I have a preference. I am, as our American friends might say, an ass man."

The crowd laughed.

"Nothing is quite so attractive as a well-shaped butt," he added, to more whoops and hollers.

Constantine paused and stood still for a moment, microphone in hand. Again, Jack was impressed by his dash of showmanship. The man knew how to milk a moment.

"When I win," Constantine said, "the ass I claim is — "

He whirled on Jack.

"His!"

CHAPTER FORTY-TWO

THE AUDIENCE GASPED.

Jack watched Constantine stride toward him, a smirk on his face, using his extra height to tower over him. The man meant to intimidate him. He expected him to be shocked, thrown off balance, and even fearful.

"When I win," Constantine yelled again, "pretty boy is mine!"

Sergei grabbed the microphone back. "Constantine, that is not intent of rules. You must select another prize instead of … ass of your opponent."

Jack kept his face deliberately neutral. Constantine's move was bold and psychologically astute, intended to frighten and demoralize him before a single punch was thrown. He would need to go beyond that. Far beyond. He gestured to Sergei for the microphone. Still agitated, Sergei handed it over.

"Can I ask our lovely volunteers to exit the cage?" Jack said. "Give us some room?"

Hazel looked at him with a question in her eyes as she and the others left the cage.

Slowly, deliberately, Jack walked around Constantine, who stood in the center of the ring, proud and spiteful. He made a full circle, looking the man up and down, waiting for the crowd to shift its focus toward him.

Then, into the microphone, Jack purred, seductively, "Hey there, big boy."

The crowd gasped, then laughed. Constantine's eyes flickered.

"I guess I'm supposed to be scared? Run for the hills because the big guy's got a hard-on for me?" He looked out at the crowd. "Should I be scared?"

"No!" the crowd roared.

"I'd say this fellow's offering me some pretty stiff incentive to win."

The crowd laughed.

"Should I say yes?"

Reassured by his encouragement, the crowd roared in the affirmative.

"Should I?"

The crowd roared louder.

"I can't hear you!"

The crowd's roar became deafening.

"Then it's on!"

From the side of the cage, Sergei stared at him, stunned.

He plucked at his fighter's robe, flashing it suggestively. "Should I show Constantine what he's fighting for?"

The crowd roared again, eating it up, loving it. The stories they'd tell.

He whipped off the robe to the cheers of the crowd and felt their gazes lingering on his muscular arms, his defined pecs, and the curve of his ass under the tight shorts. They'd all seen the tabloid photos and the sex tape. Now they wanted a live performance.

"A chair for my friend?" he said into the microphone.

Instantly, a folding chair was rushed into the cage and placed dead center.

He turned to Constantine. "Have a seat, big boy."

Constantine glowered at him, and then, remembering the crowd, smiled as if he was cool with what was going down.

"A show, yes!" Constantine laughed, trying to regain the upper hand. "Show everyone what I will be having!"

"Can we get some music?"

Within seconds, the big band, trombone-led oomph of the classic "The Stripper" filled the room, and Jack swayed his hips to the beat. He began with small shakes and twists, then raised his arms above his head to let the crowd — and Constantine — take in his muscled chest and tight abs.

He positioned himself above Constantine, astride the chair, facing him. Constantine's hand rose, and he slapped it away.

"No touching," he purred into the microphone, playing for laughs. "Not until you beat me to a pulp, you big sexy brute. Rowwwrrr!"

With the crowd, his intent was entertainment. With Constantine, the intent was different. When he whispered in Constantine's ear, he wanted the man hot and bothered. When he raised his arms and threw his head back, he wanted Constantine's eyes to travel down his torso to his crotch.

He leaned against his opponent and whispered in his ear, "You fuck with me, big guy, and I fuck with you. Just not the way you'd prefer."

He sprang up and yelled to the crowd, "Are we ready for a cage fight?"

The crowd roared back.

He turned back to his opponent, who remained sitting, unable to take his eyes off him.

"Something wrong, big guy? The excitement get to you?"

He said to the crowd, "I think our friend's embarrassed! Something's come up, and he's shy about us knowing it!"

Constantine's face flamed red. For a split second, the man's eyes telegraphed uncertainty, but only for an instant. Rising from his seat, Constantine stepped up to him and, leaning in, pressed his nose to his. The man's body radiated heat.

"I will defeat you without knocking you out," Constantine said quietly, in a voice meant only for him. "You won't require medical attention. You won't be able to avoid your end of the deal. Your ass will be mine. I will take you right here, in this cage, in front of all your wealthy friends."

Jack put a pout on his face and whispered back, "Aw, you're gonna hold back? But I like it rough, you big bruiser, you."

He turned again to the crowd. "Are you ready for a rumble?"

As the crowd roared, he raised his arms above his head and yelled, "Let's get this party started!"

CHAPTER FORTY-THREE

POW!

Crunch.

Splat!

He was in a cartoon — in an exaggerated, choreographed caricature of Hollywood-style violence.

Except he wasn't.

Two rounds in, one to go, and Constantine was crushing him — totally dominating. The man moved with speed and precision. His technique was nearly flawless, outclassing him in every way. Every kick, every punch, every takedown added to his point total.

The roar of the crowd reverberated in his ears. Constantine landed another punishing blow to his midsection — *bam!* — then backed off. The man danced around him, smirking. He meant to win on points, and avoid knocking him out. Avoid giving him an excuse to save his ass.

He tasted blood from a cut above his left eye. Nothing serious, but Constantine wasn't hitting there now, despite several opportunities for a well-placed kick or punch. His opponent was holding back.

Exactly what he'd hoped would happen.

He needed Constantine looking past the fight, anticipating his reward, infused with over-confidence, and not fully focused on the here and now. He needed him out of his fighter's zone to have any chance in hell of pulling this off.

The guests were on their feet, yelling themselves hoarse. Through a haze of sweat, he caught the gleam in their eyes, the whites of their teeth, their fists in the air, their faces flushed, urging him and Constantine on. A crush of dark suits and evening dresses and shining jewels and bared skin vibrated with bloodlust, their hands already roaming. The cage battle was sparking exactly what Sergei had intended: it was turning the crowd on.

Pow! Another blow, this time to the right side of his face.

He staggered and almost went down, but regained his balance and backed away. Constantine outweighed him and outmuscled him. If the big guy got him on the mat and kept him there, the fight would be over in a flash.

He continued moving around the cage, in a deliberately predictable pattern. The cage was an octagon, with a structural post in each of the eight corners. He'd retreated into the corners throughout the match, acting like a wounded dog, offering his shoulders and legs — fuck, they'd hurt in the days ahead — as easy targets for his opponent's relentless but restrained attacks.

The clock showed less than a minute. It was now or never.

He backed into a corner, leaning his back against a support post. As before, Constantine moved in to land more blows on his midsection.

But this time, faster than he had before, he feinted left. Constantine's left hand slammed into the post.

He heard the crack of a bone breaking.

Constantine reared back, shocked by Jack's unexpected speed and no doubt the pain in his hand.

Now! *Ferociter!*

He slammed into Constantine's midsection, moving in tight, getting inside his opponents reach, and pounded away. He heard the *oof* of surprise as Constantine lost his breath.

Now! He leaped up and clamped his thighs around Constantine's chest, knocking his opponent off his feet. Constantine fell full force on the mat and involuntarily exhaled from the impact.

Jack tightened his legs around Constantine's ribcage like a vise, leaned down, positioned his forearms on either side of Constantine's neck, and squeezed.

He saw the shock and panic in Constantine's eyes.

The Kaan Krush, named for MMA champion Kaan Karaman, was a move where a fighter clamped his legs around an opponent's ribcage (constricting his opponent's ability to breathe) and pressed his forearms against each side of his opponent's neck (reducing blood flow to the brain). Success depended on having thighs of steel, because the opponent's instinctive response would be to buck his attacker like a bronco and use his arms to push or punch him away. If a fighter could remain on his opponent for more than a few seconds, his opponent would weaken and lose consciousness. The Krush was particularly effective on big guys with big ribcages and big oxygen needs, especially after the big guy exhaled and had no air left in his lungs.

Constantine tried to square his legs and toss Jack over his head, but Jack held on. With the last of his reserves, Constantine pounded away at Jack's head.

But it was too late.

The blows faded and then stopped. Constantine's angry eyes glazed over and his arms fell limply to his sides.

Jack heard the rasp of his own breathing.

He'd won. Holy fucking crap, he'd won!

CHAPTER FORTY-FOUR

THROUGH HIS GASPS, Jack became aware of the crowd around him. They were on their feet, cheering thunderously. They couldn't believe it either. Somehow, that lucky sunovabitch Jack Ford had won!

Jack rolled off Constantine and collapsed on the mat.

Sergei jumped into the cage.

"The victor!" he yelled as the crowd roared.

Jack shakily got to his feet, and Sergei raised Jack's arm above his head. "The first champion of Synkonos!"

Hazel rushed in and hugged him. At his feet, Constantine began coming to. Support staff helped him sit up.

"He broke a bone in his left hand," Jack said to Sergei. "He'll need to get it set."

Sergei gestured to the staff. "Take Constantine to medical room. Get scan of hand. Monsieur Le Coq is doctor. Ask if he can set bone."

Constantine tried to wave off the people helping him. "I'm fine."

"No," Sergei said. "You let team do scan and set bone and check you. Is direct order."

Constantine rose to his feet, still woozy.

Jack stepped up to the big guy. "Great fight, man. I got lucky."

His opponent looked at him, focusing in.

After a pause, the big guy said, "Luck had nothing to do with it. Well played, Mr. Ford."

Constantine exited the cage. Jack took a bottle of water and dumped it over his head, the coldness a welcome shock to his overheated skin. He grabbed a towel and wiped the sweat from his body. He felt Sergei's eyes on him.

"Constantine thinks you hold back on purpose? Is that what you do?"

"Dude gives me too much credit. I got lucky. My ass got lucky."

A hand touched his shoulder. Hazel again, her eyes alive with desire.

"Feeling refreshed, Mr. Ford? Ready to claim your prize?"

He let his hand wander to her bikini-clad rear. "Please, call me Jack."

Hazel moved into his arms and pressed her body in close.

"You smell like an animal," she said. "I love it."

Sergei laughed. "Evening moves to next stage. Lights and music!"

The brightness in the cage dimmed to a warm yellow glow. The music returned, a slow, suggestive, jazzy instrumental.

Hazel pressed her hips to his and eased him toward the center of the cage. She moved her body to the music, coaxing him into the flow of the dance. Instinctively, his body adjusted to her rhythms. Her hair smelled of flowers.

An image of Lucy flashed through his mind, smiling her cute little smile — the one she tried but failed to suppress as he unpacked her suitcase, the smile she got from the pleasure of making him laugh.

Focus, dude. His mission partner was tucked safe and sound in the cabana. No muss, no fuss, no distraction. No need for his head to be anywhere but here and now. He had a role to play and a mission to accomplish.

Another flash — Calhoun's concerned face in the interrogation room, asking if his cover still fit. What the hell?

Then another flash — Moms in the sunroom, drilling into him with her bunker-buster stare.

Fuck. Focus, dude. He loved his job. He was made for this.

The girl moved in his arms, her breasts pressing against his chest.

"You okay?" she asked.

"I am now," he said.

The girl's body trembled in his arms, arousing him. He leaned in and kissed her neck and tasted honey.

A single spotlight shone on him and Hazel. Deftly, he loosened the tie of her bikini top. She laughed as he cupped her generous breasts in his hands.

"I want you," she said. "Now."

The crowd hollered in appreciation as she grabbed his shorts and yanked them down his thighs. He'd led the crowd down this path — had deliberately inflamed their imaginations — for a reason. He wanted them thoroughly engaged here and not wandering around the villa, getting in his way. The more guests who stayed here in the event room, fucking and playing on these wonderfully comfortable beds and sofas, the more easily he could make his next move.

Hazel grabbed his shoulders and jumped up, wrapping her legs around his waist. He was ready. Still standing, without preliminaries, he thrust inside her. She gasped. The crowd roared. All around them, pants slid down, dresses slid off, and thongs were ripped free. Hands and mouths and hips moved as the laughs and cries of passion filled the room.

He'd always enjoyed being the center of attention — got off on it, to be honest — and Hazel's enthusiastic cries spurred him on.

"I'm taking you to one of the beds," he said. She tightened her grip. He nearly came right there but managed to carry-fuck her out of the cage and onto one of the beds in the viewing stand, where eager guests cleared a spot for them.

He lay her down on the soft cushions and commenced his attack in earnest, her cries urging him on.

He felt hands on his back, roaming. Fingers slid further down. He glanced back. Marie Le Coq was behind him, wearing a strap-on dildo, advancing on him with two other women — Erica and Jenny. Below him, Hazel wrapped their arms around his neck and held him down tight. He was trapped. Before he could decide how to respond, the women were on him. He felt a finger slide between his asscheeks, and then a lubed finger thrust inside.

He groaned. The finger was joined by another, loosening him up. Then they vanished, replaced by the pressure of Marie's rubber phallus pressing firmly against his sphincter.

He could break free, if he wanted to. Should he? What would Jack Ford do?

He gritted his teeth. It seemed his ass wasn't going to escape a hard fuck after all.

Madame Le Coq's cock plowed into him. He grunted.

"Yee-haw!" she said, her eyes dancing. "Ride that cock, boy!"

The initial pain faded quickly as he adjusted to the thrusts of her thick rubber tool.

And then, as suddenly as it had begun, the tool was gone. Jack glanced back. Marie had been pushed away, by Vienna.

"Jack's ass is mine! All mine!" Vienna said, laughing

hysterically, high as a kite. She pushed Jenny away and collapsed next to him in giggles.

"Mine," she whispered, looking deep into his eyes. "You're all mine."

He glanced past Vienna, over her shoulder, to the edge of the event room.

And found himself staring into the shocked, hurt eyes of Dr. Lucy Kimball.

Fuck!

CHAPTER FORTY-FIVE

SHE'D BEEN BORED, restless — a modern girl could only take so much Dr. Kildare — and irritated, too. Jack had no basis for insisting she stay cooped up in the cabana. He'd misread a simple accident. No one was out to kill her.

At least that's what she'd told herself when she'd turned to Greta and said she was tired and wanted to get some sleep, and ushered Greta out of the cabana.

And that's what she'd told herself when, two minutes later, she'd slipped into a blouse and slacks and sandals and headed toward the villa and the fight. There was no reason to be scared. Nevertheless, as she walked down the dimly lit garden path, the shadows larger and darker than before, she'd picked up her pace.

She'd arrived in time to see the whole damn thing. Standing at the back, away from the rest of the crowd, she'd watched Jack accept Constantine's shocking challenge. She'd seen him regain the psychological edge with his provocative striptease. She'd felt her stomach clenching with ever-increasing anxiety as he got pummeled in the first two rounds. She'd found herself cheering his victory when he'd somehow turned the tables at the last moment, jumping on Constantine and winning.

And then she'd watched, stunned, as he and that brazen facilitator followed through on their promised sexual display. She'd stood rooted to the spot, unable to tear herself away, as that hideous Marie woman turned the tables on him with her Le Coq.

She was beyond shock. She was angry, disgusted, furious — and aroused.

Yes, *aroused*. Which made her even angrier.

So when Jack saw her — his eyes locking onto hers — and when she saw his surprise and dismay, she did what any rational person would have done.

She ran, fast, to get as far away from Jack Ford as she could.

She made it out of the villa and into the courtyard before hearing the sound of bare feet running on pavement behind her.

"Hey!" he said, catching up.

She stopped and turned to face him. He'd pulled his shorts up and was breathing hard. He skin was slick with sweat. Blood seeped from a cut over his eye.

"Are you okay?" she asked, unable to stop her instinctive concern. "How badly are you hurt?"

"Those were my questions for you," he said. "I know a place we can talk."

He took her arm, very firmly, and walked her down the garden path toward the small cave they'd explored that morning.

"Why did you leave the cabana?" he asked, each word clipped and precise. Boy, was he pissed. She could tell he wanted to yell at her.

"I was restless."

"We can talk in here, if we whisper."

His hand still on her arm, he guided her into the cave and into a small alcove. The darkness was near complete.

He removed his hand from her arm, then took a deep breath and exhaled as though willing himself to stay calm. She could smell the sweat on him, the blood, the sex.

"You know the reason for tonight's fight," he said in a whisper, his mouth inches from her ear. "Why I set it up."

Actually, she didn't. "Tell me."

"To get into the security room. With only one guard, I can."

"Why do that?"

"To see what's on video and what's not. To find the blind spots. If Sergei's the seller, he might use the blind spots for message drops. We might be able to intercept communications about the next round of the game."

"How is that related to the fight?"

"With Constantine out of commission, there's only one man in the security room, and that dude will have to leave the security room to use the bathroom."

"How can you know that?"

"The plate of baklava in our refrigerator? In a few minutes, I'll be delivering it to the security room. It's laced with a strong laxative."

It took her a few seconds to absorb this. "So you get him out of the security room — "

" — and into the bathroom. Once he's there, the sonic nausea pen — remember that gadget? — will keep him there, praying to the porcelain gods."

"Seems you've figured it all out," she said, and couldn't resist adding, "and managed to enjoy yourself to boot."

"So it looked like I was being myself? Fully engaged in the moment?"

"To the hilt."

"Good," he said, in a tone that she sensed was deliberately casual. "You know, I'm reminded of something my mother said."

"Your *mother*?" She couldn't believe what she was hearing. He was bringing his mother into this?

"She was talking about my party-boy persona. She said if I'm not having fun, if I'm not embracing the moment, people will see it. Instantly."

Her logical, cautious side knew she should pretend to go along with this ludicrous rationalization (provided oh-so-helpfully by his mother, of all people). The man's appetite for violence and fornication was none of her business. She needed to keep her mouth shut.

Yet she couldn't.

"Just so I'm clear," she said, maintaining a neutral tone. "You have fun beating people up?"

"Sometimes," he said, again casually. "Listen, my looks have attracted the wrong kind of attention since I was a kid. I've learned to defend myself. Every single thing I've done in my life, I've had to prove myself."

"And the sex?" she asked, unable to stop herself. "You don't care about people watching?"

"Total exhibitionist. It's all good."

"No hangups? At all?"

"The usual few, before I joined Special Exploits. But the training helped."

"The training?"

He paused. "You're way too easy to talk to, Lucy Kimball."

"I could never do what you do."

"Few people can."

She forced herself to stay quiet. To not say anything more. The silence hung between them, heavy in the darkness.

"You have a problem with this," he said.

"I didn't say that."

"You're broadcasting it from every pore."

"You can't see that."

"I don't need to see it to know it."

"I don't want to talk about it."

"We need to."

"No, we don't."

He grabbed her arm again. "You don't get it. We're partners here. What's going on here is not about what you or I want."

"I get it, okay?" Lucy shot back, wrenching her arm free, barely able to keep her voice at a whisper. "Your job description includes sex. Calhoun explained it. And you...."

"And I what?"

"You're just doing what you're paid for."

"Finally," he said. "It's out. Now let me say this, because you really need to hear it: You and your judgmental attitude can go fuck yourselves."

"No," she said, pushing back. Her anger broke free. She found herself whisper-yelling. "You can't avoid it like that. You get paid to have sex with people. You're a salaried sex worker. A prostitute."

In the darkness, she heard him take a deep breath and sigh — a world-weary, oh-so-aggravating, oh-so-condescending sigh.

Fuck him.

"Let me be very clear," he whispered. "I have a job. I get paid to do that job, even though I don't need the money. As part of my job, sometimes because it's necessary, and sometimes because I just goddamn feel like it, I have sex."

"I don't know how you do that. How you live with yourself."

"Would you rather I kill someone?"

"What do you mean?"

"Which spycraft techniques are acceptable to you?" He leaned in closer, his mouth brushing her ear. "How about, instead of fucking people, I beat them up, blackmail them, frame them for crimes they didn't commit, threaten their loved ones, kidnap them, torture them, or kill them?"

She heard the disbelief in his voice. "Compared to everything else I can and will do — and have done — to complete a mission, why is sex a bad thing?"

She couldn't speak. She didn't know what to say.

"It's time you understand how the world works," he said, voice bitter. "You're a grown-up. Deal with it."

"My world doesn't work like that," she said, finding the words.

He snorted.

"Your safe, sheltered, civilized world. The world I'm out here protecting, putting my ass on the line for — literally — every single day. That world?" His tone battered her. "Get over your hypocrisy. Go ahead and ignore reality if that makes you feel better, but stop with the fucking judgment."

She didn't say anything. A heavy silence filled the alcove.

"Well, partner," she finally said, "you got what you wanted. We talked it out. Satisfied?"

"I need to be in the security room in thirty minutes," he said. "I'm taking you back to the cabana."

"No. I don't want to be near you right now."

"You're not safe out here."

"I'm going for a walk."

"No."

"Yes."

"No."

They stepped out of the cave. She saw his face. He was furious and in no mood to compromise. He'd carry her back to the cabana kicking and screaming if he had to.

She relented. “I’ll go to the bar, and I’ll stay there until you come get me.”

He moved closer and stared at her face, at her pupils, at her tells.

“Sit right at the bar,” he said, his voice tight. “Order your own drink and stay put.”

CHAPTER **FORTY-SIX**

JACK STEPPED INTO the shower.

Ninety seconds.

He soaped up vigorously. The fight had been tough. His ribs and shoulders ached. He touched his nose, testing it. A miracle it wasn't broken.

Dr. Lucy fucking Kimball. He scrubbed harder, then squirted shampoo on his head and lathered his hair.

Sixty seconds.

He'd warned Grant. Sure as shit, right as rain, his so-called partner, this civilian who insisted she was open and game and ready and cool, had shown her true colors. Revealed her uptight, judgmental core. Proved she lacked the self-control to keep her goddamned opinions to herself. Fucked with his equilibrium — messed with his mojo — and for what? To make herself feel better?

Thirty seconds. He rinsed off, the hot water pounding against his skull.

Fuck her. Not literally. Not that he wouldn't; she was hot.

She didn't even know how hot she was. With a bit of encouragement —

No, no, no. Lucy Kimball was just a problem to manage. A pain in the ass and possibly a target. She'd have to come around on the safety concern, which meant he'd have to take the edge off her anger by tossing her a bone to placate her. Not that he cared what she thought. Hell, no. What mattered was the mission. He couldn't let her prissiness put her — and him — at risk.

Protect her, but stop listening to her? Yeah, that sounded right.

Zero seconds. He turned off the shower and grabbed a towel. Prudie McPrudester had no idea who she was up against.

But first thing first:

Time to check out a surveillance system.

CHAPTER **FORTY-SEVEN**

LUCY SLID ONTO a stool and signaled to the bartender.

"Something strong," she said.

"A vodka martini?" the bartender suggested.

"Perfect."

The room was empty except for Boris, Sergei's right-hand guy, sitting by himself three stools down. He glanced her way but without curiosity.

Clearly, the man wanted to be alone.

The martini appeared in front of her. She leaned in for a sip. The alcohol slid down her throat, cool and crisp and bracingly strong.

She should take Boris's lead — sit there with her drink and stew silently.

But she couldn't.

She turned toward him. "Boris, right?"

"Good evening, Ms. Keen."

She gestured toward the fight room. "Why aren't you with everyone else?"

"Sex doesn't interest me."

She blinked. People rarely admitted that. His tone was very matter-of-fact. No embarrassment. No apology.

He turned toward her. "What is your reason?"

"Orgies are disgusting," she said without hesitation.

She stopped to consider what she'd just said. Had she just learned something about herself? Before this evening, had she given, even once, a nanosecond's thought to orgies?

"Ah," he said, "you're jealous."

Her anger flared. Why this sudden epidemic of people telling her how she felt?

"First of all? No, I'm not jealous. Second, you may be comfortable sharing personal information, but I'm not."

"I propose a deal," he said. "We share equally, one personal detail at a time. Either of us can end our sharing session whenever we please."

She took another sip of her drink. Why the hell not?

She swiveled on her stool to face him. "Why doesn't sex interest you?"

"Too much work for too little reward," he said, moving to the stool next to hers. "What did your date do to disappoint you?"

She took a deep breath. The martini was starting to hit. In her brain, alcohol molecules were crossing the blood-brain barrier and interfering with the release of dopamine (essential for brain and body function) and glutamate (key to nervous response). She felt herself becoming slower, dumber, and less inhibited by the second.

"You're evading, not answering," she said, "but fine. I'm not upset with Jack Ford. I'm upset with me for believing he could change. No, that's not right. I am upset with him. He's a fucking slut."

Whoa. Had she really said that out loud?

"Leopards can't change their spots."

"People suck." She looked at her glass. Empty. She should slow down. She signaled the bartender for another.

Boris looked at her keenly. "I agree with you, completely."

"Who burned you? Why such a gloomy Gus? This time, a real answer."

"My wife," he said. "Ex-wife. When she left me, she said our marriage felt like a job. A tiresome, draining, joyless job. Her words."

"I'm sorry to hear that."

The bartender arrived with her new drink and moved away. Lucy took a gulp.

"She wasn't wrong," Boris said. "I'm not much fun."

"Why's that?"

"My turn. I do not know Jack Ford, but it appears he is — I hope we can be frank? — a spoiled alcoholic with poor impulse control. What made you think he was capable of change? And, frankly, why do you care?"

She had to be careful. The urge to open up to this stranger was nearly irresistible.

She sighed. "He's charming. He's attractive. He can be sweet when he wants to be."

"You're falling for him."

"That's ridiculous. And that was two questions, not one."

"Then you must rectify the balance," he said. "I pride myself on my ethics. A deal is a deal."

"Why aren't you fun?"

"I have too much on my mind."

"An evasion. Do better."

Now it was his turn to sigh. "For too long, I have been consumed by my work. Gang Bang has taken all of my energy. I feel removed from my true passion, which is protecting the environment. I have chosen to get back to that. Now I'm working out how."

"Does your boss know you're planning to move on?"

"Not yet."

"Have you been with him long?"

"Since the beginning. I was Sergei's academic adviser at university."

"He's not going to be happy?"

"No," he said, sadness clouding his voice. "He's not."

"You said you're working out how you're going to leave."

"Yes." He looked at her curiously.

"I like to approach decision points as if they're experiments. Test my hypotheses. Try and fail, try and fail. Eventually, if you're fortunate, try and succeed."

Boris nodded. "Most certainly, I agree. That is why my departure will only be after careful consideration and deliberation and even testing, as you say. You are a doctor, yes?"

"Yes. I mean I will be."

"I appreciate the scientific mind. It's one of the best features of our species."

"Are you as drunk as I am?" she asked. "Have we reached the point where we have deep discussions about philosophy and the meaning of life?"

A smile threatened to appear on his face. "Shall we apply the scientific method to the question? Test that hypothesis?"

"Careful," she said, threatening to smile back. "You and I might end up having fun."

CHAPTER
FORTY-EIGHT

JACK GLANCED AT his watch. Any minute now.

The security room opened and Durgos stepped out. Clutching his stomach, he ran down the hall and into the men's restroom.

Jack sidled up the security room door and, after glancing up and down the hallway to make sure he was alone, bent down and applied his picks to the lock. Seconds later, he was in.

The plate of baklava was on a small table, next to a mug of coffee. Durgos had eaten four pieces, more than enough to keep him unpleasantly occupied, especially with the sonic nausea pen in the bathroom adding an extra unpleasant layer of bad. He didn't envy the man the next hour of his life.

He surveyed the room. A wall of twenty monitors — five across, four down — showed live footage from digital cameras placed throughout the villa. Every ten seconds, the views switched. A keyboard and control monitor stood on a long, narrow table under the wall of monitors. Underneath the table was the server that controlled the cameras and stored the digital footage.

Jack took out his smartphone, slid open a hidden compartment, removed a micro-USB drive, and inserted it into the server.

The drive, one of three he always carried with him, was loaded with executable malware designed to disrupt digital video software in a specific, non-standard way. Rather than shut down the video or create a repeating loop — disruptions that were easily discovered and thwarted — the malware corrupted any recorded footage more than twenty-eight minutes and seven seconds old. The ruined recordings would, when discovered, appear to be the result of a software crash, with the randomness of the time cutoff arguing against a hack.

The malware needed three minutes to work its magic. While it crunched away, he stood back and watched the twenty screens, familiarizing himself.

Two minutes in, he'd seen enough to know he wasn't seeing what he'd expected. The cameras captured multiple views of the main public areas — the courtyard, dining room, bar, hallways, and garden paths — but almost nothing of the compound's perimeter. The beach had just two cameras. The pier had one and ditto for the helipad.

Blind spots were everywhere. Avoiding the cameras would be child's play. Incredibly, it appeared the cameras did not capture audio.

Surely there was more than this? As the monitors cycled again, he noticed one of the views hadn't changed. The camera was aimed at an unmarked door in a remote corner of the courtyard, hidden behind a stand of tall bushes.

He counted to ten and watched the monitors cycle to new views — all of them, that is, except the monitor aimed at the unmarked door.

Bingo.

He checked his watch. Three minutes. He turned toward the USB drive. It flashed twice in quick bursts — the malware's signal that all was good with the hack.

He removed the drive from the server and slipped it back into his phone.

Time to check out what was behind the unmarked door, but first....

He used the mouse to click to the fight room, where the orgy was in full swing. He could make out Sergei, surrounded by three women and enjoying himself immensely, as well as Erica Sandoz, Prince Ali, and Dick Hould.

He clicked over to the bar.

As promised, Lucy was sitting there.

But she wasn't alone.

CHAPTER FORTY-NINE

WITH HER RIGHT index finger, Lucy traced a line over the chilled glass of her third vodka martini. Really, she should stop. She was a lightweight. Always had been. A lightweight with a knack for getting herself drunk. So much for her supposed concern about a head injury, and so much for staying at the top of her game.

Her game. Ha ha. What game? She had no game. The last time she'd been this drunk was, what, two months earlier? Girl's night at Joanie's. Bad movies, good wine, detailed discussions about careers and parents and men (urgh). She'd passed out on the couch and had awoken at dawn with a pounding headache, her mouth coated in gunk, and a puddle of drool on the pillow Joanie had placed under her head.

Boris was still talking, very earnestly. What was he saying?

"I will tell you why," he said. "It seems we consume without understanding the consequences. For example, data consumption. Gang Bang's storage and bandwidth needs are skyrocketing. We can't grow capacity quickly enough to meet the demand."

Ah, environmental angst. She could talk that.

"Can't argue," she said. "Jack and I flew here on his private jet. I feel bad for our ozone layer."

"We're all guilty, in some way."

The poor man was such a gloomster. He needed something — someone? — to loosen the tension in his tight, hunched-up shoulders. Someone to help him stretch out, relax, take a deep breath, and appreciate the good parts of life.

The line of thought reverberated. She was missing something, but what?

"So, a different question?" she said.

Boris looked at her expectantly.

"Surely you still have hope?"

Boris drew back. "Hope?"

"Of meeting someone new. Of fun. Of — "

"Love?"

"Yes. Surely you haven't given up on love?"

Boris looked at Lucy with sudden intensity. "Hope is for dreamers. Naive, foolish dreamers. Love is not in my future."

He stood up abruptly, clearly ready to leave.

"Can I ask you one more question?" Lucy asked.

Boris hesitated, then nodded.

"Why were you and your wife unhappy? The real reason."

He looked at her with an expression she had trouble defining — a mixture, perhaps, of irritation and resignation. "This conversation was my idea. I should have realized you would want to continue asking questions. It's in our nature to always want more — to satisfy our curiosity."

He sat back down and faced her. "Because I can't have children. I'm infertile."

She breathed in sharply. How rudely — how inappropriately — she was behaving.

"Boris, I'm sorry," she said. "I didn't mean to.... I'm sorry."

Boris gave her a sad smile. "There is no need to apologize. I agreed to provide an answer, and I feel I should clarify. My wife was unhappy. I was relieved."

Her eyes widened. At that moment, she heard a man's voice behind her say a rough, aggressive, "Hello."

She swung around.

Dick Hould was walking toward them, fresh from the orgy room, pants on, shirt unbuttoned, and barefoot. Not drunk, judging by his gait, though not far from it. His mouth was smeared with lipstick.

"I was looking for you," he said, then turned to the bartender. "Whisky, on the rocks. Use the good stuff."

She saw Boris's eyes narrow with distaste. The bartender gave Hould his whisky.

Hould turned toward them.

"Lucy Keen," he said, his eyes raking her body. "Missed you in the fight room."

"Not my scene," she said.

"Your date was into it."

She didn't respond. If she didn't take the bait, would he go away?

"A sore spot," he said. "I can help with that."

He reached out and took hold of her arm above the elbow. She stiffened and tried to shake free, but he didn't notice or care. With a tug, he pulled her off the stool and onto her feet.

He pressed himself against her.

"I know what you need," he said, his breath in her face. "Revenge is a dish best served hot."

Later, when she attempted to analyze the two seconds that followed, she was forced to conclude, reluctantly, that she would never be able to isolate which specific distasteful element had proved to be the initiating trigger. Was it her knowledge of the deadly bioweapon he was attempting to buy? What she'd learned about his background and methods? His unwelcome interest in her? The smell of booze? His hand on her elbow? How he'd yanked her off the stool? His grossness pressed against her? The fact that he, along with everyone else, wanted to tell her exactly what she was feeling?

With a surge of anger — a shocking and welcome rush that she knew, instantly and deeply, fully and overwhelmingly, was good and just and liberating and so, so right — she slammed her knee hard into Dick Hould's groin.

CHAPTER **FIFTY**

JACK'S MOUTH DROPPED as he walked into the bar. He couldn't believe what he'd just seen: a fantastic, well-placed move, with excellent form and against such a deserving target!

He nearly burst out laughing.

Hould was doubled over, gasping for air. Lucy stood over him, her face flushed, her eyes glittering with — what? Excitement? Pleasure?

Hould turned a murderous eye on her.

"You bitch," he wheezed.

They hadn't seen him yet. He walked up behind them.

"Wow," he said. Lucy and Boris turned, surprised.

"Honey, I had no idea. Next time we argue, I'll stay out of range."

He reached down, grabbed Hould around the shoulders, and pulled him upright. "Looks like she got you good, Dickie boy. Let's get you to a chair."

As he leaned in close, he quietly slammed a fist into

Hould's gut. Lucy gasped as Hould cried out in pain and collapsed again.

"What's the matter, Dickie?"

"Bastard," Hould wheezed. "You'll pay."

"Aww...." He pulled him upright and slammed him in the gut again. "I guess you didn't hear me the first time."

Hould struggled to breath.

"Please," he begged.

"Karma, dude. Look it up." He dragged Hould to a booth and dropped him into it, then turned and extended a hand to Lucy.

Wordlessly, her eyes on his face as if she couldn't believe what had just happened, she slipped her hand into his.

As he led her away, he glanced back at Boris.

"Awesome first day, dude. Totally awesome. Can't wait for day two!"

Lucy was barely out of the bar before her mission partner started laughing. He was looking at her with such sincere pleasure and appreciation that she got a little freaked out. Wasn't he supposed to be angry with her?

Apparently not.

With a joyful whoop, he scooped her into a hug and swung her around as if they'd just won the big game.

"What are you doing?" she said, half-protesting, half not. She was all jangled and raw, awash in a sea of excitement and guilt and pleasure and shock — emotions that rarely disrupted the focus and precision of her day-to-day existence. So unlike Jack, who always seemed to dive right in, impervious to consequences, and who'd not only backed her without hesitation, but had added an exclamation point to her statement.

"You were fantastic," he said, a huge grin on his face. "I loved it. Total badass babe. Flawless technique."

He stopped swinging her around but didn't let go. Instead he held her close, staring into her eyes, their faces inches apart. She felt the moment sliding toward danger. His strong arms around her felt wonderful.

What was she doing? Her body stiffened. She reached up to push him away, but before she could, he anticipated her move and let go.

"You okay?" he asked.

"I'm fine," she said, struggling to regain her composure.

"You were amazing in there."

"I'm not so sure."

"Trust me, you were." He paused, then added, "I'm tired, but how about we take a walk before we turn in?"

She looked at him and held his gaze. "You're tired?"

"Yep."

"Really?"

"Yep."

She looked at the cut on his forehead. "When we get back to the cabana, you'll let me check your face."

"Deal." He took her hand and led her to the courtyard. "We'll need to be quick about this."

Wordlessly, he steered her through the courtyard to an unmarked door obscured by tall bushes. He took his smartphone out of his jeans pocket, slid open a hidden compartment on the side, and removed two slim pieces of metal. He bent down to the lock, inserted the two pieces of metal, and moved them around.

Her heart thumped. Her first illegal act. How would they explain this if they got caught?

She heard a faint click. He stood, put the picks back into his smartphone, and opened the door.

"Inside," he said.

The room was small, with cloth-paneled walls, wall-to-wall carpeting, and just two pieces of furniture: a comfortable leather reclining chair in the center of the room and, next to it, a small side table. The chair faced a huge white screen on the far wall. A small kitchenette and a door to a small bathroom completed the setup.

Lights turned on automatically as they entered. Jack ran his eyes over the room for a few seconds and snorted.

"What are you seeing?" she asked.

"This," he said. From the side table, he picked up a remote control and pressed a button. Immediately, the lights in the room dimmed, and the giant screen on the wall came to life.

Up popped a list of options, displayed like a TV channel guide. Jack used the remote control to select the option marked "Cabana 1." The screen showed six different high-quality video feeds of what appeared to be their cabana, with multiple angles of the bed and shower.

"Sergei is such a perv," Jack said and snorted again.

He clicked through each channel — a dozen in total — showing other cabanas, massage rooms, hot tubs, and the pool. The final channel was of the fight room, where, even now, the orgy was raging.

He looked down at the remote and pressed another button. One of the fight room's six video feeds expanded, taking up the whole screen, and showed a life-size view of a guest and a hospitality facilitator fucking. Jack pressed another button, and the camera zoomed in for an even tighter shot of the guest's hands cupping the facilitator's breasts. He pressed another button, and the cries and grunts of the impassioned couple filled the room.

"Welcome to the Masturbatorium," he said.

"Shouldn't we get out of here?" she asked.

"Yep." He clicked quickly but methodically through each

of the channels one more time, paying careful attention to each, then turned the screen off.

He ushered her out the door and led her through the deserted courtyard to the Synkonos Express, which they boarded and zoomed down to the beach. The shoreline was deserted. From the villa above, they heard the faint sounds of music, barely audible over the soft sounds of the wind and waves gently brushing the shore.

Jack chose a spot at the end of the beach and sat down.

"Here," he said, patting the sand.

"Is this okay?" she asked as she sat next to him.

"The beach only has two cameras and no audio."

"What about the camera facing the door we just broke into?"

"You saw that, huh? No worries. The video will auto-delete in twenty-eight minutes."

Which meant his surveillance room plan must have succeeded. "What have you learned?"

Jack shrugged. "Not much. Sergei's gone state-of-the-art with the surveillance in a few key spots in the villa, but elsewhere, it's like he doesn't care. There are tons of ways to slip around unnoticed."

"The key spots are wherever there's likely to be sex."

"Yep."

She frowned. "So he's seen me naked."

"Totally."

She had every right to be offended, and part of her was, but she also couldn't help feeling a certain odd sadness for their host.

"He's lonely, isn't he?"

"Very much so," he said.

"Am I the only person here who wasn't part of the orgy?"

"Seems like it. You and Boris, that is. What did you talk about?"

Briefly, she recounted their conversation. "I don't see him as the master criminal type."

He nodded. "Dude's depressed. Can't see a motive."

"We haven't learned much yet, have we?"

He picked up a rock and tossed it into the water. "Nope. Still don't know who Yoko is, or where the phosphorin is."

"So we keep looking."

"Pushing. Prodding. Nosing around."

He tossed another rock into the water. He was calmer now. His anger and exuberance gone, he seemed content to sit here with her all night. She took a deep breath. Should she ask?

Yes, her inner voice said. *Ask*.

"Jack," she said, "tell me about your dismissal from the military."

He turned toward her and held her gaze. For just an instant, his lips pressed together. Then he shrugged.

"Okay," he said. He lay next to her, on his back, facing the heavens above.

She followed his lead and settled next to him. Above them, stars filled the black sky.

"What really happened?" she asked.

"Sex happened. Your favorite subject. My dismissal was about sex."

"What did you...." She stopped herself and rephrased. "Tell me what happened."

"Before I tell you," he said, his voice low but clear, "I want to explain something about military service. In combat, you become closer than close with the guys you're with. You rely on each other and trust each other in ways you can't understand unless you're part of it. You're brothers. In the civilian world, you might have nothing in common — hell, the guy might be an ass-wipe and you might even hate him — but the bonds of combat are stronger than just about any other. You'll literally do anything for each other."

She didn't say anything, allowing him to continue.

"It was like that with our commanding officer. Captain Joe, we called him. Smart. No bullshit. Levelheaded. Committed. Fair. Tough. Worked harder than we did."

His voice sounded thick, almost as though he was getting choked up. She looked toward him, surprised.

He cleared his throat. "He got hit. Landmine. Shrapnel in the legs and abdomen. The surgeons saved him, stitched him up, and he got reassigned. Six months later, I ended up stateside, and he was there, a major on track for a promotion to colonel.

"I met his wife, Susan. Great gal. I spent a lot of my free time with them. Dinners, ball games, nights out. I'd bring a girl, and we'd double-date.

"After a while, I saw they were having trouble as a couple. Not one of the usual issues, like money or an affair. They loved each other, but they were sad.

"One night, Susan pulled me aside. She wanted my help. Joe was pulling away from her. He was becoming withdrawn, frustrated, angry, bitter, because of sex. She told me he couldn't get an erection anymore, because of the shrapnel. She told me she wanted me to help him over that hump."

Lucy blinked. This was *not* what she'd expected.

"Why did she ask you?"

"I had a reputation for being something of an … expert. And Joe trusted me."

"Go on."

"So one night, Joe and I, we had a few beers, and I created an opportunity for him to share what was going on."

"You mean you manipulated him into telling you."

"I mean," he said, turning onto his side to look at her, "I created an environment, a moment, where he felt safe talking about it. You're a woman. You know how hard it is for men to talk about anything other than sports or the weather."

"Okay, fine," she said, following his lead and turning onto her side to face him. "I don't mean to be judgmental about you manipulating people for the greater good."

She held his stare and saw him suppress a grin. Clearly, he didn't mind when she pushed back.

"So Joe finally told me," he said, getting back to the narrative. "The shrapnel sliced through key nerves in his groin. Susan kept insisting she didn't care, that she loved him and all she cared about was that he was alive and with her, but he didn't believe it. They'd had a great sex life before the injury, and he hated that she didn't have that now."

"That must have been really tough," she said.

"He was hurting. He'd lost his confidence. He couldn't see past his injury. He was starting to mistrust and pull away from the woman he loved. And then he surprised me."

"How?"

"He knew I had a fair amount of experience. He said he wanted me to teach him — you know, tricks in the bedroom, for him and Susan."

"So, you did."

He shrugged. "What else could I say but yes?"

"You became his sex tutor."

"Pretty much."

He went quiet. Lucy tried to keep still and let the silence draw him out, but her impatience was rising. What was it about these Special Exploits people? How did they turn silence into a weapon?

She gave in. "So what happened then?"

"At first, I'd give him a tip, he'd go off and try it, then come back and report. And then he surprised me again."

"How so?"

"He told me he wanted me to be there. He wasn't getting

it right. He'd talked about it with Susan, he'd told her what was going on, and she was game. Hands-on instruction, that's how he put it."

She pictured Jack in a bedroom, standing at the foot of the bed, or seated in a chair by the side of the bed, coaching a couple on how to make love.

"Of course he wanted more than that. We both knew what he wanted."

"What? What did he want?"

"He wanted me to fuck her. To give her what he couldn't."

She did her best to keep her face neutral. This was *so* not what she'd expected.

"And so…?"

"And so I did." His eyes didn't leave hers. "I'd been around the block. I knew I liked being watched. And Susan was — is — a beautiful woman."

"And Joe?"

"He needed it most of all, to give his wife the only thing he couldn't give her himself."

"Did it work? Did you help?"

"Yeah. I introduced toys — dildos, strap-ons, vibrators, pumps, you name it — and once Joe got over the hump, things really took off. They found a new groove — a good one. And you know what? It felt right. I was making a difference by helping people I cared about."

He grinned. "And having great sex, of course. I'm no saint."

"How long did this go on?"

"A couple months."

"And then?"

"A neighbor saw me and Susan through an open window, snapped a photo, and texted it to their friends. The gossip started. And then, because of my family's public profile, it got in the media and things went to hell."

"Is adultery a military offense?"

He sighed. "Technically, yes, but what usually happens is, the CO orders you to end the affair, shovels you shit duty for awhile, and sweeps it under the rug. But the CO couldn't do that with me. With the photos and the media, the chain of command had to go by the book."

"So you got charged."

"Article 134. Adultery. Charged, tried, and dismissed."

"That's it? One bad act and your military career is over?"

"Yep."

"No way around it?"

"I was too high-profile."

"What about Joe?"

"He just made general."

Her eyes widened. "He wasn't charged?"

"I made sure of that." Even in the near darkness, she felt the intensity of his gaze.

"You took the fall. You protected him."

"He's my brother," he said. "I'd do anything for him. Don't get me wrong — he fought me on it. Hard. I had a hell of a time convincing him. But I wasn't going to let our therapy sessions deprive the military of a damned good soldier. I told him his penance was to be the best leader he could be, as well as the best husband, every single minute, every single day."

He turned and sat up abruptly, then picked up a rock and tossed it into the water.

"Joe and Susan are doing great, by the way. Just had their second kid."

She sat up with him. Their shoulders brushed. He turned toward her. She knew what would happen next. His eyes fell to her lips. His hand went to her cheek, then slid to the back of her neck, his fingers rough yet smooth. He smelled so clean. A jolt of desire shot through her. His lips found hers and pressed in. Oh, God, a good kiss. His arms slipped around her, then rolled her gently onto her back, leaning his body over hers. Her arms were around him, pressing down his muscular back, urging him in.

Yet she couldn't. She just couldn't. She'd promised herself. *Not again.*

He must have sensed her tension, because he pulled back. "Lucy...."

"We can't," she said.

He swallowed and said, "Of course." He pulled away and sat up. "I get it. You don't trust me."

"No," she said, and she couldn't keep the regret out of her voice. "I don't."

He stood and extended his hand to her. "Shall we?"

A sea of unwanted emotions washed over her again, tossing her with a vengeance. "You'll let me look at your cut?"

"Of course." In silence, they made their way back to the cabana.

A short while later, in the bright lights of the bathroom, as she applied a bandage to the cut over his eyebrow, he said, "You're doing really well here. You know that, right?"

"You're all set," she said as briskly as she could.

His blue eyes held her gaze for a moment. "Thank you."

She felt an urge to say something substantive, something meaningful, something honest and real. But what? What in the hell was there to say?

"Time to get some sleep," she said instead. "Doctor's orders."

He gave her a sad smile. "As you wish."

She was still kicking herself when, an hour later, exhaustion finally claimed her and she slid into unconsciousness.

CHAPTER
FIFTY-ONE

JACK AWOKE INSTANTLY from the vibrations from his wristwatch. He switched the alarm off and allowed the sounds of the darkened cabana to wash over him. Lucy was on her side next to him, snoring softly.

In retrospect, her rejection of him was a good thing. Dealing with her was already complicated enough. Still, that kiss had been damn good, and the way she'd melted into him was —

Stop. It was time to focus and get moving. In seventy-two minutes, the sun would rise over the edge of the Mediterranean and cast its golden light on the mermaid queen in the courtyard. When it did, something — he had no clue what — would happen. Thus, Item 2 on today's mission to-do list: scope out the waterfall near the pool to figure out the best position to intercept Yoko's clue while remaining invisible to anyone who might be there.

As for Item 1: stop lollygagging around in bed and sneak in some quality time for tunnel and cave exploration. As Lucy had pointed out, the cave system offered ideal environmental conditions for live phosphorin. If the bacterium was on the island, it was possible Yoko had it stashed in one of the island's many caves, hidden yet easily accessible.

As quietly as he could, he slid out of bed and stood, nearly gasping aloud as his battered muscles screamed in protest. For a second, he felt lightheaded. The fight had taken more out of him than he'd realized. Was he getting too old for this game? Even as the traitorous thought surfaced, he batted it away. The pain would ease once he got moving. He'd loosen up and feel better in no time.

"Jack?" Lucy said from the bed. "Where are you going?"

Dammit. He turned around. His partner was sitting up, her hair tousled and her nightgown falling off one shoulder.

Man, she had a knack for looking good in bed. If he slid back in, maybe he could persuade her to massage his aching back with her lovely, slender hands. Hell, maybe she'd even change her mind and be in the mood to —

No. Focus.

"Go back to sleep," he whispered.

"What are you doing?"

"Going for a walk."

"I'll go with you."

"No need."

Ignoring him, she got out of bed and, in the darkness, started looking for her clothes.

He sighed. She wasn't going to do what he wanted — last night had proved that — so he could either keep her close and watch over her, or let her stumble around on her own. If he brought her, she might even be helpful in identifying phosphorin-friendly spots in the caves.

"Wear your dark blouse and black pants," he said.

A minute later, both dressed in casual dark clothes, they moved to the cabana door. On the floor were two golden envelopes — their next tasks for the Hotel Synkonos game. The envelopes had been slipped under the door.

Lucy picked them up. "Should we open them now?"

He took them from her and slipped them in his jeans pocket. "In a bit."

Quietly, they made their way down the garden path to the deserted courtyard. The villa's neon wall decor had been turned off. Not a soul stirred.

He led her across the courtyard and down the garden path that led to the caves. He stopped at a bend in the path.

"Duck down." At a crouch, they stepped off the path, slipped behind a clump of trees and bushes, and made their way to the small cave they'd argued in the previous night. "If we stay low, the surveillance cameras on the path won't catch us going in."

He led her into the cave, past the small alcove near the entrance, then removed his smartphone from his pocket and pressed a button to activate the flashlight. A focused beam of light revealed the path they'd taken during Sergei's tour the previous morning.

"Look for spots where it might be hidden," he said.

She nodded, needing no clarification about what "it" was. He cast the light over the walls and ceiling as they moved deeper into the cave. A couple of times, she asked him to focus on a nook or cranny more carefully.

Gradually, methodically, they made their way toward the spot where the cave widened into the large, open circle.

The stench, foul and all-too-familiar, hit him when he got closer.

"Lucy, stay back."

His flashlight ran along the edges of the circular space, then to the center of the space, and stopped.

Lucy gasped.

A man had been impaled on spikes made of construction

rebar. Four iron bars through his midsection, intestines spilling onto the ground.

They stepped closer, and Lucy gasped again as she recognized him.

Dick Hould, hedge fund asshole, would never grab her elbow again.

CHAPTER
FIFTY-TWO

JACK LOOKED UP from the body to the opening at the top of the cave. Apparently, Hould had fallen through the hole in the cave's ceiling and onto the rebar. The long metal bars had torn through his back, exiting through his abdomen.

Covering his mouth with his shirt, he aimed the flashlight on Hould's face, which was contorted in a rictus of agony, then moved the light over and around the body.

"There's not much blood," he said. "He didn't bleed out."

He reached out and touched Hould's arm. "The body's still warm. He lingered for a while. Terrible way to go. Even if he'd cried out, no one would have heard him."

"Awful," Lucy whispered, her eyes taking in the details of his wounds.

"Dude got what he deserved." He heard the vehemence in his voice and felt her attention shift onto him.

"Why do you say that?"

"A sociopath in a suit. He preyed on society. He caused way more pain than he received in the end."

Her eyes stayed on him. "It's about the responsibility of wealth and power, isn't it?"

"What do you mean?"

"With his resources, Hould had the ability to do tremendous good. But he didn't."

He shrugged. "He did shit with his power."

"So, is what you're doing enough, Jack?"

"What do you mean?"

"I understand your job," she said. "I know it's important. It matters. But is it enough? You have resources, too. Are you doing enough good?"

He didn't answer. Something welled up inside him, something deep, threatening to burst forth.

Not now. He needed it — whatever *it* was — to stay the fuck down.

His eyes caught on something — faint marks on the floor.

"What's this?" he said, grateful for the distraction. He bent to examine them closely, then looked up again at the hole in the ceiling.

He directed Lucy's attention to the markings. "This was no accident. The box of rebar was dragged from where it was at the edge of the cave and deliberately positioned. Hould was lured to the ledge above, and pushed."

"Murdered?"

"By one person. Two people could have picked up the box of rebar and moved it into position without dragging it across the ground."

"Why was he killed? To eliminate the competition?"

"Could be."

She shivered. "Somebody really wants that phosphorin."

"We can't stay here. Let's go."

Quickly, they made their way out of the tunnel and back onto the garden path.

He did a slow three-sixty to confirm they were alone, then glanced at his watch. Sunrise was in nine minutes.

"What do we do about Hould?" she asked.

"Nothing. We were never there."

"Okay."

"Are you? Okay?"

"Yes." She shivered again.

"You're cold. Come here." He pulled her toward him, wrapped his arms around her, and whispered in her ear, "At least you didn't puke this time."

She went still. "This time?"

"You know, like in Professor McGillifuddy's anatomy class."

She glanced up at him. "So you did see my file. You said you hadn't read anything about me."

"I lied."

She smiled. "You're very good at that."

"Yep."

"Because you have to be."

So she was still chewing on that. He felt an urge to protest, to explain to her again — as apparently he had to explain, over and over again, to all the women in his life — that he was fine and that they could all stop looking at him with concern in their eyes, thank you very much.

Instead, he glanced at his watch. "We have a rendezvous at the pool in seven minutes. Our next clue is at dawn. Something to do with the mermaid."

To the east, the sun, still below the horizon, brightened the sky. In minutes, the first rays would hit the mermaid rising from the waterfall behind the bar.

He led her to the tall bushes that hid the doorway to the room they'd snuck into a few hours earlier. From behind the bushes, they had a view of the entire courtyard, including the mermaid.

They heard the sound of wheels on pavement, and seconds later a waiter appeared from a service entrance, pushing a breakfast trolley across the courtyard and down a garden path toward the cabanas.

"Guests are waking up," she said.

He took the golden envelopes out of his back pocket and opened the one for Bruiser.

Together they read, "The future of Hotel Synkonos lies in your hands. After lunch, you are invited to participate in the first annual Synkonos Motocross Grand Prix. Your participation will bring honor (and points) to the Funicello family. If you win, your points will increase by a factor of ten."

At the bottom, a handwritten note added, "Jack, why do you leave party early? I hope fight is not too hurtful? No pressure for race today if pain is too much. I can give you different task for Bruiser character. Your friend, Sergei."

Lucy looked at him. "Are you going to race?"

"Yep."

She took her envelope, opened it, and found two cards inside. The first read, "The future of Hotel Synkonos is in your hands. Yesterday, you introduced yourself to Daddio Donatelli. This afternoon, you must persuade him to defect from the Funicello family and join the Avalon family. Use every means of persuasion at your disposal."

He snorted. "Lucky you. Afternoon off. Unless you can flip a dead man."

She turned to her second card, which read, "Tonight, your grace and skill will be seen by all. You have been hired to perform as a showgirl in this evening's entertainment extravaganza. Rehearsal is at 4:00 p.m. in the main event room."

He watched her lips compress and shoulders tighten as she read the note. Shocked as she had been by Hould's corpse, the prospect of performing a choreographed dance routine was apparently even more disturbing.

"I can't do that," she said.

"Then don't. We'll tell Sergei you're sick."

"Really?" Her shoulders loosened with relief.

"Don't do anything you're not comfortable with, okay?" he said. "Remember that, and you'll be fine."

"Vienna predicted this," she said. "She found a showgirl costume in her cabana, too."

"Girl knows the score."

The horizon steadily lightened. He glanced at his watch. Sunrise was just seconds away.

Out of the corner of his eye, he caught the barest hint of movement from behind the bar. Someone was hiding there, in the shadows.

"Dawn," his mission partner said.

As the first sliver of the sun rose above the sea, light hit the mermaid queen, and something in the queen's right hand glinted and flashed.

"A mirror!" Lucy whispered. "In her right hand."

"What's it shining on?" Jack asked.

The reflected light from the mirror cut through the shadows that still covered the far side of the courtyard and landed on the billboard for the Synkonos Theater. The light illuminated, for a brief moment, the words written on it:

Magical! One Time Only!

Robbie Armand & Carrie Esposito

Live in Synkonos Theater

Exciting 'N' Sensational! Tremendous! A Rare Treat!

"More wordplay?" Lucy whispered.

"First letters," Jack said, his eyes firmly fixed on the bar.

Lucy spoke it out: "Moto Race Listen Start."

Someone — he couldn't tell who — slipped out from behind the bar and dashed down the garden path.

He felt it then — the excitement of the hunt, the thrill of competition.

He turned back to Lucy. "We need to be at the start of this afternoon's motocross race and listen for the next clue. Can you be on hand?"

"Of course." She hesitated, then said, "Are you sure you want to race? After what you went through last night, no one would be upset if you bowed out."

He shook his head. "I should do it. It'll give me a different perspective on the race than what you'll see and hear in the stands."

"You just want to race," she said. "But I'll defer to your superior in-field operational expertise."

"Mad jargon-handling skills. Very Grant-esque."

"High praise. So what now?"

"Back to the cabana. Breakfast. Pool. Mingle."

"Listen and learn?"

"Listen and learn, babe. Listen and learn."

CHAPTER FIFTY-THREE

LUCY STARED AT herself in the bathroom mirror, a frown on her face, and adjusted the towel she'd wrapped around her so-called bathing suit. She reached to turn off the light and paused. The cabana was quiet, the only sound the in-and-out of her breathing.

Jack was already at the pool, doing his socializing-schmoozing-spying thing, and she'd promised to follow. This time, with Dick Hould's gutted corpse flashing across her mind, she was keeping her word. From now on, she'd do whatever her partner wanted, at least when it came to spying. Before this morning she'd understood, at least on a rational level, that the phosphorin thief was deadly serious; the videotaped massacre of the women in Zurich had proved that. But actually seeing and smelling Hould's body had hammered the horror home. A killer walked in their midst. A brutal, efficient murderer who had, more likely than not, tried to eliminate Prince Ali (and possibly her) the day before on the cliff. An enemy who might, even now, be planning another attack.

She'd always prided herself on her ability to stay calm

and be the sane person in the room. But all of this — this whirlwind of chaos and artifice and death — was too much. She was caught in the center and couldn't see her way out. She was stuck on an island like no other, where everything was beautiful and exceptional and false. With wealthy elites who considered themselves superior yet acted like greedy children. On a mission with maddeningly unclear outlines. And, swirling at the heart of it, with a partner who pushed, confounded, annoyed, and attracted her in equal measures.

In just the past day, she'd donned a piece of string and pretended it was a swimsuit, come close to kissing a prince, nearly died in an avalanche, crashed an orgy, called bullshit on her partner's unbelievable sexual rationalizations, kicked an asshole in the balls, broken into her host's secret sanctum of voyeuristic thrills, explored a cave for an unstable weapon of mass destruction, and discovered a gutted corpse.

If she had more time, she could take a step back, throw the jumble of facts and impressions and hunches skyward, and watch the patterns they made as they fell. The clues and links were there — the answers were there — yet she couldn't see them. Events were rushing at her too quickly. She couldn't be the sane person in the room if she didn't have time to breathe.

At least she'd had the good sense to save herself — barely — from what would have been an extremely ill-advised roll in the hay with her sexaholic partner. But boy, had that been close. One minute she'd been furious with him for his orgiastic antics, and even angrier with herself for not being stronger, for not remembering who this man was and what he did, for not being able to free herself from his charismatic pull. Then, in the next, she was inviting him to share a painful event from his past, allowing herself to be drawn in by his willingness to open up, and moving all-too-eagerly into his arms, feeling the heat of his body against hers, his mouth on hers....

Urgh. He hadn't made it easy on her either, being so damn accepting of her rejection. When they'd returned to the cabana, he'd sat quietly while she'd cleaned the cut on his forehead and taped a bandage over it. She'd seen understanding and respect in his dazzling blue eyes, which, perversely and predictably, had made him even more appealing. She'd almost leaned in again — had almost invited another kiss — and had pulled back only when she became aware of what her body was urging her to do.

God, she needed a drink. No, wait, not that. She needed to talk — to pick up the phone and call Joanie and get wrapped up in her best friend's wisecracks and sarcasm. She needed to share the craziness of the past two days, spill her fears, and air her doubts. She and JoJo were polar opposites in so many ways — cautious vs. impulsive, shy vs. out-there, "yikes-what's-that" versus "ooo-look-what's-that-shiny-new-thing" — but they'd been inseparable since freshman year. She could hear her too-loud voice now, filled with equal parts affection and exasperation, saying, "Oh. My. God. Stop obsessing about Mr. Secret Agent Man's flaws. He's a man — of course he's flawed. But he's hot and smart, and he's a great kisser, and he has the good sense to be into you. So jump him already. Geesh!"

She wanted to call her mom, whose temperament matched hers so closely, and lay out possible next steps, every silly and serious idea and angle and consideration that popped into her head, and hear her mom tell her, in her soft, measured voice, which of her silly ideas weren't actually silly at all. She wanted her mom to pass the phone to her dad so she could hear him say, "Luce, you've been charting your own course since you were a little girl. Whatever you want to do, I know you can do it."

Loneliness twisted her gut. She couldn't call them. She couldn't share. Ever. She couldn't talk about any of this —

about being halfway around the world, on a billionaire's bizarre island, engaged in a shadowy game with a murderer who'd stolen a weapon of mass destruction. She couldn't share her fears, or listen to their advice. She couldn't even tell them what might, in time, seem humorous, like the fact that, legally speaking, she was now a criminal. A criminal guilty of assault, breaking and entering, interfering with a crime scene —

God, she had to stop it. Just. Stop. It.

It was all happening way too fast.

Way.

Too.

Fast.

She took a deep breath and held it, then exhaled.

One piece at a time. If she couldn't take a step back, if she couldn't slow time, she could at least ignore most of the insanity engulfing her and look at one insane piece of it at a time. For example, Dick Hould's abdominal wounds. Yes, that was a good start. The murder weapon — a box filled with iron bars — had been positioned directly under the cave's skylight to maximize the potential for damage. Hould had fallen backward, which suggested he'd been pushed, or tripped, while facing his attacker.

The rest was simple gravity. Four pieces of rebar had stabbed him through his back in a line along his spine, starting near the third thoracic vertebrae and ending near the fifth lumbar. The rebar had perforated his stomach, large intestine, and colon before slicing through the peritoneum and abdominal muscles. As Jack had noted, the relatively small amount of blood indicated the rebar had missed the major arteries and veins. Death, when it finally came, would have been from shock. Hould may have been conscious during his final moments.

She blinked, realizing that she'd been frozen in place, her

hand hovering by the light switch, while her mind churned in overdrive.

A swim to clear her head? *Yes.*

The bathroom went dark as she hit the switch and stepped out.

CHAPTER
FIFTY-FOUR

COOL AND WEIGHTLESS, Jack floated up toward the surface of the pool, enjoying the flow of water over his arms and legs. He reached air and breathed in. A scan of the courtyard showed that, while many of the guests were elsewhere — at brunch in the dining room, or still recovering from the previous night's exertions — people were finding their way to the pool and bar.

Erica Sandoz was in the same lounger she'd occupied the day before, under the same umbrella. Her online persona was ruthless, which meant her flesh-and-blood persona had to be the same. Ruthless enough to commit murder? To lure Hould out for a walk and push him to his death?

Of Prince Ali, there was no sign. No surprise there. The previous night, the old dog had been thoroughly and enthusiastically entangled in a pile of nubile flesh. Even if Special Exploits was right about Ali playing the Borlando character, Jack knew they were wrong about his motive. The dude was a player, not a bad guy, though that didn't preclude him from killing Hould — not if Hould knew who Borlando was and had tried a spot of blackmail. Prince Ali Saad Bandar, third in line to the throne of the Royal Kingdom of Gudan, would not take kindly to blackmail.

A familiar voice called his name. He squinted through the light reflecting off the water and saw Sergei, in his black rugby swimsuit, walking toward him from the bar, a drink in each hand and swaying slightly. Not even noon, and already his host was drunk.

Sergei gestured to two loungers. "You join?"

"Yep!" With two easy strokes, Jack made his way to the ladder, pulled himself out of the pool, then walked over and eased himself onto the lounger next to his host. Another hot day. The sun felt great on his wet skin.

Sergei handed him a margarita. "How do you feel? Do you recover from fight?"

"Sore in all the usual places, but on the mend." He took a sip. "How's Constantine?"

Sergei downed half his drink in a single gulp and set the glass down. "He is fine. Bone break is clean. Francois Le Coq sets it. Constantine has philosophical outlook about losing. He says he loses because you are better fighter." He threw him a sharp look. "Is he right? Are you better fighter?"

The same question as last night, which meant Sergei wasn't satisfied with the answer he'd provided, which wasn't good. If he was questioning one aspect of his cover, then he might start questioning others.

Time for a charm offensive.

He gave Sergei his widest, most easy-going grin. "Dude, you're kidding, right? A monster like Constantine? I got lucky. End of story."

Sergei wasn't done probing. "Even before I meet you, I think, I know Jack Ford. But last night, you are full of surprise."

"You mean the fight?"

"Before fight. After fight."

He meant the sex, an infinitely safer topic. "You mean…?"

"I mean you are wild man," Sergei said. "Wild man!"

Jack laughed.

"Can we speak, as men of world? Speak truth?"

"Sure."

"What if Constantine wins fight?"

Jack held Sergei's gaze. "A deal's a deal."

"But you are not …" Sergei said, looking too uncomfortable to finish the sentence. He picked up his margarita and took another big gulp.

"Nope."

"But you would let him...."

"Better than going back on my word."

Sergei stared at him with something approaching wonder. "You have experience with…?"

Jack leaned in slightly and lowered his voice. "You want to know what it feels like, don't you?"

Sergei swallowed. "I do not think about … I do not have attraction for … But I...."

"You wonder what it feels like."

Sergei nodded.

"Nothing beats a finger up the ass."

Sergei's eyes widened. "But what if…what about…bigger than finger?"

"Not my thing, but not bad. The key is prep."

"But does it not do … damage?"

"Not if you do it right."

"After last night, after Madame Le Coq, do you have damage?"

Jack shook his head.

"Really?"

"Would you like to examine the scene of the crime?"

"Examine scene of — no, no, no!" Sergei said, shocked by the idea.

He watched Sergei formulating his next question. "Do you not feel … shame? Worry people think you are … less a man?"

He shook his head. "Dude, if you know me at all, you know I don't care what people think, unless they're people I like, and even then, only sometimes."

Sergei looked puzzled. "You do not care what people think?"

He twirled the ice in his drink. "You know what? I like you, so I care what you think. Do you think less of me now? After what you saw last night?"

Sergei didn't answer right away. He looked past him, into the distance.

"Before yesterday, I think because I see you on TV, hear about you from different people, I know you. But last night, I see I do not know all of you. Last night, I feel … confused." He sat up straighter. "But now, I see why. I see true man. Man with no fear!"

Out of the corner of his eye, Jack spied Lucy walking into the courtyard. He waved her over. She suppressed a smile as she took in the spectacle of him and Sergei lying side by side on identical loungers, in identical rugby swimsuits, holding identical drinks.

"What are you two so chummy about?" she asked when she reached them.

He shot Sergei a conspiratorial glance. "Nothing. Just talking about an asshole we both know."

Sergei burst out laughing. "Asshole we both know!" He laughed some more.

Lucy slipped out of her sandals, unfastened her towel, and tossed it on the lounger next to Jack's. She did it casually, with quiet confidence, unlike the day before.

Jack felt an unexpected surge of pride. His newbie partner was catching on. Adapting. Growing.

Lucy did her best to keep the smile off her face. Whatever Jack and Sergei were talking about, they wouldn't tell her. Peas in a pod, the two of them. Boys defending their tree fort against a yucky girl.

"Swim time," she said. She pivoted to the pool and dove in.

The coolness was bracing — exhilarating. For a few seconds, the water over her skin became her universe. As she sank, she looked up at the sparkling reflections on the surface. Her hair flowed freely in front of her eyes, then along her neck. She rolled her head, feeling her tension ease, and stretched her limbs in all directions. Anyone looking might wonder about her odd underwater contortions, but in this moment, she didn't care.

She felt a disruption in the water and turned. A man had jumped in and was swimming underwater toward her, his movements sure and powerful.

Jack.

She rose to the surface and breathed in. He followed, inches away, close enough for her to feel the movement of water from his strokes.

"Can we talk here?" she asked quietly.

He glanced around. "If we whisper. What's up?"

"Why does everyone think you're wild and crazy and out of control?"

"Why are you asking?"

"Because you're not wild and crazy. You're the opposite: calculating, pragmatic, disciplined, social, and outgoing, but in a directed way."

"Your point?"

"I barely know you, but I can see this."

He moved closer. His shoulder brushed against her chest. His arms and legs flowed on either side of her.

"My reputation is what people want to see. They're looking for wild and crazy. They're as invested in it as I am. They want something to talk about later."

"So you give it to them."

"They pay less attention when they think they have my number, which means I can act — how did you put it? — calculating, pragmatic, and disciplined, and not be noticed."

"So the camouflage is about the mission."

His eyes narrowed, just slightly. "What else would it be about?"

She held his stare. "You might be using it to keep everyone at an emotional distance."

A small smile touched his lips. "Ah, my supposed inner turmoil."

"Your words, not mine."

"Mmm … I think I know what's going on here." His arm slid around her and he pulled her in close.

She didn't push away.

"Do tell," she murmured in his ear.

"You had me all figured out, and now I'm not cooperating. Turns out I'm actually, like, complicated and stuff."

She smiled. "Turning the tables, are we? Best defense is a good offense?"

"I keep forcing you to change your mind, forcing you to rethink. All that extra work — very annoying."

He was right, especially about the annoying part. "Did anyone ever tell you that arrogance isn't the least bit attractive?"

He pulled back and gave her a big grin. "Aww … so now you find me attractive."

Urgh. There was no winning with this one.

"I find you inane," she said and pushed free. "Go back to your new best friend."

She heard him laugh as she dove back to the bottom of the pool.

The grin refused to leave Jack's face. Flirting with her was fun. She was enjoying it too, he could tell, despite trying super-hard not to.

He glanced at his new best friend and found him engaged in an animated conversation with Vienna. Or rather, Vienna was animated and Sergei was stiff, looking like a trapped animal. Was Vienna drunk, too? The way she was waving her arms around, it sure as hell looked like it.

He pulled himself out of the water and made his way back to his lounger.

"I tell you," he overheard her saying to Sergei, "she's a mystery. Says she's a friend of Vince's sister. All I know is that she appears out of nowhere with Jack wrapped around her little finger!"

Another possible crack in Lucy's cover.

He quickly toweled off, then sat behind Vienna on the lounger. He leaned in and wrapped his arms around her waist, then kissed her neck and nuzzled his head next to hers.

"Hey, you," she said. "We were just talking about your club."

"Have you been to Naked Lunch?" he asked Sergei.

"I go last time I am in Los Angeles," Sergei said. "But staff say you travel on business."

"You'll have to come next time you're in town."

"It's great," Vienna said. "An intimate vibe."

"Vienna says you meet Lucy there," Sergei said, eyeing him.

"That's right," Jack said. "I didn't know her, so I introduced myself."

"How do you end up dating?"

"Called her. Asked her out." He shifted back in the lounger so that Vienna could turn and look him in the eyes. "You know me, I like variety."

Vienna sat up, slid onto Sergei's lounger, and wrapped an arm around him.

"Jack and I have been friends for a long time," she said. "I like giving him a hard time."

Sergei grinned. "I read tabloids. I know you, how do you say, hook up?"

Vienna smiled. "Friends with benefits."

"'Benefits'? Meaning is?"

"In the case of me and Jack, we are friends who sometimes have sex. Is that a fair statement, Jack?"

She said it lightly, with a smile on her face, but tension rippled beneath the breezy, casual confidence.

Jack kept his eyes on hers. "We are very good friends who sometimes have amazing sex. What is it I always say? In Vienna I trust. Unlike so many people I meet, who come and then go, Vienna's a constant. I'm lucky to have her in my life."

The words were designed to reassure her, which they did. He saw her shoulders relax.

It helped that every word was true. She was a friend — a good friend — of his party-boy persona.

But the implication of his words? That Lucy would be one of the many women who would come and then go?

Before he could process that, he felt drops of water on the lounger. Lucy had joined them from the pool and was toweling off.

There was a pregnant pause as they all looked up at her.

"Beautiful morning," she said.

"Yes, beautiful," Sergei said. "Like you."

"Lucy, I love your swimsuit," Vienna said. "Where did you get it?"

"You'll have to ask Jack," Lucy said as she ran her hands through her wet hair. "It was a gift from him."

Jack was saved from having to improvise an answer by the arrival of Natasha and Boris.

"Sergei, could we pull you away for a moment?" Natasha asked. Her eyes took in Lucy in her barely-there swimsuit, then Vienna with her arm around Sergei. The look was calculating. What was she assessing?

Lucy gave Boris a smile. "Good morning, Boris."

"Good morning," he said, giving her a quick nod. "I see you and Mr. Ford are … enjoying the morning."

His manner, while courteous, seemed stiff, almost as if he was disappointed. Did he feel that he and Lucy had bonded in the bar? Was it possible he'd become interested in her?

"I go now," Sergei said, extricating himself from Vienna and the lounger. "I see you all at race?"

"Count on it," Jack said.

CHAPTER
FIFTY-FIVE

AT THE MOTOCROSS COURSE
IN THE RACERS TENT

AH, THE JOYS of the mandatory safety briefing. Even here, on an island as remote from the mundane bullshit of the real world as could be imagined, there was no escaping the inevitable, pointless lecture and disclaimers that preceded any type of organized fun. Jack sat obediently in a folding chair and listened, along with the five motocross professionals who had arrived on the ferry that morning.

Sergei stood in front of them, decked out, like the rest of them, in racing gear. He pointed to a map of the course on an easel.

"Before race starts, we do two practice laps to become familiar with course, yes? Race has many twists and turns. Lap is two kilometers. Race is eight laps in total. Start and finish is at viewing stand. Guests do not see every part of course, but they see us in straight segment near viewing stand and also here." Sergei pointed to a spot on the map. "This is white hill near viewing stand. At top of hill, you have opportunity for big jumps, yes? Guests in viewing stand can see you fly through air."

He turned away from the map to address his fellow racers. "As I explain, we pretend we are in Las Vegas in 1965. Three of you race for Avalon gang, three of you for Funicello gang. I race for fun only, but if I beat you, your gang loses points. So you must try to beat me, yes?"

Sergei gestured to a hospitality facilitator in the back of the tent. "Race is part of battle for Hotel Synkonos. So we, too, go back in time. We ride best technology from long-ago era."

Jack's pulse quickened. Old school? He turned around as a hospitality facilitator stepped into the tent, pushing in an utter impossibility: a 1963 Husqvarna Racer, the lightweight legend that transformed the world of motocross. A two-stroke, single-cylinder, air-cooled, 250-cc wonder, red and gleaming and achingly beautiful. His competitors breathed in; they recognized it too. He wanted to leap up and run his hands along its curves, rev the engine, and feel it roar — become one with it as he and that incredible machine tore through the world.

His jaw dropped as another identical Husqvarna Racer followed, then another, and another, until he was looking at seven of them lined up in a row. What he was seeing simply could not be. Only one hundred of these babies had ever been made.

"As you see," Sergei said, "we have seven Husqvarna Racers, built in 1963. All restored to excellent working condition."

"Mr. Eristov," one of the racers said, looking as stunned as Jack felt. "How did you manage this? I thought only one still existed."

"Yes, until now. Now there are seven. I track history of every one sold. Much planning and time and effort and cost. Very difficult, with many obstacles. I confess at times I am afraid I fail. But worth it, yes?" He glanced at Jack, his eyes lighting up when he saw Jack's awe.

Jack swallowed and cleared his throat. "I can't believe we get to race them."

"Would be shame not to, yes?" Sergei said. "Come, everyone. Select bike."

The riders rushed up.

Sergei motioned Jack to the bike at the end of the line. "I know you have special appreciation, so I make this one gift to you."

The bike was identical to the others in all ways but one: stenciled into the leather seat were the words, "Property of Jack Ford."

Jack suddenly had trouble breathing.

This baby was his? *His*? Holy fucking crap.

His heart lurched and he realized, with shock, that this odd, needy, lonely geek had slipped into his zone of caring. Sergei Eristov, pervy billionaire, had just become his bud, for reals.

Impulsively, he grabbed his host in a supertight bear hug. "Best. Gift. Ever."

Still holding Sergei's shoulders, he pulled away to look him straight in the eyes. "Dude, I am so glad I met you. You are the greatest. The best. The bomb."

What was he gonna do if the little fucker turned out to be Yoko?

Sergei's eyes filled up.

"You are welcome for gift. I am very happy you like." He wiped his eyes. "Now, we stop display of unmanly emotion, yes? Time for race."

CHAPTER FIFTY-SIX

LUCY HURRIED ALONG the path that wound from the villa to the racecourse. The top of the island was craggy and uneven, its black volcanic terrain dotted with clumps of bushes and trees. She passed a striking hill of white limestone that rose up from the igneous rock like a giant scoop of vanilla ice cream on black pavement, then continued past outcroppings until the path turned sharply, bringing to her destination: the racecourse.

Guests were gathered on a level field under colorful tents, finishing lunch. Next to the dining tents stood the viewing stand, with a yellow line drawn in the dirt in front. Several of the competitors were already there, motorcycles revving.

Sergei's voice came over the loudspeakers. "Race starts in two minutes. I ask guests to make way to viewing stand."

She stepped into the stand and sat in the front row, near one of the loudspeakers. The mermaid's clue — "Moto Race Listen Start" — meant her ears needed to be open and ready and unencumbered. She glanced back at the crowd and picked out Erica Sandoz three rows behind her, chatting with Francois and Marie.

Her eyes zeroed in on Marie. *Ugh.* She wouldn't be able to see that woman again without envisioning a strap-on dildo.

Motorcycles roared up to the starting line, including one with a rider dressed head-to-toe in white leather. The rider pulled up his visor. His blue eyes locked on hers. He gave her a thumb's up. She smiled and returned the gesture.

The loudspeaker crackled. On the motorcycle next to Jack's, Sergei removed his helmet and gestured to Natasha, who handed him a microphone.

Sergei turned to the assembled guests. "Welcome to first annual Synkonos Motocross Grand Prix!"

The audience applauded, and the riders revved their engines.

"We have seven competitors today — very exciting race! Course is eight laps, very hilly, twisty, and winding, across top of Synkonos. Each lap is two kilometers. From viewing stand, you can see start and finish and see bikers as they complete each lap. Also," he said, pointing to the white limestone hill behind him, "from here you can see bikers race to top of hill and show off jumping skills."

Lucy felt her bench shift as someone sat next to her, and turned to find Ali.

"Three competitors race for Avalon gang, three competitors for Funicello gang, and me."

"Good afternoon, Ms. Keen," Ali said.

"Afternoon," she said, returning her attention to the loudspeaker. A bit rude, perhaps, but she had no choice. Their next clue was embedded in what she would be hearing next.

"Also, I make special announcement," Sergei said. "Tonight, in Synkonos Theater, we have pleasure of world premiere of new duet by Carrie Esposito and Robbie Armand. You will be first to hear new song, with lyrics written especially for guests here. Winner of race today wins best tables for his gang for performance tonight!"

The crowd applauded, and the motorists revved their engines in approval.

"Are we ready for start of Synkonos Grand Prix?" Sergei yelled.

The crowd roared.

"Are competitors ready?"

The bikers revved their engines again.

Sergei handed the microphone to Natasha, put his helmet back on, and gave her a signal.

Natasha raised the flag. "Ready. Set. Go!"

The flag flashed down and the riders roared away, the cries of the crowd and the motors vibrating through her.

Her breath caught. *That was it?* The start was over? What could the clue have possibly been?

"Something the matter, Ms. Keen?" Ali asked.

Once again, her face had telegraphed her thoughts. She really needed to brush up on her deception skills. "No, the motors are just very loud."

The prince had dark rings under his eyes, and his shoulders were a bit slumped. He was distracted by something, perhaps even troubled.

"You seem a bit down," she said.

"Tired from last night."

"Nothing else?"

"Nothing I can discuss, I'm afraid. I took a risk on a business deal. It was a mistake."

Again she felt an urge to confide in him, to tell him she knew about the phosphorin, and to confirm her own suspicions about his interest in it.

"Is it too late to fix your mistake?"

"I fear so."

"Everyone makes mistakes. The good thing is that most problems go away on their own."

"Your bedside manner is most reassuring." He leaned in and said, too quietly for anyone else to hear, "By the way, I do not believe you're making a mistake."

"About what?"

"About Jack."

"Jack?"

"Beneath the flash, there is substance."

"Meaning?"

"Dating him is not a mistake."

She smiled at him. "Talking about yourself again, I see."

"There comes a time, Ms. Keen, when the high life loses its luster." He stood. "I think I will take a short nap to rest up for tonight. If you'll excuse me."

She watched him leave and head back toward the villa. She was tempted to do the same, to find a quiet place to write down the exact words Sergei had used. The clue could be hidden within them — the first letters of each word or some such. She heard the roar of approaching motors. She and the crowd stood up as the seven motorcycles turned a bend, coming into view. The racer dressed in white and caked in dust was leading, with the others just seconds behind.

She slipped away from the viewing stand and nearly ran into Natasha, Boris, and Constantine, who were all in a heated conversation just inside one of the dining tents. They hadn't seen her, but she could hear them, and through a slit in the tent flap, she could see Natasha's face.

She froze. This could be a real opportunity — a peek behind the curtain, so to speak.

"No," Natasha said. "No changes. I will tell Sergei when the race ends, and we will make an announcement to the guests."

"This is serious," Constantine said. "We need to call in the Greek police."

She could guess the topic: They'd found Dick Hould's corpse.

"You know what Sergei will say. We cannot disrupt the party," Natasha insisted.

"We have no choice," Constantine said, frustration in his voice.

Boris stepped in. "Constantine is right to take this matter seriously. We need to welcome the police and ensure a full investigation."

"I do not want — "

"The investigation does not need to disrupt the plans for this evening. The party can continue."

Natasha's mouth tightened but she held her tongue.

Boris turned to Constantine. "You are fully capable of enabling this separation, with minimal interference, correct?"

"Yes," Constantine finally said.

Natasha frowned but nodded. "Fine. I will prepare an announcement for Sergei to make after the race."

She turned to Constantine. "If the police give you any trouble, remind them who's buying them their new coastal patrol boat."

CHAPTER **FIFTY-SEVEN**

JACK WAS IN love, and her name was Husqvarna. In his mind, her name translated to "pure, unadulterated joy." She purred and vibrated beneath him, her two-stroke engine resounding a high, confident note as he twisted the throttle. She handled like a dream, taking corners with impressive ease — a pitch-perfect blend of agility and performance that pulled him effortlessly forward.

He took a small dip and aggressively shifted into the sharp right turn, revving for the straightaway that led to the viewing stand. Five laps down, three to go, and he had the lead, with his competitors a good five seconds behind.

He heard the roar of the crowd as he zoomed past the viewing stand toward the trickiest part of the course. Most of the course was excellent — the overall design exciting and varied, with twists and dips and jumps and straightaways — but a couple of spots needed to be more thought-out, and he was fast approaching one of them.

The white hill rose dramatically over the black dirt that covered most of the island's plateau, an accident of geology that served as the ramp for the course's signature moment: a full-speed jump from the top that sent the racer shooting into the sky. The guests in the viewing stand couldn't see where the rider landed, and for them, it looked as if the rider, framed against the blue sky, was flying.

The jump was a blast. The landing, not so much. The sweet spot for the touchdown was perilously close to the cliff's edge and required a hard right turn to steer clear of danger. Sergei had warned them during the briefing — maybe the safety lecture hadn't been a complete waste of time — and he'd taken the jump during practice laps cautiously, holding back to test the track.

But man, there was no holding back now, not with five top racers (and Sergei, no slouch himself) hot on his tail. He revved his baby in the sweet spot of her powerband and she responded beautifully, pulling him up the hill as though he were in a slingshot.

He cleared the ground and, in that fraction of a second, took in how amazing this experience was. Only a few people in the long course of human history would know what it was like to fly like this. Only a few would ever see the edge of a steep cliff running like a ragged line below them, dividing the world between the black solidity of earth and the blue-and-white crash of waves below. Free from the clouds of dust below, he tasted the clean salty air as the wind gusted against him.

He felt it then — an anticipatory shiver honed by years of experience, a shiver that told him something was about to go really, really shitty — and snapped back to full, in-the-moment awareness as he fell from the sky.

The pop in his front tire as he landed was not, then, a complete surprise. Nor was the catastrophic response from his beautiful baby as she careened and jerked and threw him off her.

His training kicked in through pure instinct. He rolled, absorbing and distributing the impact in a flow rather than a smack.

He sensed, rather than saw, his bike fly off the cliff — his fate, too, in less than a second.

He hands reached out, grasping for something — anything — to stop his momentum.

His feet hit the nothingness of air. Desperately, he clawed at the ground for a miracle.

And found it: a rock at his fingertips — a rock that didn't dislodge when he held on.

His arm was nearly wrenched from its socket as his body came to an abrupt stop.

He cried out in pain. The lower half of his body dangled over the cliff's edge, his feet searching for — but not finding — a place to dig in.

With everything he had, he used his hands and arms and shoulders to claw his way forward. Finally, after what seemed like an eternity, his knee found purchase and he heaved himself up.

He barely had time for a breath before he heard the high-pitched roar of his competitors racing up the hill. If they landed on him — no, he couldn't go there. He inched as close as he could to the edge of the cliff to give the racers maximum room to nail their landings. If they saw him on the ground hugging the side of the cliff, if they lost their focus —

The roars and vibrations and dust tore over him. Within seconds, it was over and the riders were past him. With his white suit caked in dust against the dirty-white hill, it was possible they hadn't even noticed him.

He sat up and moved, checking for damage, and felt a sharp pain as he rolled his left shoulder. He rolled it again and felt the same pain, to a lesser degree. Not dislocated, but definitely stressed, with a possible tear. As for the rest of him:

bruised and aching and dirty and stinking of adrenaline and shock and more than a little fear, but okay.

Though almost not.

Was the blowout an accident? Had the pressure of the big landing proved too much for fifty-year-old technology?

Or had someone chosen the perfect way to kill him?

CHAPTER
FIFTY-EIGHT

HE STOOD, TOOK off his helmet, and trudged toward the finish line and viewing stand. He knew what everyone would think when they saw him: party-boy Jack Ford had foolishly wrecked another expensive toy.

Normally, negative judgments were assets for his cover and rolled off effortlessly. But not this time. This time he was pissed. Pissed that a beautiful, priceless work of art had been ruined, and even more pissed that the cause — accident or sabotage — remained unknown. With the bike at the bottom of the cliff, smashed into a thousand pieces and scattered by the waves, there could be no examination of the evidence, at least not anytime soon. And no matter how many times he replayed the moment of impact in his mind, he couldn't see anything to rule out an accident.

He was missing something, but what? Was his cover blown? If he and Lucy were in danger, who was targeting them? Yoko? One of the competitors? What were the odds that the phosphorin was even here on Synkonos?

He turned a bend on the path. The viewing stand appeared ahead. Natasha stood off to the side, facing his way, writing something on a clipboard. She glanced up and saw him, and her eyes widened with alarm.

"Mr. Ford," she said, running toward him, her eyes scanning him for injuries. "What happened? Are you hurt?"

"I'm fine," he said. "I'm sorry. The front tire burst. The bike got the best of me."

"Are you hurt? Should we get a doctor?"

"I'm fine. I got lucky."

She turned and gestured to a facilitator. "Get Constantine. Now." She turned back to him. "Is the bike in the path of the other racers?"

He shook his head. "It went over the cliff near the white hill."

She breathed in sharply. "The bike is gone?"

"I'm really sorry."

The look she gave him could have burned through steel. "Are you? That bike was not just some new toy. You have no idea the lengths Sergei went to for you, to make this weekend special for you. When he learns of this — "

"I'll tell him."

"No, you won't. You will do nothing of the kind." She took a deep breath, then continued. "It will be better for him, and for you, if he hears the explanation from me. When he talks to you, you will say the tire burst. You will tell him you feel fortunate to not be hurt. You will tell him you are devastated by the loss of that bike. I cannot emphasize that last point enough. You are *devastated*. Do you understand?"

Man, she was making him feel like shit. "Yes, fine."

Lucy had seen him too and had jumped down from the viewing stand to join them. "Jack, what happened? Are you okay?"

The anxiety on her face was real. For a second, it almost

looked as if she might hug him, but she didn't. Instead, she reached out and rested her hand on his upper arm.

"Had an accident with the bike, but I'm fine."

He heard the roar of the approaching bikes and turned to watch as the six racers zoomed by in a tight pack. Dust washed over them.

Natasha looked down at her clipboard. "Mr. Ford, please remain here so that you and I can speak with Sergei after the race. Right now, I must finish a statement. Excuse me."

Lucy glanced around, then whispered, "They found him."

It took him a second, but he got it. *Hould.*

He whispered, "What about the clue?"

She shook her head in frustration. "Unless it's hidden in code of some sort, the only thing the clue could be is in the new song they're singing tonight. A song with lyrics about Synkonos."

He led her to the side of the viewing stand, near the finish line. Several of the guests shouted over and asked if he was all right, and he gave them a thumb's up.

Boris approached, microphone in hand. "I understand you had a close call, Mr. Ford. Are you all right? Should we have Monsieur Le Coq check you?"

"I'm fine."

Boris gave him his usual serious look, then nodded. "If you will excuse me."

He stepped up to the finish line, switched the microphone on, and turned to face the guests in the stands.

"Ladies and gentlemen, we're on the final lap. Our racers will clear the white hill at any second."

Almost as if on cue, six bikes flew into the sky from the top of the hill, one after another in rapid succession, their silhouettes framed against the blue of the sky.

"Within minutes, we will have a winner!"

In the stands, Marie stood and faced the crowd, chanting, "Fu-ni-cel-lo! Fu-ni-cel-lo!"

Her gang laughed and joined in, accompanied by boos from the Avalon gang.

Francois stood up next to her, a grin on his face, and started yelling "sucks!" in the pause between the repetitions, and his Avalon gang quickly joined in. Marie laughed and shook her fists at her husband.

The approaching roar of the bikes shifted their attention to the track. The competitors surged onto the straightaway that led to the finish line, the six bikes clumped tight.

Dust flew as they hit the throttle for the final dash. The bikes screamed past, one bike barely ahead, as the crowd cheered them on.

Boris yelled, "The winner, by a nose: Sergei Eristov!"

The bikes slowed and returned to the finish line, where the racers lined them up in a row. The crowd roared as Sergei took his helmet off and waved to the crowd, a huge grin on his face.

His grin faltered when he caught sight of Jack on the sidelines.

"Are you okay?" he mouthed.

Jack nodded.

The grin returned as Sergei gestured for the microphone. Natasha walked toward him and said something in his ear. His body went still and the grin disappeared. Natasha continued to speak as Sergei listened. He stood silently for a moment, then took the clipboard Natasha handed him.

"Yes, everyone, thank you for applause and cheers. I am happy you enjoy race. First running of Synkonos Motocross Grand Prix is very successful." He paused, looked at the clipboard, and continued. "But I am afraid I must cut short celebration with announcement of serious nature."

Sergei waited for the applause to die down.

"I am afraid we have news of terrible accident. One of our own, our friend Dick Hould, has died."

The crowd gasped.

"He is found in tunnel in cliff. He falls through hole in top of cave. We think he takes early morning walk and doesn't see hole."

The crowd, stunned, fell quiet.

"We believe his death is terrible accident. We alert Greek police, who are coming for investigation. Please cooperate fully. We expect minimal impact on events."

A number of guests began whispering to one another.

"I repeat: we believe is terrible accident. Now, I would like to have moment of silence."

The whispering stopped, and the guests lowered their heads.

"Dick Hould is man who lives for opportunities. He never misses chance to make most of opportunities. I believe he does not want us to miss out on opportunities of this weekend. Many of you sacrifice time from family and business to be here. Despite tragedy, weekend goes on. In honor of Dick Hould, we announce establishment of charitable fund. We encourage all to contribute, in honor of his memory. We have more information about fund tomorrow at breakfast."

Sergei raised his head. "Thank you all. Please, I ask you to take time for quiet reflection before dinner tonight in Synkonos Theater."

The crowd stood and began to disperse. Natasha pulled Sergei aside again. As she spoke, Sergei's eyes darted to Jack. His eyes widened in shock. Immediately, he headed toward him and Lucy, Natasha a step behind. There was tension in his stance, and agitation in his voice when he said, "Jack, you have accident at bottom of hill, near cliff? And bike is" — the next word caught in his mouth — "gone?"

Natasha's eyes drilled into Jack, waiting for his next words.

"Sergei, I'm so sorry. It went over the cliff when I landed. I feel terrible."

It didn't take a mind reader to see Sergei was torn between conflicting emotions: relief that his hero was okay, and anger that his priceless gift had been destroyed. The anger was fueled, perhaps, by emerging doubts about the judgment and actions of a man he'd admired for so long. Had Jack been cavalier with his one-of-a-kind gift? If so, what did that say about Jack's feelings toward Sergei?

Natasha was right. His host needed reassurance — lots of it.

He grabbed Sergei by the shoulder and stared him straight in the eye. "By terrible, I mean completely awful. Your gift meant so much to me. I don't know if I've ever received a gift I've appreciated more. I can't tell how sorry I am that it's gone. I feel terrible. I just hope you forgive me for not being able to save it."

It helped that every word was completely true. Sergei's shoulders loosened, and the intensity of Natasha's stare lessened as it became apparent the words were having their intended effect.

His voice choked with emotion, Sergei said, "I blame myself. Tire burst must be mechanical issue. We find pieces of bike and learn from mistake."

Natasha said, "We'll organize a search and attempt a reconstruction."

"And examine race course for improvements," Sergei added, his voice brightening at the prospect. "Yes, mistakes are necessary for learning."

His eyes went back to Jack. "You are okay, yes?"

"Totally fine."

"Good. I have much to do now, but I see you at dinner?"

"See you there."

Sergei turned toward the villa. As Natasha passed him, she gave Jack a brief nod.

Lucy leaned in and whispered, "She likes you now."

"No she doesn't."

"Are you really okay?"

"Sore shoulder, but otherwise fine."

"Want me to look at it?"

"Sure."

They joined the guests making their way down the path toward the villa. They fell in behind two guests, a man and a woman conversing ahead of them.

Jack listened in as the woman said, "I barely knew the man, and hate to speak ill of the dead...."

"Go on, say it," the man said. "Dick Hould was a douche."

"Don't say that. He just died."

"If you're so sad, pack your bags and go home."

"Oh, I'm not suggesting that."

"Not after last night, huh?"

"Like Sergei said, we put everything on hold to be here this weekend."

"Who's to say he's really dead? Maybe it's part of the game."

"What do you mean?"

"Part of a secret plan. He comes back at the end and wins the game for his team."

"Oh my God. What if you're right?"

"Who's to say I'm not? In this place, who can tell what's real?"

Three steps behind the two guests, Jack could only agree.

CHAPTER FIFTY-NINE

BACK IN THE CABANA

JACK WATCHED AS Lucy picked up a pillow from the bed and fluffed it. Since returning from the race, she'd examined his shoulder for injury, made an ice pack, applied a new bandage over his eye, rinsed dishes in the kitchen sink, and opened the drapes. Now she was remaking the bed.

He was the neat freak, not her, so what was she chewing on? He got his answer when she opened the closet, looked doubtfully at the showgirl costume on the hanger, then pulled it out to closely examine the straps and sequins.

"I thought you were going to pass on the performance," he said.

She shrugged, her eyes betraying her uncertainty. "Maybe I should try."

She held his stare, her meaning clear: If I go to the practice, I can look for the song lyrics for tonight's performance.

"Only if you want to," he said.

"I'll see if it fits," she said, taking it into the bathroom.

He smiled, then sat on the bed, picked up the phone, and asked to be connected to Los Angeles.

After three long rings, Calhoun picked up and said, in her best Gracie growl, "Who the hell is this? You know what time it is here?"

"Gracie, it's Jack. Sorry to call so late."

"You mean early! Why are you waking me from the only good sleep I've had all week?"

"Sorry, I wasn't thinking," he said. "Go back to bed. I'll call later."

"Wait." He heard what sounded like mattress springs groaning in the background. "I'm up now, so talk."

"You sure?"

"Talk!"

"I called because we just got some big news. One of the guests died. An accident. They said he fell down a hole and into a tunnel and died."

"Omigod. Who?"

"Guy named Dick Hould."

"You know him?"

"Slightly. Guy was a dick. He hit on Lucy last night, and Lucy gave him a good kick in the you-know-where."

"Don't tell me they think she pushed him or something."

"He died from a fall, not a groin injury."

"Okay, okay. I'm glad you called — could be big news. I see bad press. We'll have to distance you. You're sure — no involvement from you and your new girl?"

"Very sure."

"You okay otherwise? You didn't call after your fight last night. Did what's-his-name beat you up like I said he would?"

"Yeah, but I won the fight, somehow."

"Finally, some good news."

"But I did have an accident a little while ago on the motocross course."

"What? You were racing again? You know I don't like you on those death machines. You okay?"

"I'm fine. My front tire blew out, and I lost control of the bike."

"A tire blew? Omigod! How?"

"Don't know. Honestly, I'm not sure. Probably just a random accident. It went over the cliff and landed in the water. Too bad we can't be sure."

"Oh, you give me heartburn...."

He knew Calhoun was already initiating a recovery mission for the wreckage. He waited while she formulated what he knew would be her next question. A lot would be riding on his answer.

"I don't want you getting mad at me for suggesting this," she said. "But you seem a little freaked out. That island sounds crazy. You want me to call your plane so you can leave a day early?"

That was Calhoun's code for: Is your cover blown? Should Special Exploits move in?

He didn't answer right away. Missions often came down to this: a judgment call. Someone had murdered Dick Hould. He suspected someone had tried to kill Prince Ali. And now, with his tire, it was more than possible that someone — Yoko or Messalina — had figured out his cover.

On the flip side, his gut told him he was getting closer to Yoko, and closer to winning the phosphorin, which, after all, was the point of the mission. If the phosphorin was on the island, then bringing in Special Exploits would put an end to Yoko's scheme and contain the threat. But if the phosphorin wasn't here, if it was being stored elsewhere....

"No," he said. "Not yet. I'll call if I change my mind."

"Okay, sweetie. You let me know."

"Anything to report on your end?"

"In the middle of the night?"

"So that's a no?"

"That's a no. Nothing to worry your handsome head about."

Translation: no leads, no intel, no new developments, or at least nothing she could share over an open line.

"Okay," he said. "Thanks for putting up with me, Gracie."

"You stop being crazy with the stunts, okay? Any more bad stuff happens, you get on the phone right away, okay?"

"Got it."

"Bye, sugar." With a click, she was gone.

CHAPTER **SIXTY**

LUCY STEPPED OUT of the bathroom, her eyes moving to Jack sitting on the bed. He was still dusty from the race, blond hair ragged and uneven, and was holding an ice pack against his right shoulder. He winced as he hung up the phone, eyes aimed at the floor.

Her breath caught. He wasn't radiating his usual wattage of energy. In this moment, he seemed almost normal, almost human. Still way too attractive — she resisted the urge to sit next to him and run her hands over his bare shoulders — but not an effortless charm machine.

The sequins on her costume rustled. His head swiveled toward her and his eyes lit up.

"You look great," he said.

Her stomach fluttered as he stood and stepped toward her. She thought she'd looked pretty good, too, back in the bathroom, staring at the form-fitting costume in the mirror, but she liked hearing it from him. She'd been looking for the confirmation.

That's not all you're looking for, her inner voice said. She'd been hoping he'd respond the way he had, hoping he'd walk up to her, his interest clear. Hoping he'd — what? Lean in for another kiss like last night?

Yes. She wanted that. But why?

Because she was harboring fantasies.

Because she was not being real about who this man was.

Because she was playing the fool.

Her back stiffened. He noticed, as always. Over the past two days, she'd become very aware of how bad she was at hiding her feelings, and how good he was at finding them.

He was next to her now, smelling of sweat and dust. He ran a finger over the sequins, just above her hip.

"It fits you perfectly," he said. "I'm a little tired, but how about a walk?"

She felt a pang of disappointment. He was *tired.* He wanted to talk mission specifics.

But really, this was good. After all, the mission was what mattered. The mission was why they were here. If she kept the mission front and center, she could get the breathing room to ignore, and eventually move past, her irrational physiological responses.

"Let me change out of this," she said.

Minutes later, her hand in his, they were back on the path to the race course. Aside from staff dismantling the lunch tents and viewing stand, they had the plateau to themselves.

He glanced around. "First things first. I've replayed the words from the beginning of the race over and over in my head, and the only clue I see is the one in plain sight."

She nodded in agreement. "Which means the next clue is in the song."

"You sure you want to be part of tonight's performance?"

She was aware of her heart beating. "Not at all, but I think I have to do it."

He eyed her with a mixture of doubt, concern and — if

she was reading him right — approval. "If we know the song lyrics before the performance, that might give us a head start."

"I'm in."

"Okay. Good." He led her along the racecourse, to a spot at the base of the white hill, then turned in a slow circle, surveying the terrain.

"What are you looking for?" she asked.

"If someone blew out my tire, they would have needed a clear visual. If I was them, where would I have positioned myself to watch me land?"

He pointed to an elevated ridge farther down the course. "There."

They made their way to the ridge. Jack walked along it slowly, scanning the ground.

"Footsteps," he said with a frown. "Too many of them."

"So if the saboteur were here...."

"Their footprints are mixed in with those of everyone else."

"Can you call Special Exploits and have them sneak in and examine the wreckage?"

He gave her an appreciative grin. "Already done, though it's unlikely we'll get an answer before tonight."

"An awful lot of work for a bike."

"It wasn't just any bike."

Something stirred in her. Without really understanding why, she found herself saying, "You seem more upset about the bike than you were about Dick Hould."

"I am," he said absently, his eyes back on the ground. "I'm glad Dick Hould is dead."

"I can't believe you care more about a bike than a human life." She heard the sharpness in her voice — a surprising sharpness.

He looked up. "What's going on?"

"Clearly," she said, stalling for time and ignoring whatever the hell was surging through her, "we're examining your unhealthy emotional attachments to inanimate objects."

His eyes flashed.

Dammit. She'd meant to joke, to defuse, and instead she'd struck a nerve.

"Maybe," he said, turning to face her, "we should look instead at your low opinion of beauty and craftsmanship and tradition."

Unfair and far too broad. Her eyes narrowed.

He didn't stop.

"Maybe," he said, moving a step closer, "we should look at your unhealthy attachment to ideas over reality. Maybe we should examine why you're so intent on refusing to appreciate and enjoy this world we live in."

Okay, so he wanted a fight. *Fine.*

She turned to face him directly. "You want me to appreciate and enjoy this world? Your world? Where everyone is rich and beautiful and fake?"

He didn't flinch. "Did you ever tell your colleague Gabe?"

Her colleague Gabe? What the hell?

"Tell him what?"

"That you were in love with him."

Involuntarily, she stepped back. She couldn't believe what she was hearing. "What did you say?"

"Stop stalling," he said, his tone insistent.

Blood rushed to her face. "I am not going to discuss this with you."

"Is that what you did to him, too? Shut him down?"

She didn't have to answer him. Gabe was none of his damn business. She should tell him to fuck off. But the more insistent part of her was telling her to push back. No, to do more than that: to explain herself to him, as clearly as she could, and make him understand.

She took a deep breath. "Gabe was my friend. I miss him. There isn't a day that goes by when I don't think about him, but we were never more than that."

He stepped closer. "You had feelings for him, and he for you, but you held back. You never gave him a chance to choose."

"To choose?"

"Yeah," he said. "To choose you."

He was about to say more, but stopped, looking puzzled, as if he was missing something.

"I have no idea where this is coming from," she said, sensing her advantage, "but you have it all wrong. Gabe was with Nancy. They were engaged. They got married."

"That made falling for him easier. Nothing safer than an unattainable man."

"Fuck you."

"Finally. Passion from the ice queen."

"Please stop. Just stop. You wouldn't understand."

"Understand what?"

"Sometimes," she said, doing her best to calm her tone, "chasing what you want isn't right. Sometimes, respect for other people's choices is more important."

"Right," he said. "That's why you hid your feelings: out of respect."

"Gabe loved Nancy, not me."

He moved in close, his face just inches away, and his eyes locked in. "You'll never know that, not for sure, but one thing you do know? You blew it. You know it. You feel it, like an ache deep in your bones. The ache of 'what if.'"

Her mouth tightened. What ached to break free was her quickly rising anger.

He inched even closer. "So you're never going to blow it again, are you? You're never gonna get anywhere near that possibility again. It's why you're so incredibly, unbelievably, unapproachable."

"I am not going to kiss you again!"

She gasped, stunned. Jack froze.

"You can kiss any girl you want," she said. "Consider yourself free and clear. Just remember to follow Grant's big rule."

"Big rule?"

"'Don't fall in love.'"

He snorted.

A snort? No way was he brushing this off. She pushed on. "The rule that means you have to stay damaged, emotionally stunted, and unable to commit. So you can float like a bee from flower to flower."

He shook his head, then stepped away and sat down on a slab of rock, facing the sea. "Calhoun tell you that? No, wait. Paul did. Your favorite new hairdresser."

"You're all like that. You and Grant and Paul and the man in the air vent, whatever his name is. You're all charming and smart and beautiful. Trained to fight, break into rooms, hack computers, climb through buildings. Trained to seduce. But the secret sauce? That's the key."

"Ah, the top-secret secret sauce."

"They need you emotionally neutered and focused on the mission. They can't have you thinking about someone back home."

He picked up a rock and tossed it over the cliff, wincing as he did so.

"They'll do everything they can to improve your training and performance — make you faster, stronger, smarter, more adaptable, more insightful. But they won't touch that formative trauma. No, they need that scar tissue firmly in place. The longer it sticks, the longer they have you."

She stopped. For a moment, neither of them spoke. She watched him pick up another rock and roll his sore shoulder.

"Who was she, Jack?" she asked. "Who broke your heart?"

He shot a glance at her, his face a mask.

"Is that what you do when the subject comes up?" she asked. "Shut down?"

He sighed. "Touché."

She looked at him, unmoving, waiting.

He nodded and patted the ground next to him.

After a pause, she sat down. The Mediterranean stretched out in front of her, grey-blue in the mid-afternoon sun.

"Anne Connolly," he finally said, still staring ahead. "Her name was Anne Connolly. After my dad and grandmother died, I spent all my time at the beach, in the water, surfing. It took awhile, but after showing up every morning for three months straight and proving I could handle the waves, a group of guys let me in, let me hang with them.

"Anne was nineteen. She was the sister of one of the guys. Worldly. Wise. Beautiful. One day, she took me to her apartment. She was my first. I fell hard. I'd have done anything for her. Anything.

"Of course, no one knew. When she pushed me away — ditched me and tossed me to the curb — she said she was afraid of what people would think. What they would say about my age.

"So yeah, I learned from that. Yeah, I have scar tissue."

She looked at him intently. "What did you learn, Jack?"

He turned toward her. "Don't be afraid of what other people think or say. Don't let judgment bog you down. The only people worth caring about are the people you care about."

She shook her head slowly in disbelief. "That's the lesson? Really?"

His shoulders tensed, almost imperceptibly. "What do you mean?"

"Your great, transformative love was a teenage crush. A stupid, ordinary, teenage crush."

"Don't say that." He said it fast, as if restraining his anger.

"If you hadn't been grieving, you would have moved on," she said, her words precise and relentless. "Instead, the loss of your father and grandmother got mixed in with the pain of getting dumped by a silly nineteen-year-old girl who made the mistake of sleeping with a younger boy. The loss of Anne Connolly took on life-defining importance."

He tore his eyes away from her. "You can't know that."

"You've been blind. You think your pals in L.A. didn't realize this? You think they didn't realize what they had on their hands when they recruited you?"

She stood up and brushed herself off.

"I think we're done here."

His eyes went to hers, his face a mask again.

"Right?" she asked.

He shrugged.

"I have a show to rehearse."

He stood with her. "After you."

Side by side, not hand in hand, they made their way back to the villa.

CHAPTER
SIXTY-ONE

JACK WATCHED LUCY close the cabana door behind her, heading for rehearsal, a roomful of tension leaving with her.

He exhaled. His shoulder hurt like hell. His ribs ached. He was so beat. It'd been years since a mission had hit him so hard and so fast. He was getting soft back in La-La Land, living the celebrity lie, spending too much time setting up surveillance, passing intel, chatting up scumbags, buying rounds for his Hollywood buddies, flashing his pearly whites at any camera aimed his way.

He inhaled, then exhaled again. For the first time since arriving on Synkonos, he couldn't think of a damn thing to do.

Surely he'd missed something that required his active involvement. Surely there was something....

But no. He'd identified the next clue. He knew where and when and how he'd hear it. He'd briefed Calhoun, which left a whole bunch of nothing. Nada. Zippo.

Another agent would have more options, more latitude. A

different agent could grab Erica Sandoz, take her down into the caves, and employ all the usual methods to encourage a frank discussion.

Another agent could recruit Sergei and bring him into the loop to secure his help.

Too bad that other agent wasn't here. Other agents could break cover with fewer consequences. Their fictions had shelf lives. But Jack's cover — his long-lived, useful beast — was too valuable to risk.

Which meant he was stuck. Which meant the single most productive use of his time right now was sleep. An hour, maybe ninety minutes. A chance to de-stress, de-clutter, and decompress.

He set his watch alarm, then shrugged out of his clothes and slid under the covers. The sheets were cool and crisp and oh-so-inviting on his bare skin.

Lucy was wrong about Anne — couldn't have been more off base. Anne Connolly was a once-in-a-lifetime girl. Lucy hadn't known her and would never know her. How she could pronounce judgment with such confidence, labeling their love a "stupid, ordinary, teenage crush," was beyond him. The bond he and Anne had shared had been real and deep and pure and true and irreplaceable. Her rejection had cut him to the core. Human beings were complex. Feelings were complex. Relationships were complex. It took an expert to understand and sort through them.

And Lucy, an expert? How many relationships had she had in her cloistered life? Two, maybe three? She was practically a nun, one of those people who shielded herself from the messiness of the here-and-now in pursuit of a higher calling. She'd spent her life probing the mysteries of the universe, not the human heart.

Not that it mattered. Gnawing away at Lucy Kimball's flaws was a waste of time and energy. Like he'd warned

Grant, she was proving to be a major distraction, as well as annoying and aggravating. The mission would be over in a day or two. They would either succeed or fail. Either way, she'd be out of his life, and he out of hers. Then he could get back on track, doing what he was great at, doing what he loved.

He needed sleep. He needed to turn off his brain so he could get some fucking sleep.

CHAPTER **SIXTY-TWO**

IN THE WOMEN'S restroom near the villa's bar, Lucy checked herself in the mirror one final time. The casual t-shirt and cotton slacks she'd selected for the rehearsal hung loosely on her, allowing for easy movement. She'd left her hair pulled back in a ponytail and had steered clear of makeup.

Her external appearance was okay, she allowed herself, acceptable, unlike how she felt inside. Between the lack of sleep, the endless onslaught of shocking events, and Jack with his idiotic theory about Gabe, she was wiped out.

She forced those thoughts to the side and focused on her more imminent dilemma: Why had she committed to this rehearsal? She was a terrible dancer: awkward, uncoordinated, and self-conscious. The idea that anyone would ever pick Lucy Kimball to perform, on a stage, for the entertainment of others, was ridiculous.

She should just head back to the cabana. Jack would understand. He'd flat-out told her, several times, to only do what she felt comfortable doing.

So why did her stomach churn at the thought of bowing out? Why the unwelcome glint of determination in her big brown eyes, elbowing its way forward, pushing through her trepidation?

She flashed to her ten-year-old self, paralyzed in the spotlight at her fifth-grade spelling bee, stumbling over the word "exaggerate." A word she had down cold but whose letters she could not, in that terrible moment, get out of her mouth. She heard the snickers and whispers, and felt the heated red flush on her cheeks.

Her hippocampus, amygdala, and medial prefrontal cortex had, ever since, conspired to initiate a stress response for anything performance-related. Even now, at the mere prospect of stepping onto a stage, she could feel the effects of excitatory amino acid-induced neurotoxicity.

But this new determination? Could her hippocampus be demonstrating its neuronal plasticity and regenerative capacity? Had the shocks of the past two days acted as an inoculation of sorts against the stress she felt about performing?

Was her brain, in its infinite wisdom, trying to tell her she could handle a dance rehearsal?

Ugh. She flashed to Commander Grant in the briefing room, to what he'd said after she'd thrown her doubts at him: "Never forget the stakes are enormous, and we're on the side of right. Never underestimate how much that matters. Knowing that, believing that, feeling that, makes all the difference in the world."

She sighed.

Before she could talk herself out of it, she marched out of the bathroom, down the hallway, and pushed open the doors of the event room.

Gone were the fight cage and surrounding sofas and beds. The setup was now more traditional: a raised stage at the far end of the room, curtains open, and a large, open area in the center of the room, where, she presumed, tables would soon be placed for the dinner before tonight's show.

Vienna was already here, along with Marie and Erica, having a conversation with a man facing away from her.

"Lucy!" Vienna said, waving her over. The man turned. It was Etienne, the dark-haired hospitality facilitator she'd met when the ferry had docked at the pier. He'd kept his distance since — understanding, perhaps, that neither Lucy nor Jack had much use for him — though she'd felt his eyes on her several times.

He gave her the same seductive smile.

"I am very glad you decided to join us," he said.

"I almost didn't," she admitted. "I've never done anything like this."

"Don't worry. This will be fun." He turned to the group. "Everyone, take a minute to warm up. Whatever you normally do before you exercise."

Vienna, Erica, and Marie started bending and stretching in the center of the room. Lucy followed their lead. Jenny, the blonde waiter from the ferry, and Greta, her babysitter from last night, joined them. All of the women seemed thoroughly at ease. No one else seemed worried about stepping on toes, or falling down, or making complete fools of themselves.

A seventh woman ran in. With a jolt, Lucy recognized her as the tall, beautiful woman whom Jack had vigorously fucked in this very room the previous night. The woman's skin was flawless. She moved with grace, exuding health and self-assurance.

The woman's eyes locked on to her. "We haven't met. I'm Hazel."

Lucy was surprised by how calm she felt as she took the woman's slim, elegant hand in hers. "Lucy."

"I hope you don't mind about last night," Hazel said. "I had to know."

The lie came far more easily than expected. "We're all grownups here."

"Ladies," Etienne said. "Let's form a circle in the center of the room."

Hazel gave her a nod, then turned toward Etienne.

Vienna, who had been watching closely, leaned in and quietly said, "See, that wasn't so hard."

The seven women gathered around Etienne.

"Today," he said, his eyes moving around the circle, "we will learn what it means to be a showgirl. A showgirl is, first and foremost, a way of being, an attitude. She is elegance and glamour. She is style and grace. She epitomizes an unattainable feminine ideal. With every flutter of her eyelashes, every smile, and every kick, she commands the stage. She captures the audience with her womanly beauty."

He gestured toward the empty room. "No doubt you are wondering how, in just two hours, you can learn the art of the showgirl. I am here to show you. Just remember, a showgirl is attitude. Yes, attitude."

He snapped his fingers and two staff members rolled in a tall, black, portable cabinet on wheels, six feet high and four feet wide. He walked up to it and, with a flourish, swung open the double doors.

The women gasped. Inside were rows — rows and rows and rows — of identical red showgirl shoes, sparkling and stilettoed and gorgeous.

"Attitude begins with shoes," Etienne said. "The showgirl begins with her shoes."

The seven women rushed in.

"Find your size, try them on, and get to know the shoes that you will be performing in tonight."

"Bouboumin," Vienna breathed, holding a pair with reverence. "I love Bouboumin."

Lucy found her size and slipped a shoe on. It fit wonderfully, the inside soft yet firm, cupping her ankle and comfortably hugging her toes. She stepped into the other shoe and stood up straight. Oh, boy. The heels were far higher than what she normally wore. For a second, she felt unbalanced.

But then, first with one step, then another, the wobbles vanished. She walked in a line toward the stage, then stopped, pivoted, and turned back. The shoes felt good, every step boosting her confidence.

Etienne was looking at her, at her walk.

"Ladies, I see you and your shoes are already becoming friends. This afternoon, we will spend most of our time perfecting the showgirl pose. How you stand, how you walk, how you hold your head, how you project yourself to the audience. You will show confidence! You will be the epitome of glamour!

"You," he said to Vienna, "walk to me like an elegant, perfect creature who owns the stage."

Vienna brightened. Her neck and back straightened, her chin rose, and she strode toward Etienne, one impossibly long leg following the other.

Etienne beamed. "Perfect! You are a natural. Beauty and elegance personified!"

He turned to Lucy. "Lucy, your turn. Learn from Vienna. Follow her example."

Oh, geez. Her hippocampus squirted more stress juice as she tried to remember what she'd just watched Vienna do so effortlessly. Stand straight. Stop slouching. Move one leg forward, then the other.

Etienne nodded at her encouragingly as she stepped toward him.

"For a first try, you are doing fine." He placed one hand on her lower back, and the other under her chin. "Do it again. This time, with your back very straight and your chin up" — he guided her head up with a finger — "like this."

She walked again, this time with her head higher.

"Yes, much improved. Very good. Marie, your turn."

Marie, like Vienna, was a natural, as were the others. They walked — glided — with grace, the high heels accentuating their cleavage and rear ends. Even without costumes and makeup, they emanated the essence of the showgirl.

Over the next hour, she and the other women learned two simple dance routines for the show and tried on headdresses, which were much heavier than she'd expected. Etienne brought the right blend of focus and fun, keeping their attention on the moves and poses, while giving the women the space to screw up and even laugh at themselves.

After an attempt at a move that ended with Marie and Erica in giggles, Etienne called for a ten-minute break.

Lucy turned to Etienne and asked, "Are we performing with Robbie and Carrie?"

Etienne shook his head. "Carrie and Robbie have their own backup dancers. You will open the show, and you will be on stage, in the background, while Carrie and Robbie do their set. Why do you ask?"

"I've always been a big fan," she lied, not bothering to hide her disappointment. If she and the other showgirls weren't part of Robbie and Carrie's big number, then she wouldn't have a sneak peek at the new song they would be performing.

"I will make sure to introduce you," Etienne said, then leaned in and added, "I hope you will not take offense, but I find you very attractive. Tonight, after the show, may I ask you for a dance?"

His open brown eyes and handsome face pulled her in — toward what? She halted him with a smile. "Why don't we see where the evening takes us?"

"Until this evening," he said with a nod, then turned to

the other dancers. "Everyone, one more move for us: the classic chorus-girl line kick."

She sensed a presence behind her and turned to see Vienna with a teasing smile on her face.

"He's hot," Vienna said. "You gonna go for it?"

She shrugged. "I don't know."

Vienna clasped Lucy's hands in hers. "Listen. I know we just met, but I like you. I want you to have fun while you're here. You should enjoy this place for what it is. The weekend will be over before you know it. Get what you can while you can."

Vienna's eyes were filled with sincerity and — something else. Sympathy?

Yes, sympathy, because she knew Lucy would soon be out of Jack's life. Without realizing it, her new celebrity pal was handing her the final nail to hammer into the coffin of the implausible fantasies she'd been holding on to. The fantasy where she and Jack finished the mission and, yes, started dating. The fantasy where he whisked her away for exotic weekend getaways. The fantasy where she introduced him to Mr. Snuggles, and Mr. Snuggles jumped right into his lap and refused to budge. The fantasy where he set up Joanie with one of his single pals and the four of them double-dated. The fantasy where he met her parents: dinner at her place, serving her father's favorite slow-cooked beef stew, Jack talking geography and maps with her dad, her mother following Lucy into the kitchen and, while Lucy was checking the apple crisp, whispering that she really liked this young man.

Was anything about that ridiculous nonsense even the slightest bit real? Was anything about Jack even the slightest bit real?

And to be completely, rigorously fair — and she needed to be, if only to ensure she gave herself the good swift kick she thoroughly deserved — was there anything real about *her*?

She was damaged goods and an emotional idiot. When Jack had poked at the still-raw wound of Gabe's death, had she behaved maturely? Oh no. She'd retaliated by torching the scar of his oh-so-tragic first love. A scar that probably explained, more than anything else, why he was so good at his job.

She'd fucked with him, solely to make herself feel better, influencing his ability to do a job he was good at. A job that stopped bad guys. A job that meant something in the grand scheme of things.

She couldn't allow herself to do that again. She had to let the fantasy go. She had to let *him* go.

Goodbye, Jack Ford, her inner voice said. Whoever you are.

She looked Vienna in the eye. "You're right. I should take advantage."

"Good girl," Vienna said.

Life lessons from a party girl. Who knew? But Vienna was right. She should embrace the moment and enjoy what might come her way, in the brief time she had here. Why the hell not?

CHAPTER SIXTY-THREE

Laughter and conversation and the clink of silverware on plates swirled around him. Dinner was winding up, the event room pulsing with anticipation for what was soon to come.

Jack adjusted the collar of his tuxedo and ran a visual sweep for the eighth — ninth? — time since sitting down. He was seated next to his host, who had eagerly waved him over the instant he'd walked in.

On the surface, nothing seemed amiss. But something in the room, in the moment, was off. Something he couldn't pinpoint.

Sergei seemed his usual drunken buoyant self, his earlier doubts about the bike long gone and his sole focus now on the care and feeding of one Jack Ford. He watched with pleasure as Jack savored the tasting menu of exceptional dishes placed, one after another, in front of him: Rabbit with hot apple jelly. Sardines with fish roe. White asparagus with hot mayonnaise. Oysters with smoked pancetta. Gnocci with consomme of roasted potato skin. Razor shell clam sushi with ginger spray. Bread with oil and chocolate.

Delicious, each one, and meant to impress. Like everything else about this weekend.

Jack picked up his glass of port — a rare and expensive vintage, he was sure — and took a sip, allowing the port's potent sweetness to mix with the lingering chocolate in his mouth. He swallowed and turned to Sergei. "Dude. Best. Meal. Ever."

Sergei grinned. "Tonight you get to enjoy show and not be show. Nice, yes?"

"Totally."

"Maybe tonight you keep your clothes on, yes?" With a laugh, Sergei reached over to slap him on the shoulder and nearly fell off his chair. Sergei laughed some more, sat up straight, and gave Jack a mischievous grin. "You feel okay to sit? Your asshole does not hurt too much?"

Dude was still hung up on that? He felt the rustle of a dress against his shoulder and glanced back. Natasha. She handed Sergei a microphone. "We're ready."

Sergei stood, holding on to the chair briefly to balance himself, and said to Jack, "I see you after show? This time you stay and don't go away?"

"You got it."

He watched Sergei carefully follow Natasha through the tables to the stage. The two of them made an excellent team — the dreamer and the doer. In just hours, she'd transformed the event room into a sumptuous, intimate cabaret space for tonight's performance, with dinner tables packed tightly together in a U-shape around a catwalk that extended from the main stage and into the center of the room. Vibrant red dominated the decor: rich, red velvet curtains on the stage, red cloth banners on the walls, red tablecloths, and red upholstery on the dining chairs. On each table, a single red rose rested in a slim crystal vase.

The hospitality facilitators in the room, circulating with drinks and sitting with guests to chat and flirt, wore matching red uniforms of thongs and bowties, both the women and men. The women were topless to boot, all shreds of modesty long gone.

Lucy, were she here, would disapprove of the bared flesh. She'd frown at the decadent tableau of men in tuxedoes and women in evening gowns being served by nearly nude staff. She'd decry the power imbalance and the exploitation.

But she wasn't here. She was backstage with the other showgirls, preparing for her big debut. She'd returned from rehearsal without the tension she'd been carrying earlier, but with something else instead: certainty. She'd reached a decision. Given her subdued and distant manner toward him, it was clear the decision had been about him.

He'd been hoping for this change in her, he reminded himself, ever since the start of the mission. She was finally on board with the program. There would be no more emotional outbursts, and no more digging around in his head. They'd be able to focus, fully and without distraction, on the mission.

The hollow feeling in his gut? *Relief.* Relief that he could let go of the tension. Relief that he'd received what he'd been asking for.

From his seat at Sergei's table, he was positioned to hear every word of whatever clue the song might contain. His competitors would also hear it, or at least Erica Sandoz would while backstage with Lucy.

Prince Ali, however, was still a no-show. The prince preferred late entrances, but to be this tardy? Curious.

He turned to Francois Le Coq, who was seated next to him at Sergei's table. "Have you seen Prince Ali?"

Francois shook his head. "No, I have not."

The older man had been subdued all evening and not his usual lion-like self.

Could Le Coq's mood change be the something he'd picked up on? "Hope you don't mind me saying, but I can see you're distracted."

"Yes," Francois said. "My mind is elsewhere."

"Care to share?"

"Have you ever been married, Mr. Ford?" Francois asked.

"No."

"Then you cannot know."

Ah — a marital spat with Marie. Not surprising, given how strong-willed he and his wife were.

A fork clinked on a wine glass. He turned toward the stage. Sergei stood under a spotlight, microphone in hand.

"Welcome to the Synkonos Cabaret," he said as the audience shifted their attention to him and applauded. "We have a wonderful show for you this evening. I hope you all enjoy dinner?"

The crowd cheered their appreciation.

"We are very excited to welcome you tonight for private concert with two world-class entertainers. But first, housekeeping item. I have update on fierce fight for control of Hotel Synkonos. Both gangs are racking up points. Avalon gang and Funicello gang both doing exceptionally well."

He paused, then said: "But one gang is inching ahead."

The room tensed. Sergei paused yet again.

"Stop teasing us!" a guest yelled.

The room laughed, as did Sergei.

"Must build suspense, yes? Essential for tension. Point total after second day is: Avalon gang, led by Anthony Avalon" — he pointed to Monsieur Le Coq — "133 points!"

A roar went up from the Avalon gang, Francois acknowledging the results with a nod.

"And now, point total for Funicello gang, led by Francesca Funicello: 147 points!"

The room erupted as the Funicello gang realized they'd pulled ahead. From behind the stage curtain, they heard a woman — Marie, no doubt — yelling her approval.

"Sergei, what's the prize for winning?" a guest yelled.

"Yes, I keep you in suspense for that, too? But now I tell you. Next year, in Davos, I host exclusive gathering. Focus on how we can work together to change world. More business-focused than this weekend. Opportunity to make new and important connections. The gang that wins battle for control of Hotel Synkonos will be included in invite list for Davos gathering."

Whoa. An invitation to a private meeting at one of the top gatherings of global movers-and-shakers? A valuable prize worth fighting for, and the room knew it.

"So keep firmly in mind," Sergei said, his voice dropping a notch. "Game is for play, but play is for real. Remember what we say in Vegas: Bring your A-game, baby."

He paused yet again, and this time there were no catcalls from the audience. "You all know drill. Tomorrow morning, you find envelopes with next tasks under your door and final round begins. Game is still very close. Final round will be fierce. Either side can win. I wish you all best of luck.

"But now, on with show!"

CHAPTER SIXTY-FOUR

THE SPOTLIGHT VANISHED as Sergei jumped off the stage.

Jack's eyes adjusted to the darkness. From the stage, a dim red glow grew in intensity as the curtains opened to the heartbeat — thump-thump, thump-thump — of a lone bass guitar.

He caught a hint of movement in the red gloom. A banner of red cloth, identical to the banners of the cabaret room walls, fluttered to the ground, and behind it, a nude woman rose from the floor, her curves just visible in the red glow. She wrapped herself around the banner and extended one leg and then the other, slowly, sensuously.

Drums and cymbals smashed without warning as a spotlight hit her face. Jack gasped along with the rest of the audience. The woman wore a mask of a hideous creature in agony, its mouth and eyes opened in rage and fear. Using the banner as her tether, she writhed, legs and arms jerking about as if in a panic.

The orchestra — trumpets and trombones and saxophones

— snuck in, low and discordant and ragged. Behind her, the word "Fear" flashed briefly and intermittently through the red gloom. The effect was unsettling and disturbing — violent emotion vividly expressed. Just as the dancer's contortions became unbearable to watch, the woman waved her arm, sweeping away the word "Fear" and scattering it to bits.

She whipped off her mask, revealing a different mask, this one stern and forbidding. Her movements became rigid. The band's cacophony coalesced around a single beat with clear martial overtones.

The word "Control" flashed behind her as two male dancers, clad in skintight red leggings, leaped onto the stage. They each grabbed one of the woman's arms and pulled her first one way, then another. The three shifted in unison, their movements mechanized, the woman's stone-faced mask never leaving the spotlight.

Jack leaned forward. There was a story here. The dancers were taking the audience on a journey.

Without warning, the woman broke free of the two men. With a sweep of her arm, the word "Control" disintegrated and the music seemed to scatter. The men moved in to grab her again, but she pushed back, flinging their arms away. The men fell to the ground.

The woman rose to her full height and removed her mask, revealing a new one with wide, upturned eyes and slightly parted lips — an expression of hope, even innocence. The word "Dream" flashed behind the dancers. A lone trumpet, high and supple, rose above them in a soft melody. Red silk banner in hand, the woman moved, slowly and experimentally at first, then with more confidence, twirling and dipping and rolling with the red cloth. She pulled herself up and spun down, snapping to an abrupt halt barely an inch from the ground.

The big band swelled as the two men rose from the stage. They circled the woman warily. They reached out to her, and she reached back, using them to execute increasingly complicated spins with the red cloth.

She waved her arm again, and the word "Dream" slowly dissolved. The word "Connect" flashed by, and then the word "Change." The two words repeated over and over again as the woman removed the final mask, revealing her real, animated, and exultant face. Her lips were the same red as the banner, her makeup highlighting her eyes.

The three dancers moved together like a synchronous beast. The woman's leaps and twirls grew more daring, knowing she could rely on the two men to catch her. Four more dancers joined them, two men and two women, and together they seemed to make the stage expand — explode — in size as they pushed their way deeper into the cabaret room, their movements a combination of tight choreography and free-form movements.

The band matched their sense of joyful purpose, and for the first time, they hit the brassy, bold rhythms and notes associated with the Big Band sound.

The red lighting increased in intensity, and other lights, blues and whites and yellow and greens, popped in. Behind the dancers, a bit of Vegas razzle-dazzle emerged — a tableau of the Vegas strip in neon and glitter.

The music hit a true Big Band stride, with saxophone, trumpet, trombone, and drums building toward a crescendo. The dancers' bare bodies gleamed with exertion under the red glow.

Just as it appeared that the dancers and music were about to explode, the stage went dark. The band stopped. Jack breathed in, waiting. One, two, three —

Bam! The band roared to life and the dazzling lights splashed on, revealing:

Seven gorgeous showgirls in a line on the catwalk, each statuesque and stunning, with their arms outstretched, backs straight, heads up, and right legs forward. Huge red feathers rose out of their headdresses. The red sequins of their barely-there costumes flashed in the light. Their legs went on for miles, disappearing into gleaming red shoes with impossibly high heels.

The showgirls remained motionless, letting the roar of the audiences' applause flow over them, their demeanor cool, reserved, and even haughty.

Then they moved in unison. A shift of their hips and they were facing one side of the catwalk. Their outstretched arms found each other's shoulders, and they kicked.

A simple move, really, but in that moment, Jack understood why the chorus girl had endured and why she always would. There was beauty — a breath-catching symmetry — in that row of long, gorgeous legs aiming for the sky.

The audience was on its feet, cheering. The showgirls smoothly turned around and kicked in the other direction.

They looked amazing in their costumes — Vienna, Erica, Marie, and the others — but Jack's eyes kept returning to Lucy. She was the shortest of the women by several inches and, placed at the end of the line, closest to the end of the catwalk. Beneath the makeup, she looked exhilarated and triumphant, as if she'd crossed an internal barrier by staring down a personal fear.

His throat grew tight from — what? Pride? Yes, pride. It had to be. Of course he was proud of her. Why wouldn't he be?

Her eyes shone. She had tears in her eyes. Her kicks were high and confident. The smile on her face was genuine, fueled by an inner excitement.

She and the other showgirls pivoted and strode off the catwalk, all grace and elegance, and took up positions on the stage. They fell into a new routine, where the showgirl in the center — Vienna — performed a dance move that the other women followed in a wave.

The audience loved it, cheering as each woman posed and twirled and kicked.

Throughout the routine, he couldn't tear his eyes away from Lucy and her elegant neck, which held up the headdress seemingly without effort, though those feathers and rhinestones had to be heavy. Her slim arms moved in sync with the choreography of the dance. His eyes moved to the curve of her breasts, pushed up by the form-fitting costume. Her newfound confidence infused her movements with a grace she probably never knew she possessed.

The lump in his throat got bigger. His eyes threatened to, what? Tear up? *What the hell?*

The song came to an end. One by one, each showgirl stepped forward and gave an elegant bow to the audience, who applauded enthusiastically. They stepped to the back of the stage and sat, in elegant poses, on risers, their legs and headdresses becoming one with the Vegas tableau.

A soft drum-and-cymbal beat announced the arrival of something new. In the spotlight, stage right, appeared the one and only Robbie Armand, former boy-bander turned international pop star. The world had watched him grow up and knew his songs by heart, and now he was here, with them.

The audience cheered wildly as Robbie, clad in a burgundy tuxedo, grinned and waved as he stepped to the center of the stage. The band settled into a new song, one Jack hadn't heard before.

Was this the new song? The clue? Robbie turned to the audience, brought the microphone to his lips, and sang:

A free-living lad,

A playboy! A cad!
Drawn to the wild and taboo
He thought he was glad
Not empty, not sad
'Til the Fates sent him to you

A spotlight on stage left revealed Carrie Esposito, pop megastar, in a dazzling white sequined dress that was stunning against her blond hair and ruby-red lips.

After a pause to let the audience's roars die down, Robbie sang on:

The loveliest eyes
So bright and alive
Passion that made him feel new
Rattled and shaken
There ain't no fakin'
The shock and awe of you
The shock and awe of you

With a laugh and a wave of her arms, Carrie strode to the center of the stage and sang:

A girl with ambition
Had no suspicion
Love was a-calling her name
She met him by chance
She knew with a glance
Passion would up-end her game
She didn't want it
Oh how she fought it
Love wasn't ever her aim
Rattled and shaken
There ain't no fakin'

The shock and awe of you
The shock and awe of you

Together they sang:

The game is in play
At midnight you may
Show them you're playing for real
The challenge is clear
The ending is near
With Gang Bang, go grab a steal
A phrase to remember
Synkonos forever!
Fight well and you'll seal the deal
Rattled and shaken
There ain't no fakin'
The shock and awe of you
The shock and awe of you

Robbie looked right at Carrie as he sang:

Girl, I got snagged
My heart, bagged and tagged
So thrillingly captured by you

Carrie came back at him:

My life, incomplete
My heart skipped a beat
The moment my eyes fell on you

Looking right at each other, they belted out:

You're the spring in my step

The pop in my pep
The music that makes my heart sing
Rattled and shaken
There ain't no fakin'
The shock and awe of you
The shock and awe of you

Jack cheered with the rest of the crowd, his mind awhirl.

He locked eyes with Lucy. She nodded.

The what, the how, the when — he had the clue. And so did she.

CHAPTER
SIXTY-FIVE

THE SONGS FLOWED after that, duets and individual songs, classics freshened up and newer hits given a dose of Big Band. A terrific set, with Robbie and Carrie owning the room.

But his thoughts were elsewhere. He and Lucy made a good team — no, a great team. The way they could synch up their thinking, the way they communicated with just their eyes and body language....

The show got sexier. Carrie's and Robbie's backup dancers added a high-gloss sensual oomph to the songs, their movements becoming increasingly suggestive.

The room heated up too, with the facilitators and guests getting friendlier. Hands lingered and mouths leaned in to whisper into ears....

He glanced at his watch. Ninety minutes to midnight. The show was building toward a climax. The showgirls returned to the stage, behind Carrie and Robbie, kicking up a storm. The final song ended, and everyone took a bow. The audience cheered. What a show! Fresh drinks and appetizers spread throughout the room. Laughter rose. The tables were whisked away, replaced immediately by low couches and beds. Guests and facilitators fell into them. The undercurrent of desire, stoked by the show, bubbled to the surface.

The showgirls descended from the catwalk and into the audience, including Lucy. One of the hospitality facilitators, the French dude — what was his name, Etienne? — intercepted her and whispered something in her ear.

Jack's eyes narrowed. Dude was making a move on his girl? He was about to get up and put a stop to it when Lucy's eyes looked past Etienne, toward him. Her lips compressed, just for a second, then parted into a hint of a smile.

She murmured something to Etienne, then stepped toward Jack, a new expression lighting her face.

His breath seized up.

Lucy's eyes were filled with resolve — and desire.

Holy fuck. Funny how everything changed in a heartbeat. How the world went topsy-turvy without warning.

She reached him. He breathed in her perfume and sweat. Her hands went to his shoulders and pushed him back into a comfortable leather chair. She straddled him, legs clamping down. She reached up and removed her headdress, tossing it to the ground.

She was warm and electric in his lap. Her fingers were on his face, tracing his lips. He tasted the saltiness of her sweat.

Her hand curled around his chin, cupping it.

"This doesn't mean anything," she said, staring down into his eyes. "Got it?"

He could only nod as desire surged through him.

"Tell me you understand," she said.

"Got it," he said.

She swooped in, her mouth on his, the kiss as passionate and demanding as any he'd ever known, that of a woman unleashed, taking what she wanted.

His hands ran up her costume and up her waist, finding and cupping her breasts.

"Unzip me," she said.

He hesitated, taken aback. Here? Around the others?

"Now."

With trembling fingers, he found her zipper. The costume slid down. He took her breasts in his hands.

She pushed his face into her chest. His mouth found a nipple.

"Yes," she said, holding him tighter as his tongue swirled. "Yes."

An unfamiliar emotion — doubt — tore through him. Did she know what she was doing? She sure as hell seemed to, but did she really? He was the one who fooled around, who got naked in crowded rooms and made a spectacle of himself. He felt a sudden overwhelming urge to protect her, to pick her up and whisk her away.

She pushed his head back and stared at him again, drawing him into her bottomless brown eyes. Her beautiful, determined eyes, now alive with desire.

"Embrace the moment," she said. "Now."

He couldn't breathe. His goddamn feelings were getting in the way, constricting his chest. His feelings for this no-nonsense, pain-in-the-ass, emotionally skittish, stuck-in-her-head woman. This beautiful, sexy, strong, scary-smart, unflinching woman. This woman who had captured his …

Fuck.

His heart.

So fucking corny, but so true. He loved her. He loved the curve of her neck. The way she smelled. Her incredible brown eyes, deep and penetrating and expressive. The way her mouth twitched when she held back a smile. The way her back moved under his hands, graceful and strong. The way her hands had felt on him the previous night, when she was tending to his cuts and bruises. She cared about him. He'd felt it.

He loved her. He loved the way her cheeks flushed when she was turned on. How her mouth tightened when she was embarrassed. How she kept pushing forward even after he'd rattled her. How quickly she regrouped and threw his shit back in his face. How she made him laugh. Man, she was so fucking relentless.

He sure as hell had been missing something. Without even knowing it, he'd fallen in love with Dr. Lucy fucking Kimball.

He was so goddamned fucked.

CHAPTER
SIXTY-SIX

LUCY COULDN'T STOP herself from trembling in his arms. Not from fear — oh no — but from desire and exultation. From grabbing the bull by the horns and climbing aboard. He felt so good under her, with his arms around her, and his hands and mouth on her in all the right places.

His knowing fingers teased her nipple. A wave of pleasure shot through her.

The rest of the room was fading away fast, as if it wasn't even here. Her world became her pleasure, her lust, and the smooth skin and hard muscle and smells and sensations of the man beneath her. His face was freshly shaved, his mouth wide and eager. His hardness pressed against her through his tuxedo pants.

Oh God.

Before she could stop herself, she swung off him and deftly unfastened the bottom of her showgirl costume and shrugged down her panties.

He looked at her, mouth agape, stunned.

"What are you doing?"

She didn't answer. Couldn't. Her hand went to his pants and unzipped him like a pro.

She returned to his lap. She'd needed this, wanted this since the first time they'd met, which was far too long ago. Coitus had been far-too-long interruptus.

She reached down and took hold of him, as hard and beautiful as the rest of him. She was so wet, so ready.

"Lucy," he said.

"Shut up," she commanded. "Fuck me."

He obeyed. With a single smooth motion, he thrust inside her.

She lost herself then, burying her face in his hair. She grabbed him around the shoulders and squeezed tight. His aftershave and musk infused her senses, and she lost herself in his arms, his hot, ragged breath warming her ear.

"Lucy," he said tensely, a warning.

"Don't hold back," she whispered. "Don't you dare."

She could feel it coming, building, and she cried when the wave of her orgasm rolled through her like a shockwave. She gasped for breath, hot tears on her face.

Beneath her, Jack shuddered and clasped her tightly, sweat glistening on his brow.

Her world expanded as her heart rate slowed. She became aware of the room again, and of the other guests gathered around them, cheering them on.

Cheering them on?

Oh, geez.

What in the world had she done?

Jack was looking up at her with adoration in his eyes. His hands reached up and guided her head down for another kiss — a lingering one, his mouth passionate and demanding yet tender. His fingers tangled in her hair and caressed her neck, pulling her in oh-so-close.

This was the kiss of a lover. The kiss of a man who loved her.

Oh God. What had she done?

Abruptly, she stood, her mind awhirl. She'd seized the moment, done what she'd wanted and taken what she'd wanted — and now? What the hell was she going to do now?

If she pushed him away, he'd chase her. He wouldn't give up. It was in his nature. The pursuit would energize him, and she was weak. Oh God, so weak. No defense in her arsenal would work, not against him.

He stood with her, buttoned his pants — what had she done? — and grabbed her around her waist.

"Let's go," he said.

He led her through the crowded room, now overflowing with laughter and seduction. She nestled under his shoulder, overwhelmed but not wanting the moment to end. His heartbeat thumped against her head. Everywhere she looked, clothes were coming off, guests and facilitators doing the same damn thing she'd just done.

Sergei appeared in their path, swaying slightly, his gaze fixed on Jack. "Jack, you are leaving?"

"Just for a bit," Jack said.

Their host frowned. He wasn't happy to hear that.

"You must stay," he said. "Enjoy party."

Jack clapped him on the shoulder. "We'll be back. Soon."

Someone bumped her from behind. She turned to find Francois, pale and unsteady, his wife supporting him.

"Excuse us," Marie said. "A bit too much to drink, perhaps."

She steered him out of the room.

"You come back?" Sergei asked.

"Definitely," Jack said.

He eased Lucy past their host, and they were almost to the

exit when Vienna walked in, most likely from a quick visit to the restroom.

Her face lit up with a smile. "Jack!" Then the smile faltered.

She stared at him as though she were seeing something new and unwelcome.

Her eyes went to Jack's hand holding Lucy's waist, then traveled back to his face.

"Jack," she said, a tremor in her voice. "What is this?"

"Vienna," he said. "I...."

"Really?" she said to him. "*Her*?"

"Vienna — "

"Don't. Don't even start." Vienna's face started to collapse, but she took a deep breath and, somehow, turned it to stone instead. "Get away from me."

She pushed past them, into the cabaret room.

Jack turned and watched Vienna head straight to the bar and snap out a drink order.

"She goes too far when she's upset," he said. "It gets pretty bad."

"Do you want to go after her?"

After a pause, he said, "No. Let's go."

They made their way out of the cabaret room, away from the music and laughter and sex, and walked through the villa, across the courtyard, and down the path to their cabana.

"Jack," she said into the silence.

"Shhh." He placed a finger to her lips.

He opened the cabana door and led her inside. In the darkness, he shifted to face her. His arms went around her waist, and he leaned in for another kiss.

Another good kiss. *Argh.* Another damn good kiss.

She pushed him back. "Jack...."

"I know," he said, letting her go. "We have to get ready."

Ready for what? She froze, momentarily confused.

"Did you hear the clue?" he whispered in her ear.

The clue. Yes, the clue.

"Something's happening at midnight," she whispered, "in Gang Bang. The code is 'Synkonos Forever.'"

He chuckled. "Good girl."

He turned and flipped on the lights. His tuxedo shirt was untucked, the collar open. His hair was a mess. Her lipstick was smeared across his cheek, and her makeup was smudged on his neck. She'd done that.

What did she look like? She stepped into the bathroom and stared with dismay at her equally messy face. She had to get this junk off.

He moved in behind her and laughed when he saw his reflection in the mirror. He was acting, what? Confident? Happy? Yes, happy. He was gazing at her as if she was the greatest discovery of all time.

"Are you sure about Vienna?" she asked.

A cloud passed over his eyes. "No, I'm not."

"I have to get cleaned up. Why don't you go find her and make sure she's okay?"

He glanced at his watch. "There's time. You'll stay here?"

"Yes."

"Don't let anybody in. Back in a bit."

He looked at her for confirmation. "Go," she said. "I'll be fine."

Using the mirror, he rubbed the makeup off his face and neck with a towel, straightened his hair, and tucked in his shirt. In mere seconds, he was totally cleaned up. Totally unfair.

"Go," she said. "Now, before I kick you out."

He gave her a huge grin and a peck on the cheek, and was gone.

CHAPTER SIXTY-SEVEN

THE AIR SMELLED so fresh and sweet. The lights along the path to the courtyard glowed. The flowers and plants looked terrific. His steps felt lighter, his body tingling.

So this was love. Man, it felt great. Why had he been avoiding this?

He heard footsteps ahead of him and the murmur of voices heading his way. He slipped off the path and hid behind a tree.

Natasha and Boris walked past him down the path, toward his and Lucy's cabana.

He hadn't previously considered the possibility that Yoko was two people. Maybe Yoko was Natasha and Boris, working together? Silently, he followed, listening in.

Boris sounded impatient. "A man died this morning and another is ill. The party must end."

"An accident and a case of indigestion," Natasha replied, equally impatient. "Francois Le Coq will be fine."

"According to whom?"

"Le Coq himself. He is a doctor, remember."

"You just saw him. He looks terrible. We should alert the authorities."

"We are not going to bring the Greek authorities back for a tummy ache. Boris, you worry too much."

"Someone who is not the patient should examine him."

"You mean Lucy Keen? The medical student? Is that why you brought me here?"

"She strikes me as very sensible."

Natasha sighed. "If it makes you feel better."

They knocked on the cabana door.

No answer.

They knocked again, and Natasha said loudly, "Ms. Keen, please. We have a medical issue and need your assistance."

After a long pause, the door cracked open.

"Yes?" Lucy said from behind the door.

"Francois Le Coq has taken ill," Natasha said. "We expect it is indigestion, but we would like to be sure. Could we ask you to examine him?"

From behind the tree, Jack watched Lucy hesitate. He knew what she was thinking: The request could be a trap. One or both of them could be behind the phosphorin sale. On the flip side, it was indeed possible, even probable, that Francois was sick and needed her help.

"Let me finish changing," she said. "I'll be out in a minute."

He couldn't blame her for agreeing, even though part of him was annoyed that, once again, she was ignoring his order to stay put. But she'd never stay put, he realized. She'd always choose action.

A minute later, the door opened. She'd changed into the blouse and slacks she'd arrived in, had cleaned the makeup off her face, and wore sensible sandals on her feet.

The request was most likely legit — Francois had looked

ill in the cabaret room — but he followed them anyway and watched them knock on the door to the Le Coqs' cabana. Marie immediately opened the door, still dressed in her showgirl costume, and anxiously let them in.

He glanced at his watch. If he was going to check on Vienna, he'd have to hurry.

CHAPTER **SIXTY-EIGHT**

AS MARIE USHERED her into the cabana, Lucy's attention was elsewhere, still weighing her emotions and actions. Still marveling, really, at what she'd done. She'd made love to Jack, in public, and they'd clicked. God, how they'd clicked. The crowd had vanished. She was now an orgy girl.

But what she'd done was about more than sex, wasn't it? Before she could tumble down that rabbit hole, she found herself being led by an anxious Marie through the cabana's living room and into the bedroom. Francois was in bed, propped up by pillows, under the covers. He was pale, breathing rapidly, with his eyes closed.

Lucy frowned. This could be simple food poisoning, or....

"He is going to be fine, right?" Marie asked.

Lucy picked up his arm and felt his pulse; it was fluttery and faint.

"Francois," she said, "how are you feeling?"

Le Coq lifted his other arm. "There is no cause for concern. Something I ate."

She looked at Marie. "Is he experiencing vomiting? Diarrhea?"

"Several times," Marie said. "That is hopeful, right?"

Possibly. As if on cue, Le Coq jerked upright and lurched out of bed. Marie and Lucy helped him to the bathroom, where he violently retched into the toilet.

Behind them, Natasha paled and said, "Boris and I will wait in the living room."

For a long minute, Lucy and Marie waited for Francois to recover. Lucy ran a washcloth under the faucet and handed it to him. After a minute, he gestured for help, and they guided him back to bed.

"I told my wife," Francois said, looking at Lucy once he'd settled back in, "I am suffering from food poisoning. My body is violently expelling the intruder. I have asked for ginger ale and crackers. When I am done eliminating whatever it is that must be eliminated, I will have the ginger ale and crackers and slowly recover."

Marie looked to her for confirmation. The diagnosis was reasonable, given the symptoms, but not the only possibility.

"A good doctor doesn't self-diagnose," Lucy said thoughtfully. "In this case, however, I believe you've identified the most likely cause, as well as a reasonable path to recovery, but I'm concerned about dehydration. You may need an IV to help rehydrate."

"If it comes to that, then fine." Le Coq leaned back into the pillow. "I would like to rest, until the next bout."

"Of course." Lucy gestured to Marie, and they went into the living room. She closed the bedroom door, and Boris and Natasha approached.

"So he will be fine?" Marie asked.

"Food poisoning is the most likely cause," Lucy said. "Someone needs to watch over him. In the next few hours, he will experience more vomiting and diarrhea. He may become lightheaded as he becomes more dehydrated."

"I will watch him," Marie said immediately.

"Do you know my cabana?" Lucy asked. "I want you to call me right away if anything changes. Anything. I'll return in an hour to check on him."

"Yes, of course."

"Marie, would you like someone to assist you?" Natasha asked.

"No, I will be fine. But thank you. I will call you right away if I do."

They all stood there awkwardly until Marie said again, "Thank you all so much. I'll call you if anything changes."

Marie escorted them to the door and closed it.

Natasha turned to Boris. "See? Indigestion. The person I'm more worried about is Prince Ali."

Lucy looked up sharply. "Prince Ali?"

"He's come down with a cold. A bad one, from the looks of it."

Boris frowned but didn't argue.

"Very well," he said. "Would you mind if we pay him a visit, Ms. Keen?"

CHAPTER
SIXTY-NINE

JACK FOUND HIS target by the pool. She was sitting by herself in a lounger, facing away from the courtyard and staring over the edge of the infinity pool toward the bay.

"Hey, you," he said. He pulled up a chair next to hers and sat down.

Vienna didn't respond. For a moment, silence hung in the air.

"I don't get it." She turned onto her side to face him. Tears stained her cheeks. "You've always had your secrets. You've always had your walls. I've always known that. I just thought that if I waited, if I was patient...."

Sadness welled up inside him. No matter who he got close to, there was so much he couldn't share.

Vienna hadn't shared either. His buddy, Vienna, a girl who was fun and free-spirited and sexually thrilling, had been holding back too, and he hadn't seen it because he hadn't wanted to.

She was his friend. He owed her more than denial and deception. He owed her a measure of truth.

"I don't get it either," he said, turning to face her. "It snuck up on me. Took me by surprise."

She reached over and ran a hand over his cheek, then leaned over and kissed him — a kiss of tenderness, of regret.

At exactly that moment, of course, Lucy passed by with Natasha and Boris.

Vienna pulled away. Her hand left his face.

He sat up. Lucy was looking at him with narrowed eyes.

"Lucy...."

"There you are," she said coolly. "Don't mind me. Natasha asked me to take a look at Prince Ali. Apparently, he's also ill."

"I'll go with you."

"Don't worry yourself," Lucy said. "You and Vienna go back to whatever it is you were doing."

She turned to leave, then paused and looked back at him. "I've just been with Francois Le Coq. It appears he has food poisoning. If he does, he'll begin to recover in the next few hours. His wife Marie is staying with him."

She turned and marched away, Boris and Natasha in her wake.

With a sigh, he glanced back at Vienna, who was giving him a sad smile.

"She's really gotten to you, hasn't she?"

He heard the catch in her voice.

"Yeah," he said, "she has."

"What is it? What has she got?"

"She's...." He found himself struggling to find the words. "She's never gonna cut me slack. She's gonna make me work for it and keep me on my toes."

"Shouldn't love be easy?" He saw the pain and doubt in her eyes.

"For other people, maybe, but not for me. I need hard. I need the challenge. I'm wired that way. Always have been."

"I can … I can be — "

"No." He put a finger to her lips. "Don't. You're not that girl. The great, undiscovered truth about Vienna Hastings is that, underneath the beautiful, sophisticated, savvy celebrity trendsetter, there's a warm, generous, giving woman who's ready to fall in love, easily and completely and happily and forever, with the right guy."

He pulled back his hand and said, "I came here to check on you."

"To check on me?"

"I was thinking about Pedro's party in Bali."

"That was bad, but I'm a big girl now. All grown up."

"Can I take you to your cabana?"

She shook her head. "I'm going to stay here and stare at the sky. I can't remember the last time I experienced this kind of solitude, completely cut off from everyone. It's refreshing. Makes me think."

"You're sure?"

"I'll be okay. Really. Go."

CHAPTER **SEVENTY**

BACK IN THE cabana, Jack whipped out his laptop. Midnight was fast approaching.

Time to choose which character to hijack for his rendezvous in Gang Bang. With Dick Hould dead, he couldn't use Ming, nor could he use Messalina. Erica had been in the cabaret room when he and Lucy had left, but she could be anywhere now, preparing to compete.

That left Borlando: the lamest and least powerful of the characters. If, as Lucy had indicated, Prince Ali wasn't feeling well, then Borlando was the likeliest option.

The phone rang and he picked up. "Hello?"

"Jack, it's me," Lucy said.

"What's up?"

"I'm in Prince Ali's room. He has a cold. A chest cold."

He heard the worry in Lucy's voice. In the background, Ali coughed and said, "Jack, I'm fine. Just a cold."

"Anything I should worry about?" he asked.

"Probably not. Probably just a cold."

She was right, of course, but even on the off chance....

"I'll stay here with him for a bit," she said, addressing his unspoken concern. "We'll keep him safe and sound in his room."

"Call me if you need anything."

He hung up. Two people were now sick, one with early symptoms of phosphorin exposure. But Francois's symptoms were different from Ali's, which perhaps reduced the odds, by a bit, that Ali had been exposed to phosphorin.

Either way, they wouldn't know until more time had passed. Speaking of time.... He glanced at his watch. He needed to call Calhoun. Even with nothing definite to report, she'd want the update.

As he reached for the phone, he heard a knock at the door. He stood, moved silently to the door, and listened. Another knock sounded, followed by a familiar voice saying, very loudly, "Jack, open door."

His drunk-ass host, here at exactly the wrong time. How would he get rid of him?

He opened the door. Sergei stood there, arms outstretched, a martini in each hand.

"Jack! I bring you drink." His host pushed his way past him. "Special martini made specially for Synkonos. We use your favorite vodka."

Sergei held the drink out, waiting for him to take it. Alcohol was not on his agenda, not with a Gang Bang fight looming.

But did he have a choice?

"Dude," he said, accepting the drink, "why aren't you with the others?"

"Why aren't you? You said you will come back, but you don't, so I decide to find you." He held his glass out. "I propose toast. To friendship!"

"To friendship."

They clinked glasses, and Sergei downed his drink in a long, single gulp. Jack pretended to take a big swig from his.

"I have request," Sergei said in a quieter voice. "We are friends now, yes? I want advice. I want to experience what you experience, use your life as example for me to live my life. You understand, yes?"

"Sure...." Midnight was just minutes away. He needed to get rid of this guy.

Sergei set his empty glass down, a hint of self-consciousness surfacing. But his hesitation didn't last for long. Whatever embarrassment he might be feeling couldn't withstand the obsession driving him forward. He'd devised an extravagantly themed party weekend just to get to know Mr. Jack Ford, and he wasn't going to hold back now.

"I think about what you say this morning, at pool," Sergei said. "I think about it all day. I too am ready for dildo lady to attack my ass."

What the fuck?

"What?"

"Yes, I am ready."

With a sinking feeling, Jack flashed to where this was going.

"But I still have fear of damage," Sergei said. "I need to be brave. So I need to see."

Yep. Fuck fuck fuck.

"I want to see your asshole. Inspect for damage."

There it was. He stood stock-still, staring at his bizarre, obsessed host. For four long seconds, his mind played out three different responses and rejected each one, leaving only one option.

Hell, he'd done worse.

"Buddy," he said, "for you, anything."

He unbuttoned his tuxedo pants and let them drop to the floor, then slipped out of his boxer briefs. He fell back on the bed, raised and spread his legs, and grabbed the back of his knees. As his asscheeks parted, his puckered asshole stared Sergei in the face.

"Dude," Jack said, "examine away."

Sergei approached, awe lighting his face. "Jack, every part of you is truly perfect."

"Don't be shy. Get in closer."

As his host nosed in, Jack grabbed hold of Sergei's head with both hands.

"Come on. Closer."

He moved his hands to Sergei's neck. The move would need to be subtle — invisible to the video cameras he knew were recording his actions from multiple angles.

With his fingers, he slowly pressed down on Sergei's neck, held the pressure for two seconds, then released it. Sergei shook his head to shake off the sudden dizziness.

"Hey, you okay, buddy?" Jack asked.

"Am fine," Sergei said.

"The drinks are getting to you."

"Am fine."

Jack applied pressure again. Sergei's eyes lost focus.

He released the pressure. Sergei recovered, but was now very unsteady.

"Whoa, there," Jack said. "Let's lay you down."

He jumped to his feet and laid Sergei on the bed.

"I am fine," Sergei said.

"Let's make sure." He hopped on top of Sergei and leaned in, as if to examine Sergei's face, and again pressed into his neck. This time, when Sergei dropped off, Jack kept the pressure on for ten seconds.

"Sure thing, buddy," Jack said. "You just need to sleep it off a bit."

Sergei started snoring.

Good. With luck, he'd be out for an hour, maybe two.

He sighed. The shit he had to do to complete a mission. He stood, took off his tuxedo shirt and hung it up in the closet, grabbed a pair of jeans, and slipped them on.

He sensed, rather than heard, another presence in the room, and turned around. He relaxed when he saw Lucy at the door, a pained look on her face. Clearly, she'd been watching.

"You are shameless," she said. There was no anger in her voice this time, only resignation.

"How's Ali?" he asked, turning to his laptop and powering it on.

"Not good. I came to get my medical kit. I need to get back to him."

"And Le Coq?"

"Not sure," she said, doubt in her voice. "We'll know more soon. By the way, what you did? You know how dangerous that is, right?"

She was talking about the carotid compression. Jack just looked at her.

"Okay, fine," she said, taking her bag from the closet and heading back to the door. "Good luck."

He looked at his watch as she left. Two minutes until midnight.

No time to call Calhoun. He clicked on his Gang Bang app and logged in using Borlando's credentials.

He opened a password-entry program written by the geeks at Special Exploits and typed in every variation of "Synkonos Forever" he could think of — every spelling, every combination, with and without punctuation. The program would enter each possible password far more quickly than he could type them in himself, and with the race on, every second was critical.

Thirty seconds before midnight, his laptop identified a wi-fi network: "Synkonos."

He clicked it, then pointed the password program to it, and held his finger over the Enter key.

Five seconds. Four, three, two, one. Midnight.

He hit Enter.

The first password — rejected. So was the second. Ditto the third, the fourth, the fifth.

Shit. Had he gotten the clue wrong?

Sixth, seventh, eighth variation — all rejected.

He rewound the song in his head, focusing in on the intonation, on the emotion, and on exactly how Robbie and Carrie had belted it out.

He typed in: "Synkonos4Evah!"

A message appeared: "Congratulations, time traveler! You are leaving the Las Vegas of 1965 and returning to the year 2015."

CHAPTER
SEVENTY-ONE

WITH A CLICK, he entered Gang Bang.

The monitor zoomed him over buildings and through crowds until he landed in front of a corner cafe. He dashed into a nearby alley, stopped in front of a stretch of blank brick wall, and said, "Zero Alpha Seven Five Three Three."

The Weapons Bazaar message board materialized in front of him.

One final step: the pass phrase for the instance.

"Alas," he said, "regardless of their doom, the little victims play! No sense have they of ills to come, nor care beyond today."

Immediately, he was thrust up from the alley, through the blue sky, and into the weightlessness of space, hurtling toward a bright light beyond the sun to the sound of metal under pressure that grew louder until, with a quiet *pop*, he was back in the red auction room. Yoko stood at the podium. Messalina, seated in one of the leather chairs, gave him a look of icy malevolence.

Yoko giggled. "Young Borlando, our second finalist? What a lovely surprise!"

Behind Yoko, the curtains on the stage opened to reveal a banner that read: Messalina vs. Borlando: The Final Showdown!

The auction room transformed. The red carpet became a green artificial-turf playing field. The walls vanished, and in their place, a stadium arose, complete with screaming fans, loudspeakers blaring music, and a blimp in the sky that flashed, "M vs. B! Wow!"

"Welcome, honored competitors," Yoko said. "Welcome to the final round of our joyous competition to win the right to purchase that most valuable, yet dangerous, of biological substances: phosphorin!"

She giggled, then said, "I am having so much fun I must pinch myself. Would our esteemed competitors like to know what they must do to win the day?"

"Yes," Messalina purred, her Whip of Woe flitting sinuously over her body. "Please."

"Your task: Kidnap the beautiful Princess Hope from the magic kingdom of Banishope on the shores of the Sea of Phyre. As I'm sure you both know, the virgin princess is the daughter of the powerful and terrible King Eeval Keneval. She is beloved far and wide for her tireless crusade to bring integrity and lawful behavior to Gangland. Many say she is the only protection Gangland has against her father's insatiable appetite for blood and plunder. How would Gangland survive, they say, were King Eeval not restrained by his wise and gracious daughter?"

Borlando shrank in his seat. What Yoko wanted was impossible. The princess was heavily guarded, and pissing off the King was tantamount to a death sentence.

Messalina frowned. "I have a relationship — business and

personal — with King Eeval. Kidnapping his daughter would pose complications for me."

Yoko giggled. "I know! That's what makes this challenge so much fun!"

Messalina sighed. "What else is required?"

"You are ever so clever, Miss Messalina. Indeed, the kidnapping is just the first of your adventures! After snatching this saintly young woman from her garden sanctuary in King Eeval's impregnable castle fortress, you will battle a path through the king's army of zombie marauders and bring her to the Gang Bang Arena. There, in front of a sea of concertgoers who paid top dollar to see V3, you will take the stage and seize control of the microphone from Strike, the lead singer. At that point, you will receive further instructions."

Messalina did not look happy.

Borlando cocked his head. "Wait, V3 is playing Gangland?"

Yoko laughed with amusement. "Ah, Mr. Borlando, your wide-eyed freshness is such a treat. Yes, V3 is playing Gangland — a big coup for the maker of the game, don't you agree? The biggest entertainers in the real world, playing live and virtually in Gang Bang. Ever so cutting-edge."

Messalina whirled on Borlando. "I cannot believe you're asking about a *band*. Are you incapable of focusing? The important point is: this challenge is too much. The difficulty factor is off the charts!"

Man, this dominatrix's arrogance was annoying.

"Shut the fuck up," he said.

"You insolent maggot," she hissed. "I will crush you."

Yoko held out her hand. "My honored contestants, I do so hope we will see more of your delightful banter during the challenge itself. Miss Messalina, I would be devastated if you were to allow your impressive self-confidence to abandon you now."

Messalina shot Yoko a sharp glance but said nothing.

"I have tried my best to provide a challenge that reflects the high caliber of you, our final contestants. You are both ruthless and determined. The question is: Who wants to win more?"

The challengers absorbed their seemingly undoable task.

Finally, Borlando asked, "Rules?"

"Only one," Yoko said. "You will wear a Broadcast Brooch at all times. The brooch will allow us to share every aspect of your fantastic adventures. We will share your triumphs and feel your pain!"

Two pieces of jewelry appeared in midair in front of Messalina and Borlando. In the center of each was a red mirror, surrounded by an ornate wreath of writhing, silver snakes. Like mosquitoes, the brooches hovered erratically, awaiting Yoko's signal.

"Do I have your agreement?"

Borlando and Messalina nodded, and the brooches swooped onto them. They heard a sucking sound as the brooches adhered to their clothes.

"There are no other rules?" Messalina asked. The tip of her whip flickered around the edges of the brooch, testing its grip, and deftly avoided the lunges of the tiny, angry snakes.

"Correct," Yoko said.

Messalina eyed Borlando and shifted in her chair. Her hand tightened on her whip.

"To be clear," Yoko said, "the challenge has not yet started."

"But of course," Messalina said, her hand relaxing.

"Resources?" Borlando asked.

"Anything and everything. Any final questions before we begin?"

Borlando and Messalina shook their heads.

Yoko giggled with anticipation. "This is going to be so much fun!"

A sportscasting booth appeared around her, along with a play-by-play announcer — standard-issue, middle-aged, white, male — wearing a TV-ready blue suit and an unconvincing toupee.

"Welcome, Larry!" Yoko said to her colleague in the booth, doing her best to take on the rhythms and intonations of a sports commentator. "A match for the ages. Larry, you've called some of the biggest games in Gang Bang sports. Who has the edge going in?"

Larry said, "I've witnessed some close matches in my time in this seat, Yoko, but this isn't one of them. Messalina has the clear edge. Her experience and skill will be tough for young Borlando to top."

"Is there any way a Level 2 player like Borlando can hope to defeat a Level 47 player like Messalina?"

"Only one way I can see, Yoko, and I doubt young Borlando has the experience or savvy to pull it off."

Borlando looked at Larry and Yoko with exasperation. "Guys, I'm right here. I can hear every word."

"I know!" Yoko said with a giggle. "That's what makes this challenge even more fun!"

She turned to her cohort in the announcing booth. "But enough sparkling conversation. It's time to begin."

With a click, a timer appeared in the lower left corner of the screen.

"You will have one real-world hour. Starting … now!"

Borlando vanished with a quiet pop, a fraction of a second before Messalina's whip sliced through the spot where he'd been, burning the air with its heat.

Messalina grunted in frustration. With a pop, she too vanished.

"Borlando battles Messalina!" Larry intoned. "Can the scrappy newbie overcome impossible odds to outplay his vicious, seasoned opponent?"

Yoko laughed. "Oh, Larry, I am ever so pleased to be part of this wonderful experience! So much death and mayhem, so little time!"

"Speaking of time, young Borlando is wasting none of it," Larry said. "He's materialized in front of the Hollywood Hillz Casino."

Larry and Yoko watched as Borlando walked past the line of characters at the entrance, heading straight for the massive troll manning the velvet rope.

"Tell your boss I have an offer he can't refuse," Borlando told the troll.

"Back of the line, newb," the troll growled.

"I have the secret phrase: Party Till You Die."

The troll's eyes narrowed. He spoke softly into his hand and frowned with surprise as he listened. He unfastened the velvet rope. "I've been told to escort you inside."

He marched Borlando across the vast casino floor, past endless tables of players, to a door marked "Manager."

The door opened to a hulking, fearsome creature that was half-man, half-ogre. Wulf Avenger, the powerful casino boss. He towered over Borlando.

With shocking speed, Wulf grabbed Borlando and pulled him inside, slamming the door shut.

Borlando pointed to the brooch. A warning.

Who was inhabiting his Wulf persona? Commander Grant? One of the Special Exploits techies? Probably not Calhoun, given her lack of familiarity with the Gang Bang environment.

"The deal we discussed," Borlando said.

Wulf stared at Borlando without moving a muscle.

"It's now. The deal is now."

Wulf turned to his desk and picked up the phone. "Everyone, get in here now. We have a job."

Within seconds, characters began popping in. Jack knew them well. They were his Hollywood Hillz pals, his gang.

First in: his starlet pal Tina's persona, the ogre Berserker, who was so huge he had to squat to avoid the ceiling. Next in: the dashing swashbuckler, Dorian the Dreaded, pirate and hedonist, and the persona of his agent buddy, Ed. Finally, in popped a stout, middle-aged woman, who was conservatively clad in a dark dress and carried an umbrella, a purse, and an air of mild disapproval: Edna May Barker, governess and bodyguard extraordinaire, the persona of Billy, co-owner of his Naked Lunch nightclub.

Watching his gang through the computer monitor, Jack felt a twinge of guilt. Given the difficulty level of what awaited them, chances were good that he and his pals' characters would get slaughtered. All of them would have to start over, with newbie characters, and fight and scrape and battle all over again to get back to their current levels.

Edna May, Dorian, and Berserker examined Borlando with open curiosity.

Berserker turned to Wulf. "A job, boss?"

Before Wulf could respond, they heard the static of an open microphone. Larry's voice filled the room.

"Young Borlando has done his homework," the sportscaster said. "When I alluded to a possible strategy, Yoko, this is what I had in mind."

Wulf grabbed Borland by the throat. "Who is that?"

Borlando pointed to the brooch on his chest. "Our adventures are being broadcast. We have an audience."

Wulf tightened his grip. "Not a word about our deal."

"Of course not," Borlando managed to gasp.

Yoko's girlish voice echoed throughout the room. "Rent-a-Gang! And what an excellent choice Borlando has made! The

Hollywood Hillz gang is one of the richest, most powerful gangs in Gangland."

"Their powers become his," Larry said. "His powers become theirs. With one bold move, Borlando's given himself a fighting chance."

"Has the lovely Miss Messalina made a move yet, Larry?"

"Believe it or not, Yoko, the answer is — no. Messalina appears to be — meditating!"

"Does that mean her real-world controller has hit the pause button and stepped away from the game? What an unfortunate moment for a bathroom break."

"Could be," Larry said. "Or we might be witnessing a new strategy entirely."

"Oh, Larry! I am so very excited! I feel like I am about to burst with anticipation!"

Dorian pointed to the brooch on Borlando's chest. "Who are those bozos?"

Yoko's giggles filled the room. "We are the bozos whose tune you are about to dance to."

Dorian raised an eyebrow and was about to retort when Wulf removed his hand from Borlando's throat.

Wulf asked, "What's the target?"

Borlando rubbed his neck gingerly, then waved his hand. A map of Gangland appeared in the air in front of them. With a few hand swoops, he narrowed the focus to a rugged, hostile landscape in the far north — a land where few dared to venture, and for good reason.

He narrowed the focus further, zooming in on a massive castle, dark and craggy, that rose from the center of a vast, open plain.

Dorian shook his head with dismay. "King Eeval's fortress? We're going after him?"

"Nope," Borlando said. "We're kidnapping his daughter, Princess Hope."

"Oh fuck."

Berserker laughed a deep, rasping chuckle of amusement.

Edna May's expression of mild disapproval turned into a deep frown. "We can't group-pop into the castle. The king's protections are too great."

Borlando nodded. "We'll need to walk in."

Dorian looked incredulous. "Walk in?"

He snatched the map from Borlando and widened the focus to include the ring of barren plain surrounding the fortress, then zoomed in again to show what inhabited the area: Zombie personas. Thousands of them. Abominations of the game, they were characters abandoned by the real-life humans who'd created them. Lurching without purpose, they mindlessly sought what they no longer had: contact with a real-life person.

The zombies were sickening to look at — empty shells with vacant eyes, slack mouths, and rotting skin — with a primal, desperate need to experience, if only through the annihilation of another character, the interaction with a real human they'd once had but lost.

Dorian turned to Wulf. "Really?"

"Yes." Wulf turned to Berserker. "We'll need ten. Bring them in, two at a time."

Berserker grinned and popped out, then seconds later, he was back with two writhing zombies under his arms. He dropped them to the floor. Slowly, unsteadily, the zombies stood up. The scent of live characters washed over them. Moaning hungrily, they reached out, mouths open, and groaned desperately.

Without hesitation, Wulf and his gang sliced away, ignoring the zombies' pained moans as they stripped flesh from the creatures in great tearing chunks.

Yoko laughed merrily as Wulf and his gang applied the

zombies' wet, gloppy skin to their bodies. "Oh, Larry. What fun this is!"

Larry didn't sound as enthusiastic. "An impressively … disgusting tactic."

Berserker brought in more zombies, and then more still, until their zombie-skin disguises were complete.

Wulf turned to his gang. "Now."

Borlando, Edna May, Dorian, and Berserker joined him in a circle.

They placed their hands together in the center of the circle and —

CHAPTER SEVENTY-TWO

POP!

They were on the plain, surrounded by zombies — thousands of foul, horrific shells that stumbled aimlessly and bumped into each other at random.

A few nearby zombies noticed their arrival and swung toward them, noses in the air, sniffing for the telltale aroma of real-life energy.

But the strips of freshly harvested zombie flesh covering their bodies were doing the trick of masking their scents.

Wulf and his gang lurched their way through the army of zombies to King Eeval's fortress. A bed of flowering plants lined the castle walls, incongruously beautiful. The work, no doubt, of Princess Hope.

Wulf turned to Edna May. "Invisibility shower."

"With that one here," she said, pointing to Borlando, "we'll have ten minutes, tops."

She opened her umbrella and the gang crowded under it. Above the umbrella, raindrops of light-scattering invisibility fell. Within seconds, the umbrella and the gang beneath it had vanished.

Wulf said to Dorian, "We need to slip through the wall."

They made their way over the flower bed to the fortress walls. Carefully, Dorian ran his hand slowly over the roughly hewn blocks.

Yoko said, "Larry, this is fascinating! Dorian is famous throughout Gangland for his ability to sneak in anywhere. Now, for the first time, we get to see how. "

Dorian shot Wulf another look. "Dude...."

Wulf held his stare. With a frustrated shake of his head, Dorian returned to his task. His hand stopped over a tiny crack in the mortar, then seemed to disappear into the wall.

"Hands together," he said.

The gang grabbed Dorian's other hand in the center of the circle, and Dorian muttered an incantation. Their bodies began to — there was only one way to describe it — liquefy. Their forms held their shape, sort of, but jiggled like gelatin in a stiff wind.

Berserker gasped as his form drained away, first his head, followed by his legs and arms, vanishing like water poured from a glass bottle, his essence flowing into Dorian's hand, then moving through Dorian and into the wall.

Above them, Larry said, "Ingenious technique. Turning oneself into liquid, then flowing through the tiny cracks in a wall to get through to the other side."

After the last of Berserker passed through Dorian, Wulf drained next, and then Borlando. As Borlando flowed, he saw himself in a stretched and distorted fashion, passing into Dorian's outstretched hand, then up his arm, through his upper torso, and then down his other arm and into the wall. The crack in the mortar was micro-thin and the journey was like a descent into a jagged, claustrophobic cave. Dim light appeared ahead. He found himself breathing a sigh of relief as he flowed out of the crack and into Dorian's hand, and from there he filled up, like water in a vase, into his familiar shape.

Edna May filled up shortly after him, followed by Dorian himself.

As Edna May reopened her umbrella to cloak them, the gang pulled out their BangBlaster guns.

"Set to Dechloroplastize," Wulf said.

Quietly, they made their way into the heart of the castle, Edna May's umbrella enabling them to move without detection down the stone corridors and past the armies of guards, maidens, and servants who served the king.

They reached the center of the fortress and found themselves in a courtyard open to the sun and sky, with a beautiful garden alive with a profusion of flowers and plants. The Goodness Garden, home of Princess Hope.

In the garden, they made their way to an open pavilion, and there, with her handmaidens, they found their target: Princess Hope, the kind, beautiful, and gracious protector of Gangland.

She and her handmaidens were weaving "Hope Baskets," which each had the power to protect and feed a gang of four for as long as the gang was committed to the "Hope Covenant" and its key promise: "Play nice."

Wulf unhooked a glowing green grenade from his belt and tossed it high into the air. With a silent whoosh, the grenade — a dechloroplasting bomb capable of killing any life that received its sustenance from light — exploded into a cloud of powder and settled over the plants in the garden. The plants writhed and even screamed. The princess looked up, shocked. Anger flashed in her eyes. Roots rose out from the ground, searching for the invisible intruders.

With their BangBlasters, the gang took aim at the roots and fired. Desperately, the roots sought to avoid the blasts, but couldn't withstand the Hollywood Hillz gang's experience and skill.

In seconds, it was over. Edna May folded her umbrella, revealing the gang to Princess Hope, who stood her ground and regarded them bravely.

"Reinforcements are on their way," she said.

"We're not done," Wulf said. He pulled out another grenade, this one the color of iron, and tossed it into the air, where it exploded into another cloud of powder that settled over the dead plants and roots and vines, transforming them into metallic versions of themselves.

"Robo dust!" Yoko said with a giggle. "So clever!"

The vines that had once protected Princess Hope were now under Wulf's control and slithered up and around her, trapping her. A single vine wound around her neck, but didn't squeeze, its warning inescapable.

"Tell your reinforcements to stand down," Wulf said.

Hope grimaced, but nodded her assent.

Dorian turned to Wulf. "Boss, I've tried to keep quiet, but what the fuck? Why are we here? Kidnapping King Eeval's daughter is so not in our wheelhouse."

Borlando stepped toward Dorian and said, "Your boss and I have a deal. He may not be happy about it, but a deal's a deal."

"Only until we decide it's off," Dorian shot back. "Stealing the princess? Way bad karma. Maybe we de-gang you, elf boy. Toss you to the head-munchers."

A not-unreasonable option, given the circumstances.

Edna May looked at Wulf. "We have a good thing going at the casino. A really good thing."

Wulf surveyed his gang. Clearly, they trusted him. Just as clearly, they needed his reassurance.

"The deal was for intel," he said. "The king is planning a move against us."

Berserker frowned. "But he promised his daughter he'd hold off on attacks as long as she remains a virgin."

"She's not a virgin."

"What?"

"What?" cried Princess Hope.

"Elf boy tell you that?" Dorian said.

Everyone looked at Borlando, who turned to the princess and shrugged. "Sorry, babe. You fell for the wrong guy."

"You?" Dorian said, amazed. "Princess Hope and … you?"

"I haven't had sex!" Hope cried. "Certainly not with him!"

"But you have had sex," Wulf said. He said it as a statement.

"No," Hope said quickly, too quickly, and the gang sensed it.

In that second, the universe shifted. Wulf was right. The princess was lying.

"I can prove I'm pure," Hope said in an effort to regain the upper hand.

"No, you can't."

"I can show you my hymen — my intact hymen. I have nothing to hide."

"That trick doesn't work," Berserker said, "not even in the real world."

The princess took a deep breath. "Please. This is important for everyone, including you. You may think my father knows, but he doesn't. I'm sure of it. As long as he doesn't know, Gangland is safe."

Borlando shook his head. "Sorry, princess" — he pointed to the brooch — "no secrets here. Your sex life just became everybody's business."

From the announcing booth, Larry said, "A shocking turn of events, Yoko. If King Eeval hears about this, then — "

"Then Gangland is fucked! Completely and totally

fucked!" Yoko said with a giggle. "Oh, I must tell you, Larry, I am enjoying myself so much!"

"Truly," Larry said, "Young Borlando is shaking things up in spectacular fashion."

"And what of his opponent, the delightful Miss Messalina?"

"Frankly, Yoko, I'm perplexed. After meditating, she visited an electrical substation and engaged in a civilized, non-violent discussion with an engineer about conductivity. Now she's in the back room of a repair shop, talking shop with a nerd."

"A nerd?"

"Yes, Yoko, an ordinary nerd — glasses, t-shirt, bad posture, pudgy body, no girlfriend, hasn't showered in days. A typical example of nerdus patheticus. According to his Gang Bang character profile, he spends nearly all of his time in Gangland fixing things — televisions, radios, speakers, you name it."

"What are they talking about?"

"Something about sound. She just placed his pale, trembling hand on her breast. She's using her sex appeal to open him up."

Yoko giggled. "Nerds — so easy to manipulate."

In the garden, Hope looked around, bewildered. "Who is that talking?"

Borlando pointed to his broadcast brooch. "Our play-by-play announcers."

"A game?" Hope said, aghast. "This is part of a *game*?"

Yoko giggled again, very loudly. "Yes, Princess Hope. A game to end all games. A game like no other!"

CHAPTER SEVENTY-THREE

BORLANDO FROWNED. Yoko's delight for destruction seemed excessive, unbalanced, even manic. The sooner he got the phosphorin away from that crazy schoolgirl, the better.

Wulf turned to his gang. "We can't use zombie skin to get out of here — what we have isn't fresh enough. Suggestions?"

The gang paused. In normal circumstances, zombies weren't much worry. Recently abandoned characters had trouble standing for more than a minute or two — a single step was an accomplishment — but gradually, as the zombies ate insects, roadside carrion, and each other, they gained strength and a measure of motor coordination. Their first live-character kill — their first connection to the energy of a real-life human — gave them an automatic eight-level boost. At that point, they could shuffle and lurch over long distances, and even, for a second or two, move quickly.

King Eeval's zombie army had adapted further. Unlike most zombies, they demonstrated awareness of one another. They attacked cooperatively. Some had the presence of mind to carry weapons. A few of the higher-level zombies had even developed the ability to fly, or at least rise in a controlled fashion. Their aero skills weren't perfect. While they could float up with ease, getting back down to the ground required them to lapse into a state of suspended animation. Only then, and only very slowly, could they drift back to the ground.

Somehow, King Eeval had control over thousands of them.

"I heard a new theory," Borlando said to Wulf. "About how the king controls his zombies."

"Explain."

"The theory is that he doesn't actually control them, except to keep them confined to the ring of land surrounding his fortress."

Wulf grunted. "A spell?"

"Or a repellent."

"How do you explain their behavioral advances? Their ability to organize?"

"Evolution," Borlando said. "Confined to this small ring of territory, packed in like sardines, with almost no food...."

Wulf turned to Edna May. "Analyze the land surrounding the zombie zone. Identify any materials or substances that might be keeping the zombies corralled within."

He opened his gear bag and pulled out a small round globe that glowed bright yellow.

Hope gasped. "Is that...?"

"Yes," Wulf said.

The globe was a weapon like no other: a tiny sun. The size of a baseball, it glowed a warm yellow. He tossed it into the center of the garden then pressed two buttons on his watch.

"Two minutes," he announced to the Hillz crew.

Dorian paled. "For real?"

The tiny sun began to change color — first orange, then

red — and grew ten times in size, then one hundred times in size.

Berserker tossed the princess, still wrapped in robotic vines, over his shoulder, and the Hillz gang raced through the fortress at top speed, blasting away guards who tried to stop them.

"Supernova in ten seconds!" Wulf said. "Faster!"

Behind them, the sun, now a red giant the size of a house, dimmed just for a second.

Boom!

Instantly, the Garden of Hope was obliterated. Wulf, Borlando, and the Hillz crew raced out of the fortress as the supernova consumed the castle from within.

"Faster!" Wulf yelled. "We need to get out of the range of the black hole!"

From the announcing booth, Larry said, "Whoa!"

"Indeed!" Yoko said. "Such fantastic violence!"

The supernova began collapsing on itself. Everyone felt the pull of the suck-back. The rubble of King Eeval's fortress was compressed into an ever-tinier ball of matter, into what could only be described as a black pinpoint.

The transformation took only seconds. Where once the mighty fortress of King Eeval Keneval stood, a zone of emptiness remained.

Standing at the edge of the zone, Borlando could feel the black hole's pull.

"The weapon will lose power in three minutes," Wulf said, glancing at his watch. "Until it does, we can't group-pop out of here."

"Bad news, boss," Edna May said. "Analysis of the fields surrounding the castle indicates the zombies are indeed controlled by a repellent — the repellent found in the pollen of the flowers that grew in Princess Hope's garden."

"The garden you just destroyed," Princess Hope said.

Borlando gulped. He looked across the field. The force of the supernova's blast had knocked the zombies down, but they were starting to regain their feet. Driven by their insatiable hunger for live-character energy, they lurched and stumbled toward them.

"How long before they reach us?" Borlando asked.

"Ninety seconds," Berserker said.

Wulf snapped his fingers. From the far edge of the plain, an armada of hovercrafts flew over the zombies and headed toward them.

Zombies rose to intercept, but when they reached to touch the crafts, they found themselves swiping through thin air.

"The old hologram trick," Larry said. "Excellent."

The airborne zombies screamed in frustration and lapsed into suspended animation. But instead of drifting down, the zombies were rapidly pulled down by lines tethered to their ankles. The zombies on the ground were reeling them in like kites on a string.

"Clever!" Yoko said.

Amidst the armada of holographic hovercrafts, Borlando knew that one of the crafts, owned by the Casino, was real. At Wulf's command, it attempted to clear a path through a sky now littered with rising zombies. It zoomed back and forth to capture as many zombies — and their tether lines — as possible. After several sweeps, the hovercraft steered skyward, pulling hundreds of zombies with it.

High above the plain, the craft sliced the tethers. The zombies groaned in rage and lapsed into suspended animation. At that elevation, they wouldn't reach ground for hours.

Hundreds of zombies were now out of action, but thousands remained. Too many. No matter how they worked it, they were fucked.

"Can we cover ourselves in fresh zombie flesh?" Berserker asked.

"Too late," Wulf said. "They've already sensed us. We can't hide now."

Unless....

"The black hole has a wormhole, right?" Borlando said.

Wulf frowned. "Inherently unstable. Even if we made it out of this universe, we'd be crushed by the black hole that exists in the other universe."

"But we can escape this universe through the wormhole."

Edna May added, "And use our combined powers to create an instance."

Dorian said, "And because instances exist outside space and time...."

Borlando finished the thought. "The black hole at the end of the wormhole won't touch us."

"You're suggesting we ride a wormhole out of here?" Berserker said. "Boss, that's crazy!"

Wulf looked at his watch. "The wormhole is happening for the next … twenty-seven seconds."

He regarded his gang.

Seconds passed as they looked at each other. Four seconds. Five seconds. Six. No one spoke. The zombie army was almost upon them, their lurches eager and their hungry groans keen with anticipation.

In unison, the gang formed a circle and placed their hands together.

"Now!" Wulf said.

And —

CHAPTER
SEVENTY-FOUR

POP!

They were in utter darkness, yet Borlando felt himself moving at unimaginable speeds.

A pinprick of light appeared in front of him. Like a freight train, the light slammed into him —

— and he found himself in a featureless beige cube the size of a large room. He was floating. The rest of the gang was there too, looking as disoriented as he felt.

Wulf shook his head as if to clear it, then looked at his watch. "Our default instance appears to be intact."

"Holy shit," Dorian said with relief.

"We need tickets to the concert," Borlando said.

"What concert?" Dorian asked.

"V3. We have to bring the princess to the main stage."

Edna May sighed. "This job gets better and better."

Berserker scratched his chin. "The casino bought a block of tickets for promotional purposes."

The gang joined hands, popped out of the instance and into Wulf's office, grabbed the tickets, then popped to the entrance of the Gang Bang Arena, the massive concert and sporting stadium in the center of Gangland.

Inside the arena, V3's latest chart-topping anthem had the crowd on their feet, screaming themselves hoarse as they sang along, word for word, with lead singer Strike.

Wulf scanned the stage with his watch.

"State of the art anti-popping protections," he said. "Suggestions?"

Borlando pushed the princess forward. "Hope and Strike are good friends. She's probably pop-approved. We just have to — "

" — hitch a ride," Dorian finished.

"No!" Princess Hope said. "Not a chance!"

Edna May ran her hand over the princess's forearm. "This won't hurt a bit."

A blue glow appeared over the princess's skin.

"You first," Edna May said to Borlando.

Borlando bent his head over the blue glow and was sucked in. Within seconds, the rest of the gang had done the same.

From inside the glow, Wulf said, "Now."

And *pop!*

Princess Hope materialized on the stage.

Immediately, the audience recognized her and cheered. Strike turned around, and his eyes lit up. He turned back to the arena.

"Everyone, what a wonderful surprise! Give it up for … Princess Hope!"

The stadium roared.

From inside the glow, Wulf said, "Acknowledge your fans, Princess. Play happy."

Assisted by the metallic vines still wrapped around her, the princess raised her arms to the crowd.

"Are you done with this game?" she said through

clenched teeth, a smile frozen on her face. "Do you have what you want?"

"Almost," Borlando said. "Take the microphone from Strike."

Princess Hope reached her hand out for the mic, and Strike handed it to her.

Hidden in the blue glow, Borlando said, "Yoko, we've delivered the princess and have control of the stage."

Yoko's giggle filled the stadium, carried over every sound system in the arena. The audience looked around, puzzled. What was this?

The massive screens surrounding the stage zeroed in on the blue glow covering the princess's forearm.

"Come out, young Borlando!" Yoko said, her girlish voice carrying over the arena. "Join the party. All of you!"

Inside the glow, Borlando found the Hollywood Hillz gang glaring at him.

"What the fuck have you gotten us into?" Dorian said.

"We'll be completely exposed on stage," Edna May said. "We won't be able to pop out."

Wulf frowned but said, "We have no choice."

He pressed his face to the outer edge of the blue glow and was sucked out, rematerializing within seconds on the stage next to the princess.

Berserker shook his fist at Borlando. "If we make it out of this alive, I will hunt you down and kill you. Very, very slowly."

Then he let himself be sucked out, followed by Dorian, Edna May, and finally Borlando.

On the massive screens surrounding the stage, Yoko's image appeared. She was seated next to Larry in the announcer's booth.

"Welcome, inhabitants of Gangland!" Yoko said. "You are all so blessed, for tonight you will bear witness to an ancient ceremony, a cleansing rite so rare and special and shocking that it was banned ages ago!"

From where he stood on the stage, Borlando could tell the audience had no clue what to make of this. Who was the cute little Japanese schoolgirl? What the hell was she talking about?

Yoko's giggle vibrated throughout the arena. "The beautiful Princess Hope is here with her new friends from the Hollywood Hillz gang, led by the one-and-only Wulf Avenger."

From the stage, they heard the audience members murmuring to each other. The princess, friends with the notorious badass Wulf?

"The Hollywood Hillz gang is going to complete a ritual tonight that, I promise you, will change Gangland forever."

Yoko paused to let the tension build. As she opened her mouth to continue, they all heard a sound: a low rumble that turned into a rasp, then a cry, and then a sigh like pressure being released. The sigh increased until it filled the arena and the stage, growing louder and louder until the vibrations began assuming a form. Yes, a form, on the stage.

The shape coalesced into — what was it?

Borlando's eyes widened as he recognized the sinewy shape flashing toward him.

He ducked and cried out, "Whip of Woe!"

The whip nicked his arm, immediately knocking him to the ground. From the slice, a paralytic agent raced over his body, shutting him down inch by inch.

"No!" Borlando gasped as the paralysis inched up his neck.

The whip — or rather, to be precise, the sound-based representation of it — sliced through the Hollywood Hillz gang like butter.

Berserker, the mightiest of fighters, fell like a stone beside him, with a huge, gaping gouge where his left shoulder used to be, his life force draining out of his eyes.

Edna May stared with shock at her mid-section, then watched, in her final seconds of life, as the top half of her body slid off the bottom half.

Dorian looked around wildly, searching for the attacker, then gasped and stared down at his chest as the whip drilled into him from behind, tearing out his heart and crushing it before his dying eyes.

Wulf dove for cover as the Whip of Woe sliced toward him. He feinted left, dipped right, and used all of his skills and experience to stay a millisecond ahead of the whip, but he couldn't escape forever. A single nick on the leg was all it took for Wulf to gasp and fall to the ground, the paralytic agent spreading over him.

Stunned at the carnage, the V3 band members backed away from their instruments and fled the stage.

The sound-based Whip of Woe sizzled in the air and slowly transformed into solid matter. A hand appeared at the end of it, then a slim arm, then a beautiful, curvaceous female body clad in skintight black leather.

"Messalina!" Yoko screamed with delight. "How ever did she do it?"

Larry looked incredulous. "Messalina broke through the anti-pop barriers by transforming into sound!"

"Have you ever seen anything like this, Larry?"

"Never, Yoko. Now we know why Messalina was spending time with that nerd. She was devising a way to bypass the anti-pop security of the main stage!"

Messalina picked up the microphone and turned to the big screens. She bowed to Yoko. "I have control of the main stage. What is the next task?"

Yoko laughed. "Oh, how joyous this challenge is proving to be." She turned her attention to the audience in the arena.

"Ladies and gentlemen, beasts and aliens, you are in for a treat. You will soon bear witness to an event that has never before been witnessed in Gangland.

"Tonight, Miss Messalina will perform — the Ceremony of Surreal Sacrifice!"

A murmur swept through the crowd. What was that? What did it mean? Was this Ceremony part of the show?

Messalina went pale. "You can't mean that."

"Oh, but I do!" Yoko said. "To win the prize, I will have my reward!"

Messalina turned toward the princess and regarded her silently, the Whip of Woe flickering tentatively around her.

"Messalina, please," Princess Hope said. "You've been with my father for years. You can't."

"Please hold your begging for the dramatically appropriate moment, Princess Hope!" Yoko said. "I have not yet finished. Miss Messalina, I will have my reward. I want it delivered to me in a beautiful, red hatbox. Also — very important — I want the box decorated with a big, beautiful, red ribbon. I do so love the color red."

Messalina's whip flickered, as if making up its mind.

From his prone position on the stage, Borlando could feel the whip's paralytic powers fading.

"What the fuck's the Ceremony of Surreal Sacrifice?" he whispered to Wulf. He flexed his fingers. If only he could move his arm....

Wulf grunted and shook his head, warning him to stay silent.

Yoko was still addressing Messalina. "After you complete the sacrifice, you will escape the stadium and deliver me my reward. If you do, the prize will be yours! All yours! Just think of the fun you'll have!"

Messalina turned to Princess Hope. "I hope you understand, it's nothing personal. I actually kind of like you."

"What are you saying?" the princess said, aghast.

"I'm saying real trumps virtual. Sorry."

In the announcing booth, Larry said, "Yoko, my Gang Bang mythology is a bit rusty, so can you tell us: What is the Ceremony of Surreal Sacrifice?"

"A lot of mumbo-jumbo, Larry, but with a big climax!"

"What kind of climax?"

"A sacrifice so shocking, so vivid, so painful, Larry, that it feels real, though of course it's not! Something unexpected and mind-bending!"

"Can you share specifics, Yoko?"

Yoko leaned over and whispered in Larry's ear.

"Holy crap," Larry said. "I figured when I got this gig you'd be a — "

"A what, Larry?" Yoko asked, turning toward him, her eyes flashing red.

Larry swallowed. "I knew you'd be a … a clever game-maker, Yoko. But your … inventiveness is truly exceptional."

"Why thank you, Larry. Thank you!"

On the stage, Messalina aimed her whip at the princess.

The Whip of Woe slowly wrapped itself around the princess's neck.

"Please," Princess Hope whispered.

Messalina shook her head. The Whip of Woe started squeezing.

"Larry," Yoko said, "do you think Messalina will give the princess the chance to utter a few final words?"

"I couldn't even begin to hazard a guess, Yoko. Nothing — I repeat nothing — about this matchup has been ordinary."

As the arena's big screens closed in on the princess's tear-stained face, the concertgoers booed. If this was part of the show, it had gone too far. The princess was having trouble breathing. That crazy dominatrix had to let the princess go!

The audience yelled, screaming out in protest. The front

rows tried to rush the stage but were repelled by the anti-popping barrier.

The roars of one hundred thousand outraged concert attendees surrounded Messalina and Princess Hope.

Still too paralyzed to move, Borlando and Wulf watched helplessly as the Whip of Woe suddenly tightened. With a sickening plop, Princess Hope's head dropped to the stage and rolled toward Borlando, her sightless eyes aimed right at him.

"Noooooo!" the crowd roared, aghast and horrified.

Yoko's maniacal laugh soared over the arena. "You did it, Messalina. You killed Hope! You destroyed Hope!"

The whip let the princess's headless body drop to the ground.

Yoko sighed with contentment. "Remember, Messalina. I want my gift delivered in a red box, with a beautiful red ribbon!"

Without warning, Messalina dematerialized into sound. Less than a second later, she popped inside the announcing booth and grabbed Yoko from behind by her neck.

While Larry looked on in shock, Messalina and her captive popped from the announcing booth and rematerialized onto the stage.

Yoko's eyes flashed red. She struggled against Messalina's grip, but before she could, Messalina's Whip of Woe sliced off Yoko's head.

The audience, stunned by the second beheading, grew more agitated. Concertgoers worked together, ganging up to penetrate the stage's anti-popping protection.

Messalina turned to Yoko's severed head. "I'm afraid King Eeval will require an impressive gift to distract him from what I've done to his daughter, and you did say no rules. A head for a head?"

Yoko's severed head, still very much alive, giggled. "You are so right!"

As if on cue, a shadow fell over Gang Bang Arena as a massive aerial battleship materialized in the sky. The audience gasped in fear. The mighty ship's engines shook the ground as a ramp descended from the ship toward the stage.

A familiar and terrible figure appeared on the ramp. The audience quailed as the screens captured his face — a face of malevolence and anger, with heavy brows, black eyes, and a hard, cruel mouth.

King Eeval Keneval, lord of the kingdom of Banishope, tamer of the Sea of Phyre, master of the greatest zombie army ever assembled, father of the dearly loved, freshly decapitated Princess Hope, descended from the ramp to the stage.

Messalina bowed before him.

"Your highness," she said. "I can explain."

"Is what I hear true?" King Eeval whispered. "My castle? My daughter?"

"The blame lies with Wulf Avenger, your highness," Messalina said, pointing to Wulf, who was still paralyzed on the stage. "He kidnapped the princess and destroyed your fortress."

King Eeval's eyes locked on to his daughter's headless body, then shifted to her lifeless head.

"Oh, my darling girl," he said. Lost in shock and grief, the king knelt down and closed his daughter's dead eyes.

Quietly, Messalina reached her fingers into Yoko's brain stem.

"Sorry about the intrusion," she said quietly to Yoko. "I'm looking for the 'on/off' switch."

"Oh, you are so clever!" Yoko said. "I can feel your fingers in my head!"

King Keneval slowly stood. Every movement seemed to

cause him pain. He turned to Messalina, roared an ear-splitting blast of rage and grief, then advanced on her.

"You will die at my hands!" he screamed.

Messalina took a step back, her fingers rooting through Yoko's brain. With a snap of her fingers, she generated a tiny electrical charge, pointed Yoko's head at King Eeval, and covered her eyes.

Medusa's Death Helmet roared to life. Yoko's eyes flashed red and snakes sprouted from her scalp.

The crowd gasped. Mesmerized, they couldn't look away. King Keneval, his eyes filled with hate, cried out one last time.

Then, in the seconds that followed, the sounds of the audience vanished. Eeval's angry, terrible form was frozen in place, his hands mere inches from Messalina's neck, never to move again.

Silence had fallen over the massive arena, punctuated only by Messalina's relieved gasps.

The Medusa Death Helmet reverted back to Yoko's normal head.

"Larry," Yoko's head said. "Are you seeing this? Larry?"

"I covered my eyes," Larry said. "For the first time in my long career, I turned away from the big play."

Yoko's head cried with joy. "Messalina turned my Medusa Death Helmet on King Eeval! With a single move, she killed him and the entire audience!"

"Mass murder at Gang Bang Arena," Larry said. "More than one hundred thousand Gang Bang characters turned to stone. I've never seen anything like it."

Yoko cried, "My every dream has been exceeded! Such utter ruthlessness! Such a joy to witness. I feel so honored, so special."

"But wait, Yoko. Do I see movement on the stage?"

Indeed, they did. While Messalina laughed in triumph,

the Whip of Woe was getting agitated, almost as if it resented, and was jealous of, the Medusa Death Helmet in Messalina's other hand.

Borlando, his paralysis wearing off, slowly reached over to Wulf and took hold of his BangBlaster. Wulf whispered something to Borlando, and Borlando quietly changed the gun's settings, then fired it into Messalina's back. Shocked, Messalina dropped Yoko's head, and her hold on the whip lessened just enough for Borlando, now standing, to dislodge it from her hand with a kick.

The Whip of Woe went flying off the stage, into the silent sea of forever-stoned concert-goers.

Messalina turned around and extracted a dart from her shapely rear.

"A slow-down shot?" she said with a smirk. "That the best you can do, newb?"

Relentlessly, though slowly, she moved toward Borlando, who stepped back to evade her grasp.

A hand gripped his ankle. He looked down. Though his lips could barely move, Wulf whispered, "What's mine ... is yours."

Borlando felt it then. All of Wulf's powers, all of his abilities, flowed into him. Wulf Avenger had sacrificed himself so that he, Borlando, could fight this evil maniac.

"Give her hell," Wulf said. With a final exhalation, he died.

"Garbage bag," Borlando said, using Wulf's spell for conjuring everyday items out of thin air. The bag appeared in his hand even as he was zipping behind Messalina to wrap her head in the black plastic.

A time-gaining tactic, buying him a few seconds at most, but he'd need every advantage he could get. While Messalina snarled her way free of the confining bag, he jumped off the stage and ran into the stone crowd, chasing after the Whip of

Woe, which even now was slithering through the frozen concertgoers, finding its way back to its mistress.

With a leap, he managed to grab hold of the whip by its midsection, but the whip wasn't having any of it. It lashed out at Borlando, its tip slicing at his face. The whip's handle — its control — wiggled desperately to escape his reach.

Behind him, he heard Messalina pushing the stone concertgoers out of her way as she slowly inched herself toward him.

The whip's slices cut deeper and deeper. Blindly, desperately, he reached for the whip's handle.

A stone statue crashed down on him and knocked him to the ground.

Messalina towered over him. "Prepare to die, you worthless fool!"

Borlando's hand closed over the whip's handle. A single thought pulsed through him:

Die, evil bitch, die!

The Whip of Woe lashed through its former mistress with a single, vertical slice, starting at her crotch, running up through her body, and exiting through the top of her skull. The Level 47 player known as Messalina screamed, then separated into roughly equal halves that collapsed to the ground, twitching for just a few seconds before becoming still.

Wearily, Borlando watched the Whip of Woe, which trembled in his hand, flick its tip at Messalina's bloody remains. "Stop that, you bloodthirsty piece of shit. Your mistress is gone. She split."

With a sigh, he stood up, walked back to the stage and picked up Yoko's and Princess Hope's severed heads.

"Remember," Yoko's head said with a giggle, "my prize must be appropriately wrapped."

"Fuck you," he said.

Yoko giggled again.

Heads in hand, Borlando jumped from the stage and popped into Gangland's trading district. He flew up and down busy streets until he found his destination, a store called "Hats All, Folks."

He walked into the store and up to the counter, where a sales assistant sat in a chair, filing her nails.

"I'm on break," the salesperson said to Borlando, barely looking up.

"I need a box," he said, slamming Princess Hope's bloody head on the counter.

The salesperson's eyes slid to Hope's severed head, then to Yoko's head, then up to Borlando's sliced-and-diced face. With a shriek, she dropped her nail file and fled.

Borlando sighed. Sometimes, if you wanted to do something right, you had to do it yourself. He stepped behind the counter and selected a beautiful red hatbox from a shelf against the wall, then glanced at the countdown clock: thirty seconds.

He opened the box and dropped the princess's head in with a wet thump.

Twenty seconds.

Now where were the ribbons? He opened a few drawers — nothing. Ergh.

In the storefront window, a mannequin was wearing a dress. A red dress.

Fifteen seconds.

"Slice that fabric into a ribbon-sized slice," he told the Whip of Woe.

Grudgingly, the whip did as it was told, whipping through the fabric in deft, skillful strokes.

Ten seconds.

He wrapped the ribbon around the box. Now to tie it, but how? How the fuck did you tie a bow?

Five seconds.

"Tie the bow!" he told the whip.

And the whip, with barely a second to spare, fashioned a beautiful bow tie.

Yoko's head giggled with pleasure.

"Congratulations, young Borlando. You won! Your prize will be available at 09:00 GMT Tuesday at the Bank of Zurich, deposit box 145993000, passcode 'ChangeDaWorld4Evah!'."

"I really hate you," Borlando said.

Yoko giggled again. "You're welcome!"

CHAPTER SEVENTY-FIVE

JACK BREATHED A sigh of relief and closed the laptop. He'd won — by the skin of his teeth and at the cost of his Hollywood Hillz gang and a hundred thousand Gang Bang characters. But he had the prize. The phosphorin would soon be his, assuming Yoko was on the level.

He raised his arms over his head and stretched. An hour at the computer had left him stiff and creaky. He flexed his back, enjoying the sensation of his vertebrae and muscles realigning.

He sensed movement and twisted around.

The cabana door was open. Marie Le Coq stood there, still in her showgirl costume, a laptop in one hand and a gun in the other, aimed at him.

"I'm rather annoyed with you, Borlando," Marie said, smiling. "Three years of hard work building up Messalina. Level 47. The Whip of Woe. All of that — gone."

She seemed as elegantly blonde and playful as ever. Her tone was light, even teasing, but there was no mistaking her intent. A piece of the jigsaw puzzle snapped into place. The inconsistencies between Messalina and Erica Sandoz suddenly made sense. The real-world force behind the vicious, domineering Messalina wasn't Erica Sandoz. Erica was a front: human camouflage for Marie Le Coq.

"You had it coming," he said.

"Who are you with? No, don't tell me. Special Exploits."

He shrugged. She was twelve feet away — too large a gap to rush her before she could fire — but if he shifted slowly in his chair and turned to face her —

"Keep your feet exactly where they are," she said, anticipating his plan. "Hands on your head."

Confident, this one, and extremely capable. Every inch the real-world version of Messalina. A pity he hadn't seen it sooner.

She motioned for him to get on the floor. "Face down, arms behind your back."

He eased off the chair and lowered himself onto the carpet so that he could keep his eyes firmly fixed on her face. If she gave him even the slightest opening....

On the bed, Sergei rolled onto his side, snoring. Marie barely glanced at him.

He knew what came next: the inevitable demand to hand over the phosphorin. She stood there, gun in hand, a safe distance away. What was she waiting for?

"Your partner in do-gooding," she said. "Lucy, the medical student. Who is she, really? A civilian, of course. She's no agent."

Marie wanted to talk. *Good.* "What makes you say that about Lucy?"

"Too uptight. Too much of a prude."

"You mean she's normal, unlike you and me."

Her eyes glinted with amusement. "An expert of some sort. A scientist. A biologist. An innocent. I thought Special

Exploits was all about protecting civilians, not putting them in danger."

"I assume you have a reason for asking."

Marie smiled.

"She surprised me tonight by climbing on your lap and opening your pants and fucking you." Her eyes roamed over his bare, muscular back. "Then again, how could she resist? I certainly couldn't. I enjoyed our moment after the fight — our moment of true understanding — even if our time was cut short."

"Is this the new SABRE interrogation protocol?" he asked, probing to confirm that she worked for the criminal organization. "Terrify your targets with pointless speculation? Blather on until they beg for relief?"

She placed the laptop on the table and pursed her lips, as if trying to make up her mind about something.

"You don't know, do you?" she said.

"Know what?"

"How I know Lucy is not a trained agent."

He didn't say anything. She was going to tell him anyway.

"Trained agents," she said, "do not fall for their partners."

Before he could think up a suitable retort, the cabana's phone rang.

"That will be her," she said, "calling to tell you about my husband."

Marie had mentioned Francois for a reason. A suspicion formed.

"Are you the one who made him ill?" he asked.

"A bit more than ill, I'm afraid."

He zoomed in on her eyes. She'd killed him? Her irises told him she was serious.

"Why?"

She shrugged. "I got careless. He found out about the

phosphorin. I tried to reason with him, but he kept going on about the dangers."

The phone rang an eighth time and went silent.

"So you poisoned him."

"I wanted him to use the phosphorin for his research. He needed a bigger challenge, something newer, fresher, more urgent." She gave him a surprisingly earnest look. "I really did want him to win the Nobel prize. He could have. He was very close."

"Must have been quite a shock for him, realizing he married a psychopath."

"He couldn't let go of his training as a doctor — 'do no harm' and all that nonsense. He couldn't see the bigger picture."

"So you eliminated him," he said, then added, "just like you killed Dick Hould."

"My new role will be 'widow of eminent scientist.' It suits me." She glanced at her watch. "But no, Dick Hould wasn't me. Credit for that goes to the lovely Yoko."

"You know who Yoko is?"

"A suspicion, nothing more."

"What did you use on your husband?"

"I'm glad you asked." She reached into her bosom and pulled out a small vial of clear liquid. "A SABRE specialty. A few drops, tasteless and odorless, in drink or food and the target suffers indigestion, then a heart attack, then death. The poison breaks down in the body, becoming undetectable."

She placed the vial on the table.

"This is your choice," she said. "If you give me the location of the phosphorin and drink the poison, if you behave sensibly, I will not kill Lucy."

She stood quietly for a moment to let that sink in, then continued. "But if you fight me, if you delay me, if you make me work for the information, I will torture Lucy in front of you until you tell me. Then I will pour the vial of poison down her throat so you can watch her die before your eyes. Then, and only then, will I shoot you."

She said it with a smile, her tone conversational and pleasant, as if she were describing a picnic in the park. But he knew, with a hammer blow to his gut, that this damaged lunatic meant every word.

"Lucy will be here soon," she said. "Let me tell you what happened while we have been talking. She was tending to Prince Ali. She called my cabana to check on Francois, and no one answered. That concerned her, so she left Prince Ali and went to my cabana and discovered Francois dead and me gone. She debated alerting him" — she pointed to Sergei — " and his minions, but she didn't, because she decided to inform you first."

She leaned in. "If you tell me now, I'll leave before she arrives."

His mind desperately searched for options.

"If you tell me now," she repeated, "she won't die."

The cabana door swung open. From his spot on the ground, Jack saw Lucy in the doorway, staring at them.

Shit.

Eyes wide, face pale, frozen with uncertainty.

"You're early," Marie said to her. "That's too bad. Step in and close the door behind you. Run and he dies."

"Run, Lucy!" Jack said.

"Don't even try," Marie said.

"She can't kill me until I tell her where the phosphorin is."

Marie laughed and swung the gun toward Lucy. "But I can shoot you. Step in and close the door."

"I'm feeling sick," Lucy whispered.

"Too bad," Marie said. "Close that door. Slowly."

Lucy took a step into the cabana and pushed the door shut behind her.

She clutched her stomach and gasped, "I'm going to — "

Without warning, Lucy ran into the bathroom and, from the sound of it, collapsed on the floor. From his spot on the floor, Jack couldn't see into the bathroom, and neither could Marie.

Marie said to him, "Don't move." She edged closer to the bathroom.

He knew what Marie was wondering: Had the poison she used on Francois also affected Lucy? If so, how? And was Marie also contaminated?

"Get off the floor," Marie said to Lucy, a touch of impatience in her voice. "Stand up."

"I have medicine in my bag," Lucy said weakly. "If I can get...."

Marie's face tightened. Toiletries clattered on the floor.

"Is that a satellite phone?" Marie suddenly asked.

"Doesn't work," Lucy whispered.

"Toss it to me!"

"I can't...."

"Bring me the phone."

Marie turned to Jack. "Does it work? Can it get through Sergei's jamming?"

"Fuck you," he said.

Excitement flashed in Marie's eyes. She turned back to Lucy, coaxing her forward. "Yes, give it to me...."

Lucy's hand appeared from inside the bathroom, close to the floor, as though she were crawling with one arm extended in front of her.

The phone was in her hand, her thumb positioned over the number pad. As Marie reached down to take the phone, Lucy's thumb pressed down on the 7, 8, and 9 buttons simultaneously. Fifty thousand volts shot through Marie, sending her flying against the cabana door, where she crumpled with a moan.

Jack leaped up and kicked the gun away from the barely conscious Marie and turned to Lucy, heart pounding.

"Tell me you're okay."

Her eyes went up to him, but she didn't move from the floor.

"Tell me you're okay!"

CHAPTER **SEVENTY-SIX**

LUCY STARED UP at Jack's anxious face, her heart racing, her mind still in shock.

"I'm okay," she heard herself say.

A wave of dizziness hit her as she sat upright. Had she done what she'd just done? Had she managed to remember the electroshock satellite phone in her travel kit next to the bathroom sink, then act as if she was suffering from the same poison that had killed Francois, then collapse on the floor and reach up for the travel bag, scattering the contents, then draw Marie's attention to the phone, then grab the phone and hold down the right buttons to zap the living hell out of that murderous bitch?

Jack pulled her up into his arms and didn't let her go. His warmth felt so good.

"You just saved our asses," he said. "Thank you. Don't ever do that again."

She felt shaky and jangled, her heart still pounding in her chest. "What now?"

"Lots." He guided her to the bed and sat her down, then went to his luggage and pulled out concealed plastic ties.

With a few deft twists and knots, he tied Marie's hands and feet.

"I heard what Marie said about poisoning Francois," she said.

"She's a piece of work." He inspected the ties, then picked up Marie and carried her to the closet, where he set her on the floor on her back.

"Also," she said, "I heard what she said about my feelings for you."

Jack shot her a quick glance. "That wasn't you who called?"

"No, I was outside listening." She took a deep breath, then added, "For the record, Marie was wrong about me falling for you."

"No, she wasn't."

"Yes, she was."

He stepped toward her and, without a word, pulled her into his arms again, this time for a kiss. She didn't even pretend to resist. He felt too damn good. Such a damn good kisser.

He smelled like sex. Her scent and his were mixed together.

He pulled back and grinned at her. "Nah, the bitch nailed it."

"Let's get one thing straight," she said, half-heartedly pushing him away. "I don't like you. I still don't like you."

"Whatever you say." His blue eyes didn't leave her.

"When this mission is over, we're over."

"Okay."

"I mean it."

"Sure." He gave her a wink.

The bastard.

"I like someone else," she said, the words out of her mouth before she could even think.

He brushed a stray hair from her cheek. "Your long-distance part-time boyfriend in Chicago? You broke up with him three days ago. At least in your head you did."

"Not him," she said, then added, again without thinking, "Your colleague, the Air Vent Man from England."

He stilled at that. Something indefinable shifted in his eyes. She'd found a worthy competitor.

"You didn't read the full report, did you?" she continued, pushing her advantage.

He focused on her eyes intently. "You suck at lying, Lucy Keen."

To escape his eyes, she leaned in close and whispered in his ear, "You don't think they would have let me come on this mission if I hadn't been properly … vetted?"

She felt a muscle twitch in his cheek.

"Your colleague's background investigation was very thorough, and very intense. I guess Grant and Calhoun thought, who better to handle me than the man I'd already worked with?"

His arms tightened around her. Her breasts pressed against his chest. He pulled his head back and stared deeply into her eyes. He smiled a knowing smile and leaned in for another kiss. This time, he ran his lips slowly over hers. Their breaths mingled.

He moved his mouth to her ear.

"Did he fuck you hard?" he whispered.

She tensed, startled. *Damn him.*

"Tell me about his cock," he whispered. "Was it big and thick and long? Did he fill you completely?"

His hand slid down her back and cupped her butt. He gripped it tightly and pulled her in closer.

"Did he tease your clit? Pinch your nipples? Did he make

you beg before he let you come?"

She gasped as his erection pressed against her thigh.

"Tell me what he did to you," he whispered. "Every filthy detail."

"You know I can't do that," she said, struggling to regain her composure. "Compartmentalizing information is an operational necessity."

He burst out laughing.

She couldn't help but smile. Making him laugh was ... *fun*.

"A woman of mystery," he said. "Love it!"

He broke free.

"Okay, Lucy Keen. Time to focus." He turned to the laptop and looked at the screen. "Wi-fi's gone. No surprise."

He bent down, picked up the satellite phone from the floor, and checked it briefly to confirm that it too had no signal. Then he stepped into the bathroom, where he gathered up the toiletries she'd spilled.

She followed him in. His sudden switch from lover to neat-freak agent was jarring. Unless ...

"You won the online thing," she said.

He nodded.

"You know where the phosphorin is."

Another nod. He dumped the last of her toiletries into her bag, then slid past her, opened a dresser drawer, and pulled on a t-shirt.

She gestured to Marie in the closet, then to Sergei on the bed. "What about them?"

"They'll keep. First thing's first: we report in."

He picked up the phone, brought the receiver to his ear, and went still.

"What is it?" she said.

"No dial tone." He looked past her, his mind already running through the possibilities. "The phone is dead."

CHAPTER SEVENTY-SEVEN

JACK TRIED TO keep the alarm from his face. The phone had been working just minutes earlier. If someone had cut the line to their cabana, that someone could be outside right now, watching and listening. He and Lucy would be exposed the instant they stepped outside, but they had no choice. He had to tell Special Exploits about the phosphorin handoff, and he needed a decision about the psycho in his closet.

He grabbed his mobile phone and, from a secret compartment, pulled out a tiny, one-jab hypodermic. He bent over Marie, stuck the needle into her upper arm, repositioned her on her side, and closed the closet door.

"A sedative?" Lucy asked.

"Her body weight, she'll be out for twelve hours."

On the bed, Sergei was still snoring softly.

"He'll wake up when he wakes up," he said, then turned to Lucy and handed her the golden lipstick gun. "Bring this, just in case."

She looked at it uncertainly, then slipped it into her pants pocket.

"We have to call in," he said. "Let's go to the main villa."

"You're worried," she said.

He picked up Marie's gun, checked the chamber, then turned off the lights and stepped to the sliding door that led to the cabana's rear deck. He gestured for her to follow.

Slowly, he eased the sliding glass door open and stood, still inside the room, like a statue, listening. The night was quiet, with barely a breeze rustling the leaves in the garden outside. A cricket chirped. The faint sound of laughter and music drifted from the villa.

One minute. Two minutes. Behind him, Lucy shifted position.

He waited another minute. If someone was out there, that someone was good. More waiting wouldn't help.

He turned to her, brought a finger to his lips, and motioned for her to follow. Bending low, he slipped out the door and across the deck, Lucy a step behind. He led her into the garden, to a spot behind a small tree.

He listened for another minute — still no sounds that shouldn't be there — and moved with Lucy through the garden, toward the courtyard and the villa.

The sounds of the party grew louder as they reached the courtyard. After a final glance behind them, he and Lucy stepped from the garden onto the path. He stuffed the gun into the back of his jeans, the gun's handle obscured by his t-shirt.

The orgy had expanded out of the cabaret room and into the courtyard. In the pool, a naked trio was laughing and frolicking. Several lounge chairs were occupied by guests and facilitators fucking vigorously. At the poolside bar, five half-dressed guests were laughing uproariously as they made themselves drinks.

He and Lucy moved past them, into the villa, down the hallway, and toward the courtesy phone outside the entrance to the cabaret room.

The music and laughter grew louder. Ahead of them, a couple stumbled out of the cabaret room, giggling and groping.

And then he noticed it. A hint of lemon in the air. Delightfully crisp.

He froze. A shock ran through him as he realized he couldn't un-breathe the air he'd just inhaled; he couldn't rewind time and go back outside to the courtyard. There was nothing he could do to escape the horrifying realization that he'd just been exposed to —

Phosphorin.

Beside him, Lucy stiffened.

"It's here," she whispered, shock in her voice. "They have it here."

He looked at Lucy with the unspoken question.

She breathed in and exhaled, then again, like a wine expert sampling a rare vintage.

The horror in her eyes answered him.

"It's dead," she said.

Dead phosphorin. Shit shit shit.

She looked at the air vents. "Is it coming from there?"

"From the tunnels inside the cliffs. Has to be."

"Why are we smelling it?"

"Accident. Assassination attempt. Who knows?"

"We need to quarantine the island immediately."

He picked up the courtesy phone. No dial tone. A terrible possibility pushed its way into his head. What if Synkonos wasn't the only place the phosphorin was being released?

"The lines are dead," he said.

"We need to call in now. Every minute counts."

"We'll have to try from the communications shed."

"Where is that?"

"On the plateau, not far from the helicopter pad, near the motocross course."

He turned to leave, but she remained frozen in place, her brow furrowed, lost in thought.

"What is it?" he asked.

"I need to get back to Prince Ali," she said. "He needs help."

"I want you close to me."

She shook her head. "We both have places to be. I need to talk to him to identify how he was infected. Maybe he can help us."

She was right, of course, but he didn't like it.

"We're dealing with a maniac," he said. "I don't want you hurt."

"I'll stay with Ali. I'll lock the door. I promise, I won't leave."

She seemed so earnest, so serious, and so unstoppable.

He leaned over and kissed her forehead. "Okay. But first, back to the cabana. I need my tools, and you need yours."

CHAPTER SEVENTY-EIGHT

MINUTES LATER, outside Ali's cabana, Lucy looked up at Jack's face, at his compressed lips and watchful eyes, and realized she wasn't looking at an agent, but rather at a man who cared about her. A man who — no, she couldn't go there, not now. Not when the stuff of her worst nightmares had come to life.

"How will Special Exploits get here?" she asked. "Will they invade or something?"

"As soon as we give the signal."

Without even thinking about it, she pulled him in for a kiss, one that conveyed more emotional truth than anything she could put into words.

She stepped away. The night air hung heavily around her, soft and quiet. There was no telltale lemon scent here.

She knocked on the door, then waited and listened. Silence. She knocked again, then turned the handle. The door was unlocked. She pushed the door open. The cabana was dark. Jack motioned her back and stepped inside ahead of her.

Ali was in bed, asleep, his breathing labored and shallow. Jack checked the bathroom and closet, locked the sliding door, then closed the curtains.

"I'll knock four times, then pause, then twice more," he whispered. "Lock the door when I leave."

With a tight smile, she closed the door behind him and turned the bolt, locking herself inside.

She stepped toward the bed to look at her new patient, her new case of phosphorin exposure. If only she were dealing with a case of the flu. A bottle of cold medicine sat on the nightstand, nearly empty. She wanted to question him, but for now, she'd let him sleep. Until Special Exploits arrived with the treatments, there was little she could do to help him.

She stepped into the bathroom. Ali's symptoms meant the exposure had occurred the previous day. If she were the killer — if she had processed the dead phosphorin into an easily transportable powder, for example — then how would she have done it? She picked up his tube of toothpaste. A pinch of phosphorin powder, dabbed into the paste, would work beautifully. But that wasn't the only option. The killer could have added the phosphorin to Ali's drink, or his food, or dusted in on his shirt, or....

The possibilities were endless. Why had Yoko — she had to assume it was Yoko — infected Ali? If getting rid of him was the objective, why resort to phosphorin? Why not arrange for another accident like the rockslide? Why risk having him spread the contamination? Unless — but no, that didn't make sense.

She heard her patient cough and shift in his bed. She poked her head out of the bathroom. He was sitting up and holding the bottle of medicine.

"Ali, it's me," she said.

He looked up, startled, then relaxed when he saw her.

"The good doctor," he said. He raised the bottle of medicine to his lips and downed the last of it.

He looked terrible — pale and weak and sweaty. His hand trembled slightly as he placed the empty bottle on the nightstand.

She stepped toward the bed. "I came to check on you."

"Stay back," he said. "Don't come any closer."

"Ali, I — "

"Step back! There's something I must tell you."

She did as he asked, retreating two steps, and waited.

"There is a chance I do not have the flu," he said.

She remained silent, waiting for him to continue. She'd been on the other end of this "talk to fill the empty space" dynamic several times in the past few days, feeling powerless to stop herself from falling into it even as her rational mind yelled at her for being such an easy mark. Experiencing the same dynamic from the other end was fascinating. She watched him step up to the ledge of self-disclosure, stare into the abyss, and leap.

He coughed, his chest already thick with congestion. "I came to Synkonos in pursuit of a biological substance that has tremendous potential for agriculture. The substance was for sale, and I'd hoped to purchase it."

He coughed again. "The opportunity fell through, as opportunities do. That would be the end of the story, except for this: the substance was obtained through illicit means, and the seller is dangerous and ruthless. Also this: the substance is toxic and spreads easily from person to person."

"Easily?"

"By air, exposed surfaces, through food or drink."

"Toxic?"

"Extremely."

"How do you know this?"

A pained looked crossed Ali's face. "That's not important.

What matters is that my flu symptoms are consistent with exposure to the substance. I may have spread the contamination to others."

His fear was palpable, as was his guilt. She wanted to put him at ease by telling him that she knew about the phosphorin, that Special Exploits was on its way with the treatment, and that his odds of pulling through were better than good.

As a scientist, she could tell him all that. But as a medical student who knew nothing about phosphorin? No dice.

Once again, she was reminded that being a temporary secret agent sucked. So much she could never share.

"We'll call for medical help," she said.

He picked up the phone. "I've tried. The line is dead."

"We can ask the staff for help."

"That may not work," he said, coughing again. "I suspect the seller is a member of Sergei's staff."

"Who?" she asked, keeping her tone neutral. If he knew who Yoko was, then....

From behind came the sound of metal sliding on metal — a sound she instantly recognized as a key sliding into a lock.

She whirled around. The bolt slid out of the lock. The handle turned. Heart pounding, she watched the door slowly swing open.

CHAPTER
SEVENTY-NINE

A MOONLESS NIGHT on the plateau. Jack carefully worked his way toward the communications shed, scanning the path to avoid unexpected dips or potholes. The shed stood half a mile from the villa, close to the helipad and the spot where guests had cheered the motocross racers earlier that day by the finish line.

A gust of wind hit him. Up here, away from the villa and its garden, the night sky was clear but restless, the atmosphere churning.

He brought his attention back to earth, to the shed he was quickly approaching. If he was lucky, the locks would be the same as the rest of the villa and make breaking in child's play.

Once inside, he'd send Special Exploits a brief communication, and that would be that: mission accomplished. He could go back to being Jack Ford, spoiled celebrity playboy. The island would be quarantined, and he and everyone else on the island would receive the medical treatment needed to save their lives.

It was funny how, after the initial shock, his phosphorin exposure no longer made him nervous. He'd just breathed in a highly toxic substance, and the treatment he would rely on to save his life had been tested on exactly one human being. Rationally, he had every reason to be wracked with anxiety.

Did his faith in Lucy extend that far and go that deep? He smiled to himself in the darkness. That kiss she'd laid on him at Ali's door — a helluva smack. Spoke volumes. Girl was as into him as he was into her.

He'd take her somewhere after the quarantine. Down to Baja, maybe. She'd like it there. A nice long drive, an empty stretch of beach, a tent above the high tide line. They could build a big fire, have a bit too much sangria....

First thing first. The communications shed — a concrete structure, plain and solid, with a single metal door — stood ahead, barely visible in the darkness.

He walked a silent circle around the shed, fifty yards out. Nothing unusual or unexpected. He appeared to be alone. If anyone were watching, it would be from … where? He spied a low ridge to the west. With barely a whisper, he slipped across the plateau and approached the ridge from behind.

The ridge was empty. Still, he found himself on edge. Something wasn't right.

Experience told him to go slow, to wait, to sift through what he knew to figure out what he was missing. But he didn't have that luxury. Grant and Calhoun had to know.

He crept up to the back of the shed and slid around to the door. He took his mobile device from his pocket and knelt, left knee in the dirt, in front of the door.

The lock was at eye level. He slid open the hidden compartment on his phone and took out his trusty lock picks. To steady himself, he rested his right elbow on his right knee. With his right hand, he aimed the first pick at the lock, and —

Bam!

He barely registered the overwhelming pain before his body was tossed like a rag doll and his world went dark.

CHAPTER **EIGHTY**

LUCY'S BREATH CAUGHT in her throat.

The door swung open, revealing the figure of a man with a gun in his hand — a gun aimed at her.

Boris.

The man she'd poured her heart out to last night at the bar. The man who, with Natasha, had helped Sergei build Gang Bang.

The man, she realized, who also called himself *Yoko*.

His tall frame filled the doorway. His expression was serious, even stony, but she saw tension in his eyes — anticipation. He'd planned for whatever was coming next. He knew how it would play out.

"Step back, Dr. Kimball," he said, gesturing with the gun. "We have much to discuss."

Kimball. He'd called her Kimball. For a second, she considered playing dumb, but there was no point.

"You know who I am," she said.

He stepped into the cabana and closed the door. "I know

nearly everything there is to know about phosphorin, including the identity of its leading expert."

He pointed to a chair at the dining table. "Sit."

Slowly, she lowered herself into the chair.

"Keep your hands on the table."

He turned the gun on Ali, who was sitting up in bed, his back stiff, watching their every move. "Your Highness, I suggest you stay where you are."

"Or what?" Ali said.

"I'm here to talk with Dr. Kimball, not you."

She saw his finger tighten on the trigger.

"Boris," she said to distract him. "How long have you known about me?"

His eyes, and his gun, swung back to her. He stood a few feet from the door, his stance easy and confident. "Since this morning, when you stepped out of the pool. Your hair was wet and plastered against your skull. You looked like you do in your driver's license photo, with your hair in a ponytail."

She glanced toward the door. Jack hadn't had time to reach the communications shed. She needed to stall and keep him talking.

"I got my hair done especially for the party," she said. "Glad to hear it worked."

"It's impressive what a new haircut and makeup can do to a person's appearance," Boris said. "I suppose you're wondering about your cohort."

"Cohort?"

"Jack Ford. Another impressive bit of concealment."

Lucy snorted. "Jack? He has no idea what's going on."

Boris shook his head. "That was my initial assessment. How could a spoiled, self-involved, alcoholic, exhibitionistic wastrel like Jack Ford be a spy? Clearly he was a dupe, and Lucy Kimball was using him."

A tight smile played at his mouth. "But I needed to confirm my hypothesis — I'm sure you would approve — so I decided to review the security footage. Imagine my surprise when I discovered that video was being erased. Someone had accessed the security room and hacked the video-storage settings. Who did that, I wondered, and when?"

"That's too bad," she said. "No footage, no solution. The mystery lives on."

"Not so fast," he said. "Before the days of electronic surveillance, mysteries were solved by good old-fashioned detective work."

"You became a detective?"

"Yes," he said, "I did."

"Please, lay out your case."

"Thank you." He pulled out a chair from the dining table, carried it to where he had been standing, and sat down. He was getting comfortable, enjoying the moment, but the gun never wavered.

"We have a bit of time," he said. "I've enjoyed the deductive process. I welcome the opportunity to share with someone who will appreciate the challenges I faced."

"I'm all ears," she said.

He gave her a small nod. "I began my investigation of the video hack with the security room itself. From Friday afternoon through early Saturday evening, two men were on duty, and at least one of them was inside the security room at all times. But on Saturday night, only one person was on duty, because Constantine was fighting Mr. Ford. During the match, the security room was manned by a single man, a fellow named Durgos."

He paused. "Are you with me so far?"

"Go on," she said.

He glanced at Ali, still as a stone in the bed, then turned back toward her.

"On Saturday night, Natasha told Durgos that he would have to man the security room alone. I asked Durgos if he had stayed in the security room the entire night. He told me he'd done his best, but after experiencing severe intestinal upset, he had been forced to leave the room to use the bathroom a number of times. He was very angry with the kitchen staff, because he believed their baklava had caused it. I asked him how he'd gotten the baklava, and he said a plate had been sent from the kitchen with a note from Natasha that said, 'Thank you for extending your shift this evening.'

"I asked the kitchen staff if Natasha had requested a plate of baklava, and they said no. I asked if anyone had, and they said yes, a guest had in the late afternoon. I asked which guest and learned it was the guest staying in the cabana next to yours. I asked the waiter who delivered the baklava if the guest had been there when he'd delivered it, and he said yes, but that the guest hadn't opened the door. He had told the waiter to leave the plate on the mat.

"After further inquiries, I learned that the guest was in a poker game by the pool when the baklava was delivered. I also learned that you and Jack were more than likely in your cabana at the time."

Boris paused again, his pace quickening as he moved deeper into his recap.

"I began to appreciate the mind of the person who had broken into the security room on Saturday night. This person had to remove not one, but two people. One of the two was, conveniently, taken out of action at the fight, in full view of everyone. The other was removed by a person who knew Durgos has a sweet tooth, knew he would be manning the security room alone after the fight, and knew the cabana next to yours would be empty when the waiter arrived with the plate.

"I went back to Durgos and asked if he'd had any baklava

earlier in the day and if anyone had seen him eat it. He said he had, at lunch by the pool before his shift. He said anyone near his table could have seen him eat it.

"Because the video footage was erased, I could not confirm that Mr. Ford had been at the pool while Durgos ate his baklava, so I turned my attention to the man himself. What observable facts did I have? What did I really know about him?

"He always seemed to have a drink in his hand, but I asked myself: Had I ever seen him take more than a sip? He is very fit, which requires discipline and dedication. Somehow, he ended up in the ring with Constantine — I wish I had been poolside for that conversation. He knocked out Constantine. He ignited an orgy. And then, with the crowd distracted and the security team injured or ill, he disappeared, for nearly an hour."

He looked directly at Lucy. "During that hour, you were keeping me distracted at the bar."

"That's quite a story," she said, trying her best to sound politely skeptical.

"A dupe cannot do all I just described. Therefore, Jack Ford is no dupe. The two of you make a good team."

The lights in the cabana dimmed for a few seconds, then brightened again.

Boris smiled.

Something in his smile scared her.

"What just happened?" she asked.

"The equipment in the communications shed has been destroyed by an electrical surge, triggered by someone who attempted to open the door to the shed."

Her face went immobile. He couldn't mean —

"Yes, Dr. Kimball. I set a trap. The person who tried to open that door has been electrocuted."

She willed her lower lip to not tremble. He was wrong. *He had to be.*

The certainty in his voice sliced into her core. "Dr. Kimball, it is my duty to inform you that Jack Ford is dead."

CHAPTER
EIGHTY-ONE

FROM OUT OF the blackness, Jack became aware of pain. Every inch of him buzzed, tingled, and ached.

Where was he? He opened his eyes. His vision was fuzzy and unfocused. The wind gusted against him. He was outside, under the stars, flat on the ground, with rocks jabbing into his back.

The bam came back with a rush: The lock. The door. The massive jolt.

An electric booby trap meant for him — a lethally shocking surprise. Why hadn't it worked? The current should have passed through his heart, killing him.

He moved his right arm and intense pain erupted. Gingerly, with his left hand, he reached over and touched his right elbow.

The skin at his elbow felt rough and damaged. That meant.... He reached down to his right knee and discovered a hole in his jeans and another patch of damaged skin, burnt, no doubt.

Head pounding, he reconstructed how he'd been positioned when he'd knelt in front of the door; his right elbow had been resting on his right knee. The slim metal lock pick had been in his right hand, zeroing in on the lock....

The electricity had entered through his fingers, traveling down his arm to his elbow, then continued into his knee, down his lower leg, and into the ground.

If the pick in his left hand had touched the lock first.... If his elbow and knee hadn't been in contact....

Fuck, his head was throbbing. Slowly, he sat up.

The charge had tossed him, and he'd hit the ground hard. His back was a mass of cuts and scrapes. He rolled over, onto his hands and knees, and took several deep breaths.

Very carefully, he stood and nearly fell over. Staggering, he bent down, hands on his knees, overcome with lightheadedness, wincing as he put weight on his knee. Nausea rolled through him.

He forced himself to inhale and exhale, over and over, in long, deep breaths.

Gradually, the dizziness and the urge to puke receded and his vision cleared.

He straightened his back, this time managing it without stumbling, then stretched his arms and shoulders, twisted his torso, and carefully pressed down on each foot. Nothing was broken.

The door to the communications shed had been blown open by the electrical surge. He stepped to the door and, with his rubber-soled shoe, pushed it open. The door swung in silently. The reek of burnt electronics washed over him. A quick glance inside confirmed that the equipment in the room was toast.

Until the shed was fixed, the only sound coming out of Synkonos would be silence.

Time for Plan C.

He grabbed his mobile device out of his back pocket and

removed a high-powered laser pointer. A few quick dashes of light aimed at the sky — Morse code for the heavens — and Special Exploits would come, eventually. He'd have to sit here and repeat the code every five minutes for the next three hours to guarantee that a satellite picked it up, but sometime within that three-hour window, his faint, lighted code would find its audience and his job would be done.

He pressed the laser's button. Nothing. Pressed it again. Nothing.

Dammit. He unscrewed the top and heard the faint tinkle of shattered glass dropping to the ground.

He was tired — so fucking tired.

He stared up at the star-filled sky, at the trillions of tiny, bright lights so far away. Somewhere among them, a satellite tasked to Special Exploits was awaiting his signal — a signal he couldn't send. The raddest, coolest, most astonishing communications technologies in the world, and they were useless to him.

What would the classic spies do?

Think old school.

In the darkness, the answer came.

He closed his eyes and sighed. A lot to do, and not a lot of time to do it. But it was their only chance.

CHAPTER
EIGHTY-TWO

LUCY WILLED HERSELF not to speak, fearful that whatever came out of her mouth would reveal weakness and uncertainty.

Boris kept his attention on her, glancing only occasionally at Ali, who remained on the bed.

He cleared his throat. "Yes, Dr. Kimball, whoever set off that trap is dead. There will be no communication between Synkonos and the outside world over the course of the next day. The Grid's jamming technology will remain locked in the 'on' position, since the controls were in the communications room."

He gestured with his gun. "Somewhere, presumably on a nearby island, you have a support team awaiting your signal. They haven't moved in yet, and why is that? Judging from the expression on your face when I opened the door, they do not know I am Yoko. More importantly, they do not know whether I have the phosphorin here or somewhere else. They don't want to spook me. They don't want me to panic."

"None of that matters," Lucy said, "because you won't get away with selling the phosphorin."

Boris laughed. "You don't understand, do you? The game is a ruse. There is no winner. There is no sale."

"Then why are you doing this?"

He sat up straighter, looking much like the professor he had once been. "In the next few hours, the guests at Villa Synkonos, fresh from their night of sexual abandon, will pack their bags and take their leave. They will board the ferry to Kasos. From there, they will fly home.

"Your support team will watch everyone leave. They will debate whether to intervene. In the end, despite concerns that their agents have not communicated with them, they will choose to do nothing for fear of alerting the dastardly phosphorin thief.

"Unbeknownst to everyone except me and you, most of the two hundred guests and staff at this party will be transporting dead sucronal phosphorin in their lungs. These two hundred people are ideal carriers, as they are among the most well-traveled people on the planet. In the next forty-eight hours, they will board more than three hundred jets — half of them commercial airliners — and travel to eighteen countries. On those flights, they will begin feeling the effects of what they'll believe is a cold. In the closed air systems of those planes, they will infect thirteen thousand people. Outside those planes, especially in the airports, they will infect another twenty thousand."

A wave of dread hit her. He couldn't mean what he was saying.

"In two more days," Boris continued, "the original two hundred carriers will be near death and the health authorities will know they have a crisis on their hands, but it will be too late. By that point, the thirty-three thousand will have infected another million. Within a week, the number of infected will reach thirty million. Within a month, one billion. Within a year, the vast majority of humans on this planet will be dead."

The numbers were frighteningly on-target. She'd run the projections herself: the exponential explosion of contamination; the swift, sure, unstoppable spread of death from one to many, and from many to many more; and the inevitable destruction of most of humanity and, quite possibly, the extinction of a species — her species.

"Why?" she asked faintly, barely able to breathe.

"We don't stop, do we?" Boris said.

"Who?"

"We. The people. We keep pushing forward. We don't take no for an answer."

Her breath returned.

"Why are you doing this?" she asked again, more loudly. "Why?"

"I'm hitting the reset button for the planet."

"The reset button?"

His gaze intensified. "Think of our planet as a computer game. Its operating system has been infected by malware — our wretched species. To save the earth, we need to wipe the hard drive clean."

"You can't mean that."

"I do mean that," he said, his lower lip twitching, just slightly. "Everywhere you look, we — humans — are destroying the planet."

She had to stop him. She had to find a way. He was talking with her, which meant something. Did he want her to dissuade him?

She took a deep breath. "What about your plans to change the world with Sergei?"

Boris nodded sadly. "Sergei — my last hope for human transformation. He really is a genius, with an incredible ability to see new connections. His heart is in the right place, but even he can't change us fast enough."

"You have to give him time," she said.

Blood rushed to his face. She'd hit a sore spot.

"I gave him time," he said. "Ten years! Ten years in which I stood by and did nothing. I helped him build Gang Bang because I believed social gaming had transformative potential for communications and social activism — that it could create an awareness of, an appreciation for, our global interconnectedness. Even when I saw most people using Gang Bang to recreate real-world tribal rivalries, I told myself that Gang Bang's massive wealth could fund political and social and environmental change."

He glanced at Ali briefly, then continued. "We are such an impressive species. Capable of so much artifice and imagination. Look at your partner, Jack Ford. Hiding in plain sight. Playing a jackass when he was really a spy. Here on Synkonos, he was a spy playing a fool, while also playing a gangster in a real-world simulation of a glamorized version of Las Vegas."

He was pleased with this analysis, she saw. He liked being the smartest kid in the room. She had to make that work against him.

He continued. "Then this pretender, playing a character playing a character in a real-world imagined version of a long-ago time and place, hijacks someone else's imaginary online character to compete against other imaginary characters in an imaginary world in a contest he thinks is real, which it wasn't, for a prize he believes is attainable, which it isn't. It's enough to make one's head spin."

She nodded, acting as though she were following him. "Identity is a tricky thing."

"And yet, you care — cared — about him." He leaned

forward, his curiosity evident. "How is that possible? Does — did — Jack Ford even know who he was? Did you?"

"I know enough about him."

"How can you say that? Jack Ford was a character played by Jack Ford. How many lies did he tell you? How many lies did he tell himself? His line of work isn't easy on the psyche. It must be very tempting to lose oneself in the fiction."

If she allowed herself even an instant to dwell on Boris's use of the past tense....

"I want to understand something," she said. "Why go to all this trouble? Why the online competition? Why the subterfuge? There are easier ways to release phosphorin and kill every human on the planet. You could have done it sooner, in any number of ways."

"You're right, of course. We actually discussed the main reason last night, in the bar."

"We did?"

"I'm not a monster," he said. "I want you to understand that. I feel profound regret for the manner in which people will die. If I could accomplish my goal differently, I would. I assure you, I approached my decision with great care."

In his own twisted way, he really believed he was behaving responsibly — even ethically. She had to keep him talking to find a gap in his confidence.

"Why the auction?" she asked. "Why the elaborate game?"

"Several reasons. The first: to keep myself busy and focused. I feared I might become weak and not follow through if I had time to reflect."

"I'm relieved," she said. "It means you understand that annihilating the human species means killing children. Putting small children — innocent, trusting children — through unimaginable pain."

His mouth trembled at that. "I freely admit that I do not

want to dwell on that. Painful sacrifices are sometimes necessary for the greater good."

"You don't have to do this."

"Oh, but I do."

Fearing he'd stop talking if she pushed harder, she switched gears. "What are the other reasons?"

"Another reason, I admit, was simple ego. I wanted to outsmart everyone. I wanted to prove I could do it. Designing and executing the plan has been — enjoyable."

Something came to her. "Last night, in the bar. Dick Hould wasn't coming to see me. He was coming to see you. He'd figured out who you were and that's why you killed him."

"Very good, Dr. Kimball. Yes, I was not as clever as I'd hoped. He had the gall to threaten me with blackmail."

She could imagine how it had played out: Boris pretending to agree to Dick's terms, offering to show Dick the phosphorin, then luring him up onto the plateau to the hole above the cave and ending the threat with a simple push.

"And your third reason?" she asked.

He gave her a sad smile. "Last night, at the bar, I realized that a part of me wanted to be stopped. I had made my plan intricate and complicated because I wanted it to fail. I was like a person who tries to kill himself with one pill too few."

"I'm glad to hear that. You don't have to do this."

"That part of me was wrong," he said. "That part of me was a sentimental fool."

She realized he wasn't explaining his actions to her, but rather justifying them to himself.

"Which leads me now to my main reason," he said. "The main reason for my intricate game. I felt compelled to test my main hypothesis."

"Your hypothesis that the human species — in its entirety — is irredeemable."

"Last night, in the bar, you said, 'Approach decision

points like they're experiments.' I have tried my best to approach this decision in the most serious manner possible. It's a responsibility I take very seriously."

He looked at her thoughtfully. "I conceived the theft and auction as an experiment. The results, I'm sad to report, are irrefutable and clear. The buyers I attracted are disgusting and frightening. So much greed and so little regard for anyone or anything beyond the acquisition of money and power."

"You can't say that about Prince Ali." She looked over at Ali, who was remaining quiet and still on the bed.

"Yes, Ali," Boris said, acknowledging his presence but keeping his eyes on her. "We've been working together for some months, on two promising environmental projects: a desalinization project and a water purification project. I thought his intentions were good, but when he expressed interest in the auction, I knew otherwise."

Ali sat up straighter, preparing to defend himself, but Lucy gestured for him to stay quiet.

"Are you sure?" she said. "One of the most interesting properties of phosphorin is that it will eat just about anything."

"Your point?"

"Its diet can include fertilizers and other agricultural waste that pollute the water and land."

"I see," he said. "You're saying that phosphorin has potential for water purification."

"Yes. The idea would be to develop filtration barriers that allow the phosphorin to consume the agricultural runoff — "

" — but not escape the filters," Boris finished for her.

"Yes," she said. "One of my main research areas is modifying phosphorin to maintain its omnivorous appetite while eliminating the dangers posed by it eating certain foods, like sugars."

"You are trying to tell me that Prince Ali's interest in phosphorin is due to his active engagement in our water-purification project, and not related to his family's support for terrorist activities."

Ali seemed about to interrupt, but Lucy once again waved him down. "Your definition of family is different than his. I understand he has dozens of siblings and half-siblings, and hundreds of cousins. Surely you can't blame him for what some of them are involved in."

Boris regarded her silently, then said, "Let us adopt your speculations about Ali as a working hypothesis. It is quite possible, even probable, that he attempted to acquire phosphorin for reasons that, I think we would agree, are worthy of praise."

"Then have I persuaded you?"

"Of what?"

"That human beings are capable of good. That we can act in ways that help rather than hurt."

"Dr. Kimball, I have never disputed that. My point, my conclusion, is that the human species is defined, primarily, by greed and self-interest. We are a terrible blight. The planet will breathe a sigh of relief when we are gone."

She heard the conviction in his voice — the finality. Her head was swimming. She wanted to believe he was insane, but she couldn't. His goal was horrifying, but his approach, his methodology, his reasoning were all impeccably rational.

She had to say something — anything — to penetrate his confidence. "I'll be fine, actually. I have immunity."

His eyes narrowed. "There is no immunity. I hacked your systems. I kept tabs on your research."

"I write my results by hand in lab notebooks. I don't transfer my data to a computer until I'm ready to share my results."

"How did you become immune?"

She didn't respond.

"Ah," he said, leaning forward. "You exposed yourself. That was naughty of you, Dr. Kimball. Scientists are prohibited from using themselves as guinea pigs, and for very good reasons."

She sighed. "I had to know."

"I understand that. I believe that. How did you ensure you would not contaminate anyone?"

"I made sure I was alone in the containment room. Protocol ensured that no one could enter. If I hadn't survived, the contents of the room would have been incinerated."

"How did your colleagues ensure you weren't contagious?"

"In addition to daily blood tests, two colleagues volunteered to be exposed to me."

"How long were you stuck in that room?"

"Six weeks."

"You're telling the truth," he said. "What else don't I know?"

He leaped toward her without warning and jammed his gun into her ribs.

Lucy cried out in pain.

"You will tell me what I don't know," he said, digging the gun in deeper. "You will tell me about this antidote of yours."

"Stop!" Lucy gasped, and he did.

He pulled back and whirled around, and Lucy heard why.

There was a knock at the door.

CHAPTER
EIGHTY-THREE

LUCY'S HEART THUMPED.

Three knocks in a row. Not Jack. So who?

Boris turned to Ali. "You were contaminated thirty-two hours ago — a sprinkling of phosphorin powder in your drink. You will be dead in four days. You are facing ninety-six hours of extreme pain and suffering. What I do now is a mercy."

He aimed the gun at Ali's chest and pulled the trigger. Ali's mouth opened in shock. His body jerked and shuddered. He sunk into the bed.

Lucy's mouth opened. She couldn't breathe. She couldn't believe — no, it couldn't be. She hadn't heard a gunshot — he couldn't have fired — but blood was soaking through Ali's shirt, and Ali's eyes, though open wide, were staring into nothingness.

If the gun had a silencer....

Boris pulled the bed sheet up to Ali's neck and, with his hand, closed Ali's eyelids. The prince looked as if he was asleep, but he wasn't. Prince Ali Saad Bandar, gentleman farmer and third in line to the throne of the Royal Kingdom of Gudan, was dead.

Dead.

Boris turned to Lucy, pulled a plastic tie out of his jacket pocket, and tossed it to her. "Sit on the floor. Tie your legs together."

Shakily, she did as she was told.

The knocking at the door came again, this time louder.

Boris tossed her another plastic tie. "Now your hands, then extend your arms to me."

Silently, she slipped the tie around her wrists. He reached down and pulled them tight, the plastic digging into her skin.

"A single sound from you and they die," he said, gesturing to the door. "Do you understand?"

She didn't need convincing. She nodded.

He turned off the lights, plunging the room into darkness.

Boris stepped up to the cabana door and opened it. From her vantage point, tied at the foot of the bed, she could see Sergei and Natasha in the light of the doorway. And she knew, from where they stood, that they wouldn't be able to see her through the gloom in the darkened room.

Boris put his finger to his lips. He stepped outside to join them, but kept the cabana door open.

"Ali is sleeping," he said to Sergei and Natasha, just loud enough for Lucy to hear. "Lucy Keen is tending to him."

Natasha said, "We have just come from Francois Le Coq's cabana. He is dead. Marie isn't there."

"Lucy told me. She believes his death was due to an infectious bacteria — Legionnaires' disease — which was most likely found inside the tunnels. She recommends we evacuate the island right away."

"Evacuation, based on the opinion of a medical student?" Natasha said.

"She is very intelligent."

Natasha shrugged as if to concede the point, but said, "If we have an infectious disease here, wouldn't it be wiser to quarantine ourselves?"

Boris shook his head. "Legionnaires' disease isn't transmittable from person to person. Infection is from heavy exposure to contaminated air. In addition, it has no effect on most individuals. Older people like Le Coq are the most susceptible. If any of the guests were exposed, their doctors can provide appropriate treatment."

Sergei frowned. "How can we be sure?" From the sound of his voice, he was no longer drunk, but not sober either.

Boris said, "I can arrange for medical staff to examine each guest after they leave the ferry in Kasos and before they board their jets. We can ask each to provide swabs to test for possible exposure. Would that work?"

Sergei looked at Natasha, who seemed uncertain.

At that moment, Durgos, the security man, joined them.

"We have a problem," he said. "Communications are down."

"Even land lines?" Sergei asked.

"Yes. We are completely cut off."

Natasha frowned. "Then we cannot arrange for medical tests after guests leave the island. We will need to keep everyone here."

"Yes," Sergei said. "Is responsible thing to do. I tell guests at breakfast. Now we must fix communications."

"No," Boris said. "I'm afraid you can't do that."

Natasha turned toward Boris. "Why — " she started to ask, then stopped.

Boris was aiming his gun at her.

"Inside," he said, gesturing with the gun toward the cabana.

Sergei stared at the gun, confusion on his face. Then his expression cleared. "Is joke, yes? You play role of bad guy?"

Boris smiled sadly. "Yes, Sergei. I'm playing the role of bad guy."

A deathly pallor came over Natasha's face.

"Boris," she said. "Please."

"You play role very well," Sergei said, delighted. "We can use in party next year. Theme can be — Bad Guy Takes Over Resort!"

"I'm afraid that won't be possible, my friend," Boris said. "All of you, inside."

Sergei grinned. "More surprises, yes? Come, Natasha, Durgos, we go in."

Natasha, tense and clearly terrified, nodded to Durgos.

They stepped into the cabana. Boris followed them in and shut the door.

"Turn on the lights," he said.

Durgos, closest to the switch, hit the lights.

Sergei's eyes widened when he saw Lucy tied up at the foot of the bed. He turned to Boris, confused. "Boris, game goes too far."

Sergei dashed to Lucy and knelt down. "I untie you now. You are okay?"

"Stay away from her, Sergei," Boris said, a tremor in his voice.

"Why?" he asked, turning to look up at Boris. "What are you saying?"

"I'm saying this is not a game."

Sergei's eyes moved from Boris's face, to the gun in his hand, then back to his face. His mouth opened, then closed, then opened again, as if his brain and mouth weren't working.

"Why?" he finally asked — a single word that carried with it a world of bewilderment and shock and hurt.

Boris's resolve seemed to falter. He pressed his lips tightly together and swallowed.

"I did not want it to end this way," he said, his voice thick with emotion. "I have plans for us, for you and me, my friend. I will not have you suffer."

"What are you doing?" Sergei cried.

"You must be calm."

Sergei stood. "You point gun at me? You want to hurt me? Go ahead. Shoot me! If you want to hurt me, do it now. Now!"

Boris trembled.

"No," he said as much to himself as to Sergei. "No. I will not have that memory in my head. I will not shoot you."

Without warning, Boris aimed the gun at Durgos and fired.

A bloom of red appeared on Durgos's forehead. With a gurgle, Durgos dropped to the ground.

Boris yanked Natasha to him and jammed the gun into her neck. "She's next, unless you cooperate."

No one protested after that. Quickly and efficiently, Boris rolled Ali's body to the floor, ordered Natasha and Sergei onto the bed, and tied them to the bedposts.

"I have something for all of us later," he said. "A strong narcotic. A simple injection, and we slip away gently. It will be painless for us, I promise.

"But first," he said, bending down and slicing through the tie binding Lucy's feet, "Lucy and I are going for a walk."

CHAPTER
EIGHTY-FOUR

Special Exploits command center
Los Angeles

DEPUTY COMMANDER CALHOUN took the pen she was chewing out of her mouth and set it on the workstation in front of her, frustrated that she had nothing to do but pace the floor. With Commander Grant called away to meet with the Director, the command center was hers.

Across the globe, agents were chasing down leads, reporting in, and receiving new instructions — all except Agent Ford. She'd watched him play Gang Bang as Borlando and win the phosphorin. She'd been waiting for him to report, but he hadn't called. She hadn't heard a thing, and she didn't like it.

On an island near Synkonos, a combined medical and security team was standing by, waiting for her signal to move in. They could be there in twenty-two minutes, if needed.

Agent Ford should have called. Something wasn't right. Something nibbled away at the outer edges of her thoughts.

"Replay the satellite feed," she said.

The footage came up. The satellite had passed over Synkonos an hour earlier. For six precious minutes, it had zoomed in on the island. Through the darkness, it had picked up heat signatures of people walking near the compound, swimming in the pool, and fucking on the beach.

"Pan back," she said.

The image zoomed out to reveal more of the island. She noticed a single heat signature on a barren hill near the main compound.

A security guard, most likely, but his movements were odd. She watched with increasing interest. He would bend over, stand up, walk up the hill, bend over, and then run down to where he'd started. Then he would do the same thing again. In the six minutes of captured imagery, she saw him do this three times.

"What is he doing?" she asked out loud.

She looked at her team for input, but got only shrugs.

"It's a hill," an analyst offered. "He could be running up and down to train for a sporting event."

"He could be bored," another said. "People do the weirdest shit when they're alone."

"When do we get satellite again?" she asked.

"Seventy-two minutes, shortly after sunrise," came the reply.

"Include the hill in the sweep when we get our eyes back," she said. "Better safe than sorry."

CHAPTER
EIGHTY-FIVE

AT THE SLIDING GLASS DOORS
OUTSIDE PRINCE ALI'S CABANA

JACK LEANED IN closer and listened. With the curtains closed, he couldn't see inside. He knocked again on the sliding glass door. Four knocks, a pause, then two knocks.

Nothing.

The time for covert action was over. He picked up a large rock from the garden and slammed it into the door.

The glass splintered. With a kick, he cleared the glass from the door and stepped inside.

Shit.

Sergei and Natasha were on the bed, gagged and tied to the bedposts and staring at him bug-eyed.

Ali and Durgos were on the floor beside them, dead.

Heart racing, he dashed into the bathroom — empty. Same with the closet.

Where was Lucy?

He stepped over Ali's corpse and loosened Natasha's gag.

"Where's Lucy?" he asked.

She gasped. "Boris took her."

Boris!

"He's dangerous," she said. "He has a gun."

He had to save her. He dashed into the bathroom, rooted through Ali's items until he found a straight razor, and ran back to Natasha and sliced through the tie binding her wrists.

"Where did he take her?" he asked.

"I don't know," Natasha said, "but I heard luggage rolling down the path. I think Boris is telling guests to leave."

He went still. That made no sense. Why encourage the guests to leave? Unless....

Boris wanted the contamination to spread.

And that would mean....

He'd encountered this mindset before — one far removed from the petty concerns of profit or power or personal glory. It was the mindset of an activist, a society-changer, an idealist who was ready to sacrifice others to realize his twisted version of a better world.

His gut clenched. Nothing riled him more — or frightened him more — than messianic self-righteous psycho nutjobs.

For the first time in six years as an agent with Special Exploits, he felt a stirring of bitter anger, mixed with sadness, about what his job required of him and the priority it forced on him now.

"Did Boris threaten to kill himself?" he asked.

"And us," Natasha said. "I've never seen him like this."

He handed her the razor. "Be careful. Stay out of his way. I have to go."

CHAPTER
EIGHTY-SIX

IN THE GONDOLA CAVE

THE MORNING SUN cast early shadows on the cave wall as Boris helped a frightened guest place her luggage in the gondola.

"I promise, you will all be fine," he said to her as the others packed into the crowded gondola. "A short trip down to the pier, and the ferry will have you on your way."

He closed the door, signaled to the operator, and watched the gondola glide through the mouth of the cave and toward the pier and ferry on the other side of the bay.

As expected, he'd had no trouble convincing the guests to cut their weekend short. In small groups, he'd pulled them aside and told them the island was experiencing an outbreak of Legionnaires' disease. Monsieur Le Coq was dead, he'd told them, and Prince Ali was infected. Yes, he'd agreed, very tragic. Fortunately, he'd told them, Legionnaires' disease didn't spread from person to person, so there was no cause for concern once off the island. Of course, the Greek authorities would undoubtedly institute a quarantine as soon as they organized their response. The quarantine would likely drag on — the Greeks were not known for their efficiency. Very troublesome, yes, and pointless.

Although, he added, a ferry was leaving for Kasos shortly. To avoid being stuck on Synkonos for days or even weeks, it might make sense to pack up and head to the pier. But time was of the essence.

More than eighty guests and hospitality facilitators had rushed to ensure they were on that ferry. In their lungs, dead sucronal phosphorin was triggering their good bacteria into reproductive overdrive. They didn't feel anything, of course — not yet. In eighteen hours, they'd notice a small cough and would wonder whether they were coming down with Legionnaires' disease. Some would rush to see their doctors, but most wouldn't. Most would shrug it off. Just a cold, they'd tell themselves. A simple cold.

He stepped up to the mouth of the cave and took in the view of the bay. A beautiful morning on planet Earth, which would soon be even sweeter with humans gone. Nature would cleanse itself of mankind's damage — atmospheric carbon, industrial pollutants, decimated seas, vanishing rain forests — within a few hundred years. A few thousand years more, and nearly all evidence of mankind's existence would rust and decompose and crumble away. In some distant future, if the planet was unfortunate enough to evolve another intelligent, greedy, rapacious, shortsighted, vicious species, they might discover evidence of humans in the fossil record, and wonder what had brought about their sudden end.

The gondola was halfway across the bay, several hundred feet above the water and fast approaching the pier. He reviewed his operational checklist: Sergei and Natasha — incapacitated. Durgos and Prince Ali and Jack Ford — dead.

Constantine — down at the pier and out of the way, overseeing the guests' departures. The ferry's departure — imminent.

Everything was in hand. Should he head for the helicopter now? Fly up above the Grid and, with a single call, set in motion the other phosphorin releases that would bring about the end of the human race? Or should he remain on the island a bit longer, to directly oversee the dispersal of more phosphorin-carrying guests into the world?

The latter course was wiser, he decided. The guests' transmission potential was too vast — their capacity for travel too important — to treat casually. He turned to the staffer manning the gondola controls.

"I have an errand, but I will be back shortly. As more guests arrive, tell them the next ferry will leave in one hour. Encourage them to take the gondola down to the pier to await the ferry's arrival."

He left the cave and headed into the tunnel system that ran under the plateau. There was one particular item on his operational checklist he wanted to check off.

An item named Dr. Lucy Kimball.

CHAPTER
EIGHTY-SEVEN

SPECIAL EXPLOITS COMMAND CENTER
LOS ANGELES

ON THE BIG screen in front of her, Calhoun watched the island come into focus as the satellite crossed overhead.

Morning light bathed Synkonos. The satellite captured a wide-angle shot of the island.

"Zoom in," Calhoun said. "Scan for heat signatures."

Nothing unusual. All seemed quiet.

Then she remembered. "Scan the hill on the plateau."

Long seconds passed as the commands were relayed to the satellite and the cameras and sensors focused in.

The hill came into view. The ground was almost white, unlike the rest of the black rock on the plateau.

"Closer," she said.

Then she saw it — dozens of black rocks the size of bowling balls arranged in a pattern on the white hill, making up four letters:

P H O S.

Calhoun breathed in sharply. Jack would have had to run up and down that hill dozens of times to pick up the dark rocks from the plateau and lug them up the hill. He would have done that only if he had had no other way to communicate. Which meant, as Jack might have put it, shit had hit the fan and splattered big-time.

She turned to the satellite controller. "Where is the ferry?"

The tech clicked away at his keyboard. A few seconds later, the screen widened, then zoomed in again on the ferry.

At sea, approaching Kasos.

"It left Synkonos twenty minutes ago," the tech said. "It will dock in Kasos harbor in eight minutes."

"Tell the local authorities not to let the ferry land and to keep everyone on board."

Another tech spoke up. "Deputy Commander, the harbor master on Kasos isn't responding. Neither are the police."

"Have the communications been hacked?"

"It appears so. If the passengers disembark — "

"I know!" Calhoun snapped. "Dammit."

She took a deep breath. She'd known it might come to this and hated the thought.

"Are the F-18s at the ready?" she asked.

"Yes, ma'am."

"On my order," she announced.

"Wait," the tech said. "The ferry — it's slowing down."

They watched as the ferry, still outside the harbor, slowed. Then it turned, its engines roaring into overdrive as it aimed itself back toward Synkonos.

Calhoun exhaled in relief.

"Listen up, people," she said. "We are at Level Five biohazard status. Notify the advance team. Alert NATO and the Greek authorities. Monitor the ferry and make sure it returns to Synkonos. As soon as the ferry arrives, move in."

She paused, then said, "We have nearly three hundred civilians on that island, along with two of ours, but know this: No one — no one — can leave Synkonos without medical clearance. No one. No matter the cost."

CHAPTER
EIGHTY-EIGHT

LUCY STRUGGLED AGAINST the plastic ties cutting into her wrists — futilely, she knew.

Not a shred of light penetrated the cave where Boris had stashed her. Gun in her back, he'd forced her underground, down a tunnel she hadn't been in before, to a small passage barely waist-high, and told her to get down on her hands and knees and crawl through the narrow fissure into the small cave she found herself in now.

The air in the cave was dry and cool and carried something else: the cheerful aroma of phosphorin.

"Lay on your stomach, hands behind your back," he'd told her. He followed her in, then positioned his flashlight on the floor, aiming the beam upwards to illuminate the small space.

Quietly and efficiently, he used plastic ties to bind her feet and hands. He then used another plastic strip to hogtie her feet and hands together behind her back.

He pulled at the bonds to satisfy himself, then stood.

From her spot on the ground, she watched him remove a clear plastic bag of gray powder from a nook in the cave wall.

"A kilo," he said, giving the bag a shake. "Finely ground and barely a tenth of a micron in size."

The man had done his homework. Particles that size could travel effortlessly across long distances, carried by the faintest of air currents.

He kneeled down again and fastened a gag over her mouth. "I'll be back, Dr. Kimball."

And then he was gone.

How much time since he'd left? Half an hour? An hour? All she really knew was that she was captive and immobile in utter darkness, at the mercy of a madman who would soon kill her.

She grunted in frustration, pulling uselessly against the ties, her arms and legs and back screaming in pain.

She heard footsteps and saw a bloom of faint light. Boris appeared in the narrow fissure, flashlight between his teeth. He ran the light over her to make sure her bonds had held, then crawled forward and removed her gag.

"All is well," he said. "Only a few items left to check off my list."

She worked her mouth and moved her jaw.

"Boris," she said, her voice hoarse and scratchy.

"Are you ready to talk?" He cut through the tie binding her arms to her legs, then sliced through the ties binding her ankles and wrists. "No heroics. I have my gun."

"What do you want?" she asked in an exhausted voice. She stretched her arms and shoulders, trying not to cry out in pain.

"Time for a walk."

"Where?"

"We'll talk while we walk."

"About what?"

"Your antidote."

Like hell.

She must have broadcast her resistance — her eyes must have flashed, her mouth must have tightened, or her neck must have tensed — because Boris chuckled.

"I admire your spirit, Dr. Kimball. Still not ready to concede."

"Never," she said.

"Let's go."

She dropped onto her hands and knees and crawled through the fissure, exiting into the larger tunnel, Boris behind her. The thought of escape teased her, tempting her, but the darkness, and her wobbly legs, quashed that idea.

Boris joined her and stood. He aimed the flashlight to the left.

"Walk that way," he said.

She took a few shaky steps, her strength slowly returning. She walked ahead of him, his flashlight pointing the way. After a few minutes, they reached the entrance to the gondola cave.

"Stop," he said.

She looked back at him.

"Let us be clear," he said. "I expect you to act normally. If you do anything or say anything to warn or alert anyone, I will shoot you and the witnesses. Do you understand?"

She nodded. "Where are you taking me?"

"For a walk. But first, we'll make sure everything is running smoothly."

She stepped out into the gondola cave. A small group of guests had gathered and were waiting with their bags for the next gondola.

Vienna was among them. Her eyes found and stayed fixed on Lucy, looking torn about whether to speak to her.

"Where's Jack?" she finally asked.

Lucy struggled to keep her face from showing the fear the simple question triggered, the upwelling of uncertainty and doubt and — grief? No, not grief. She couldn't go there. Grief required loss. Uncertainty was better than loss. Infinitely better.

"He's on his way," she said to Vienna as calmly as she could manage.

Boris turned to the gondola technician. "How are we doing?"

The tech said, "Guests have been heading to the pier for the next ferry."

Boris glanced at his watch. "Good."

He turned to Lucy. "Ms. Keen, shall we?"

A guest approached him. "Boris, where is Sergei? I wanted to say goodbye."

Boris turned to face the assembled guests. He addressed them with calm authority, displaying the ease of a man with years of public speaking under his belt.

"Sergei has asked me to apologize on his behalf. As you may have realized, in addition to our medical issues, we've experienced a communications glitch. Sergei is working to fix it. He will be in touch with each of you in the next few days to thank you personally for coming to Synkonos this weekend. Again, we're very sorry these sad occurrences cut our weekend short. The ferry will be returning to Synkonos in a few moments to take you all home. We wish you all a safe and speedy journey. If you'll excuse us."

His eyes went to Lucy, and he gestured toward the stairs leading up to the garden and courtyard. "Shall we?"

She had no choice, she realized. With a final glance at Vienna, she turned and made her way up the steps.

"You did well," Boris said once they'd reached the garden path at the top of the steps. "To the courtyard."

Lucy started walking, Boris at her side. There had to be

something she could do. Surely an opportunity would present itself.

In a calm voice, Boris said, "I've been giving some thought to your supposed immunity. There will be, of course, a few people who, like you, even after exposure, won't die from the phosphorin. Not many, but a few. Perhaps one out of every hundred thousand will have a natural resistance. Very few survivors will come from the young and healthy segment of the population; those with robust immune systems will, ironically, suffer most from the phosphorin. No, the survivors will more likely have weaker immune responses — older people and those whose health is already poor."

They reached the courtyard. Several guests hurried past them with their luggage, heading for the gondola cave.

Boris guided her toward the path at the opposite end of the courtyard. "The few who survive the phosphorin will face a very dangerous world. Most will die from the usual causes: starvation, exposure, accidents, other diseases, isolation. Or from each other, assuming they find each other.

"Your city of Los Angeles, for example. A population of nine million reduced to ninety people, the majority of them old or sick. Reproduction, when it does occur, will be sporadic. It is doubtful enough new humans will be birthed to outpace the mortality rate.

"No," he said. "Odds are quite good my plan will succeed."

He could easily be right, she knew. Even if his assumption of lethality was off by an order of magnitude — if survival was one in ten thousand, or one in one thousand — the odds of the human race coming back from the brink of extinction were slim to....

None?

No. She couldn't go there.

They reached the pavilion for the Synkonos Express elevator-rollercoaster.

"Stop," he said.

He walked her to the edge of the pavilion, to a spot that offered an unobstructed view of the bay. Just two nights earlier, she and Jack had danced in that very spot.

In the bay below, she saw the ferry slip through the passage in the cliff and head toward the pier.

The ferry's return seemed to please Boris.

"Ahead of schedule," he said.

He glanced at his watch, then frowned. His stance shifted from confident to tense. He reached behind him and pulled out his gun, his eyes fixed on the ferry below.

What was going on? She heard the roar of revving engines. The ferry picked up speed. She spotted people on the ferry's upper deck — guests.

What the — ?

The ferry wasn't slowing down. Rather, it was speeding up and barreling toward the beach.

Without even the slightest hesitation, the ferry rammed itself ashore, its bow rising out of the water, beaching itself like a suicidal whale.

She gasped as guests went flying, screaming in terror.

Then she saw him. He jumped from the ferry and dashed up the beach, racing toward them.

Jack!

CHAPTER EIGHTY-NINE

NEXT TO HER, Boris uttered a word — "mudak!" — which probably wasn't very complimentary.

He whirled on her, his eyes filled with rage. The gun inched closer to her head.

Was this how she would die? She closed her eyes, unable to breathe, her heart thudding in her chest.

Seconds passed. She hazarded a look. Boris's face was still flushed, his eyes still vivid, but his anger was subsiding. He took a deep breath and exhaled, then inhaled and exhaled again, forcing himself to calm down, to think, to assess, to adjust. A remarkable display of self-control — control that he'd lost, for a second or two, as he'd neared his breaking point.

"Change of plans," he said. He grabbed her arm and shoved her down the path.

"The game's over," she said. "The team's moving in. The island will be quarantined. The phosphorin will never leave Synkonos."

He laughed. "For someone so clever, you really are naive."

The path led to the plateau.

"Faster." He grabbed her by the elbow and forced her into a jog.

She realized where they were headed before she saw it: to the helicopter pad and the old Vietnam War-era helicopter that Boris and Sergei had used, two days before, to replace one of the weather balloons holding up the Grid over the island.

Was he trying to escape? Or — more likely — was there more to his plan than she'd seen so far? What if Synkonos wasn't the only dispersal point for the phosphorin? Given how determined and thorough he was in his planning, he would —

And she saw it, in a single panicked flash: He'd set up multiple dispersal points, probably in crowded transportation hubs in major cities. Ready to be activated at his command, as soon as he flew above the Grid and made the fateful phone call.

She had to stop him, but how? Could she delay him long enough for Jack to reach them?

They reached the edge of the landing area. Ahead of them, a man — the pilot, she guessed — was removing a fuel nozzle from the chopper.

Boris turned to her and said quietly, "I expect you to behave."

"You won't shoot me," she said. "Not now."

"You overestimate your importance."

"Jack's coming. The team is coming. I'm insurance — leverage."

He smiled grimly. "You're a fool."

"You won't shoot me, and you won't threaten to shoot the pilot. You need both of us."

"I'm a trained helicopter pilot, Dr. Kimball. I'm surprised my dossier didn't reveal that."

Was he a trained pilot? For the life of her, she couldn't recall what she'd read about him. All she knew as she looked at his determined face was that he seemed triumphant, as if he was still in control and knew it, as if he was telling her the truth.

"Let's go," he said. He stuffed his gun into the back of his pants, took her by the arm, and walked her to the helicopter.

The pilot glanced at them.

Boris gestured to the chopper. "Are we ready?"

"Three minutes," the pilot said. "Climb in."

The pilot had been expecting Boris. The ride had been planned all along. Jack's arrival had merely sped up the timetable.

She climbed into the chopper. Unlike the sleek, modern craft she'd flown in three days earlier over Los Angeles, this helicopter was old and worn, with walls of rough metal. The inside was bigger, and tall enough for her to stand in while bent over.

"Sit there, Dr. Kimball," Boris said, indicating a low bench against the rear wall of the cargo area.

She sat. As she did, her right hand brushed her pants pocket — the pocket with the lipstick gun! She'd forgotten about it. A flare of hope surged through her.

How did the gun work again? What had Jack shown her? Open it and — turn right? Turn left? Was there a button she needed to push? How accurate was the bullet? How close did she have to be?

For the life of her, she couldn't remember. But she had to try — had to.

Boris followed her in, his eyes darting from her to the plateau and back. He was expecting Jack, just like she was expecting him to appear, running his ass off to stop the man who now stood, hunched over, at the open cargo door, ready to pull out his gun and shoot him down.

The pilot climbed into the chopper, glanced at her with curiosity, and strapped himself into the pilot's seat. He adjusted his glasses and pressed a button on the instrument panel.

The engines revved to life. The massive blades started turning, round and round until they blurred together.

The pilot flipped a switch on the instrument panel, grabbed levers on either side of him, then pushed the left lever forward.

The chopper rumbled and shook as it prepared for liftoff.

Her fingers traced the outline of the lipstick gun in her pocket.

Jack wasn't going to make it. He hadn't had enough time to get from the beach to the helicopter.

Which meant she was on her own, with just one shot at stopping a madman.

With a lurch, the helicopter rose off the ground.

CHAPTER **NINETY**

BREATH RASPING, heart pounding, arms and legs pumping, Jack reached the top of the plateau and saw the two objects of his concern:

Lucy — alive and in the helicopter, seated on a bench in the cargo bay.

And Boris, standing at the cargo bay door, his eyes scanning the plateau, looking for him. But looking in the wrong direction.

Boris hadn't seen him yet, nor had Lucy. Her gaze was fixed on Boris, her hand inching into her pants pocket.

The helicopter lifted off the ground.

He raced up to the helicopter from the front. The pilot stared at him in surprise and shook his head.

"It's dangerous," he mouthed.

No shit.

He leaped onto the landing gear, grabbed the edge of the cargo bay entrance, and swung in feet first, using his forward momentum to body slam into Boris.

They crashed to the floor, Jack on top. The gun in Boris's waistband went flying. Boris exhaled in surprise.

Jack gripped Boris by the head and slammed it into the metal floor, but the man wasn't going gently into the good night. Boris wrapped his legs around him and, with a move that spoke of serious wrestling chops, flipped Jack onto his side, which was a problem. Boris was bigger than him: taller by two inches, twenty pounds heavier, and, apparently, really good at close fighting.

Boris pushed something into his face — a plastic bag. He was trying to suffocate him. A piece caught in Jack's teeth. He bit down and tore through the plastic. Powder — lemony powder — filled his mouth.

Fuck.

Boris's hands moved down to his neck. Before he could even gasp for air, the hands started crushing his throat.

Double fuck.

"Stop!" he heard Lucy yell. "I'll shoot!"

Boris glanced up and froze.

Jack followed his gaze. Lucy was standing over them, aiming something at them.

The lipstick gun. The one he'd given her.

Her eyes had a wild edge to them, mixed with determination. "Let him go!"

Boris's hands loosened, and Jack gasped for air. Phosphorin powder whirled into his lungs, triggering an uncontrollable coughing fit.

With a single fluid movement, Boris backed away from Jack and, on his knees facing Lucy, inched toward the door of the cargo bay. His hand reached behind him.

Too late, Jack saw why. Boris's arm swung around, gun in hand.

Jack rolled up, grabbed the arm holding the gun, and pulled Boris toward him.

Down they went. Jack slammed the arm holding the gun against the floor.

Boris pulled the trigger — a silent shot.

The helicopter gave a sudden lurch.

"Jack," he heard Lucy scream. "The pilot!"

Boris looked up, and Jack saw his chance. He slammed his elbow as hard as he could into Boris's temple. With a groan, Boris went down.

The chopper spun like a malformed bowl on a pottery wheel. Lucy grabbed an overhead strap and her lipstick gun went flying.

"Hold on!" Jack yelled. He got onto his hands and knees and pulled himself toward the pilot. The man was dead, slumped in his seat, a crimson splatter dripping from the windshield in front of him.

Jack unbuckled the pilot and pulled him clear of the seat as the helicopter shot up, its nose lurching toward the sun.

"Hang on!"

He climbed over the man's body and into the seat, then took a split second to glance back to reassure himself that Lucy was still there.

She was, hanging desperately to an overhead strap as the helicopter swung them around.

In that second, he saw her eyes widen in shock as she realized what was covering his face.

Gray powder. Too much gray powder, her eyes said. With that much exposure —

The helicopter shuddered, the morning sun nearly blinding him as he turned toward the controls and to the impossible task of setting the machine down in one piece.

"Jack, look out!" he heard her cry.

He glanced back again. Boris had awakened and, in a single, fluid movement, grabbed an overhead strap.

With a cry of triumph, he aimed his gun at Lucy's head.

"Leave her out of it, Yoko!" Jack yelled. "The game's over. You can't win."

Boris burst into laughter at the sight of Jack's phosphorin-covered face.

"Maybe not, Mr. Ford, but neither can you."

Laughter edged into hysteria as he repeated, with unhinged glee, "Neither can you!"

CHAPTER NINETY-ONE

LUCY GASPED. Madness. Insanity. Never in a million years would she have imagined this, fighting for the fate of mankind against a madman with a gun, alongside a man she —

Never in a million years.

She lunged at Boris.

Boris's hand hit the roof, and the gun went flying.

The gun! She dove for it, Boris right behind her.

They clawed and kicked at each other.

Her hand reached out, her fingers on the gun —

Boris pulled her back by the legs.

She kicked at him, but he absorbed the blows and dropped on top of her.

Breath knocked out of her, she gasped.

Boris reached over her and grabbed the gun.

With his other hand, he grabbed her by the hair.

She cried in pain as he jammed the barrel into her ribs.

Her head swam. God, the pain.

She couldn't breathe.

"Lucy!" Jack cried, rage in his voice. "Boris, let her go!"

Boris laughed. "Get this helicopter under control, Mr. Ford. Do it now!"

"Let her go!"

"You will fly this helicopter above the Grid, now!"

She cried out again as Boris dug the gun in deeper.

"I'll do it!" Jack yelled. "I'll do it! I'll fly you there! Just leave her alone!"

Boris pushed away from her. He sat up, still on his knees, and fell back onto the bench.

Lucy gasped in pain. Boris had cracked a rib when he'd landed on her.

"Lucy!" Jack yelled. "Are you okay?"

She breathed in and felt a sharp stab, and then breathed again, this time with a smaller breath. The sharpness of the pain eased.

"Cracked rib," she said, surprised to find her voice steady. "I'll be fine."

"Turn around, Mr. Ford, and focus on flying," Boris said.

The helicopter was still spinning. A gust of wind hit, causing the chopper to lurch sickeningly.

"Focus, Mr. Ford!"

Jack returned his attention to the controls.

Through the open cargo bay door, she saw they were over the bay, several hundred feet up. Another gust of wind hit them, and the chopper shuddered. With difficulty, Jack worked the levers on either side of him.

The chopper hovered in the air uncertainly, then stabilized as Jack gradually gained control.

"Position yourself below the hole in the Grid, fly up for three hundred meters, and then head north," Boris said, then turned his attention to Lucy. "Sit up on the bench."

She pulled herself up and did as ordered.

He reached into his pants pocket and pulled out another one of those damn plastic ties.

"My last one," he said. "Attach your arm to the overhead rail. I will not underestimate you again."

He tossed the tie onto her lap. She looked at it, then at him. She'd be helpless, at his mercy, and she was so goddamn sick of being at his mercy.

"No," she said.

"What?" Boris said.

"No!" she yelled.

Jack glanced back. "Lucy, do what he says!"

Boris's mouth tightened.

"You won't kill me," Lucy said. "I'm your leverage against Jack."

Boris regarded her in silence, his breathing returning to normal. Such exceptional equilibrium.

"Dr. Kimball, you never cease to surprise."

He pulled a phone out of his pants pocket and turned it on. He frowned.

"Mr. Ford, keep yourself facing forward. Position us below the hole in the Grid. Dr. Kimball, I will shoot you in the leg if you don't tie yourself to the upper rail."

"I don't care!" she said, yelling to make sure every word carried over the deafening roar of the chopper's blades and engines. "I'd rather Jack crash this helicopter than give you the chance to trigger your devices."

Jack turned around again. He saw the phone in Boris's hand. He locked eyes with Lucy.

In that second, time expanded. She saw that he understood. She saw sadness in his eyes, as well as regret for all they would never experience. She saw respect for her choice, for her sacrifice — for their sacrifice.

"Hang on!" Jack yelled.

"Mr. Ford!" Boris said, swinging the gun toward him.

Jack swerved hard on the controls. Lucy grabbed the upper rail and hung on for dear life as the helicopter lurched hard to the right.

Boris slammed against the cabin roof but hung on. Enraged, he aimed the gun again at Jack and fired, missing and splintering the front window.

Lucy let go of the railing and flung herself onto Boris, making a grab for his arm.

The helicopter swerved over Villa Synkonos, barely missing the roof, and shot out over the bay.

She fought desperately for any tiny advantage. She didn't stand a chance, but she didn't care. With everything she had, she grabbed at Boris's arm, which even now was aiming at Jack's back.

Boris shot again, this time missing Jack's head by inches.

Another hard swerve sent them both rolling toward the open cargo bay door.

Wind rushed at her. The cliff loomed ahead, the chopper heading straight for it.

Boris's eyes widened. With an enraged cry, he rolled onto his feet and grabbed Jack from behind with one arm and, with his other arm, jammed the gun against Jack's head.

"Turn!" Boris screamed.

At the last second, Jack yanked right and up, and the helicopter went almost straight up. The engine roared in protest. Boris lost his grip and fell back.

And so did Lucy, through the open door.

She heard Jack's anguished cry as she slipped out the cargo bay door.

So this was it, her last seconds on this earth — a fall through nothing, and then death.

The thought barely had time to register before her legs caught on the chopper's landing gear. Like an acrobat, she hung from her knees, hundreds of feet above the cobalt blue of the bay.

The chopper twisted and shuddered, swinging her like a girl on a trapeze as the helicopter twirled out of control.

With everything she had, she willed her legs to hold on to the landing gear. As the torque on her body increased, she went almost horizontal.

Inside, she caught glimpses of Jack on top of an unconscious Boris, pounding his face with punishing blows. He'd abandoned the controls and had attacked. The powder on his face was streaked with tears.

"Nooooo!" he screamed, hammering away. "Noooooo!"

"Jack!" Lucy yelled. "Jaaaaack!"

Her shouts penetrated his kill zone. His eyes shot up in disbelief.

He bounded to the door and, with a sharp cry, saw her.

"Hang on!"

The helicopter spun even more erratically.

With one hand on the door handle, he reached out and grabbed at Lucy. "Reach up!"

The torque increased. Desperately, Lucy tried to sit up — tried to reach Jack's hand.

"Reach up! Come on! You can do it!"

The helicopter pitched to the side. Lucy's legs lost their grip.

"Jack!"

She was loose and untethered. And then she felt it — his rough hand grabbing her arm — but they weren't falling. He'd leaped out and had caught her. His legs were wrapped around the chopper's landing gear.

Spinning through the air, the helicopter now truly out of control, swinging in ever-wider arcs through the air. A gust of wind hit them.

"Lucy!" Jack said. "The gondola!"

With horror, Lucy looked down and saw the gondola moving from the pier toward the villa, and realized the helicopter was rushing toward it.

"Jack?"

"On the count of three!"

"What?"

"One!"

Lucy saw what he wanted to attempt. It wasn't possible!

"Two!"

The helicopter, still spinning, swung through the sky and over the cable, the gondola approaching fast. The chopper reached a high point in its arc and dipped back.

The gondola zoomed up the cable. The chopper's angle shifted. They were on a collision course!

"Three!"

Jack let go. And for the second time in two minutes, she fell.

She landed hard, Jack right behind her, on the roof of the gondola. Her legs buckled beneath her.

Before she even had time to register the pain, the gondola's automatic wind sensors misinterpreted their midair landing as a gust and brought the gondola to a screeching halt.

The sudden lurch sent her sliding toward the edge until a strong hand on her arm stopped her.

Jack pulled her up into his arms, and she buried her face in his neck. She gripped him as if she'd never let go.

"We're gonna be okay," she heard him say, but his voice wasn't comforting; it was distracted. She looked up.

Above them, the helicopter climbed higher, continuing its uneven arc.

His face was grim.

He let her go, stood up, and unzipped his jeans. Why was he undressing?

"What are you doing?" she yelled.

"Stand up!"

"You're getting naked? Again?"

The chopper reached the top of its arc and headed back down — toward them.

He threw one leg of his jeans over the cable and gripped each pant leg as tightly as he could.

"Grab hold of me, arms around my neck, legs around my waist! Don't let go!"

She threw her arms around him. His skin was slick with sweat.

"Whatever you do, don't let go!" he yelled in her ear.

She wrapped her legs around his naked hips and locked her ankles.

The helicopter roared toward them.

"Hold tight!"

He jumped. She felt his shoulders flex and strain as he bore their weight. The jeans started sliding down the cable. They picked up speed, hurtling downward.

"We're going too fast!" she yelled. "We'll never slow down!"

"We don't have a choice!" he yelled back.

As he said it, the helicopter slammed into the gondola and exploded.

She screamed and nearly lost her grip.

She heard a voice yelling, "Faster!" and realized it was her own.

The heat of the blast hit them. Pieces of helicopter flew past them.

The cables held fast for three agonizing seconds and then snapped. The gondola and helicopter fell, taking the entire cable system with it.

And then they were falling. This time, nothing would stop them.

She hit the water with a shocking smack. For several seconds, she couldn't move, stunned. She opened her eyes and felt the sting of the salt water. Her instinct to survive took over and she kicked her way toward the surface.

Her head burst out of the water, and she inhaled as if she'd never breathed before.

Jack's head popped up twenty feet from hers.

"Dive!" he yelled. "The cable!"

Without even looking up, she dove. The cable smacked the surface where she had just been and bore down on her, catching her midsection right where Boris had cracked her rib. The sudden pain caused her to exhale, costing her precious air.

She couldn't break free. The weight and speed were too much. The cable sank her like a stone to the floor of the bay.

She wasn't far down, maybe twenty feet. She could do this. With her remaining strength, she pushed against the cable pinning her down.

She couldn't. She wanted to cry but couldn't. Her lungs threatened to explode.

Then came a flutter of movement. A hand on the cable somehow lifted it and pulled her loose, then yanked her to the surface.

Sunlight exploded in Lucy's eyes.

She gasped.

CHAPTER
NINETY-TWO

On Greek Island, a Deadly Duel with Legionnaires

The New York Times

ATHENS — The Greek government reported "significant progress" today in efforts to contain a deadly outbreak of Legionnaires' disease that has killed a dozen people and endangered hundreds of vacationers on the Greek island of Synkonos. A spokesman for the Greek health ministry said medical treatments are "working effectively" for most of the nearly 300 people who remain in quarantine.

"Treatment is proving efficacious for nearly all of those who suffered exposure," said Theodoris Onassis, director of Disease Prevention for the Greek Ministry of Health.

Onassis would not speculate on how much longer the quarantine would continue. "We are monitoring constantly," he said. "The guests of the resort are anxious to return to their busy lives. We will lift the quarantine as soon as medically appropriate."

The U.S. Centers for Disease Control said scientists are

focusing on World War II-era tunnels on Synkonos as the likely source of the infection.

"The resort used the naturally cooled air in the tunnels as air conditioning," said CDC spokesman Jameson Franks. "The tunnels offer ideal growth conditions for Legionella, the bacterium that can cause Legionnaires' disease."

Authorities stress that there is no risk of infection by anyone not on the island.

Legionnaires' Toll in Greece Rises to 17

Associated Press

ATHENS — Greek authorities reported an additional fatality from the outbreak of Legionnaires' disease on the Greek island of Synkonos, bringing the death total from the outbreak to 17. The death of twenty-two-year-old American model, Jennifer Lynn Sparks, was due to respiratory infection and organ failure.

Other casualties of the Legionnaires' disease outbreak include French scientist Francois Le Coq, Prince Ali Saad Bandar of Gudan, and Boris Ignatiev, COO and co-founder of online gaming company Gang Bang, Inc.

In addition to the Legionnaires' disease deaths, noted hedge fund owner Dick Hould died from an accidental fall, said Greek authorities.

Jack Ford, younger son of Abernathy Industries chairman Abigail Ford, and Marie Le Coq, the wife of the deceased French scientist, have reportedly been evacuated to a secure medical quarantine facility in Germany and remain in critical condition.

Vienna's Ordeal!

Them Weekly

Plucky paparazzi princess Vienna Hastings is hanging tough despite being trapped with a deadly disease on the remote Greek island of Synkonos, sources say.

"I don't know if I can bear this any longer!" she reportedly told close friends, who fear Vienna may succumb to the horrible Legionnaires' disease — a deadly scourge that is now killing off her friends, one by one, on the gorgeous private Greek isle.

Complicating matters for Vienna's terrified family and friends: Gang Bang founder Sergei Eristov has issued a Soviet-style directive that no computers or phones are allowed on the island! Vienna's twelve million Twitter followers will have to wait until she's freed from her Greek island prison to hear how she's holding up amidst the fear and uncertainty of infection and death. Friends say Vienna is nearly out of her mind with worry over the fate of sometime beau, Jack Ford, whose condition reportedly continues to worsen.

It's a Cover-up! End of the World is Near

Survivalist message board

Don't believe the lamestream media's lies! Legionnaires doesn't exist. It's just a stupid cover story the government trots out after a bioweapon attack. They can't even come up with something original!

CHAPTER
NINETY-THREE

DEEP UNDERGROUND
IN A SECURE UNDISCLOSED LOCATION

THE TELEX MACHINE came to life. He heard the gentle click-click-click of words being printed to paper.

An indulgence, in this age of mobile communication. But one he preferred. A reminder of times past.

Carefully, he made his way across the room and let the telex do its work.

TO: DIRECTOR

FROM: COMMANDER

RE: SPECIAL EXPLOITS CASE 11348-X

PRELIMINARY ASSESSMENT:

PHOSPHORIN THREAT CONTAINED.

CONTAGION LIMITED TO SYNKONOS. ISLAND QUARANTINED UNDER CDC/WHO CONTROL WITH NATO AND GREEK NAVY SUPPORT.

SEVEN PHOSPHORIN BIOWEAPONS RECOVERED WITHOUT INCIDENT AT GARE DU NORD (PARIS), PADDINGTON (LONDON), GRAND CENTRAL (NEW YORK), SHIBUYA (TOKYO), TSIM SHA TSUI (HONG KONG), CHHATRAPATI SHIVAJI (MUMBAI), AND CARIOCA (RIO).

COVER STORY (LEGIONNAIRES) PROVIDED TO MEDIA. NO LEAKS. TRACKING USUAL MESSAGE BOARD ASSERTIONS FROM KNOWN CRANKS.

TREATMENT PROTOCOL (REF: LUCY KIMBALL) ADMINISTERED AND 92% EFFICACIOUS.

CASE SUMMARY:

19 DEATHS FROM 294 INFECTED INDIVIDUALS, 4 ADDITIONAL DEATHS LIKELY. SEE FULL LIST IN ADDENDUM.

BORIS IGNATIEV ELIMINATED. MASTERMIND OF OPERATION. UNLIKE MOST WOULD-BE MURDERERS OF ENTIRE HUMAN SPECIES, IGNATIEV WAS A ONE-MAN SHOW. EXTREMELY WELL ORGANIZED. EMPLOYED STRICT NEED-TO-KNOW PROCEDURES. HIRED SPECIALISTS FOR KASSON THEFT. HIRED ZURICH CRIME GANG TO KIDNAP, VIDEOTAPE, AND MURDER ZURICH PROSTITUTES. UPON DELIVERY OF VIDEO PROOF, HIRED SPECIALIST ASSASSIN TO KILL ZURICH GANG TO PREVENT LEAKS. HIRED LOCAL COURIERS TO TRANSPORT PHOSPHORIN BRIEFCASES TO TRAIN STATIONS. COURIERS WERE TOLD BRIEF-CASES CONTAINED INDUSTRIAL SECRETS.

DICK HOULD ELIMINATED BY IGNATIEV. PLANNED PHOSPHORIN RELEASE AT MAJOR THEME PARK (ORLANDO, FLORIDA) TO DAMAGE SHARE PRICE OF THEME PARK'S PARENT COMPANY TO AID IN HOSTILE TAKEOVER. ADDITIONALLY, EXPECTED TO BOOST STOCK PRICES AND CONTRACT OPPORTUNITIES FOR

DEFENSE COMPANIES BY INFLUENCING PUBLIC OPINION TO SUPPORT MORE INTRUSIVE SECURITY FOR PUBLIC EVENTS AND LOCATIONS.

MARIE LE COQ DETAINED. SABRE ASSOCIATE. PLANNED TO PROVIDE PHOSPHORIN TO HER HUSBAND, FRANCOIS LE COQ, TO SUPPORT HIS DESIRE TO EXPAND INTO NEW, HIGH-PROFILE AREAS OF SCIENTIFIC INQUIRY. INSTEAD, POISONED HIM WHEN HE OBJECTED TO HER PLAN. NOW BEING QUESTIONED (STANDARD TACTICS). WILL UPDATE WITH RECOMMENDATION TO TURN OR TERM.

PRINCE ALI SAAD BANDAR OF GUDAN: EXPOSED TO PHOSPHORIN, THEN SHOT BY IGNATIEV. MOTIVE FOR INVOLVEMENT IN AUCTION/GAME WAS APPARENTLY LAUDATORY (ENVIRONMENTALLY RESPONSIBLE FOOD PRODUCTION). EVIDENCE INDICATES REACTION OF REGRET UPON REALIZING HE WAS PARTY TO KIDNAPPING AND MURDER.

FRANCOIS LE COQ: POISONED BY WIFE, MARIE LE COQ, AFTER DISCOVERING HER INVOLVEMENT WITH PHOSPHORIN. POISON IS SABRE INVENTION, NOT PREVIOUSLY KNOWN, WHICH MIMICS INDIGESTION AND HEART ATTACK, LEAVING NO APPARENT RESIDUE. LE COQ'S BODY RETAINED FOR RESEARCH.

SOURCE OF PHOSPHORIN IDENTIFIED AT CDC AS VISITING RESEARCHER ALEXANDER FOLEY. MOTIVE WAS FINANCIAL DIFFICULTIES (ALIMONY). TERMED (CAR CRASH).

MIDDLEMAN BETWEEN PHOSPHORIN SOURCE AND KASSON REMAINS UNKNOWN. IDENTIFICATION OF MIDDLEMAN ADDED TO PRIORITY QUEUE.

KASSON RESPONSE ON HOLD AT DISCRETION OF DIRECTOR.

ERICA SANDOZ CLEARED OF INVOLVEMENT.

ONLINE IDENTITY USED AS DISGUISE BY MARIE LE COQ.

SERGEI ERINOV CLEARED OF INVOLVEMENT.

NATASHA DUBRONOVITCH CLEARED OF INVOLVEMENT.

LUCY KIMBALL CLEARED OF INVOLVEMENT AS SOURCE OF PHOSPHORIN. DEMONSTRATED SKILL AND INITIATIVE IN THE FIELD. SAVED LIFE OF AGENT FORD TWICE. USED STUN GUN TO DISABLE MARIE LE COQ. HELPED PREVENT IGNATIEV FROM REMOTELY RELEASING PHOSPHORIN IN TRANSPORT HUBS. ORGANIZED QUARANTINE. TRAINED CDC/WHO IN TREATMENT PROTOCOLS. WITH AGENT FORD, QUITE LITERALLY SAVED THE WORLD.

AGENT JOHN ABERNATHY FORD EXPOSED TO EXTREMELY HIGH LEVELS OF PHOSPHORIN. EVACUATED TO RAMSTEIN AFB BIO-CONTAINMENT FACILITY. CONDITION CRITICAL. NOT EXPECTED TO SURVIVE. FAMILY ON SITE: MOTHER (ABIGAIL), BROTHER (DANIEL), AND FAMILY ASSOCIATES (HAROLD AND ROSITA BURTON). PRESENCE OF FAMILY NOT DESIRABLE BUT IMPOSSIBLE TO AVOID GIVEN STATUS AND HISTORY OF INVOLVEMENT WITH SPECIAL EXPLOITS (AS YOU WELL KNOW, SIR).

The hand holding the telex trembled, then crushed the printout.

CHAPTER
NINETY-FOUR

A HOSPITAL ROOM

JACK OPENED his eyes.

Tubes. Lights. Monitors. With every breath, pain sneaked in through the fuzzy haze of the morphine drip. Individual cells writhed in agony, screaming as they burst.

Flashes of consciousness: Memories. Fragments from the past day or days — he didn't know which. His mother. Harold and Rosita. His brother, Danny, whispering a single word in his ear: *Ferociter*.

A vigil, for him.

One person in the room now.

Lucy, at his side, in hazmat gear and struggling to smile. So beautiful.

"We're going to put you under while we try something," she said.

"Put me under?" he asked, willing himself to stay conscious, to stay lucid.

"A medically induced coma." She was afraid, but trying to mask it.

His eyes closed. He was so tired. But he forced his eyes open and aimed them straight at her.

"You know why I love you," he whispered.

He willed himself to hold her gaze. She needed to know this was him talking, and not the fever or drugs.

"Why, Jack?"

"The way you try to hide your smile," he whispered. "The way you surprise me. The way you make me laugh."

A small, trembling smile appeared on her lips.

"Yeah, like that," he said, his eyes not wavering. "I love that."

"We'll have you back soon," she said.

"You know why I love you?"

"Why, Jack?"

"You kiss like a demon. You have no idea how hot you are."

A cough welled up and exploded into a round of horrible heaves and gasps. He struggled for breath, struggled to settle himself.

"Jack, you need to rest," she said, her eyes sliding to the numbers spiking on the monitor.

Excellent advice, which he ignored.

"I love that you're a slob," he said as soon as he could. "And eat like a horse. And snore. I love that."

"You really know how to woo a girl," she said, forcing lightness into her tone.

"I love that you don't hold back. You called me a whore."

"I believe my exact words were 'salaried sex worker.'"

"See? That's why I love you."

The coughs hit him again.

"Jack, you need to rest."

"I love how uptight you are," he said. "So fucking uptight."

"Jack...."

"Keeping it bottled up, controlled. But when the cap comes off — pow."

"Jack...."

"I want to be there when you explode. When you lose it. I want to be with you."

Another terrible round of hacking coughs shook him.

Her eyes teared up.

"Will I?" he asked her when he could.

"Will you what?"

"Be with you."

"We're trying something new," she said. "I need you to hang on."

"Lucy...."

"Do you hear me, Jack Ford?"

"Lucy...."

"What is it, Jack?"

"I love you," he whispered.

Fresh tears filled her eyes. "Goddamn it, Jack Ford. I love you, too."

"Lucy...."

"What is it?"

He saw the fear in her eyes.

Fuck it. Now or never. "Marry me."

Her eyes widened. "What did you say?"

He heard the shock in her voice.

"Marry me."

Another terrible cough, his body breaking apart. More blood.

"How dare you."

"Marry me."

"How dare you ask me when — "

"When what?"

She didn't respond, couldn't get the words out.

He answered for her. "When I'm at death's door?"

A tear rolled down her cheek.

"Marry me," he repeated, barely able to whisper.

He was fading. He needed more time. His hand gripped hers.

The last thing he heard, before darkness engulfed him, was her answer.

CHAPTER **NINETY-FIVE**

FORD FAMILY CHAPEL
FORD ESTATE, SOUTH OF LOS ANGELES

COMMANDER GRANT sat down heavily in the pew next to Deputy Commander Calhoun. The chapel was warm with people — too warm. His dark suit clung to him. Sweat trickled down his neck. He adjusted his collar and looked at Calhoun.

She glanced his way, sympathy in her eyes. She knew he blamed himself.

Up in the front, the minister stood and faced the crowded room. "We are gathered here today...."

He barely listened as the minister droned on. Saying goodbye to an agent was never easy, but losing Agent Ford was particularly hard. He'd been an exceptional operative — daring, inventive, insightful. Worth the wisecracks, the instinctive rebelliousness, and the constant challenges to his authority.

The fault was his. All his. The mission had been his idea.

Involving Dr. Kimball had been a mistake. Agent Ford had been right. She'd distracted him.

He looked at Calhoun sitting next to him, focused on the action up front.

Goddamn, he hated weddings.

Hated the sight of the two lovebirds up in front. Staring into each other's eyes, grinning ear to ear. Radiating joy. Two smart, capable, useful people, turned into mushy, mindless automatons for love. Next to the goddamned minister, who was urging anyone with an objection to speak now or forever hold his peace.

Hell, he had a dozen objections. But Calhoun grabbed his arm before he could move an inch.

He didn't fight her. The way those two were mooning at each other, nothing he could say would make a damn bit of difference.

The bride was beautiful: elegant and poised in a simple, flowing white dress, her hair in the style she'd worn on the mission, her brown eyes shining with tears.

And staring at her with wonder and disbelief and gratitude and love — yes, love — was the groom, still too thin and still too pale. A streak of white flecked the hair at his temples. The treatment had nearly killed him, and the recovery had been slow, but he'd held on, pushed on, for her. He couldn't stop grinning now, his eyes seeing only her.

And then the dreaded words.

"Lucy," the minister said, "do you take this man, Jack, to have and to hold, to honor and to cherish, in sickness and in health, from this day forward, till death do you part?"

"I do," she said.

"Jack, do you take this woman, Lucy, to have and to hold, to honor and to cherish, in sickness and in health, from this day forward, till death do you part?"

"I do," he said.

"By the powers vested in me, I now pronounce you husband and wife. You may kiss the bride."

Goddamn it.

And then they were kissing.

The church erupted in cheers.

Weddings were the worst. He wanted to hit someone.

He really had to do something about his agents falling in love. Next time he brought in an outside expert, he'd make sure it was someone with bad teeth and bad hygiene. Someone who hated sex and commitment.

He saw Calhoun wipe a tear from her eye.

She caught his look and, embarrassed, said briskly, "We need to mingle. Promise you won't bite anyone's head off."

He sighed. It was going to be a long day.

Lucy stared, yet again, at the ring on her finger, still not fully accepting it as real. A beautiful piece of jewelry — a single diamond, not too small, not too large, on a simple silver band. Nothing flashy about it. Subtle but substantial. Elegant. Appropriate.

She felt the hug of the band around her finger as the stone sparkled in the afternoon sun. Was she really here, on Jack's family estate, in a large renovated barn decorated to the rafters — literally — to host their wedding reception, standing in a white wedding dress, surrounded by a hundred guests, being served champagne and appetizers by tuxedoed waiters?

A soft breeze carried the scent of tall grass from the surrounding hills. The air was dry and warm; later that afternoon, after the toasts and cake, when they danced, they'd get sweaty.

Unless, of course, she was dreaming and would soon

wake up in her own bed, back in her previous reality after a restless night's sleep, realizing, with a small measure of relief and a large dose of regret, that her crazy-insane adventures had been just a fantasy. That she hadn't been recruited by a secret spy organization to save the world from a madman. That she hadn't kicked a dirt bag in the balls, zapped a psycho, danced the can-can, initiated public sex, fallen from a helicopter, leaped from a gondola, and nearly drowned. That she hadn't organized a must-succeed response to a deadly contagion.

If she woke up soon, it meant she hadn't fallen for her partner, the charming, distractingly handsome heir to a billion-dollar fortune.

And it meant her partner hadn't fallen, improbably, in love with her.

His hand on her waist felt very real, as did his body next to hers — still too thin, but increasingly energetic and on the mend. She warmed inside at the sound of him laughing at something his brother had said.

His older brother, Danny, who stood next to him, was real too. He was four years older, as handsome as Jack but with a more serious demeanor, with close-cropped brown hair showing flecks of gray at the temple. His mother, Abigail, stood next to Danny, as poised and watchful as ever.

And next to Abigail were her own parents. She felt a protective urge as she watched them struggle not to be overwhelmed by their surroundings, by this influx of glamorous and wealthy strangers into their quiet lives, and by the startling suddenness of their ever-solitary daughter's whirlwind romance with a man she barely knew.

Did she know him, this man she'd just married? Not in the traditional sense, no. But her gut told her that despite her innate cautiousness, she knew him enough. After what they'd been through, she knew his core.

"Hey," she heard him say.

She looked up into his blue eyes. She'd never tire of looking into those eyes.

"Lost in your head again, I see," he said.

She smiled. "An occupational hazard of being me."

He leaned in and kissed her forehead. She breathed in his scent.

Yes, crazy-insane, and also real.

Now was not the time for self-reflection — not with a deluge of well-wishers crashing over her. Her colleagues from the lab, amazed that their quiet, serious, workaholic research partner had picked a playboy for a husband, and vice-versa. Her best friend and maid of honor, Joanie, who knew instinctively that Lucy's lies about how she'd met and fallen for Jack were bullshit, but who had chosen, for now, to pretend to believe her. All too soon, there would be a girl's night, with a bottle or two or three of wine, and Lucy knew her commitment to discretion would be sorely tested.

She found herself being introduced to Jack's former commander, Captain Joe — now General Joe — and his wife, Susan, and their two adorable children. They were happy together — a family. They'd figured out how to make it work, with help that only Jack could provide.

Paul, her Special Exploits hair stylist, walked up with a man she recognized from his photo in the Special Exploits makeup studio: Carlo, the man Paul had fallen in love with and given up being an agent for. They made quite the pair in their stylish dark suits.

Carlo kissed her on both cheeks and said, in lightly accented English, "You and I have something in common. We'll have you and Jack over for dinner. You and I can be a support group. Share strategies for handling our men."

"Hey," Paul said, pretending to protest.

"I'd love that," she said.

She felt a presence behind her and heard a voice, one she'd heard once before, say, "Dr. Kimball."

"Excuse us," Paul said, and he and Carlo slipped away.

She turned. It was the man from England — Air Vent Man — in a tailored dark suit with a thin black tie. His dark hair was longer and wavier than when she'd met him, though his gaze was as intense as ever.

"I am pleased Jack has treated you with the respect you deserve," he said.

Such controlled energy in his voice, like Commander Grant. She felt short of breath. Her stomach fluttered.

What was it with these Special Exploits men?

"I never learned your name," she said.

"Mohammed," he said. "Mohammed Monroe."

He paused, as if weighing his next words. He glanced at Jack across the barn, surrounded by a group of his Hollywood friends.

"I wish you every happiness. I'm afraid I must go. Please give my regards to Jack. He is a lucky man."

To his gaggle of H-town buds, Jack was explaining — yet again — how he'd met Lucy, when a familiar drunken voice said, "Jack! My friend!"

Two arms grabbed him from behind in a fierce bear hug.

Jack grinned. He extricated himself and turned around.

Sergei stared at him, face flushed, his eyes anxiously taking in every detail of Jack's appearance.

"We are late because plane is delayed," he said. "We come straight from airport. I am so happy to see you alive and standing and recovering, yes?"

"Definitely on the mend."

Sergei impulsively pulled him in for another bear hug

and, in a quieter voice, said, "I am happy you recover well. We must talk."

Jack freed himself again and turned to his Hollywood pals. "Later, okay?" He allowed Sergei to pull him to a quiet spot away from the crowd.

"Talk about what?" he asked.

"My friend, my good friend...." Sergei looked at him with bleary, teary eyes. "I don't know why I cry. I have much to drink. I am happy to see you."

A surge of affection rolled through him. "You too, buddy. I'm glad you're here."

A cloud passed in front of Sergei's face. He wiped the tears from his eyes. "But we must talk."

"About what?"

"I have news you may not like. But we are true friends, no secrets."

An alarm bell went off. "Sergei, what is it?"

Sergei looked around to make sure no one could hear them. "We had secret agent at Villa Synkonos."

Clang clang clang. He did his best to look doubtful. "Really? Why do you say that?"

"We are true friends. I tell you now. I install camera system at villa. For security, you understand."

"Go on."

"Somebody breaks into security room. The lock is — how do you say?"

"Jimmied? Tampered with?"

"Yes. And video erased."

"You're sure?"

Sergei gave him an indignant look. "Is my system. Of course I am sure."

Time for the million-dollar question. He focused in on Sergei's pupils — his tell. "Do you know who it was?"

"That is what I ask myself," Sergei said. "Who can it be?

And then — it comes to me. I know who it is."

Sergei was telling the truth. The dude believed he knew.

Jack steeled himself for the accusation.

Sergei looked around again, then leaned in. "My friend, I am sorry to say, the spy is your wife."

Shit. "What?"

"While I am in quarantine, I watch footage from last day there. I notice Lucy. I see patterns. I connect dots."

Sergei's speculations needed to be shut down — pronto. "I gotta tell ya, dude, what you're saying is crazy. Lucy is not a spy."

"I tell you evidence, then you decide. Okay?"

"Tell me."

"First item. Nobody knows her. She appears from nowhere. She is unknown quantity. Only you know her, and you only know her for few weeks."

"Sergei, I invited her. I met her. She's a doctor. She doesn't move in our circles."

"Second item. I find out she kicks Dick Hould in balls. Bartender tells me. He says she uses very professional move. Expert training."

"Dick Hould was a predator. He hit on Lucy, and she kicked him when he wouldn't take no for an answer."

"Then, next morning, he is dead. Accident, but very suspicious."

"Lucy had nothing to do with that."

"Wait, I have more. I see her standing in door to your cabana, watching." Sergei lowered his voice to a whisper. "The night I was very drunk, the night I do not remember."

At least the dude had the grace to look embarrassed for drunkenly barging into his cabana and demanding an impromptu asshole inspection.

Adopting a patient tone, Jack said, "Sergei, she was there

because it was her room, and she heard us, and she wasn't sure if she should interrupt."

Jack began to relax. If the rest of the evidence could be explained away as easily, they'd be fine.

Sergei shook his head. "She is very beautiful, charming, intelligent. Natural leader. She has qualities of successful spy."

Jack smiled and said, in his most persuasive voice, "Lucy is a doctor. I promise you, from the bottom of my heart, she's a doctor and a scientist."

Sergei stared at him, then nodded slowly. "I understand. I see now."

"Good."

"You already know she is secret agent."

Jack started to protest, but Sergei plowed on. "You are chivalrous man. You protect her."

Before Jack could rebut him, Sergei held up his hand. "Jack, my friend. I too am chivalrous man, so I keep her secret. Do not fear. I too am admirer of strong women."

Jack sighed.

"Sergei, I am going to trust that you, as my friend, will not tell anyone you think my wife is a spy. That kind of talk would hurt her professionally." He leaned in close and, emphasizing each word, said, "Because she is not a spy."

"Yes, fine. She is not spy. I know nothing. I say nothing." A look of anxiety flitted across Sergei's face. "But I have to ask something else. I have concerns."

"About what?"

"How women capture men."

"What?"

"You are paragon of man. You have women of the world at your beck and call. But now you are married man. One woman trapped you."

"Sergei — "

"How did she do it?" Sergei whispered. "Is she insatiable in bed? Does she tame you with sexy spy techniques? Does she wrap you in feminine wiles?"

"Sergei — "

"I always want to be playboy, live exciting life, like you. And now, I achieve my dream. World is my oyster. You show me way. But how do I stay free when one woman can have such power over man's heart and soul?"

"What are you talking about?"

"I am failure as playboy," he whispered, misery in his voice. "Yes, failure. I think I...."

"What?"

"I think I am in love!"

At that moment, Natasha stepped up behind Sergei. She looked dazzling in an elegant red dress. Her hard edges had softened, and she glowed.

"Congratulations, Jack," she said, leaning up to give him a kiss on the cheek. "I could not be happier for you and Lucy."

She stood next to Sergei, leaned her head on his shoulder, and linked her arm through his.

Ah.

"Do I detect a change in your relationship status?" Jack asked.

Sergei leaned over and kissed Natasha's head.

"Yes, I have girlfriend now. I was about to tell you." He looked at him, an anxious plea in his eyes.

"I'm really happy for you guys."

"Thank you," Natasha said.

"When you walked up," Jack said, looking directly at Natasha, "I was about to tell Sergei why I got married."

Sergei stiffened.

Jack kept his focus on Natasha, but his message was for Sergei. The kid needed reassurance that what he was feeling was okay.

"For as long as I can remember," he said, "I've wanted to experience the world. I've always done that through women — wonderful, intelligent, lovely, talented, sexy women. I never thought I'd want to settle down. I thought marriage was a trap."

Sergei eyed him warily.

"But when I met Lucy, I realized something important: I still wanted to experience the world, but with someone — a wife."

He saw a light go off in Sergei's head.

"When love hit, it hit me hard, like an express train. If I denied that, I'd be lying. I try very hard to be honest with myself, and my honest truth is: I can't imagine life without Lucy. "

Sergei's shoulders loosened, and the tension in his face eased.

"Well, I'm very happy for the two of you," Natasha said. "You make an excellent match."

"So," Jack asked, "how'd it happen with you two? How'd you make the leap from friends and colleagues to … more?"

"The quarantine," Sergei said, looking at Natasha. "Fourteen days, no outside world, no distractions. We are talking, on day four, I see something new. All these years, working together, under my nose, a beautiful woman. Perfect woman. I ask, 'Why do I not see?' And she says — tell him what you say."

Natasha looked straight into Sergei's eyes and said, "I told you I was waiting for the gap between your chronological and emotional ages to narrow to less than a decade."

Sergei laughed.

"She says I am ready for her, because I am no longer emotional jailbait!" He turned to Natasha and said, "I tell Jack what I discover about Lucy."

"Sergei!"

"Don't worry, we keep Lucy's secret, yes?"

Natasha frowned and said to Jack, "I do not share Sergei's conclusion. He has created an exciting story out of unconnected details, which is something he's very good at, but I do not accept it as the truth. And because his story could have real consequences, we will keep it to ourselves."

"Thank you," Jack said.

"Darling," she said to Sergei, "will you get me a glass of champagne?"

He leaned in and kissed her cheek. "For you, my dear, anything. World is our oyster."

They watched him weave through the tables, stumbling slightly.

"He's right about one thing," Natasha said quietly.

"Right about what?"

"There was a spy at our party."

"You can't think it was Lucy."

"No," she said, looking directly into his eyes. "I think it was her husband."

Clang clang clang.

He shook his head. "You two really are made for each other. Full of crazy."

"Your cover is quite clever, and unexpected. Don't worry, it's our little secret."

"Natasha, I don't know what you mean."

Natasha ignored him. "If I told Sergei that you — his hero — were a spy, then he would want to be a spy, just like you. I can't have that. Sergei is a genius and a visionary and I love him, but his emotional intelligence is limited. He would be a terrible spy."

She stepped closer and stared at him with the same fierce intensity as when they'd first met.

"Sergei is a good-hearted person. His essential impulses are toward generosity and kindness. He would be very troubled by the decisions you must make in your line of work. I do not want him to have a guilty conscience — ever — about his decisions."

She'd thought this out. He remained silent.

"Right now, he suspects Lucy. I will see to it that he transfers his suspicions to … Madame Le Coq?"

He wouldn't be able to dissuade this one; she was too damn sharp.

Screw protocol. He went with his gut. "An excellent choice."

"I understand she's still sick. Does that mean she's … detained?"

"Something like that."

"I thought so." Natasha's face relaxed. She took a sip of her wine.

"Sergei's lucky to have you," he said.

"Yes," Natasha said with a smile, "he is."

The music — a classic swing number from the 1940s — guided Jack across the dance floor, with Lucy in his arms. It felt so natural to hold her, to feel her body move with his. His hand rested on her waist, sensing the flow of muscles beneath her dress as they glided together. He inhaled the scent of her hair against his cheek as he picked her up and twirled her around.

The song ended and the guests applauded. Jack gave a signal, and the sound system pumped out a modern thumper. The guests cheered and joined them on the dance floor.

From the edge of the dance floor, he caught sight of Deputy Commander Calhoun. She held up two fingers and pointed to the outside of the barn.

Jack gave her a nod. A minute later, when the song ended, he took Lucy's hand.

"We've been summoned," he said.

They found Calhoun and Grant standing outside the barn, under the massive oak tree Jack had climbed countless times as a child.

"You know what I'm going to say," Grant said, as serious and monolithic as ever.

"Yep," Jack said.

"You're fired."

"Yep."

Calhoun coughed softly.

Grant grimaced, then added, "Congratulations to both of you."

"Thank you," Lucy said.

"Something for you," Grant said. He pulled an envelope out of his jacket pocket and handed it to Jack.

Calhoun coughed again. If it were possible for a slab of granite to flinch, then that's what Grant did.

"A wedding gift," the Commander said through gritted teeth.

Jack slid open the flap of the envelope and pulled out a single folded sheet of paper.

He froze as the words flew out at him:

To: Lieutenant John A. Ford

Following subsequent review of evidence related to your dismissal, your discharge from the U.S. Army has been changed to HONORABLY DISCHARGED.

Tears threatened his eyes.

"Thank you, Commander," he said, his voice thick with emotion.

Lucy leaned in and gasped as she read the letter. She grabbed him around the waist and hugged him.

"My family will appreciate this almost as much as I do," he said to Grant and Calhoun. "Thank you."

He heard a faint beep.

Grant pressed his ear. "Yes." He listened for a moment. "Right away." He turned to Calhoun. "Time to go."

He extended his hand to Jack. "Agent Ford, it has been an honor and a privilege. You have served with distinction."

Jack grabbed his hand and gripped it tightly. "The honor is mine, Commander."

Grant turned to Lucy. "Dr. Kimball, the entire world owes you a debt of gratitude."

He held out his hand, and Lucy shook it.

Grant turned and strode toward his SUV.

Calhoun hugged each of them. "I'm going to miss you both."

She turned and ran to catch up with her Commander.

A moment later, as their black SUV pulled away, Jack felt a tug of longing. Already, he was missing it. The anticipation. The adrenaline. The agents of Special Exploits were off on a new adventure. Without him.

"Honey, you okay?"

At the sound of her voice, Jack turned and looked at his wife. He felt himself tearing up again. *His wife.* This amazing, incredible woman was *his wife*.

He pulled her in close. "More than okay."

Since teaming up with Dr. Lucy Kimball, he'd been beaten up, dildo-fucked by a sociopath, tossed from a speeding motorcycle, electrocuted, shot at, and poisoned with lethal bacteria. He'd watched helplessly as the woman he loved fell from a helicopter — to what he'd believed for one terrible moment was her death. And as phosphorin ravaged his body, he'd faced, and in his final moments accepted, his end.

"You know what I feel like?" he said.

"Tell me," she said as she wrapped her arms around him and squeezed tight.

"Like the luckiest man in the world."

THE END

BEFORE MOST OF THIS HAPPENED

13 MONTHS EARLIER
SKY HIGH AIRLINES FLIGHT 32
LONDON TO LOS ANGELES

LUCY SANK INTO her business-class seat, surprised and grateful to have been bumped from economy. She could only assume the upgrade was the work of the man in the air vent or his organization. A way to thank her for helping him, perhaps.

If so, she wasn't complaining. The rollercoaster ride of the past two days had left her exhausted. Thank goodness she was headed home to her lab, to her colleagues, to her cozy cottage, to Mr. Snuggles, to her normal, steady, boring life. She needed a dose of the dulls in the worst possible way — even ached for it. She couldn't wait to catch up on her lab work, scrub the bathtub, plop down on the couch and dip into her DVR, shop for groceries, talk to her mom and dad, and invite Joanie over for a girl's night in.

A flight attendant appeared next to her seat. "Welcome

aboard, Dr. Kimball. Can I get you something before takeoff? A glass of freshly squeezed orange juice? Champagne? Water?"

"Orange juice, please," she said, then paused. She'd had a rough two days — what the heck. "Actually, if you have Chardonnay...."

Jack's phone vibrated as he approached the boarding gate. A text from Special Exploits: "Before you meet your friend, find out if 4D is chatty."

He looked at his ticket: seat 4C.

Before tackling his main goal for the flight — befriending a high-end coke dealer and scoring an invite to the scumbag's underground poker table — he now had a last-minute task: find out how easily he could persuade 4D to spill the beans. About what, he didn't know; all he knew was that it involved a fellow agent. "Chatty" was code for a civilian asset's likelihood to blab about what he or she had done to help Special Exploits complete a mission.

Most assets talked — it was simple human nature. Most were excited by their brush with intrigue and danger and were bursting to share.

Jack stepped into the plane and identified his coke-dealer target in seat 1A, next to a man who Jack instantly tagged as a plainclothes Homeland Security air marshal.

So Special Exploits had arranged for Jack to pull a seat switcheroonie. No problemo.

He moved down the aisle and got his first look at the occupant of seat 4D: A woman. Thirty years old, give or take. Glasses hanging off the end of her nose. No makeup, no wedding ring. Brown hair pulled back in a sensible ponytail. Attractive, but not doing anything to advertise it. Hints of a slim, trim bod under a shapeless sweater and loose jeans. A glass of white wine in one hand, and an open magazine — the page filled with words, not photos — in the other.

The woman glanced up at him. Intelligent brown eyes took him in quickly, but without a flicker of recognition.

Dammit. A smart one. An introvert. Emotionally closed. No interest in pop culture.

Didn't know world-famous, fun-loving, celebrity playboy Jack Ford from a hole in the wall.

It didn't take a keen observer to recognize how attractive the man was. She wasn't dead, after all.

Though she could have been, several times in the past two days — the gun in her face, the mysterious stranger in the air vent, the pill she'd swallowed and blacked out from....

Somehow, despite leaping before she looked, she'd survived.

The man seemed familiar. Had she met him somewhere? He placed his travel bag in the overhead bin and dropped into his seat.

"Hi, I'm Jack," he said, turning toward her and extending his hand. "Jack Ford."

"Lucy," she said, setting her magazine down and extending hers.

A jolt shot through her as their palms touched. Her breath quickened.

A reaction to the excitement of the past two days — that explained it. She glanced again at his face, mere inches from hers — unruly blond hair and a wide, easy grin. And *crap,* dazzling blue eyes.

Quickly, she pulled her hand back.

"Don't worry, they treat us right here," he said as he settled in.

She gave him a polite smile in response and pretended to return to her *New Yorker*.

"You fly often?" he asked.

So he was a talker. She'd have to engage.

"Not really."

"Traveling for business? Pleasure?"

"Business."

He looked at her expectantly, letting the silence lengthen.

She tried to resist falling into his conversation trap, but failed. "For a conference," she said.

"Let me guess."

"Guess what?"

"Your business."

A challenge? Interesting tactic. She gave him a skeptical look. "Based on?"

"Observation." His eyes really were an extraordinary blue. "Visual clues."

"Okay," she said, her curiosity piqued.

"All right." He sat up straight and rubbed his hands together. "No smartphone, so you're not a slave to email, which means you're probably not a consultant, or in sales, or in operations."

Good observation and reasonable deduction — not bad. "Go on."

"I see you take your work seriously. It matters. Whatever it is, it kept you very busy while you were here. You're happy to be flying home."

Right again. She did her best to keep her face immobile. No hints.

"You mentioned a conference. I'll go out on a limb — government, academic, maybe scientific?"

She nodded.

"On a roll!" he said with a grin. "Okay. You're not with the government."

"Why do you say that?"

"Because bureaucrats are boring, and I can tell you're not."

She felt a smile coming on and suppressed it.

"So maybe you're a professor, or a scientist, or an analyst, or...." He paused. "You're not making this easy on me."

"You're doing well so far."

"So I'm close." He leaned toward her, just a bit, and she watched his eyes slowly roam over her, head to toe. Then he grinned.

She caught a whiff of aftershave and felt her face heat up. *Dammit.*

"Process of elimination? You're not a professor — too young. Jobs in academia are tough to come by these days, and the professors with tenure are sticking around longer."

He inched slightly closer. "Am I right?"

"I'm not a professor."

"On a roll."

She almost told him what she did right there, but stopped. She was missing something. Without looking away from him, she mentally assessed her space. Her appearance. Her — *aha.*

This time, she didn't hide her smile. Should she call him out, or play along a bit longer?

She made her decision. "Please, go on."

"Okay," he said. "This is where it gets tricky. Scientists and analysts both use their brains. Both want to figure stuff out, find answers, develop solutions."

He made a show of deliberating and stroked his chin thoughtfully.

"I'm gonna go with my gut. You're a scientist. Definitely a scientist."

"What kind of scientist?"

He leaned in. "Um, beautiful?"

She blinked and pulled back. "That's not what I meant."

"I know," he said. "But I did. Let's see … what kind of beautiful scientist are you?"

She was enjoying this, she realized, and so was he. Understanding the game made things … fun.

"This is totally based on instinct, all right?" he continued. "I have a feeling you care about people. You want to help people and do right by them. Which means, maybe you were drawn to medicine. So I'm gonna say you're a doctor, or you at least trained as one."

Her smile widened. "I do medical research."

"So I nailed it?"

"You nailed it."

"So tell me I'm good."

"Well," she said, "I suppose it's possible you arrived at your conclusion via a series of astute observations, like you said. Or you saw this." She pulled a magazine out of the reading slot in front of her and dropped it into his lap.

Jack stared down at the latest issue of the New England Journal of Medicine.

He laughed. "Busted!"

She couldn't help herself; she grinned.

"You know what, doc? You are a doctor, right? Dr. Lucy, M.D.? I think we're gonna have fun on this flight."

And they were having fun, Jack realized. Too much fun. They'd been in the air for more than two hours, and the clock was ticking.

Yet here he was, lingering. There was something about this woman. They clicked. The chemistry was real, and she was feeling it too. He saw interest — desire — in the depths of her warm brown eyes.

The wine was helping, of course. The girl liked her wine, but not enough to spill.

She'd told him about the scientist at the lab who'd taken her hostage at gunpoint. She'd shared how she'd slipped the guy a sedative and accidentally swallowed one herself.

And he knew, from her pupils, she was glossing over how she'd gotten her hands on the sedative. The sedative hadn't just been "there," and she hadn't "happened to notice it." One of his Special Exploits colleagues had given it to her and told her to use it.

But she hadn't let that slip, not even a hint. Even with three glasses of wine in her. Even with him piling on the charm and doing all he could to encourage her to share.

Impressive. She was no ordinary woman.

"I'm amazed you managed all that," he said.

Her lips compressed. "I got lucky."

She was one of those people who were uncomfortable with credit or praise, especially when inaccurate. Uncomfortable being part of a misunderstanding or lie, even by omission. She'd feel the urge to speak up, to set the record straight.

"You're amazing," he said, lathering it on. "You single-handedly stopped a bad guy. You're like a one-woman rescue squad."

"Stop," Lucy said. "I was lucky."

"To think that you did it on your own. You must be really pleased with yourself."

She desperately wanted to correct him, he could tell, but instead she said, "Enough about me. Really, enough. I'm tired of talking about myself. Tell me what brought you to England."

The soul of discretion, this one, and unlikely to spill. Which meant the first item on his in-flight to-do list was complete. He'd report back and tell Grant and Calhoun that Dr. Lucy, despite a full-on charm offensive, had resisted mentioning his fellow agent. She'd been tested and had passed.

Now for the shitty part. More and more, there were moments in his job — and this was one of them — where he resented what was required of him.

He unhooked his seat belt and prepared to stand, but her eyes stopped him. They stared at him unwaveringly. Her gaze was watchful and serious, but swirling with emotion beneath the still, quiet surface. She was open to him — ready.

On impulse, he leaned in and kissed her. She didn't pull back. Rather, she leaned in, joining him.

Damn. The kiss was good — astonishingly good. His lips pressed against hers as he inhaled her natural scent and tasted the wine on her breath. His hand went to the back of her neck. Gently, he pulled her closer.

Then he backed away with a sharp stab of regret.

His plan.

Could he change his plan? *No.*

Could he explain? *No.*

Fuck.

"Excuse me," he said, then abruptly slid out of his seat and stepped to the front of the cabin.

Holy crap. What had she just done? Her heart was racing, her blood pulsing. Her senses were alive and tingling.

She'd kissed a total stranger, that's what.

Not her usual thing — not at all — but damn, the kiss had felt good. His lips on hers, his hand on her neck ...

It was good that he'd stepped away. She needed a breather. She needed to get hold of herself. She'd been through a lot and had had too much to drink. For all she knew, her surprising and sudden loss of inhibition had been a side effect of the sedative she'd swallowed — or of mixing it with alcohol. She should have known better. She should have held back.

Of course, it wasn't just anyone she'd kissed. She'd kissed Jack Ford, the famous rich guy who looked like a surfer, and who, by all rights, should have been an entitled jackass but wasn't. He was clever and funny and charming.

And sexy. She lingered over the fading sensations of the kiss and felt a rush of arousal. He was into her too, his interest in her clear.

She sensed a presence standing in the aisle next to her seat and looked up.

It was one of the flight attendants. Jack stood behind the attendant, three steps back.

"Dr. Kimball," the flight attendant said with an edge to her voice.

"Yes?" Lucy said. What was going on?

"I understand you may have had a bit too much to drink."

True enough, but — wait. *What?*

The flight attendant's gaze darted to the glass of wine in front of Lucy. "I know it can be exciting to come into contact with celebrities, but they're people, too. They have boundaries, just like regular people."

Wait. *What?*

Lucy looked over to Jack, who stared back at her with a stony expression. "Jack, what's going on?"

"I was just trying to be polite," he said, his voice cold and tinged with anger. "You shouldn't have kissed me like that."

What?

She froze, shocked.

"Why are you doing this?" she said, too loudly.

Around them, heads turned. She felt her face flame red.

What the hell was going on?

The flight attendant turned to Jack. "Mr. Ford, I'm so sorry. Maybe I can find a passenger to change seats with you."

Jack nodded. "I'd appreciate that."

The attendant lowered the overhead luggage bin. Without even glancing at her, Jack removed his bag and marched away, to the front of the cabin.

What the hell?

Three rows up, the flight attendant leaned down and whispered in a passenger's ear. A huge hulk of a man rose from his seat, barreled down the aisle, and dropped into the empty seat next to her.

"Let's be clear," the man said, his eyes hard and angry. "I'm in no mood for your bullshit. You misbehave, and I'll arrest you."

"I — "

"I don't care. Zip it."

She gaped, speechless.

"We clear?"

Nothing is clear, she wanted to scream. *Nothing*! But she bit her tongue. Shock gave way to anger, then fury.

Three rows up, ten feet away, she watched Jack settle into his new seat. The guy next to him said something, Jack said something back, and the guy laughed. Jack signaled to the flight attendant for drinks. Before long, he and his new buddy were getting on like gangbusters, gabbing and laughing and getting louder by the minute.

What the hell had just happened? Why had he set her up? Why had he lied? Clearly, the bastard was playing a sick, twisted game.

In a drunkenly loud voice, Jack's new buddy laughed and said something about "stalker chicks."

Jack laughed. "An occupational hazard of the fame game."

From deep within, a righteous rage arose, white-hot and pure. If she ever got her hands on him, she'd kill him; she'd skewer him and wring his lying, manipulative, traitorous neck.

For the sake of Jack Ford's personal safety, she hoped she never saw the bastard again!

THE REAL END

ABOUT THE AUTHOR

Michael Ryder worked as a journalist in Tokyo, New York, and Hong Kong before moving to San Francisco and getting involved in tech and banking. Now a full-time purveyor of fiction, he's currently writing *Bring It On,* the second thriller in a trilogy featuring Jack Ford and Lucy Kimball. His short stories have appeared in *Compelling Science Fiction, Penumbra,* and *Fiction River*. Most days, he can be found in neighborhood cafes, typing madly into his trusty laptop.

To sign up for his newsletter, go to

MichaelRyderBooks.com.

Thank you for being a reader.

www.ingramcontent.com/pod-product-compliance
Lightning Source LLC
Chambersburg PA
CBHW021958040826
48979CB00045B/2305/J
* 9 7 8 1 9 4 5 3 2 0 2 4 8 *